TOPSY TURVY TALES

THE LOST STORIES OF W. S. GILBERT

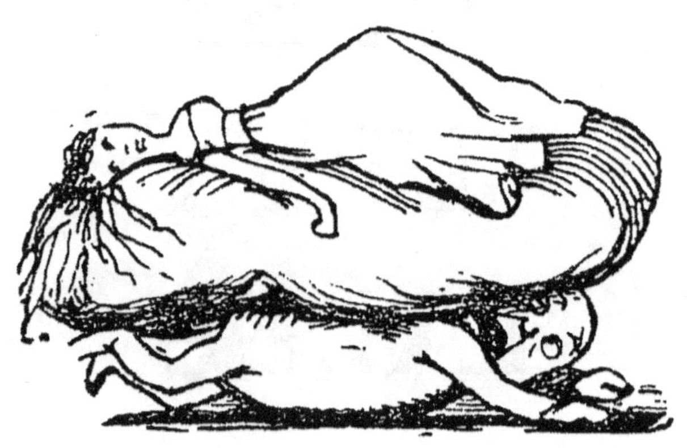

TOPSY TURVY TALES

THE LOST STORIES OF W. S. GILBERT

Creator of the Gilbert and Sullivan operas
"Trial by Jury," "The Mikado," etc.

Compiled and Introduced
by Peter Haining

the apocryphile press
BERKELEY, CA
www.apocryphile.org

For KEITH LARKMAN, AFR

Take of these elements all that is fusible,
Melt them all down in a pipkin or crucible,
Set them to simmer and take off the scum,
And a Solicitor Bold is the residuum!

With apologies to W.S. Gilbert and *Patience*

apocryphile press
BERKELEY, CA

Apocryphile Press
1700 Shattuck Ave #81
Berkeley, CA 94709
www.apocryphile.org

First published by Robson Books, Ltd in 1982.
First Apocryphile edition, 2007.

For sale in the USA only. Sales prohibited in the UK.
Printed in the United States of America.

ISBN 1-933993-30-8

CONTENTS

INTRODUCTION 7
MY MAIDEN BRIEF 26
THE POISONED POSTAGE STAMP 37
MAXWELL AND I 40
THE TRIUMPH OF VICE 69
JONES' VICTORIA CROSS 82
DIAMONDS 89
AN ELIXIR OF LOVE 106
TOM POULTON'S JOKE 125
CREATURES OF IMPULSE 134
THE WICKED WORLD 143
WIDE AWAKE 157
COMEDY AND TRAGEDY 166
FOGGERTY'S FAIRY 174
THE BURGLAR'S STORY 199
THE FINGER OF FATE 206
LITTLE MIM 216
ANGELA 222
THE FAIRY'S DILEMMA 228
THE LADY IN THE PLAID SHAWL 245
TRIAL BY JURY 252

The History of the Sensation Drama that Jack wrote.

INTRODUCTION

'It's a topsy-turvy world, ain't it?'
Ruth Tredgett in *Charity* (1874)

THE COMIC operas of W. S. Gilbert and Arthur Sullivan have rightly been described as a hugely popular national possession—rivalled only in their widespread and apparently permanent appeal by the plays of William Shakespeare and the novels of Charles Dickens. They hold the record for the longest continual presentation by theatrical companies (second only to Shakespeare's plays) and it can be fairly claimed that on any day of the year, somebody, somewhere is performing one or other of their works.

Indeed, with the passage of time, the term 'Gilbert and Sullivan' has come to mean far more than just the collaboration of these two men; it has become rather a synonym for light-hearted, often satirical, occasionally ludicrous and always melodic entertainment. Yet despite the undoubted quality of Sullivan's music, at their heart lies Gilbert's genius as a wit—and in particular his creation of a style of humour in which only the possible never happens: a world of sense upside down—a place called 'Topsy-Turvydom'. Speaking of this invention in their classic biography, *W. S. Gilbert: His Life and Letters* (1923), Sidney Dark and Rowland Grey have said, 'As a framework for his humour Gilbert invented the Topsy-turvydom, which has come to be generally known as "Gilbertian", and which consists in giving to his characters qualities exactly opposite to those that they would possess in real life. This land came into being when he wrote the first *Bab Ballad*, and it was the scene of almost all his libretti.'

Such is the international fame of the Gilbert and Sullivan operas, however, as well as the general paucity of biographical work on the two men—especially for the phases of their life before their collaboration began in 1871, and following its rather ridiculous severance in 1889 as the result of an argument over a carpet—that Gilbert's achievements in particular as a writer of work other than the operas, has been largely ignored. Certainly for generations few of the other contributions from his pen beyond the operas have been in print, a factor which this book in part sets out to remedy. For Gilbert's talents extended far beyond his brilliance as a humorist and the constructor of plays: he was also a writer of satirical verse (the still highly regarded *Bab Ballads* published in 1869 testify to this), a forceful and perceptive drama critic, a skilful comic illustrator, and the author of a body of varied short stories which he himself believed to be amongst his finest work. So before the reader dips into a selection of the best of these stories brought together for the first time—tales witty and grim, humorous and even romantic—it makes for a better appreciation of them to take a fascinating journey back to the forgotten days of Gilbert's life before he rose to world fame . . .

William Schwenk Gilbert was born in the heart of London at 17, Southampton Street, Strand on 18 November 1836. He was the only son of four children born to Anne Morris, a doctor's daughter, and William Gilbert, a descendant of Sir Humphrey Gilbert, the Elizabethan navigator who established the first English colony in America in 1583. William Gilbert had himself been a sea-faring man, a naval surgeon, but he abandoned this career at the age of 25 when he inherited a small fortune. The young W.S. Gilbert in turn inherited a love of the sea (typified in one of his most popular comic operas, *H.M.S. Pinafore*) as well as his father's fierce and often irrational temper. The peculiar middle name was the surname of his godmother and not surprisingly he grew to loath it!

Freed from the normal restrictions of having to earn a living, William Gilbert the elder travelled a great deal with his family, and in his infancy W.S. crossed many miles of Europe. He also had his first taste of comic opera at the tender age of two when he was in Naples, according to another biographer, Hesketh Pearson, who writes in *Gilbert and Sullivan* (1947):

Two courteous Italians stopped his nurse on the road one day and informed her that the English gentleman had sent them to fetch the baby. Captivated by their pleasant speech and charming manners, the nurse did not hesitate for a moment, but made them a present of William, who was then carried through some fine mountain scenery, which impressed him so much that he remembered it when visiting the country in after years, and a request for the equivalent of twenty-five pounds sterling was despatched to his parents. He was redeemed by return and about forty years later made use of the incident in a less realistic form! [In *The Pirates of Penzance*—Editor.]

It was during his childhood that W.S. earned the nickname 'Bab' which he later used to sign his sketches and also employed as the title for his collection of ballads. ('Bab' was a shortened form of 'Babe' or 'Babby', a dialectal word for a child much in use at that time in England.) When he went to Great Ealing School—and later King's College, Oxford—he quickly revealed an interest in the stage by first making up the cardboard cut-out theatres and actors which were then widely sold—the 'penny plain and two-pence coloured' items that so delighted Robert Louis Stevenson—and even wrote for his schoolfellows a number of plays which have, sadly, been lost.

At King's College, Gilbert also began to show an interest in literature and writing, contributing verse to the college magazine. Then, after an ill-fated attempt to join the Royal Artillery so that he might serve in the Crimean War (thwarted because the war ended before he was old enough to gain enlistment), Gilbert spent four less-than-happy years as an assistant clerk in the Education Department of the Privy Council Office. An unexpected bequest of £300 enabled him to quit this job and take up another career that had attracted him—and was to remain one of his main interests throughout his life—the Law. With the money from his inheritance he was able to fund his training and furnish his own chambers.

But the life of a barrister-at-law proved an unrewarding one for the young Gilbert, and when clients failed to beat a path to his door, he began to look for other means of augmenting his income. Like many a legal man before him (and since) he chose the pen. In an essay which he later wrote for the journal *The Theatre* in 1883, he tells us about his literary début:

> My very first plunge took place in 1858, I think, in connection with the late Alfred Mellon's Promenade Concerts. Madama Parepa-Rose (at that time Mdlle. Parepa), whom I had known from babyhood, had made a singular success at those concerts with the laughing-song from 'Manon Lescaut', and she asked me to do a translation of the song for Alfred Mellon's play-bill. I did it: it was duly printed in the bills. I remember that I went night after night to those concerts to enjoy the intense gratification of standing at the elbow of any promenader who might be reading my translation, and wondering to myself what that promenader would say if he knew that the gifted creature who had written the very words he was reading was at that moment standing within a yard of him? The secret satisfaction of knowing that I possessed the power to thrill him with this information was enough, and I preserved my incognito.

Although during the years from 1858 to 1863 Gilbert averaged only five clients per year, he did not waste his time, as Hesketh Pearson recognized. 'With a packet of quill pens, a few wood blocks, and a quire or two of blue foolscap paper at his side, he spent the hours waiting for clients in writing and illustrating articles for the weekly papers. Nearly all were returned with the usual editorial regret.'

But a man of W.S. Gilbert's determination, and temperament, was not easily discouraged—nor did he fail to profit from his few experiences at the bar: even those which worked against him. His very first brief, for instance was to defend a lady pickpocket, and although he applied himself to her defence with great resolution, he failed and was rewarded with a string of abuse and a boot hurled at his head by his ungrateful client! But he never forgot the incident, and later utilized the facts for one of his earliest short stories which *was* accepted, 'My Maiden Brief'. This amusing, not to say clever, tale appeared in the popular *Cornhill Magazine* of December

1863, and as it shows some of the first flowerings of Gilbert's later famous comedy techniques, it makes a most suitable opening story for this collection.

At about this time, Gilbert also began contributing to the humorous weekly magazine *Fun* which had been started in late 1861 as a rival to *Punch*. As none of his work was signed at this period, it is difficult to establish precisely *when* his first pieces were published, but from 1863 he was certainly supplying the magazine with verse, humorous observations on the social scene, and art and dramatic criticism. And although he had no formal artistic training, he found the little comic drawings he made to accompany his words were also popular with the editor. Writing in *The Theatre*, Gilbert explains how this association with the magazine came about:

> In 1861 *Fun* was started, under the editorship of Mr. H.J. Byron. With much labour I turned out an article three-quarters of a column long, and sent it to the editor, together with a half-page drawing on wood. A day or two later the printer of the paper called upon me, with Mr. Byron's compliments, and staggered me with a request to contribute a column of 'copy' and a half-page drawing each week for the term of my natural life. I hardly knew how to treat the offer, for it seemed to me that into that short article I had poured all I knew. I was empty. I had exhausted myself. I didn't know any more. However, the printer encouraged me (with Mr. Byron's compliments), and I said I would try. I did try, and I found to my surprise that there *was* a little left, and enough indeed to enable me to contribute some hundreds of columns to the periodical throughout his editorship, and that of his successor, poor Tom Hood!

Ideas were indeed soon pouring from W.S. Gilbert—and this fact can be readily substantiated by glancing through the pages of the now-rare copies of *Fun* from 1863 onwards when his pen-name 'Bab' appeared on most of his contributions. Although it was not until 1865 that he began writing the series of wickedly satirical verses that became known as *The Bab Ballads*, there can be no doubt of the importance of all his early work, as Sidney Dark and Rowland Grey have suggested: '*Fun* is indeed the cradle of the operas, and by no means through the 'Babs' alone. The prose sketches are sown with embryo ideas, often developed later with triumphant effect. The Gilbertian spirit—tricksey, elusive, magical—speedily begins to haunt these columns. The Pucklike imp of Topsy-turvydom plays pranks foreshadowing those of the libretti.'*

Among his contributions to *Fun* it is possible to identify one or two short stories, and the most suitable of these to my mind is 'The Poisoned Postage-Stamp' published in the issue of 16 February 1867. It is particularly interesting because it undoubtedly mirrors some of the frustrations Gilbert himself must have experienced when he was trying to get started as a writer. The piece also hints at Gilbert's fascination with crime, for as Hesketh Pearson has said, 'he was keenly interested in crime and criminals, and was an authority on the famous murders of the past.' It can also be fairly described as typical of his prose work for *Fun*.

Once Gilbert had made his literary mark, so to speak, he did not confine himself to *Fun*, but began contributing essays and drawings to other magazines, as well as developing his skill at short stories, a form of writing which seems to have been well suited to his mercurial temperament. He himself has written of this period in *The Theatre*:

> From time to time I also contributed to other magazines including the *Cornhill*, *London Society*, *Tinsley's*, *Temple Bar* and *Punch*. I furnished London correspondence to the *Invalide Russe* and I became the dramatic critic to the now defunct *Illustrated Times*. I also joined the Northern Circuit (in 1866), and duly attended the London and Westminster Courts, the Old Bailey, and Manchester and Liverpool Assizes, and Liverpool Sessions

*The most striking example of this occurred in the issue of *Fun* for 11 April 1868 when Gilbert published a page of verse and sketches entitled 'Trial by Jury'. This later formed the embryo of his first major collaboration with Arthur Sullivan in 1875. For all those readers who regard *Trial by Jury* as one of the partnership's most outstanding collaborations, this remarkable 'first draft' from *Fun* is reprinted at the end of this book.

> and Passage Court. But by this time I was making a very decent income by my contributions to current literature, and the Bar went by the board. I was always a clumsy and inefficient speaker, and, moreover, an unconquerable nervousness prevented me from doing justice to myself or my half-dozen unfortunate clients.

The contributions which Gilbert began making at this period of his life to these various magazines—then highly regarded and well-read, though now all long since defunct (except *Punch*, of course)—form the major part of this book. However, even with the coming of the success of the operas written with Arthur Sullivan, and the natural clamour for more which followed, Gilbert never gave up writing short stories, 'which he alone rated highest of his literary output', according to *Chamber's Literary Dictionary* (1961). It is doubtless the overwhelming fame of the operas that has caused these stories to slip into oblivion—a fate they ill deserve and the primary reason why I have rescued them from the dusty tomes in which they have lain forgotten for so many years.

The comic operas which made the names of Gilbert and Sullivan world famous, such as *Trial by Jury* (1875), *H.M.S. Pinafore* (1878), *The Pirates of Penzance* (1879), *Iolanthe* (1882), *Princess Ida* (1884), *The Mikado* (1885), *Ruddigore* (1887), *The Yeoman of the Guard* (1888) and *The Gondoliers* (1889), need no more than listing, so familiar are they and their themes. The public acclaim and knighthoods which were conferred on the two men are also well-known, just as is the perplexing quarrel which developed between the pair of them over the price of a carpet being installed into the newly built Savoy Theatre which staged their work. The collaboration of Gilbert and Sullivan never recovered from this bizarre argument, and their three further works together before Sullivan's death in 1900 are well below the standard of the rest. To those unfamiliar with their working life together and in particular the interaction of their very different personalities, I can do no better than recommend Hesketh Pearson's perceptive biography.

But to return to our study of W.S. Gilbert's early life. It

was as a direct result of his dramatic criticism for *Fun* that Gilbert was drawn to the theatre, and through his admiration of the work of the then very popular playwright, Tom Robertson, that he began to write plays himself. In his theatre column, 'From Our Stall', Gilbert often praised Robertson for his 'strongly individualized and thoroughly spontaneous' comedy, and once the two had met a friendship naturally enough developed. The next step was equally inevitable, as Hesketh Pearson explains:

> The first of his plays to be produced was written to order on the advice of Tom Robertson, who was thus his theatrical godfather as well as his chief influencer as producer and playwright. Gilbert finished it in a few days, and under the title *Dulcamara*, it appeared at the St. James's Theatre on December 29, 1866. Only thirty years of age, and therefore sanguine of success, Gilbert invited a few friends to supper after the performance. Fortunately the play was well received and the party was an appropriate close to a happy evening.

At a stroke, Gilbert had found his true métier, and in the next dozen years comedies, dramas, farces, burlesques, plays in blank verse, plays in stilted prose, plays in rhymed couplets, flowed from his pen. Though Gilbert was never noted for specifically acknowledging the help of others, he was grateful to Robertson and said so in his autobiographical essay for *The Theatre*:

> Of the many good and staunch friends I made on my introduction into journalism, one of the best and staunchest was poor Tom Robertson, and it is entirely to him that I owe my introduction to stage work. He had been asked by Miss Herbert, the then lessee of St. James's Theatre, if he knew anyone who could write a Christmas piece in a fortnight. Robertson, who had often expressed to me his belief that I should succeed as a writer for the stage, advised Miss Herbert to entrust me with the work, and the introduction resulted in my first piece, a burlesque on *L'Elisir d'Amore*, called *Dulcamara*.

Gilbert adds somewhat wryly to this that because of the haste of production, he did not discuss terms for his work until the play was a hit. When this matter did arise he suggested a fee of £30 would not be unreasonable.

> Mr. Emden (Miss Herbert's acting manager) looked rather surprised [says Gilbert], and, as I thought, disappointed. However, he wrote a cheque, asked for a receipt, and, when he had got it, said: 'Now take a bit of advice from an old stager who knows what he is talking about—never sell so good a piece as this for £30 again!' And I never have!

As he had done previously with his experiences at the bar, Gilbert used this period of his life as the basis for another short story, 'Maxwell and I' which was published in *London Society* in December 1866. The two playwrights who feature in it, Maxwell and Bailey, are clearly modelled on himself and Tom Robertson, but whether or not they were actually involved in trying to help an unfortunate woman escape from the bullying attentions of her husband—as described in the tale—is something we have no record of. There are also strangely prophetic elements in the relationship of Maxwell and Bailey which foreshadow the partnership of Gilbert and Sullivan themselves!

After Tom Robertson, the only other person Gilbert freely acknowledged as an influence on his career was Charles Dickens. Like many of his contemporaries, Gilbert had grown up reading Dickens's tales as they appeared in serial form during the 1840s and 50s. There is no doubt, too, that like Dickens he was fascinated by the supernatural, and he had an affection for fairies and humorous supernaturalism which shows up not only in certain of his short stories but also, of course, in a good many of the *Bab Ballads* as well as the comic operas. The first of his stories to exploit this vein in comic terms was 'The Triumph of Vice' which he wrote for the *Savage Club Papers* in 1867. It shows Gilbert clearly getting into his stride in his world of Topsy-turvydom, and the enthusiastic reception it received from readers was to prompt him to write similar stories which, as we shall see, he ultimately used as the basis for several of the operas produced with Arthur Sullivan. (As a matter of interest, Gilbert later adapted Dickens's novel *Great Expectations* into a three-act play which was produced with some success at the Court Theatre in London in 1871.)

The year 1867 in fact revealed Gilbert stretching his literary skills and imagination as far as possible. Not content with just writing humorous tales, he tried his hand at more general storytelling, and how well he succeeded can be judged from 'Jones' Victoria Cross', a story of personal heroism which was published in the magazine *Once a Week* on 2 November 1867, and 'Diamonds', a grim tale of tragedy complete with a vivid dénouement which he contributed to *Routledge's Christmas Annual* for 1867. The motivation for writing 'Jones' Victoria Cross' was clearly his interest in warfare, for as Hesketh Pearson has written,

> At the beginning of his life Gilbert had wanted to take part in the Crimean War, and ever since his failure to see it as a soldier he had pictured the Crimea as a land of romance. The subject constantly cropped up in his conversations, and one unfortunate lady was forced to listen to his views on that famous campaign during the greater part of a dinner.

This story, and 'Diamonds' which follows, are both far cries from the work by which he is best remembered—although both contain examples of his sly humour—yet they do demonstrate that he was a writer of wider scope than most people suspect. As Benjamin Fisher has commented on 'Diamonds' in *Horror Literature* (1982): 'It shows that even the consumate punster and vitriolic wit, W.S. Gilbert could turn his comic talents to horrific themes.' (The year 1867 also saw Gilbert married to Miss Lucy Blois Turner, the daughter of an Indian officer. Although the couple were evidently devoted to children, they were to have no family of their own.)

Two years passed before the appearance of Gilbert's next important short story, although he had been constantly busy in the interim on new plays, verses, essays and sketches. The tale was called 'An Elixir of Love' and it was published in *The Graphic* Christmas Number for 1869. The story is notable because it is the first short story that Gilbert was to utilize specifically as the basis for a play. It is a tale of fantasy with strongly humorous elements about the effect of a love philtre on the inhabitants of a sleepy parish. According to Sidney Dark and Rowland Grey it was the basis of the plot for *The Sorcerer*, the first collaboration by Gilbert and Sullivan to be produced in connection with Richard D'Oyly Carte, the entrepreneur, in November 1877:

> The idea of the story is the idea of the play, and some of the dialogue is taken almost word for word from the earlier work. In *The Sorcerer* we are introduced to 'the firm of J.W. Wells and Co., the old established sorcerers in St. Mary Axe.' In 'The Elixir of Life' we are told, 'In S. Martin's Lane lived Baylis and Culpepper, magicians, astrologers, and professors of the Black Art. Baylis had sold himself to the Devil at a very early age, and had become remarkably proficient in all kinds of enchantment. Culpepper had been his apprentice, and having also acquired considerable skill as a necromancer, was taken into partnership by the genial old magician, who from the first had taken a liking to the frank and fair-haired boy. Ten years ago the firm of Baylis and Culpepper stood at the very head of the London family magicians.' In 'The Elixir of Love' the Rev. Stanley Gay bought a nine-gallon cask of love-philtre from Messrs Baylis and Culpepper. In *The Sorcerer*, Mr. Wells tells Alexis that he sells his patent Oxy-Hydrogen Love-at-first-sight Philtre 'in four-and-a-half and nine gallon casks'. And there are many other resemblances between the play and the story.

Messrs Dark and Grey also believe that 'the germ of the idea of *Trial By Jury* may be found in "An Elixir of Love" in which, at the end, the Bishop marries the young lady as the judge marries the plaintiff in the play.' Despite the fact that Gilbert had already written the verses for *Fun* in 1868 entitled 'Trial by Jury', all these facts go to make this a most important story.

With the growth of his stature as a humorist and dramatist, Gilbert naturally began to assume some of the trappings of the successful Victorian gentleman. He took to riding each morning in Rotten Row, bought himself a small yacht in which he sailed with his wife and some of their friends, and joined the famous Junior Carlton Club. Although club life appealed to part of his nature, it also brought out the sarcasm in him, and he gave vent to this in the hilarious tale 'Tom Poulton's Joke' which appeared in *The Dark Blue* in March 1871. The tale was also, in part, inspired by a little circle of people he had belonged to during his early days as a contributor to *Fun*. Hesketh Pearson explains in his biography,

> At first Gilbert's fellow contributors looked upon him with disfavour . . . he was not, like themselves, a born journalist; he was an interloper, an outsider; and he was treated with scant courtesy in the weekly *Fun* dinners. Gilbert set himself to remedy this state of affairs.
>
> Moving to chambers in South Square, Gray's Inn, he founded a small coterie of young dramatists, critics and journalists, which was called 'The Serious Family'. Tom Hood (who succeeded Byron as editor of *Fun*) was elected father of the family, Gilbert became known as the *enfant terrible*, and H.J. Byron, Clement Scott, Tom Robertson, Artemus Ward and a score of others made up the family circle. They met weekly in Gilbert's chambers and the annual subscription was two guineas, from the payment of which Gilbert alone was exempted, on the understanding that he should supply a rump steak pie, a joint of cold boiled beef, a Stilton cheese, whisky and soda and bottled ale, every Saturday night for the rest of his life; an expensive way of becoming popular, though it probably paid him to know the sort of people it paid to know.

As the reader will come to appreciate after reading 'Tom Poulton's Joke', there is more than a little of this group in Gilbert's story which is, once again, filled with his sly humour and a situation straight from the world of Topsy-turvy.

During 1871 two more short stories by Gilbert appeared

which were destined to become stage successes. The first, 'Creatures of Impulse', was a delightful tale about a strange old woman who throws an inn and its residents into total confusion when she defies their efforts to remove her and begins casting spells on them! It appeared in *Tinsley's Magazine* in April 1871, and was produced as a musical in one act at the Court Theatre that same month with a score composed by Alberto Randegger. The second tale, 'The Wicked World' was another of Gilbert's excursions into supernaturalism and portrayed a battle between the good fairies and the evil forces at work in the world of humankind. The story was published in *Hood's Comic Annual* of 1871, but it was not until January 1873 that Gilbert's three act 'Fairy Comedy' based upon it opened at the Haymarket Theatre. Interestingly, the story itself inspired a burlesque version in 1873 written by Gilbert à Beckett entitled 'The Happy Land'. However, this play was suppressed after a short run at the Royal Court Theatre because 'it ran into censorship troubles as a result of its political satire', according to Jane W. Stedman, the author of *Gilbert Before Sullivan* (1969).*

Gilbert and Sullivan had actually first met casually in 1870, a year before these two stories were published, but it was in their immediate aftermath that the two men began their collaboration. In 1871 they were, of course, both well-known figures: Gilbert was regarded as one of the country's leading dramatists, and Arthur Sullivan one of its best composers. The suggestion that they collaborate on a musical opera resulted in *Thespis*, which was produced at the Gaiety Theatre in the December of that year. Although it was not a success, it attracted the attention of a man named Richard D'Oyly Carte, the manager of the Royalty Theatre in Soho, and when in 1875 he happened to meet Gilbert in the street he invited the dramatist to work on something for him in conjunction with Sullivan. 'Curiously enough', says Hesketh

*In 1873 Gilbert himself wrote an essay about the trials and tribulations of writing, producing and launching 'A Stage Play' which he inexplicably published under the pen-name of Horace Facile, though it is not difficult to recognize his unmistakable style. The essay appeared in *London Society* in 1873, and as it gives such a fascinating insight into what is clearly Gilbert's own theatrical world and experiences, I would direct the interested reader's attention to it.

Pearson, 'Gilbert had recently dramatised a story he had written for *Fun* and Carl Rosa had agreed to do the music for it: but the death of Mrs. Rosa had resulted in the return of the libretto, and Gilbert promised to let Carte read it. Carte immediately saw its possibilities and arranged a meeting between Gilbert and Sullivan. 'The 'story' from *Fun* was the page of verses entitled 'Trial by Jury' (reprinted at the end of this book) and the resulting collaboration which opened at the Royalty Theatre on 25 March 1875 saw the blossoming of arguably the most famous partnership in stage history.

As I mentioned earlier, the demands which success made upon W.S. Gilbert did not make him abandon short story writing, and the remaining selections, dating from the 1870s until just before his death in 1911, bear witness to this fact.

'Wide Awake' which he contributed to *Mirth: A Miscellany* in 1878 at a time when he was much absorbed in the third great collaboration, *H.M.S. Pinafore*, shows how easily he could slip from one medium to another, expressing his wit and humour as easily in the form of a comic opera or a short story like this one about a bachelor's cunning scheme to rid himself of a woman he had inadvertently become engaged to. By contrast, 'Comedy and Tragedy' is a tale of tragic irony against a historical background about an eighteenth-century French actress and her desperate ploy to rid herself of the unwelcome attentions of a persistent nobleman. The story, published in *The Stage Door* of Christmas 1879, was written with the specific idea of being dramatized, according to Gilbert, and when this was carried out, provided a most successful costume drama for the Lyceum Theatre in 1884. Writing of the short story in his essay, 'The English Aristophanes' in *The Fortnightly Review* of 1911, Walter Sichel comments, 'It is not so much the words said, but the situation and the feelings flashed on us by a few bold strokes after an elaborate prelude of artificial gaiety... examples of Gilbert's pathos are not often remembered, nor is the ironical pathos of his absurdities borne in mind.' And of the play, Sidney Dark and Rowland Grey observe, 'It is curious to note that Gilbert wrote best when he did not write at any length. The libretti of the operas are all very short. The short *Comedy and Tragedy* is superior to many of his comedies, and *The Hooligan* the best of his dramas, is in one act.'

'Foggerty's Fairy' which follows is another example of a story that Gilbert later turned into a stage comedy as a form of relaxation from the demands of the collaboration with Arthur Sullivan. Once more he turns romance and realism alike topsy-turvy through the adventures of a man who is given three wishes and catapults himself into a variety of extraordinary situations. The story was published in the *Temple Bar* magazine in March 1880 and was performed in its adapted form at the Savoy Theatre in December 1881. Biographers Sidney Dark and Rowland Grey who particularly admired this story have stated that it 'possibly may have supplied Mr. Hackett with the germ of the idea which he developed so cleverly in his farce, *Ambrose Applejohn's Adventure*.' And Walter Sichel has also said of it, 'Nowhere is a better example of his union of the practical and the poetical, and he was practical enough to repeat long afterwards several of his 'Foggerty' lines in his *Yeomen of the Guard*. ('Foggerty's Fairy' was also used as the title story for a collection of Gilbert's short stories—the only one prior to this book—which was published in 1890. The collection was only published in a limited quantity, and then had to be withdrawn when a theatrical producer claimed copyright in two of the short plays which were included to make up the length: hence it has become an extremely rare book today.)

'The Burglar's Story' is one of my favourite pieces of work by Gilbert and for this reason I wanted to find it a place—I believe many readers will share my view that this humorous episode of a burglar who has the tables turned on him by a householder is an example of Gilbert's Topsy-turvydom at its very best. 'The Burglar's Story' was published in *Routledge's Annual* for 1890 along with 'The Finger of Fate' which displays something of Gilbert's own temperament in its story of a bad-tempered man and his bizarre adventure with a negress. One has a distinct feeling when reading this particular tale that a psychologist might be able to tell us much about its author by reading between the lines!

Gilbert's talent was not just confined to humour; and in the next two stories he shows a fine mastery of pathos as well. 'Little Mim' is a moving story about some children and one appreciates some of its deeper feelings all the more when one recalls that Gilbert was only able to contain his vitriolic temper in the company of boys and girls, and that one of the major disappointments of his life was having no children. 'Angela' is a love story, but a love story tinged by tragedy as a young man dreams wistfully of the girl he can only admire from his sick bed. Both stories were published in *The Century* magazine in August and September 1890 in the aftermath of Gilbert's famous quarrel with Sullivan. Although we cannot be sure precisely when Gilbert actually wrote these stories, it is impossible not to wonder whether the circumstances of the time played any part in their generally pessimistic tone.

The last two items, which date from 1900 and 1908, just three years before his death, hark back again to themes that had absorbed Gilbert throughout his life, and had emerged time and time again in his plays, his verses, his stories and even his drawings: supernaturalism and personal experience. 'The Fairy's Dilemma' was his contribution to *The Graphic* Christmas Number of 1900, and was later adapted by him for the Garrick Theatre in May 1904. Although the piece was generally well received by the critics, Gilbert himself was pessimistic and confessed to a friend that 'the little piece is rather in the nature of a dramatic "lark".' He could never rid himself of the appeal of the fairy world, however, and what was to prove his last opera, *Fallen Fairies*, also dwelt on the theme. According to Hesketh Pearson, 'the libretto was taken holus-bolus from a blank-verse play of his called "The Wicked World", produced in the early seventies, and described by a critic as "coarse" and "foul" because one of the characters said, "I go to that good world where women are not devils till they die".' Gilbert's final short story, 'The Lady in the Plaid Shawl' was a contribution to a charitable fund-raising compendium entitled *The Flag* published by the *Daily Mail* to raise money for the Union Jack Fund in 1908. Gilbert was one of several grand old men of letters who provided items for the book—others included Rudyard Kipling, George Meredith, Robert Hitchens and Edgar Wallace. He sub-titled the story, 'A Scrap of Autobiography' and said in a note that it was 'literally true in every detail, even to the singular coincidence at the end'. Reading the story today, one suspects that this was yet another Gilbertian joke!

By a strange twist of fate, W.S. Gilbert died in a similar manner to his famous ancestor, Sir William Gilbert, who was drowned in the Azores. On 29 May 1911, while entertaining some friends at his home, Grim's Dyke at Harrow Weald, a young lady who was swimming in the lake cried out that she was out of her depth and drowning. Without hesitation, the 75-year-old host plunged in to rescue her, but moments later he disappeared from view. When his body was finally recovered from the bottom of the lake he was found to be dead—but not from drowning: the sudden coldness of the water had brought on a fatal heart attack. As Isaac Goldberg has observed in his essay, 'W.S. Gilbert's Topsy-turvydom' (*Bookman*, 1928), 'True to the pantomimic traditions of his beginnings, he died like a Harlequin in a gallant attempt to rescue Columbine from drowning . . . It was a romantic end for one of the most realistic, yet most fanciful, of the late Victorians. It crowned the paradox that was his life.'

The coincidence concerning the manner of Gilbert's death does not end with this, however. There was also an eerie coincidence surrounding the closing words he had written in what was to prove his last play, *The Hooligan*, a chilling little drama about the final hours of a condemned criminal. Reginald Allen has pointed out this strange quirk of fate in his *W.S. Gilbert: An Anniversary Survey* (1963):

> Not quite three months earlier Gilbert's final dramatic work, a grim little one-act play called *The Hooligan*, had opened at the Coliseum. Its terminal direction and curtain line—the last words written by Gilbert for the stage—were:
>
> (*The Doctor turns his face upward, feels his heart, and puts his ear to Solly's mouth*)
>
> DOCTOR: Heart-failure. Dead.

William Schwenk Gilbert, the writer of biting invective and cruel satire, the 'King of Topsy-turvydom', the man who always liked to have the last laugh when he was alive, had also managed to achieve this in death, as well!

PETER HAINING

'Gilbert's works are like a hall of mirrors—trick mirrors that work every distortion—along which he passes with an antic gait, delighted not least with the mirrors on the ceiling. Topsy-turvy? Yes and No. As when one inverts the figure eight; or turns upside down an hour-glass.'

Isaac Goldberg
W.S. Gilbert: A Century of Scholarship and Commentary (1970)

'No literary artist was ever less a realist than he. Fairyland was his home, and in his short stories, as in his plays, he is happiest and most successful in the fantastic land of make-believe. It is obvious that it is infinitely more difficult to make the fantastic convincing in a play than in a story. Gilbert was triumphant in the more difficult task, and in the easier he was sufficiently successful in his short stories to make one believe that, had the theatre not called him as its own, he would have won a considerable reputation as a story-writer.'

Sidney Dark and Rowland Grey
W.S. Gilbert: His Life and Letters (1923)

My Maiden Brief

LATE ON a certain May morning, as I was sitting at a modest breakfast in my 'residence chambers,' Pump Court, Temple, my attention was claimed by a single knock at an outer door, common to the chambers of Felix Polter, and of myself, Horace Penditton, both barristers-at-law of the Inner Temple.

The outer door was not the only article common to Polter and myself. We also shared what Polter (who wrote farces) was pleased to term a 'property' clerk, who did nothing at all, and a 'practicable' laundress, who did everything. There existed also a communion of interest in tea-cups, razors, gridirons, candlesticks, etc.; for although neither of us was particularly well supplied with the necessaries of domestic life, each happened to possess the very articles in which the other was deficient. So we got on uncommonly well together, each regarding his friend in the light of an indispensable other self. We had both embraced the 'higher walk' of the legal profession, and were patiently waiting for the legal profession to embrace us.

The single knock raised some well-founded apprehensions in both our minds.

'Walker!' said I to the property clerk.

'Sir!'

'If that knock is for me, I'm out, you know.'

'Of course, sir!''

'And Walker!' cried Polter.

'Sir!'

'If it's for me, I'm not at home!'

Polter always rejoiced if he could manage to make the conversation partake of a Maddisonian Mortonic character.

Mr. Walker opened the door. 'Mr. Penditton's a-breakfasting with the Master of the Rolls, if it's him you want; and if it isn't, Mr. Polter's with the Attorney-General.'

'You don't say so!' remarked the visitor; 'then p'raps

you'll give this to Mr. Penditton, as soon as the Master can make up his mind to part with him.'

And so saying, he handed to Walker a lovely parcel of brief-paper, tied up neatly with a piece of red tape, and minuted—

'Central Criminal Court, May Sessions, 1860.—The Queen on the prosecution of Ann Back *v.* Elizabeth Briggs. Brief for the prisoner. Mr. Penditton, one guinea.—Poddle and Shaddery, Hans Place.'

So it had come at last! Only an Old Bailey brief, it is true; but still a brief. We scarcely knew what to make of it. Polter looked at me, and I looked at Polter, and then we both looked at the brief.

It turned out to be a charge against Elizabeth Briggs, widow, of picking pockets in an omnibus. It appeared from my 'instructions' that my client was an elderly lady, and religious. On the 2nd April then last she entered an Islington omnibus, with the view of attending a tea and prayer meeting in Bell Court, Islington. A woman in the omnibus missed her purse, and accused Mrs. Briggs, who sat on her right, of having stolen it. The poor soul, speechless with horror at the charge, was dragged out of the omnibus, and as the purse was found in a pocket on the left-hand side of her dress, she was given into custody. As it was stated by the police that she had been 'in trouble' before, the infatuated magistrate who examined her committed her for trial.

'There, my boy, your fortune's made!' said Polter.

'But I don't see the use of my taking it,' said I; 'there's nothing to be said for her.'

'Not take it? Won't you, though? I'll see about that. You *shall* take it, and you shall get her off, too! Highly respectable old lady—attentive member of well-known congregation—parson to speak to her character, no doubt. As honest as you are!'

'But the purse was found upon her!'

'Well, sir, and what of that? Poor woman left-handed, and pocket in left of dress. Robbed woman right-handed, and pocket in right of dress. Poor woman sat on right of robbed woman. Robbed woman, replacing her purse, slipped it accidentally into poor woman's pocket. Ample folds of dress, you know—crinolines overlapping, and all that. Splendid defence for you!'

'Well, but she's an old hand, it seems. The police know her.'

'Police always do. "Always know everybody"—police maxim. Swear anything, they will.'

Polter really seemed so sanguine about it that I began to look at the case hopefully, and to think that something might be done with it. He talked to me to such effect that he not only convinced me that there was a good deal to be said in Mrs. Briggs's favour, but I actually began to look upon her as an innocent victim of circumstantial evidence, and determined that no effort should be wanting on my part to procure her release from a degrading but unmerited confinement.

Of the firm of Poddle and Shaddery I knew nothing whatever, and how they came to entrust Mrs. Briggs's case to me I can form no conception. As we (for Polter took so deep a personal interest in the success of Mrs. Briggs's case that he completely identified himself, in my mind, with her fallen fortunes) resolved to go to work in a thoroughly businesslike manner, we determined to commence operations by searching for the firm of Poddle and Shaddery in the *Law List*. To our dismay the *Law List* of that year had no record of Poddle, neither did Shaddery find a place in its pages. This was serious, and Polter did not improve matters by suddenly recollecting that he had once heard an old Q.C. say that, as a rule, the farther west of Temple Bar, the shadier the attorney; so that assuming Polter's friend to have come to a correct conclusion on this point, a firm dating officially from Hans Place, and whose name did not appear in Mr. Dalbiac's *Law List*, was a legitimate object of suspicion. But Polter, who took a hopeful view of anything which he thought might lead to good farce 'situations,' and who probably imagined that my first appearance on any stage as counsel for the defence was likely to be rich in suggestions, remarked that they might possibly have been certificated since the publication of the last *Law List*; and as for the *dictum* about Temple Bar, why, the case of Poddle and Shaddery might be one of those very exceptions whose existence is necessary to the proof of every general rule. So Polter and I determined to treat the firm in a spirit of charity, and accept their brief.

As the May sessions of Oyer and Terminer did not commence until the 8th, I had four clear days in which to study my brief and prepare my defence. Besides, there was a murder case, and a desperate burglary or two, which would probably be taken first, so that it was unlikely that the case of the poor soul whose cause I had espoused would be tried before the 12th. So I had plenty of time to master what Polter and I agreed was one of the most painful cases of circumstantial evidence ever submitted to a British jury; and I really believe that, by the first day of the May sessions, I was intimately acquainted with the details of every case of pocket-picking reported in *Cox's Criminal Cases* and *Buckler's Short-hand Reports*.

On the night of the 11th I asked Bodger of Brazenose, Norton of Gray's Inn, Cadbury of the Lancers, and three or four other men, college chums principally, to drop in at Pump Court, and hear a rehearsal of my speech for the defence, in the forthcoming *cause célèbre* of the Queen on the prosecution of Ann Back *v.* Elizabeth Briggs. At nine o'clock they began to appear, and by ten all were assembled. Pipes and strong waters were produced, and Norton of Gray's was forthwith raised to the Bench by the style and dignity of Sir Joseph Norton, one of the barons of her Majesty's Court of Exchequer; Cadbury, Bodger, and another represented the jury; Wilkinson of Lincoln's Inn was counsel for the prosecution, Polter was clerk of arraigns, and Walker, my clerk, was the prosecutrix.

Everything went satisfactorily: Wilkinson broke down in his speech for the prosecution; his witness prevaricated and contradicted himself in a preposterous manner; and my speech for the defence was voted to be one of the most masterly specimens of forensic ingenuity that had ever come before the notice of the court; and the consequence was, that the prisoner (inadequately represented by a statuette of the Greek Slave) was discharged, and Norton (who would have looked more like a Baron of the Exchequer if he had looked less like a tipsy churchwarden) remarked that she left the court without a stain upon her character.

The court then adjourned for refreshment, and the conversation took a general turn, after canvassing the respective merits of 'May it please your ludship,' and 'May it please you, my lud,' as an introduction to a counsel's speech—a discussion which terminated in favour of the latter form, as being a trifle more independent in its character. I remember proposing that the health of Elizabeth Briggs should be drunk in a solemn and respectful bumper; and as the evening wore on, I am afraid I became exceedingly indignant with Cadbury because he had taken the liberty of holding up to public ridicule an imaginary (and highly undignified) *carte de visite* of my unfortunate client.

The 12th May, big with the fate of Penditton and of Briggs, dawned in the usual manner. At ten o'clock Polter and I drove up in wigs and gowns to the Old Bailey; as well because we kept those imposing garments at our chambers, not having any use for them elsewhere, as to impress passers-by, and the loungers below the court, with a conviction that we were not merely Old Bailey counsel, but had come down from our usual sphere of action at Westminster, to conduct a case of more than ordinary complication. Impressed with a sense of the propriety of presenting an accurate professional appearance, I had taken remarkable pains with my toilette. I had the previous morning shaved off a flourishing moustache, and sent Walker out for half-a-dozen serious collars, as substitutes for the unprofessional 'lay-downs' I usually wore. I was dressed in a correct evening suit, and wore a pair of thin gold spectacles, and Polter remarked, that I looked the sucking bencher to the life. Polter, whose interest in the accuracy of my 'get up' was almost fatherly, had totally neglected his own; and he made his appearance in the raggedest of beards and moustaches under his wig, and the sloppiest of cheap drab lounging-coats under his gown.

I modestly took my place in the back row of the seats allotted to the bar; Polter took his in the very front, in order to have an opportunity, at the close of the case, of telling the leading counsel in the hearing of the attorneys, the name and address of the young and rising barrister who had just electrified the court. In various parts of the building I detected Cadbury, Wilkinson, and others, who had represented judge, jury, and counsel, on the previous evening. They had been instructed by Polter (who had had some experience in 'packing' a house) to distribute themselves about the court, and, at the termination of the speech for the defence, to give vent to their feelings in that applause which is always so quickly suppressed by the officers of a court of justice. I was rather annoyed at this, as I did not consider it altogether legitimate; and my annoyance was immensely increased when I found that my three elderly maiden aunts, to whom I had been foolish enough to confide the fact of my having to appear on the 12th, were seated in state in that portion of the court allotted to friends of the bench and bar, and busied themselves by informing everybody within whisper-shot, that I was to defend Elizabeth Briggs, and that this was my first brief. It was some little consolation, however, to find that the unceremonious manner in which the facts of the cases that preceded mine were explained and commented upon by judge, jury, and counsel, caused those ladies great uneasiness, and indeed compelled them, on one or two occasions, to beat an unceremonious retreat.

At length the clerk of arraigns called the case of Briggs, and with my heart in my mouth I began to try to recollect the opening words of my speech for the defence, but I was interrupted in that hopeless task by the appearance of Elizabeth in the dock.

She was a pale, elderly widow, rather buxom, and remarkably neatly dressed, in slightly rusty mourning. Her hair was arranged in two sausage curls, one on each side of her head, and looped in two festoons over the forehead. She appeared to feel her position acutely, and although she did not weep, her red eyes showed evident traces of recent tears. She grasped the edge of the dock and rocked backwards and forwards, accompanying the motion with a low moaning sound, that was extremely touching. Polter looked back at me with an expression which plainly said, 'If ever an innocent woman appeared in that dock, that woman is Elizabeth Briggs!'

The clerk of arraigns now proceeded to charge the jury. 'Gentlemen of the jury, the prisoner at the bar, Elizabeth Briggs, is indicted for that she did, on the 2nd April last, steal from the person of Ann Back a purse containing ten shillings and fourpence, the moneys of the said Ann Back. There is another count to the indictment, charging her with having received the same, knowing it to have been stolen. To both of these counts the prisoner has pleaded "Not guilty," and it is your charge to try whether she is guilty or not guilty.' Then to the bar, 'Who appears in this case?'

Nobody replying in behalf of the crown, I rose and remarked that I appeared for the defence.

A counsel here said that he believed the brief for the prosecution was entrusted to Mr. Porter, but that that gentleman was engaged at the Middlesex Sessions, in a case which was likely to occupy several hours, and that he (Mr. Porter) did not expect that Briggs's case would come on that day.

A consulation then took place between the judge and the clerk of arraigns. At its termination, the latter functionary said, 'Who is the junior counsel present?'

To my horror, up jumped Polter, and said, 'I think it's very likely that I am the junior counsel in court. My name is Polter, and I was only called last term!'

A titter ran through the crowd, but Polter, whose least fault was bashfulness, only smiled benignly at those around him.

Another whispering between judge and clerk. At its conclusion, the clerk handed a bundle of papers to Polter, saying, at the same time,

'Mr. Polter, his lordship wishes you to conduct the prosecution.'

'Certainly,' said Polter; and he opened the papers, glanced at them, and rose to address the court.

He began by requesting that the jury would take into consideration the fact that he had only that moment been placed in possession of the brief for the prosecution of the prisoner at the bar, who appeared, from what he could gather from a glance at his instructions, to have been guilty of as heartless a robbery as ever disgraced humanity. He would endeavour to do his duty, but he feared that, at so short a notice, he should scarcely be able to do justice to the brief with which he had been most unexpectedly entrusted. He then went on to state the case in masterly manner, appearing to gather the facts, with which, of course, he was perfectly intimate, from the papers in his hand. He commented on the growing frequency of omnibus robberies, and then went on to say:—

'Gentlemen, I am at no loss to anticipate the defence on which my learned friend will base his hope of inducing you to acquit that wretched woman. I don't know whether it has ever been your misfortune to try criminal cases before, but if it has, you will be able to anticipate his defence as certainly as I can. He will probably tell you, because the purse was found in the left-hand pocket of that miserable woman's dress, that she is left-handed, and on that account wears her pocket on the left side, and he will then, if I am not very much mistaken, ask the prosecutrix if she is not right-handed, and, lastly, he will ask you to believe that the prosecutrix, sitting on the prisoner's left, slipped the purse accidentally into the prisoner's pocket. But, gentlemen, I need not remind you that the facts of these omnibus robberies are always identical. The prisoner always *is* left-handed, the prosecutrix always *is* right-handed, and the prosecutrix always *does* slip the purse accidentally into the prisoner's pocket, instead of her own. My lord will tell you that this is so, and you will know how much faith to place upon such a defence, should my friend think proper to set it up.' He ended by entreating the jury to give the case their attentive consideration, and stated that he relied confidently on an immediate verdict of 'Guilty.' He then sat down, saying to the usher, 'Call Ann Back.'

Ann Back, who was in court, shuffled up into the witness-box and was duly sworn. Polter then drew out her evidence bit by bit, helping her with leading questions of the most flagrant description. I knew that I ought not to allow this, but I was too horrified at the turn matters had taken to interfere. At the conclusion of the examination in chief Polter sat down triumphantly, and I rose to cross-examine.

'You are right-handed, Mrs Back?' (*Laughter.*)

'Oh, yes, sir!'

'Very good. I've nothing else to ask you.'

So Mrs. Back stood down, and the omnibus conductor took her place. His evidence was not material, and I declined to cross-examine. The policeman who had charge of the case followed the conductor, and his evidence was to the effect that the purse was found in her pocket.

I felt that this witness ought to be cross-examined, but not having anything ready, I allowed him to stand down. A question, I am sorry to say, then occurred to me, and I requested his lordship to allow the witness to be recalled.

'You say you found the purse in her pocket, my man?'

'Yes, sir.'

'Did you find anything else?'

'Yes, sir.'

'What?'

'Two other purses, a watch with the bow broken, three handkerchiefs, two silver pencil-cases, and a hymn-book.' (*Roars of laughter*.)

'You may stand down.'

'That is the case, my lord,' said Polter.

It was now my turn to address the court. What could I say? I believe I observed, that, undeterred by my learned friend's opening speech, I *did* intend to set up the defence he had anticipated. I set it up, but I don't think it did much good. The jury, who were perfectly well aware that this was Polter's first case, had no idea but that I was an old hand at it; and no doubt thought me an uncommonly clumsy one. They had made every allowance for Polter, who needed nothing of the kind, and they made none at all for me, who needed all they had at their disposal. I soon relinquished my original line of defence, and endeavoured to influence the jury by vehement assertions of my personal conviction of the prisoner's innocence. I warmed with my subject, for Polter had not anticipated me here, and I believe I grew really eloquent. I think I staked my professional reputation on her innocence, and I sat down expressing my confidence in a verdict that would restore the unfortunate lady to a circle of private friends, several of whom were waiting in the court below to testify to her excellent character.

'Call witnesses to Mrs. Briggs's character,' said I.

'Witness to the character of Briggs!' shouted the crier.

The cry was repeated three or four times outside the court; but there was no response.

'No witnesses to Brigg's character here, my lord!' said the crier.

Of course I knew this very well; but it sounded respectable to expect them.

'Dear, dear,' said I, 'this is really most unfortunate. They must have mistaken the day.'

'Shouldn't wonder,' observed Polter, rather drily.

I was not altogether sorry that I had no witnesses to adduce, as I am afraid that they would scarcely have borne the test of Polter's cross-examination. Besides, if I had examined witnesses for the defence, Polter would have been entitled to a reply, of which privilege he would, I was sure, avail himself.

Mr. Baron Bounderby proceeded to sum up, grossly against the prisoner, as I then thought, but, as I have since had reason to believe, most impartially. He went carefully over the evidence, and told the jury that if they believed the witnesses for the prosecution, they should find the prisoner guilty, and if they did not—why, they should acquit her. The jury were then directed by the crier to 'consider their verdict,' which they couldn't possibly have done, for they immediately returned a verdict of 'Guilty.' The prisoner not having anything to say in arrest of judgment, the learned judge proceeded to pronounce sentence—enquiring, first of all, whether anything was known about her?

A policeman stepped forward, and stated that she had been twice convicted at this court of felony, and once at the Middlesex Court.

Mr. Baron Bounderby, addressing the prisoner, told her that she had been most properly convicted, on the clearest possible evidence; that she was an accomplished thief, and a most dangerous one; and that the sentence of the court was that she be imprisoned and kept to hard labour for the space of eighteen calendar months.

No sooner had the learned judge pronounced this sentence than the poor soul stooped down, and taking off a heavy boot, flung it at my head, as a reward for my eloquence on her behalf; accompanying the assault with a torrent of invective against my abilities as a counsel, and my line of defence. The language in which her oration was couched was perfectly shocking. The boot missed me, but hit a reporter on the head, and to this fact I am disposed to attribute the unfavourable light in which my speech for the defence was placed in two or three of the leading daily papers next morning. I hurried out of court as quickly as I could, and, hailing a Hansom, I dashed back to chambers, pitched my wig at a bust of Lord Brougham, bowled over Mrs. Briggs's prototype with my gown, packed up, and started that evening for the West coast of Cornwall. Polter, on the other hand, remained in town, and got plenty of business in that and the ensuing session, and afterwards on circuit. He is now a flourishing Old Bailey counsel, while I am as briefless as ever.

The Poisoned Postage Stamp

A Sensation Romance

I

AUGUSTUS DE Vere Billingsby was, as his name would divulge, the assistant in a chemist's shop. But he had a soul above *fiat mistura*—a mind that spurned *mane sumend*—an intellect that soared higher than *pillulae sex*. He wrote for all the principal magazines and papers. You will observe that I am careful in saying he wrote *for* them. I am compelled to admit that his efforts never went beyond that, for his articles were never printed.

Only one of Augustus's works ever reached posterity. It was the following poem written after a visit per London, Chatham and Dover to the Crystal Palace, and suggested by painful, commingled with pleasant, reminiscences:

Little Miss Muffet
Sat at a buffet,
  'Neath Spiers and Pondian sway.
There came a young rider,
Who asked for some cider,
  And then was unable to pay.

These verses—which Billingsby used fondly to speak of as 'a poem which was the fruit of much Spiers and Pondering'—was sent to various journals, but without success. But it was fated that the public should not lose it. He left a copy inadvertently on the counter, and his employer, Mr. Squills, used it to cover a pot of *unguentum* for Mr. Potherby's bad leg. Mr. Potherby opened the parcel and read the lines before he destroyed the paper. And that was a large public for Billingsby!

Billingsby had written a story for the (but no! Prudence forbids our mentioning the name of the periodical in question—Ed.), and one of the rules of the periodical (the name of which prudence forbids us to mention—Ed.), was that no MSS could be returned if they were not accompanied by a stamped and directed envelope (and a very good rule, too—Ed.).

'Ha, ha!' cried Augustus, as he enclosed a directed envelope (adhesive) and a stamp (ditto) to the editor, with his manuscript.

He had smeared the flap of the envelope, and the back of the stamp, which he had not affixed to the envelope, for an object which will be seen hereafter, with that most prompt and deadly poison (name suppressed for obvious reasons—Ed.).

'Ha, ha!' he had better not reject my MS' said Billingsby.

II

Billingsby was engaged in the manufacture of antibilious pills. Possibly the aroma of these beneficent creations of the pharmacopoeia affected his brain with benevolence.

He started!

He sneezed!

'Ha!' he exclaimed, rubbing a pill wildly into the roots of his hair in the excitement of the moment, 'He may—he may—he may use the envelope to send me a cheque for my article. I have heard of such things. And if he should die—they may refuse to cash it! Let me fly to preserve him. Mr. Popkin's pills can wait.'

III

Billingsby clamoured at the portals of the (name suppressed for the obvious reason—Ed.), office. A mild person put his head out of the window and said, 'What the doose are you a-kicking up that row for?'

'I must see the editor. It is a matter of life and death.'

'What name, sir?'

'My name is Norval for all practical purposes, for he would not know me by name.'

The mild being disappeared and returned to usher the trembling Billingsby into *THE PRESENCE*. (The printer is requested to put that in caps for obvious reasons—Ed.). In the Editor's right hand was a manuscript, which the unhappy Billingsby recognized as his. In his left was an envelope. Before him lay a stamp. Billingsby was the prey of conflicting emotions. His MS. was about to be rejected—should he let 'venom do its work'?

While he hesitated, the editor—with the sweet placid smile editors are wont to use—slipped the MS. into its cover, drew the flap of the envelope over a Patent Damper, did the same for the stamp, and affixed it! Then looking up, said:

'May I ask the reason of your visit?'

The unhappy Billingsby saw a large bluebottle, attracted by the moisture, settle on the Damper, taste the fatal spring, and then fall on his back, with his six quivering legs upwards, on the blotting-pad. Poor bluebottle!

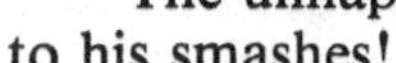

An hour later all that remained of Augustus De Vere Billingsby was a powder triturated to impalpability in the bottom of Mr. Squill's mortar.

The unhappy wretch had thus committed suicide. Peace to his smashes!

MAXWELL AND I

I

IT WAS a dull Christmas night that Ted Maxwell and I were spending, boxed up in our chambers on a top-floor of Garden Court, Temple. Not but that we had plenty of friends in London who were keeping it up merrily that night—friends whose merriment was tempered by the fact that circumstances beyond our control required that we should spend the afternoon and evening in chamber solitude. But that Grand Fairy Christmas Extravaganza, the One-Eyed Calendars, Sons of Kings; or, Zobeide and the Three Great Black Dogs, was due on the boards of a minor metropolitan theatre by ten o'clock on the following night, and there were two scenes still unfinished, and three or four songs still unwritten.

For we were dramatic authors, Maxwell and I. Of course we were a great many other things besides, for dramatic authorship in England is but an unremunerative calling at the best of times; and Maxwell and I were mere beginners. We wrote for magazines, we were dramatic critics, we were the life and soul (such as they were) of London and provincial comic papers, we supplied 'London Letters,' crammed with exclusive political secrets, and high-class aristocratic gossip, for credulous country journals; we wrote ballads for music publishers, and we did leaders and reviews for the weeklies. I had almost forgotten to add that we were barristers-at-law of the Inner Temple, esquires, because that fact was only brought under our notice twice a year; once when the treasurer of the Inn applied to us for our term fees, and once when the Directories and Court Guides made ironical application to us for information concerning our titles and country seats.

There had been an aggravating rehearsal of our extravaganza that morning. It was then discovered that a 'carpenter's scene' must, absolutely, be introduced in order to allow time for the elaborate 'set' with which the piece was to conclude.

The last scene was, as a matter of course, unfinished; the chorus that opened the piece had not yet been written; and several 'cuts' had to be made in our favourite scene. Moreover, the leading lady, Miss Patty de Montmorenci, had expressed her intention of ruining everything if she were not permitted to introduce the '*Miserere*' from the *Trovatore*, after the comic duet between Mesrour and Zobeide; and Mr. Sam Travers, the leading low comedian, had insisted on our finding occasion for him to get over a brick wall with glass on the top of it for him to stick in.

Three or four hours' incessant work enabled us to overcome these difficulties with greater or less success. The 'carpenter's scene' was written (goodness only knows what it had to with the plot!); the opening and final choruses were determined on, the necessary cuts were made, and the excised good things carefully stowed away for our next production. Miss de Montmorenci had her '*Miserere*,' Mr. Sam Travers his broken glass.

'Now,' said Maxwell, 'let's see how that bit goes, after Travers' scene—the bit between Scherazade and Zobeide, I mean.'

SCHER. One morning early when I sought my bower
Without spec-*tater* just to *cull-a-flower*,
I found my cavalier astride the wall,
And in the glass entangled, cloak and all.
And then I heard the wretched youth, alas!
Casting some strong reflections on the glass;
And, after having to perdition booked it,
He first *un*hooked his cloak, and then—he hooked it!
ZO. You did not see his face!
SCHER. Alas! He fled
Ere I could make remarks upon that head;
But as I scanned the footsteps in the mould
With eager curiosity, behold
I found—

'Open the door! For God's sake, open the door!'

Maxwell and I started to our feet. We had 'sported our oak,' as we did not want to be disturbed, and the voice (a woman's) was accompanied by a violent knocking, as if the applicant were beating at the door with her open palm.

We ran to the door, and as soon as we had opened it a couple of women rushed violently past us into our sitting-room.

'Shut the door—don't stop to ask any questions—shut the door, I say!'

We closed it in mute astonishment. One of the women, the younger, had fallen on the hearthrug in a swoon; the elder was leaning against the mantelpiece, her head resting on her right hand, and her left hand pressed to her side. Both were soaked with rain and splashed with slushy mud, but they appeared to be dressed in clothes of good quality, and made with some taste. The elder woman, as she stood against the mantelpiece, appeared to be about forty years of age, tall, thin, and notwithstanding her pitiable condition, ladylike. The younger woman was evidently her daughter, and appeared, as well as we could judge as she lay crouched upon the hearthrug, to be about sixteen or eighteen years old.

'I beg your pardon for entering your rooms so unceremoniously,' said the elder woman, as soon as she had recovered her breath. 'If you will allow me to sit down for a few moments, I will explain all.'

Maxwell placed her in a comfortable armchair near the fire, and then busied himself in getting out the brandy. I prepared, in a confused sort of way, to pick up the young girl who had fainted, and who, by this time, gave some evidence of returning consciousness. After two or three attempts, I contrived, rather clumsily I am afraid, to get her on to the sofa; and by that time she had so far revived as to be able to express her thanks for the attention. I then saw that the estimate I had formed of her age was rather over than under the mark, for she was not more than fifteen or sixteen at the utmost. She was very pale, and apparently in delicate health; her features were pretty, without being strictly handsome; and she had a quantity of light yellow hair, which fell in masses over her shoulders as I loosened the strings of her bonnet.

'Now,' said Maxwell, as he placed a steaming tumbler of brandy and water before each of the women, 'put that away, and then tell us all about it.'

'I thank you very much,' said the elder woman. 'We—'

'I'll not hear a word while there's a drop of brandy left in that tumbler. Drink it off directly.'

But that was clearly impossible, for he had mixed it on the Jack-tar principle of 'half-and-half.' So on my representing this to him, he was pleased to pass a more lenient sentence, and to reduce the punishment, in each case, by one half.

'I am very grateful to you for your kindness,' said the elder woman. 'My daughter and I have fled from the violence of my infuriated husband, who, but for your kindness would certainly have killed us.'

'May I inquire the particulars?' said he.

'My husband is a master mariner, and we occupy a house in Essex Street, Strand, where I let apartments. He is a dreadfully violent man, and this evening he was brought home, after an absence of three days, by two policemen, quite drunk. He insisted upon having more drink as soon as they had left, and he gradually worked himself into a frenzy of excitement. It unfortunately happened that one of our lodgers left yesterday without paying his rent, and as soon as this fact came to his knowledge he flew into a violent rage, and struck me here,' laying her hand upon her side. 'He then seized a life-preserver, and, in an agony of terror, Emmie and I rushed into the street, with the intention of seeking shelter from his violence in my nephew's chambers, which are nearly opposite this house. In my excitement, I could not find them for some time, and we wandered about Temple for, I should think, a quarter of an hour, before we found Garden Court; and when at length we did find it, we discovered to our great sorrow, that his chambers were closed, and a notice posted on his door to the effect that he had gone out of town for a week. I heard my husband's voice in the immediate neighbourhood, and seeing only one window with a light in it (owing, I suppose, to its being Christmas-day), my daughter and I made our way to it as quickly as we could, and affected the unceremonious entrance for which we have to offer you our humblest apologies.'

'If your story is true,' said Maxwell, '(and I see no reason to doubt it), you shall have an asylum here until we can place you beyond the reach of your husband's violence. But you are wet through. How in the world are we to remedy that?'

'I have it,' said I. 'I'll run round to Mrs. Deeks, and get a change of some kind for these ladies.'

Mrs. Deeks was one of that remarkable and much-abused class of women, the Temple laundresses. She was a pleasant, cheery little old woman, with a quiet chirruping voice, and so big a heart, that you wondered how she could find room for it in her particularly little body. She had 'done for' us during the three years we had lived in the Temple, and had nursed me through two severe illnesses. She was our adviser in all circumstances of social difficulty, and the present embarrassment appeared to be, pre-eminently, a case for her interference. So Maxwell agreed that we could not do better than take counsel with her immediately; and I started off to lay the delicate circumstances of our case before her without a moment's delay.

I hurried through the half-melted slush, and driving rain, to Gate's Court, Clement's Inn, where the old lady lived. She was entertaining a select company of laundresses and their 'good gentlemen,' and seemed to be enjoying the gentility of her position as hostess so completely, that I felt I was doing a brutal thing in interrupting her proceedings. It was a case of urgency, however, which could not wait, so I did not hesitate to lay the particulars before her, and claim her assistance.

The old lady had herself had some experience of conjugal existence under difficulties, for the late Mr. Deeks, of no occupation worth mentioning, was much given to knocking her down and dancing upon her, during the twenty years of their married life. His chief cause of complaint was that she was 'much too good for him,' but a merciful Providence, pitying his conscientious difficulties, had eventually removed him to a sphere in which he probably had no difficulty in meeting with congenial companionship. By virtue of her personal experiences with Mr. Deeks, and the fact that she had lived for many years in a neighbourhood where gentlemen of his stamp are common, she set herself up as a judge of bad husbands, and in that capacity entered with considerable zeal into the study of the case I placed before her.

The old lady made up a bundle of dry clothes with all

expedition, and, after apologizing to her guests, started off with me to the chambers.

Our visitors were still drying themselves by the fire, and overwhelmed me with their thanks when I entered with Mrs. Deeks. Maxwell and I then made a hollow feint of having important business in a man's chambers in the immediate neighbourhood, which would detain us half-an-hour or so, and left the two ladies and Mrs. Deeks to their devices.

It was still pouring with rain, so Maxwell and I sat on the bottom step of the staircase, and took counsel together.

'Now, Ted, my boy, what are we to do?'

'This,' said Maxwell, who had a turn for stating cases, 'is a case of peculiar delicacy. Here we have two bachelors in chambers, to whom, in the dead of night, enter two sopping females—one middle-aged and not otherwise remarkable; the other very young, and I think I may add interesting.'

'Decidedly interesting,' said I.

'And decidedly interesting. They come round with an account of themselves, which on the one hand, may be as true as gospel, and, on the other, may be a story of a cock and a bull.'

'That's not likely,' said I.

'I did not say it was likely. I am not dealing with probabilities, I am dealing with facts. Whether it is true or not, the fact remains that two sopping females have quartered themselves on two dry bachelors.'

'One dry bachelor and one wet one,' was my rather captious amendment.

'Now, don't interrupt me unnecessarily; they were both quite dry when the women entered. The fact that one of them has since been out in the rain cannot be taken to act retrospectively. The two sopping females quartered themselves upon two dry bachelors.'

'Be it so.'

'The question then arises,' said Maxwell, dropping the argumentative form in which he had opened the case, 'what the devil are we to do?'

'Precisely. And what do you suggest?'

'There are three courses open to us: firstly, to allow these ladies to occupy our chambers until we can dispose of them satisfactorily, and get rooms at Sams' Hotel for ourselves: secondly, to allow them to occupy our chambers and *not* get rooms at Sams' Hotel for ourselves—to occupy them conjointly in short; and thirdly, to wash our hands of the whole affair, and, by placing the sopping ladies on the landing and once more sporting our oak, reduce the present complicated state of things to its normal simplicity.'

I am bound, in justice to Maxwell, to admit that I believe that he placed his last course before me, simply that the beauty of his argument might not be impaired by the omission of any of its features. As he himself expressed it in reply to my expostulations, he did not suggest it as a prudent course—he simply threw it out for my consideration.

It did not take us long to determine that the first and second propositions alone demanded our serious attention.

'You see,' said Maxwell, 'you get two ladies and two gentlemen on the one hand, and a sitting-room and a double-bedded bed-room on the other. There is an utter want of proportion between the two groups, to say nothing of the fact that a cold and critical society is looking quietly on, eager to pounce upon and make the most of any step which is not characterized by the nicest discrimination.'

'The upshot of all this would seem to be, that we had better let them occupy our rooms until tomorrow, and that the best thing we can do is to go and secure a couple of beds at Sams'.'

'That is the conclusion to which I should have come in time, if you had allowed me to argue it out my own way,' said Maxwell, rather pettishly; 'but I suppose we had better let our guests know what we propose to do, before we take any further steps in the matter.'

So we went upstairs again, and finding from Mrs. Deeks that the ladies were in as presentable a condition as circumstances would permit, we walked in with the intention of obtaining their agreement to our suggestion.

They were sitting by a blazing fire, comfortably wrapped up in shawls and flannel petticoats, while the dresses they had taken off were steaming away on the backs of two chairs. There was a quiet, cosy look about the old chambers, which was partly due to the fact that Mrs. Deeks had laid a substantial supper, partly to the presence of the ladies themselves under circumstances which generated mutual communicativeness, and partly to the contrast that the room afforded to the miserable splashing pavement which we had been contemplating for the last half hour. I daresay that the appearance presented by our visitors, muffled up as they were in Mrs. Deeks's underclothing, would have been sufficiently ridiculous, if it were not that their pale appealing faces, thinned as they were by hard usage and insufficient food, their utter helplessness in our hands, and an exaggerated sense of the intrusion of which they had been guilty, brought the pathetic side of their case so forcibly before us that even Mrs. Deeks's flannel petticoats were glorified by their association with it.

We sat down to supper; Maxwell doing the host in a pleasant, cheery, country gentleman sort of way, intended to convey the impression that we were not at all taken aback by the events of the evening, and that, in point of fact, this sort of thing happened to us three times a week, or so.

'I beg your pardon,' said Maxwell, 'may I venture to ask whom I am addressing?'

'Talboys, sir—Mrs. Talboys; and this is my daughter Emmie Talboys. I should have told you our names before, but in the excitement of the events that brought us into your chambers, I forgot to do so.'

'Pray don't mention it. I am Maxwell, my friend here is Bailey—Bob Bailey; and now that we all know one another, I'll tell you, Mrs. Talboys, what we—that is, Bailey and I—propose to do. We propose to give up our chambers to you for the night—Mrs. Deeks will see to the necessary alterations—and to take up a temporary abode in an adjoining hostelry—at Sams', in fact. Now, Mrs. Talboys, have you, or has Miss Talboys, any objection to urge to this arrangement.'

Mrs. Talboys was, of course, exceedingly and unnecessarily grateful to us for our hospitality, and as the only objection she could urge was the sorrow she should feel at putting us to so much trouble, the matter was soon decided, and Mrs. Deeks received instructions to make our room as suitable to the necessities of two ladies as circumstances would allow, while we finished supper.

We soon became very pleasant and chatty together, a state of things for which, I believe, we were in no small measure indebted to the fact that tea formed one of the items in our repast, and that Mrs. Talboys presided at the tea-pot. There are no circumstances better calculated to make an Englishwoman look and feel thoroughly at home, under difficulties, than the sitting at the head of a table pouring out tea. It is a position that comes naturally to her, and she fits into it as a ball fits into a socket. She handles your tea-pot, and your milk-jug, and your sugar-basin, and your cups and saucers with an air of understanding their various relations, properties, and proportions, to which no bachelor—or married man, for matter of that—was ever known to attain. It puts her on good terms with herself and her surroundings, and Maxwell and I agreed that tea in chambers, presided over by a lady, although in Mrs. Deeks's underclothing, was as different a thing altogether to tea under bachelor circumstances as rum-punch to curds and whey.

Maxwell and I took our leave of Mrs. and Miss Talboys with as much ceremony as if they had been our hostesses and we their guests, and started off for Sams', which then stood opposite King's College. After passing an unsatisfactory night at that dingy establishment, we returned to our chambers to breakfast. Mrs. Talboys and her daughter had, it appeared, passed as comfortable a night as circumstances would permit, and after a pleasant breakfast, we took further counsel with our *protégées* as to what was to be done.

It appeared from Mrs. Talboys' statement, that her impulsive husband was expected to leave London for Melbourne the next day; so Maxwell and I determined that our course, as far as Mrs. Talboys and her daughter were concerned, was to afford them the protection of our chambers for another night; after which they would be enabled to return to their house without dread of further molestation. This arrangement appeared to set the mind of Mrs. Talboys completely at rest, and she overwhelmed us with expressions of gratitude. She expressed herself, however, with so much anxiety as to the condition of her husband, the lodgers, and the furniture, after the *fracas*, that Maxwell and I determined to call at the house in Essex Street on our way to rehearsal, and, in the assumed character of intending lodgers, ascertain whether any harm had resulted to the establishment or its inmates in consequence of the previous night's disturbance.

II

The rehearsal was called for eleven o'clock, and as we had upwards of an hour to spare, Maxwell and I made our way at once into the heart of Captain Talboy's social privacy. The house in Essex Street had all the appearance of a carelessly conducted lodging-house. The windows were dirty, the blinds were awry, one of the area railings was broken, and the place generally conveyed an impression of insolvency, which the presence of a canary in the parlour window did little to remove. The street-door was open, for a drabby girl of fourteen, in ragged brown stockings, was cleaning the steps, and a rusty cat sat by her side, looking up and down the street wistfully with an expression of countenance that seemed to say, 'This is a very hopeless concern of ours; I wonder if there's an opening for me at No. 15.' That there was at least one inmate, however, whose spirits were not damped by this state of things, was testified by a huge voice that came rolling out at the open door, bearing upon it the refrain of some old-fashioned nautical song, and which ran, I think, as follows:

> 'Oh, Jenny, she cock'd her eye at me,
>   A long time ago!
> A long time ago, you lubber!
> A long time ago, you lubber!
>   A long time ago!'

Maxwell and I listened a few minutes, and eventually the singer stopped, and applause, as from a solitary tumbler, appeared to reward his efforts. We then asked the wretched servant-girl, as a matter of form, if Mrs. Talboys was at home?

'No, sir, missis is just gone out, sir. Is it about the lodgings?'

'Yes, it's about the lodgings.'

'Master's in sir,' said she, 'I'll tell him, and p'raps he'll show 'em.'

The unhappy girl, who appeared to be suffering from a chronic cold, which she relieved from time to time on the back of the hearth-stone, gathered herself together, and limped into the dining-room, whence the sounds of revelry proceeded. She came out almost immediately, with a ducking, dodging action, as if something had been thrown at her, and told us to step in.

We obeyed her instructions, not without much misgiving, and, passing two corded chests, labelled 'Captain Talboys, ship *Heart's Content*, Limehouse Reach,' which stood in the hall, we found ourselves in the presence of the carousers whose voices we had heard in the street. One, evidently Captain Talboys, was a big, muscular, hairy sailor, with a low square brow, a bull neck, great brown hands, and shoulders of enormous breadth. His coat was off, and was lying on a chair hard by. He wore square-cut black trousers, a black satin waistcoat, and thick square-toed Wellington boots. His companion was a small, unwholesome-looking, fat, Jew, with a pasty complexion, black moustache and whiskers, a massive gold chain, and several thick rings on his dirty squabby fingers.

'Come in shipmet,' said Captain Talboys, in a thick husky voice, 'come in; and what'll yer take? Here's brandy, rum, whisky, gin, anything. Help yourself shipmet! Yo ho! help yourself!'

'Thank you, I don't think we'll drink anything,' said I, as I stumbled over the coal-scoop, which appeared to have been the missile with which the announcement of our appearance by the drabby servant girl was greeted. 'We have come about some apartments which you advertise in your window.'

'Here, you gal!' shouted Captain Talboys.

The drabby girl made her appearance at the door.

''Partments. Take 'em up,' was the brief form of words in which he explained the object of our visit to the servant.

The fat Jew had been staring at Maxwell and at me rather anxiously for a minute or two, and just as we turned to leave the room he said, 'Beg your pardon, gents, but I think I'm speaking to Messrs. Maxwell and Bailey, ain't I?'

We had determined on two imaginary names, which we had arranged to give if any names had been demanded of us; but as the small Jew appeared to know us, we were fain to admit the truth of his assertion.

'I thort so. Here, Captain, these gents is Maxwell and Bailey, the dramatic horthers. You've 'eard on 'em, Captain; don't say yer ain't 'eard on 'em! Saw that farce o' yourn, *Up in the World*, gents. Best thing eversornalmilife! best thing eversornalmilife! *You* know, Captain; chap up the chimney—*you* know!'

'Oh, ah!' said the Captain, '*I* know fast enough.'

'Very 'appy to make your acquaintance, gents. I'm Mister Abraham Levy, of the Parnassus Music Hall; p'raps you may have 'eard on me. Any night you like to look in upon me, your card's quite sufficient, gents; either on you, or any friends o' yourn.'

I said some matter-of-course words, to the effect I should be delighted, I was sure.

'By the way, p'raps we can do some business together; who knows? Yer 'avent got anything in the comic duologue line on yer hands, 'ave yer? Somethin' that would suit my Bob Saunders and little Clara Mandeville, yer know. *You* know the sort of thing I mean.'

Maxwell and I regretted that we had nothing on hand that would suit him. An impatient growl from Captain Talboys warned us that he considered that the audience had lasted quite long enough; so we beat a rapid retreat, and proceeded, in company with the servant, to go through the hollow form of inspecting the apartments.

I am sorry to say, that the rooms to which our attention was principally directed were at that moment in process of being vacated by a gentleman, who had given notice of his intention to quit on the preceding evening, immediately after, and in consequence of, the disturbance between Captain Talboys and his unhappy wife. There was only one other lodger, an undesirable Irish tenant, whom Mrs. Talboys had made repeated but fruitless efforts to get rid of.

We mumbled out something to the servant about returning tomorrow, and giving a definite answer, and then made the best of our way to the theatre. The rehearsal was unsatisfactory; no one was perfect, or anything like it; properties had to be made, music to be scored and learnt, and comic dances to be decided on. At two o'clock we were all cleared off in order that the rest of the afternoon might be devoted to the last scene—a complicated absurdity, that took ten minutes to develop, and looked, eventually, more like a gorgeous valentine than anything I ever saw. The stereotyped assurance that everybody gave us, that 'it would be all right at night,' afforded us but little consolation, for we had often heard it before, in cases where it was very far indeed from being all right at night. So we returned to the Temple in evil spirits.

We gave Mrs. Talboys and her daughter an account of Captain Talboys' then condition, and we told her of the first floor's indignant departure. I am afraid that the result of our mission did little in the way of raising her spirits. The fact, however, that the captain's luggage was prepared for sea revived her a little; and it was settled that, if, on our calling the next day, we found that he had joined his ship, Mrs. Talboys and her daughter were to return home. As the day wore on our respective spirits revived; and, after a pleasant makeshift dinner, which we ordered in from the 'Cock,' we began to look upon our respective prospects with more hopeful eyes. We had a piano in the chambers, and Emmie Talboys sang some simple old English ballads, with a delightful untutored pathos which was inexpressibly charming. Maxwell, who had a fine baritone voice, also employed it to the best advantage; and so with songs and quiet chat we passed the afternoon and evening, until it was time for us to go to the theatre. We left the two ladies in possession of our chambers, and betook ourselves to the first representation of the Grand Fairy Extravaganza of 'The One-Eyed Calendars, Sons of Kings; or, Zobeide and the Three Great Black Dogs.'

My private impression of the One-Eyed Calendars is that it was irreclaimable nonsense; but, as everyone had the necessary number of verbal contortions to deliver, and as every song was followed up by a nigger 'breakdown,' and as the management had the combined *maximum* of (stage) beauty with the *minimum* of petticoat, it was practically a great success. The authors were honoured with the customary 'call,' and the papers on the ensuing day endorsed (as they usually do) the opinions expressed by the audience. It is true that our satisfaction at the favourable character of the notices was somewhat damped by finding ourselves invariably alluded to as 'those twin sons of Momus;' but, on the whole, we had no reason to complain of the manner in which we were treated.

The next day on my inquiring in Essex Street, I found that Captain Talboys, his Jew friend, and the two big boxes had taken themselves off. The drabby servant was in a terrible state of mind at the non-appearance of her mistress, who (she now told me) had been absent with Miss Emmie ever since Christmas night. 'She was a good missis to her,' she said, 'and so was Miss Emmie, right good; and she'd go right off to the pleece and have them looked for, if she'd only someone to mind the house for a quarter of an hour.' But the woman who usually came to cook had been drunk ever since Christmas Day, and she was at her wits' end to know what to do. And the poor little drab, who had made many gulpy attempts to keep the tears down (for she was a brave little drab), fairly gave way, as her responsibilities stood forth in all their naked magnitude before her, and cried away as if her heart would break.

Maxwell and I made the best of our way back to the Temple, and placed the facts of the little servant's anxiety and helplessness before Mrs. Talboys and Emmie who lost no time in putting on their bonnets and returning to Essex Street, after thanking us most emphatically for our kindness and hospitality. She sincerely hoped that we would kindly call on her from time to time; Emmie and she were always at home in the evening, and they would be most happy if, when we had an evening to spare, we would spend it with them.

By degrees Maxwell and I became very intimate with Mrs. Talboys, and we took an interest in assisting her with our counsel, whenever she found herself entangled in a social difficulty with which she was unable to grapple single-handed. For I am afraid that no course of training under the sun could possibly have made a good manager of Mrs. Talboys. She was a mild, weak, good-hearted, unsystematic woman, who was as unfit to manage a London lodging-house as Maxwell and I were to command a man-of-war. A very short experience of the nature of difficulties with which the poor lady was surrounded, convinced us that she was more or less the dupe of everyone with whom she had dealings. We contrived, in course of time, to establish a system of check upon her lodgers and her tradespeople, we lent her a little money to make a few indispensable additions to her stock of furniture, and we procured her a tenant for her drawing-room floor. In a couple of months after Captain Talboys' departure, matters had so far improved that Mrs. Talboys was in a position to substitute a permanent cook for the intermittent functionary who had hitherto been in the habit of looking in from time to time to ascertain whether her services were required.

We passed a great many pleasant evenings with the Talboys, to the enjoyment of which little Emmie's unpretending musical powers contributed in no slight degree. I have not dwelt at any length on Emmie Talboys' appearance and characteristics, for, when I first knew her, she did not make any very decided impression on me. She had a quiet, retiring, unassuming way with her, that appeared rather to shun observation than to court it; and, at first, her extreme nervousness made us feel that the ordinary matter-of-course attentions which we should have paid to any other young lady, would have frightened the poor little woman out of her senses. But as she came to know us more intimately, her extreme shyness wore off, and we found beneath it a sweetness of disposition, combined with a simple unaffected pleasure in our society, which to me was irresistibly charming. She was not absolutely pretty, but her big blue eyes, her thick yellow hair, and the bright smile with which she welcomed us when she came to know us well, stood her in good stead of the advantages which mere regularity of feature would have conferred upon her. I am afraid that I must own that before I had known the little woman many weeks, I fell desperately in love with her. As I have already implied, it took some little time to bring this about; for her beauties of disposition broke upon us so gradually that to have fallen in love with her, at first sight, would have implied the possession of a discrimination of character to which I lay no claim.

They were very pleasant evenings, those that Maxwell and I spent with the Talboys. Maxwell, I think, enjoyed them almost as much as I did. He was not a man who was given to falling easily in love, and, although he was about my own age—that is to say eight-and-twenty, or thereabouts—he had a fatherly protecting way of treating little Emmie Talboys that was really very amusing. He looked upon her as a mere child, and bought playthings and sweetmeats without number for her. He had no hesitation in calling her by her Christian name, as soon as he knew what it was; and his elderly didactic manner caused her to look upon his doing so as a matter of course. We used to sit by the fire-light on the long winter evenings, and Mrs. Talboys would take counsel with Maxwell on such points of domestic economy as had turned up to perplex her during the day, while I sat by the battered old piano, and listened to Emmie's pure and gentle voice, as she sang 'On the Banks of Allan Water,' 'The Bailiff's Daughter of Islington,' or some other simple plaintive ballad which lay within the compass of her unpretending powers. Maxwell and I used often to take them to the theatre, to which we had no difficulty in obtaining free admission; and it was refreshing to a couple of battered theatrical hacks like ourselves, who had seen every piece that had been produced in London during the last ten years or so, to witness the childlike interest that the little woman took even in the common-place hackneyed incidents of the wretched farce that played the audience out. At other times, Mrs. Talboys and Emmie would spend the evening with us at our chambers; on which occasions we would ask Cranley of the Home Circuit, O'Byrne of the *Advertiser*, and one or two other fellow-Templars, to drop in; and then we always wound up the proceedings with an oyster or lobster banquet from Prosser's. We always gave out that Mrs. Talboys was the wife of Captain Talboys (impliedly of the Royal Navy), now at sea; concerning whose health and prosperity, by-the-bye, O'Byrne invariably made well-meant but most awkward inquiries of Mrs. Talboys whenever he met her.

This sort of thing went on for about twelve months. The

more I saw of little Emmie Talboys, the more desperately I loved her. I don't think I ever hinted to the little woman in the most remote manner at the existence of this attachment, but I cannot suppose she was ignorant of it. In point of fact I am sure it was marked by Mrs. Talboys, and I am equally sure that she placed no impediment in the way of our being together. I had almost made up my mind to speak openly to Emmie, when an event occurred which upset all my plans.

One morning (it was in the January twelve-month after our first meeting with the Talboys) Maxwell and I returned to London after a fortnight's absence in Liverpool, where we had been to superintend the production of a Christmas piece. Among the letters that awaited us was one addressed to Maxwell from Mrs. Talboys, with a date a week old. He opened it, read it, and handed it to me. It was to the following effect:—

Essex Street,
30*th Dec.*, 1859.

My Dear Mr. Maxwell,

I have grievous news to tell you of myself. My husband contracted a great many debts before he left England, and as he has not been heard of for twelve months, his creditors have become most impatient. You will be distressed to hear that all my furniture has been seized under a bill of sale, that my tenants have been obliged to leave the house in consequence, and that Emmie and I are absolutely ruined. We start for Chester to-day—we used to have friends there, who may still remember us, and place us in the way of earning a respectable living; God only knows what is to become of us should they fail. Forgive me, dear Mr. Maxwell, for taking this course without consulting you or Mr. Bailey. After your exceeding kindness to me and mine, I am afraid that you will think I am acting most ungratefully in thus leaving London without speaking to you on the subject. But, when I tell you that I do so because I know that your generous nature would have prompted you to offer further assistance if I had placed our case before you, I am sure you will see that I could not, with propriety, have acted otherwise than I have done. If my husband should return soon, my present difficulties may be got over, for he will receive a large sum of money on his arrival;

but, in the meantime, Emmie and I must do our best to earn a living by ourselves. Trusting that a very short time will elapse before we meet again, and with the deepest gratitude to both of you for your extreme and, to me, unaccountable kindness, believe me to be, my dear Mr. Maxwell, ever yours, most thankfully,

Emily Talboys.

We were thunder-struck at the contents of the letter: in point of fact, I had to read it two or three times before I could grasp its contents. Some minutes elapsed before either of us spoke. I sank on my armchair, completely overwhelmed at the misfortune that had happened to them and to me. At length Maxwell broke the silence.

'We must take steps to find them instantly!'

'But what, in Heaven's name, can we do?' said I.

'Advertise; we will also write to the post-office at Chester—it is not improbable that they will think it likely that we have written there, and will make inquiries accordingly.'

'But they don't want to hear from us.'

'Yes, they do. Besides, if a woman knows, or believes, that a letter is waiting for her at a post-office, she will go and apply for it, whether she wishes to hear from the writer or not.'

Maxwell had an intellectual pinnacle of his own, from which he looked down upon woman and her ways. From some cause or other (perhaps owing to its giddy height) it appeared to be unfavourable for minute examination; at all events, woman at large was one of those topics of discussion upon which Maxwell and I seldom agreed. However, I was only too glad to catch at the small crumb of comfort that he offered me, and I agreed that there might be something in that, too.

We hurried off to the house in Essex Street. It was empty, and a torn advertisement pasted near the door, together with the litter and straw on the steps and in the road, spoke of the recent sale. A notice to the effect that the eligible premises (adapted for a lodging-house) were to let, and that application might be made to the housekeeper within, or to Messrs. Puddick and Crowby, auctioneers and estate agents, in

Catherine Street, Strand, adorned the parlour window.

We made application to the housekeeper, as advised, believing that she would be more likely to give us information about Mrs. Talboys' movements, than Messrs. Puddick and Crowby. However, she turned out to be a sodden old lady, who knew nothing more of Mrs. Talboys except that she was a precious bad lot, as ought to be rope-ended if all on us had their jew. No, she didn't know nothing about no addresses—Mrs. T. took precious good care as nobody should—and for a good reason too.

We left this impracticable old female in depressed spirits, and turned our attention to Chester generally. We sent carefully-worded advertisements to *The Times* and to the Chester papers; and Maxwell wrote a long letter to Mrs. Talboys, Post Office, Chester, begging her to afford us some information as to her proposed movements, if she objected to telling us her address.

Day after day elapsed, but no letter came to us from Mrs. Talboys. I will not attempt to paint my intense grief at losing my little Emmie. Suffice it to say, that, after six weeks' interval of mental depression, which seriously affected my powers as a writer of light literature, I began to recover my usual spirits, and, excepting that I could never make up my mind to leave the Temple at the Essex Gate or to look down Essex Street as I passed it in the Strand, matters went on pretty well as they did before the events of which these chapters have told.

III

TWO years had elapsed since the disappearance of Mrs. Talboys and little Emmie. During that time neither Maxwell nor I heard anything of either of them, and I am afraid I must own that they had both completely faded from our thoughts. With the exception of an occasional 'Wonder what's become of the Talboys?' they were hardly ever alluded to by either of us.

Time had not treated us particularly well. We had long ago attained that well-known five pounds a week that so many writers of light literature attain, and so few go beyond, and at an average of five pounds a week, apiece, our income steadily remained. Not so, however, our expenditure. I am bound to honour to state, that Maxwell and I were both inconveniently in debt. We were not men of decidedly extravagant habits, but each of us had his hobbies, and a hobby-horse is the most expensive riding that a beggar can indulge in. In our cases, our respective hobbies carried us considerably beyond the constable, and we were obliged to accept all sorts of work to enable us to keep our enemies at bay.

One morning, as Maxwell and I set to work, in extreme ill-humour, to complete a series of 'Drawing-Room Comic Songs,' which we were doing for a cheap music publisher at a guinea per song, we were interrupted by a single knock, which Maxwell rose, impatiently, to answer. He opened the door and found a flabby, shabby-genteel man in rusty black, waiting on the landing—

'Mr. Bailey, sir?'

'No—Maxwell.'

'That will do, sir. I have come—'

'I know. It's steel pans; I don't want any.'

'No sir, it's not steel pans—'

'Then it's ketchup. Be off!'

'No, and it isn't ketchup neither,' said our visitor, with an impatient air of injury. 'A letter, wait for answer.'

And, so saying, he put a dirty, thumby envelope into Maxwell's hands. He opened it, and read as follows:—

Parnassus, Oxford Street
April 4*th*, 1863

Dear Sir,

I am in want of a short dualog for two people—self and wife—with songs. Something short and smart, to play twenty minutes or thereabouts, with practical fun, such as suits my audience. My terms for such is a ten-pound note, and if either of you got anything to suit, shall be glad. Must have it by the 6th, as we open with it on the 7th. Please send answer by bearer, and beg to remain, yours, etc.,

Abraham Levy

Owing to the fact that the demands for light farce had not kept pace with our literary fecundity in that respect we had a good deal more theatrical capital lying idle on our hands than we had at the time when we first made Mr. Levy's acquaintance at Captain Talboys'. So we sent an answer by the seedy messenger, to the effect that we had something that would doubtless suit the requirements of a Parnassus audience, and would look in upon Mr. Levy that evening, and talk the matter over with him.

That afternoon, however, we were favoured with a visit from Mr. Levy, who, having occasion to call at his solicitor's in Clement's Inn, to instruct him to defend an action by the Dramatic Authors' Society for an infraction of copyright, availed himself of the fact of his being in our neighbourhood, to look upon us, and to arrange preliminaries.

We submitted our plot to Mr. Levy. A lady and gentleman, of high rank, who have been betrothed in early infancy (as is customary in the best English families), but who had taken the deepest dislike to each other, owing to the fact that the gentleman was said to possess an inordinate and unnatural passion for baked sheep's head—a dish which the lady held in aristocratic abhorrence—and that the lady was never happy unless she was devouring peppermint—a confection for which the gentleman entertained the profoundest disgust—meet unexpectedly in the centre of the maze at Hampton Court. The mutual embarrassment and annoyance caused by this most awkward *rencontre* is enhanced by the fact that, owing to the ingenious disposition of the labyrinth, neither of them is able to find a way out of it. Thus thrown together by a fate with which it is impossible to contend, they determine to put up with each other's society as best they may. The limited area at their disposal is divided into two equal parts by an imaginary line, and each undertakes to keep to his or her own territory until such time as somebody shall appear who can give them a clue out of the perplexing labyrinth. The lady thinks she cannot do better than employ her enforced leisure by singing some of the favourite ballads of her early infancy, and the gentleman (whose tastes are more material) proceeds to devote himself to the lunch which he has brought with him in a basket. The lady's attention is arrested by his movements, and in an agony of dread at the anticipated appearance of the detested dish, implores him (in a parody on 'Robert, toi que j'aime') to postpone his meal until she can escape from the maze. In a comic duet (a community of proceeding not forbidden by the terms of their treaty), he declines to entertain her suggestion, and proceeds to lunch off—not a sheep's head, but a magnificent *pâté de foie gras*. The whole truth flashed upon her in a moment. A wicked marquis, who seeks her hand, has spread the detestable calumny which has caused her detestation for her betrothed lover! She rushes to his arms and embraces him, and the gentleman, as soon as he has recovered from the astonishment with which this proceeding not unnaturally strikes him, is amazed and delighted to discover the lady is absolutely free from all suggestion of peppermint. He at once perceives that a wealthy (but hideous) duchess, who adores him, is the author of the abominable rumour that has estranged him from his beloved—an explanation ensues, and matters end as happily as a comic duet can make them.

Mr. Levy was delighted with the plot, and after suggesting that the gentleman must accidentally sit upon the pie, and put a fork or two into his pocket, and by otherwise misconducting himself contribute to the actual fun of the piece; and impressing upon us that we must on no account go in for 'comedy dialogue,' he took his departure. The dualogue was duly finished, christened 'Love in a Maze,' and sent in. By the next post we received a cheque for ten guineas on the Union Bank.

The ensuing morning, as we sat at breakfast, Maxwell, who had been amusing himself with *The Times* supplement, suddenly sprang to his feet exclaiming,

'By Jove! here's something about the Talboys!' and he handed me the paper, pointing to an advertisement that ran as follows:—

'TALBOYS OR TALBOT.—If this advertisement should meet the eye of Mrs. Emily Talboys or Talbot, widow of the late Esau Talboys or Talbot, master mariner, who died in Australia on the 14th or 18th of November last, and late of Essex Street, Strand, she is requested to send her address to

Tenby and Campbell, solicitors, Brabant Court, London. Any person who can furnish such a clue to the present residence of Mrs. Talboys or Talbot, as shall lead to her discovery, shall receive a reward of Ten Pounds.'

We bolted our breakfast and hurried, as fast as a Hansom could carry us, to Brabant Court. Of course we could give no information as to her whereabouts, but giving our cards, and informing Messrs. Tenby and Campbell that we were intimate friends of the Talboys, they were good enough to tell us that Captain Talboys reached Melbourne in safety, and that he had shortly afterwards made his way to the diggings, where, after several weeks' labour, he had made a find of surpassing magnificence; that he had returned to Melbourne, that he fell overboard as he went up the ship's side in a state of intoxication, that he was drowned, and that his widow was entitled to a sum of seventeen thousand five hundred and sixty-four pounds—the net proceeds of his labour in the gold fields. They further told us that the news only reached them two days since, and that no clue had as yet been afforded as to their present address.

We left the office in good spirits, for the hope that we should eventually hear something of Mrs. Talboys and Emmie revived within us. As we were in the City we made our way to Mr. Levy's bankers, with the view of getting his cheque cashed, for that gentleman's reputation as a pay-master was not so unimpeachable as to warrant our looking upon his cheque as a negotiable security of a wholly unquestionable character. Accordingly, we were not altogether surprised to find it returned to us dishonoured, with the announcement that Mr. Levy had considerably overdrawn his account, and that no further advance would be made to him. So, as we were particularly insolvent at that moment, Maxwell and I repaired the same evening to the Parnassus Music Hall, with the view of inducing him to substitute a cash payment for his worthless cheque.

Mr. Levy was all apology. He had paid a large sum of money in yesterday, and found himself unexpectedly compelled to draw it that morning. But if we would take a seat in his private room, he would see if a sufficient sum of money had been taken at the doors to enable him to settle our claim.

On inquiring he found that up to that time (nine o'clock) only five pounds and some odd shillings had been received, but if we would sit down and make ourselves comfortable, he had no doubt but that he should be able to square it up in half an hour or so. We were fain to agree to this, and placing a bottle of whisky and some cigars in a tumbler before us, he left us to attend to his duties.

Mr. Levy's private room was situated at the extreme end of the Parnassus, and as the glass door commanded the stage, we amused ourselves by watching the performance until such time as ten pounds should have been taken at the doors.

The principal element of entertainment at the Parnassus Music Hall was comic singing. A stout man, who looked like a churchwarden out of work, occupied the platform as we entered, and sang a series of dismal comic songs, 'all of his own composition, sir!' as a waiter informed me.

'I'm told sir,' added my informant, 'that that gent is always a-writin' songs in his 'ed. To look at him as he walks through the 'all, talkin' affable to a gent here and a gent there, and a-smokin' with this one and a-drinkin' with that, you'd little think that all the time he was a-composing the verses as he sings five minutes after on the platform. But he is, sir—rhymes and all!'

We listened with increased interest to the singer after this description of his peculiarities. He was extremely political, and was very hard upon Lord Derby, and very patronizing indeed, when he had occasion to allude to the Royal Family—every member of which appeared to enjoy *ex officio* the advantage of his protection and his encouragement—which was the more remarkable as he was for upsetting every other constituted authority. He touched upon the American differences, and having demolished the North at a blow, proceeded to slap General Garibaldi on the back, annihilate the police system, and to tell us that we had a great many more bishops than was good for us. He was vociferously encored (my friend, the waiter, going into ecstasies over him), and he obligingly favoured us with another of his composition, in which he advised Britons generally to go in for their rights, which he described as,

'A pipe, my brother; a bowl, my brother;
A maiden fair of a beauty rare,
To comfort your jolly old soul, my brother;
Sing cheerily ho! sing ho!'

Then a terrible woman with big bones, a raw brazen voice, and her hair parted at the side, came on to the stage and screamed and roared, and slapped her hands, and danced, and then sang again, and then danced and sang and banged herself once more, which was her energetic way of advising you, under all circumstances of life, to 'speak up like a ma-a-n!' And then we had a fiddler who could play under a chair, and over a chair, and through a chair, and on his head, and with his head between his legs, and under all circumstances of contortion under which a man could reasonably be expected to play a fiddle. The fiddler was followed by two Bounding Brothers, who, at first, were so mutually polite (as they bounded about the stage) that you would think they had only been introduced to each other; but when (in the course of the performance) they came to know one another better, you found that the elder brother was haughty, for he repelled the ingenious advances of the younger brother by turning him head over heels in the air. But the younger brother's fraternal love was too strong to be at all affected by these repulses, although as often as he ran up to embrace the elder brother, he was turned about by his unnatural relative in a most distressing manner. Eventually the elder brother began to lose his temper, and seizing the younger brother by the middle, twirled him violently round and round, and eventually threw him over his head, standing over him (as he came down) in a threatening attitude which there was no mistaking. The younger brother, who began to feel that matters were getting desperate, fell on his knees and prayed. The elder brother was softened, relented, clasped the younger brother in his arms, and the two went off, over each other's heads, in a burst of fraternal ecstasy.

A depressed and faded middle-aged lady, dressed in a scanty black silk dress, with a small arrangement of artificial flowers in her bosom, and wearing black mittens on her hands, then stepped nervously on the platform, and began to sing, in a weak faltering voice, a few verses of an Italian song, the purport of which did not reach us at our end of the room. She was suffering from extreme nervousness, and broke down twice or three times in the song she was endeavouring to sing.

I don't think I ever witnessed a more melancholy spectacle. The poor lady was received with an ironical cheer, which in her innocence, she accepted as compliment, and every verse was hailed with derisive shouts, which even she was unable to mistake; so uttering an apology to the conductor who appeared to be remonstrating with her in no measured terms, she left the stage amid a whirl of hooting and cat-calls, which did not cease until a Favourite Delineator of Negro Peculiarities appeared, when it changed to a shout of applause.

'Maxwell,' said I, 'don't you know that poor woman's face?'

'No; I didn't notice her, poor creature.'

'It's Mrs. Talboys,' said I.

'Impossible!'

'But it is. I'm nearly sure of it. Here, waiter, who was the last singer?'

'What, her as made a mess on it?'

'Yes.'

'Bernardini—Madame Bernardini. It's her first night—she's on trial for an engagement. And,' he added, 'I expect it's her last.'

There was little else to be got out of the waiter, so we were compelled to wait until we saw Levy. More comic singers, more acrobats, more niggers, and eventually poor little Emmie Talboys!

She was announced under a different pseudonym to that which her mother had adopted; but I had little difficulty in recognizing her. If anything else were wanted to place it beyond a doubt that Mrs. Talboys and Emmie, mother and daughter, had appeared before me that evening, it would have been found in the fact that the wretched bit of faded finery which Madame Bernardini had worn in her bosom, had been transferred to that of the poor trembling little woman who stood before me.

My heart seemed to rise to my throat as I looked upon

the old love I had so long lost. The same gentle timid voice bore the accents of the same old pathetic air to my ears—she was singing the 'Banks of Allan Water'—and the same mild appealing face, sadly changed by privation, looked timidly on the audience as she concluded her song. She was received with insolent cheers, such as had greeted her poor mother half an hour before, and as she left the stage she stumbled, in her nervousness, over a nail on the floor, and fell heavily against the wing.

Maxwell and I started up to seek Levy, and we met him at the door, with our ten guineas in shillings and sixpences in his hand.

'Levy,' said Maxwell, 'who is that young girl who has just gone off?'

'Ah, Mister Maxwell, what a chap you are!'

'Tell me her name, for God's sake, man!' said Maxwell, stamping with impatience.

'No, no, Mister Maxwell; she's a good girl, she is—I don't like that sort of thing—she's a good girl, and you must leave her alone.'

'Confound it, Levy, stop your infernal—no, no, I beg your pardon—there, you're a good fellow, and mean well—I respect you for it, but you mistake my meaning.'

'Oh, it's all right, is it, Mister Maxwell? Well, you're a gentleman, and I don't believe you'd do a dirty thing. Her name is Tolboysh—Tolboysh.'

'Then she and her mother are old and intimate friends of ours, and they are advertised for in to-day's *Times*. For God's sake let us go to them!'

'You don't say so! Vell now, only to think! Come along with me—come along with me!'

And the good-natured little Jew led the way to the wretched apartment dignified by the title of 'Artistes' Room.'

It was a square whitewashed room, furnished with a deal table, a small cracked looking-glass, and half-a-dozen Windsor chairs; a pot of coarse *rouge* with a hare's foot stood upon the mantelpiece, and a well-filled subscription list for an injured acrobat hung upon the wall. The room was strewn with comic hats, banjoes, wigs, and other properties in immediate use by the performers. Poor little Emmie lay on two chairs, nearly insensible, while the vulgar big-voiced woman (who had a big heart too) was bathing a wound in her forehead with a motherly tenderness which would have atoned for her vulgarity twice told. Mrs. Talboys was hovering about her daughter in a helpless anxious way, invoking blessings on the comic lady who had taken the affair into her own hands, and who announced her intention of sending them home in her brougham after it had taken her to do her 'turn' at the Polyhymnian.

We were not long in making ourselves known to Mrs. Talboys, and eventually to Emmie. She was at first distressed at our having discovered her under such circumstances, but very delighted to see us notwithstanding. We all went home to her poverty-stricken lodgings in the Camberwell Road together, and when there, we gradually told Mrs. Talboys of the good fortune that awaited her.

It would be affectation to pretend that she felt any sorrow for her husband's death, and we spent a couple of hours that night in mapping out the future which was to be invested with such golden surroundings. They had had a hard time of it since they left London; their friends at Chester had procured her a little employment as a teacher in a National School, but poor little Emmie fell ill of scarlet fever, and Mrs. Talboys lost her situation in consequence. She then advertised as a morning governess, and obtained a little work in that capacity; but she was totally unfitted for the charge of children, and that source of income eventually failed her. Then she obtained a little employment as a dresser and wardrobe-woman at a provincial theatre, and eventually little Emmie made her appearance on the stage, but the poor timid little girl failed absolutely. For some months they obtained a precarious living by hanging about theatres and provincial concert-rooms, getting a little employment here, and a little employment there, until at length Mr. Levy, who happened to hear her sing at a provincial music-hall, offered her an engagement in London at one pound ten a week, if, after a week's probation, she should be found up to the requirements of his audience.

That all went merrily with us after this, it is, I suppose, unnecessary to say. We took a pleasant cottage at Twickenham for Mrs. Talboys, with a pretty garden and a lawn sloping down to the Thames, and Maxwell and I used to pull up the river on fine summer evenings after our work was done and take tea with them in the open garden. I leave you to imagine the happiness these evenings afforded me. I leave you to imagine also, that it was not very long before I found out that they afforded equal happiness to little Emmie. And I leave you to imagine how it all ended.

THE TRIUMPH OF VICE

A Fairy Tale

THE WEALTHIEST in the matter of charms, and the poorest in the matter of money of all the well-born maidens of Tackleschlosstein, was the Lady Bertha von Klauffenbach. Her papa, the Baron, was indeed the fortunate possessor of a big castle on the top of a perpendicular rock, but his estate was deeply mortgaged, and there was not the smallest probability of its ever being free from the influence of the local money-lender. Indeed, if it comes to that, I may be permitted to say that even in the event of that wildly improbable state of things having come to pass, the amount realized by the sale of the castle and perpendicular rock would not have exceeded one hundred and eighty pounds sterling, all told. So the Baron von Klauffenbach did not even wear the outward show of being a wealthy man.

The perpendicular rock being singularly arid and unproductive even for a rock, and the Baron being remarkably penniless even for a Baron, it became necessary that he should adopt some decided course by which a sufficiency of bread, milk, and sauerkrout might be provided to satisfy the natural cravings of the Baron von Klauffenbach, and that fine growing girl Bertha, his daughter. So the poor old gentleman was only too glad to let down his drawbridge every morning, and sally forth from his stronghold, to occupy a scrivener's stool in the office of the local money-lender to whom I have already alluded. In short, the Baron von Klauffenbach was a usurer's clerk.

But it is not so much with the Baron von Klauffenbach as with his beautiful daughter Bertha that I have to do. I must describe her. She was a magnificent animal. She was six feet in height, and splendidly proportioned. She had a queenly face, set in masses of wonderful yellow hair; big blue eyes, and curly little mouth (but with thick firm lips), and a nose which, in the mercantile phraseology of the period, defied competition. Her figure was grandly, heroically outlined, firm as marble to the look, but elastically yielding to the touch. Bertha had but one fault—she was astonishingly vain of her magnificent proportions, and held in the utmost contempt anybody, man or woman, who fell short of her in that respect. She was the toast of all the young clerks of Tackleschlosstein; but the young clerks of Tackleschlosstein were to the Lady Bertha as so many midges to a giantess. They annoyed her, but they were not worth the trouble of deliberate annihilation. So they went on toasting her, and she went on scorning them.

Indeed, the Lady Bertha had but one lover whose chance of success was worth the ghost of a halfpenny—and he was the Count von Krappentrapp. The Count von Krappentrapp had these pulls over the gay young clerks of Tackleschlosstein—that he was constantly in her society, and was of noble birth. That he was constantly in her society came to pass in this wise. The Baron von Klauffenbach, casting about him for a means of increasing—or rather of laying the first stone towards the erection of—his income, published this manifesto on the walls of Tackleschlosstein:

'A nobleman and his daughter, having larger premises than they require, will be happy to receive into their circle a young gentleman engaged in the village during the day. Society musical. Terms insignificant. Apply to the Baron von K., Post Office, Tackleschlosstein.'

The only reply to this intimation came from the Count von Krappentrapp; and the only objection to the Count von Krappentrapp was, that he was not engaged in the village during the day. But this objection was eventually overruled by the Count's giving the Baron in the handsomest manner in the world, his note of hand for ten pounds at six months date, which was immediately discounted by the Baron's employer. I am afraid that the Baron and the Count got dreadfully tipsy that evening. I know that they amused themselves all night by shying ink-bottles from the battlements at the heads of the people in the village below.

It will easily be foreseen that the Count von Krappentrapp soon fell hopelessly in love with Bertha; and those of my readers who are accustomed to the unravelling of German legendary lore will long ere this have made up their minds that Bertha fell equally hopelessly in love with the Count von Krappentrapp. But in this last particular they will be entirely in error. Far from encouraging the gay young Count, she regarded him with feelings of the most profound contempt. Indeed, truth compels me to admit that the Count was repulsive. His head was enormous, and his legs insignificant. He was short in stature, squat in figure, and utterly detestable in every respect, except in this, that he was always ready to put his hand to a bill for the advantage of the worthy old Baron. And whenever he obliged the Baron in this respect, he and the old gentleman used to get dreadfully tipsy, and always spent the night on the battlements throwing ink-bottles on the people in the village below. And whenever the Baron's trades-people in the village found themselves visited by a shower of ink-bottles, they knew that there was temporary corn in Egypt, and they lost no time in climbing up the perpendicular rock with their little red books with the gilt letters in their hands, ready for immediate settlement.

It was not long after the Count von Krappentrapp came to lodge with the Baron von Klauffenbach, that the Count proposed to the Baron's daughter, and in about a quarter of a minute after he had proposed to her, he was by her most unequivocally rejected. Then he slunk off to his chamber, muttering and mouthing in a manner which occasioned the utmost consternation in the mind of Gretchen, the castle maid-of-all-work, who met him on his way. So she offered him a bottle of cheap scent, and some peppermint-drops, but he danced at her in such a reckless manner when she suggested these humble refreshments, that she went to the Baron, and gave him a month's warning on the spot.

Everything went wrong with the Count that day. The window-blinds wouldn't pull up, the door wouldn't close, the chairs broke when he sat on them, and before half his annoyances had ceased, he had expended all the bad language he knew.

The Count was conscientious in one matter only, and that was in the matter of bad language. He made it a point of honour not to use the same expletive twice in the same day. So when he found that he had exhausted his stock of swearing, and that, at the moment of exhaustion, the chimney began to smoke, he simply sat down and cried feebly.

But he soon sprang to his feet, for in the midst of an unusually large puff of smoke, he saw the most extraordinary individual he had ever beheld. He was about two feet high, and his head was as long as his body and legs put together. He had an antiquated appearance about him; but excepting that he wore a long stiff tail, with a spear-point at the end of it, there was nothing absolutely unearthly about him. His hair, which resembled the crest or comb of a cock in its arrangement, terminated in a curious little queue, which turned up at the end and was fastened with a bow of blue ribbon. He wore mutton-chop whiskers and a big flat collar, and his body and misshapen legs were covered with a horny incrustation, which suggested black beetles. On his crest he wore a three-cornered hat—anticipating the invention of that article of costume by about three hundred years.

'I beg your pardon,' said this phenomenon, 'but can I speak to you?'

'Evidently you can,' replied the Count, whose confidence had returned to him.

'I know: but what I mean is, will you listen to me for ten minutes?'

'That depends very much upon what you talk about. Who are you?' asked the Count.

'I'm a sort of gnome.'

'A gnome?'

'A sort of gnome; I won't enter into particulars, because they won't interest you.'

The apparition hesitated, evidently hoping the Count would assure him that any particulars of the gnome's private life would interest him deeply; but he only said—

'Not the least bit in the world.'

'You are poor,' said the gnome.

'Very,' replied the Count.

'Ha!' said he, 'some people are. Now I am rich.'

'*Are* you?' asked the Count, beginning to take an interest in the matter.

'I am, and would make you rich too; only you must help me to a wife.'

'What! Repay good for evil? Never!'

He didn't mean this, only he thought it was a smart thing to say.

'Not exactly,' said the gnome; 'I shan't give you the gold until you have found me the wife; so that I shall be repaying evil with good.'

'Yes,' said the Count musingly: 'I didn't look at it in that light at all. I see it quite from your point of view. But why don't you find a wife for yourself?'

'Well,' said the gnome diffidently, 'I'm not exactly—you know—I'm—that is—I want a word!'

'Extremely ugly?' suggested the Count.

'Ye-e-es,' said the gnome (rather taken aback); 'something of that sort. *You* know.'

'Yes, I know,' said the Count; 'but how am I to help you? I can't make you pretty.'

'No; but I have the power of transforming myself three times during my gnome existence into a magnificent young man.'

'O-h-h-h!' said the count slyly.

'Exactly. Well, I've done that twice, but without success as far as regards getting a wife. This is my last chance.'

'But how can I help you? You say you can change yourself into a magnificent young man; then why not plead your own case? I, for my part, am rather—a—'

'Repulsive?' suggested the gnome, thinking he had him there.

'Plain,' said the count.

'Well,' replied the gnome, 'there's an unfortunate fact connected with my human existence.'

'Out with it. Don't stand on ceremony.'

'Well, then, it's this. I begin as a magnificent young man, six feet high, but I diminish imperceptibly day by day, whenever I wash myself, until I shrink into the—a—the—'

'Contemptible abortion?'

'A—yes—thank you—you behold. Well, I've tried it twice, and found on each occasion a lovely girl who was willing and ready to marry me; but during the month or so that elapsed between each engagement and the day appointed for the wedding, I shrunk so perceptibly (one is obliged, you know, to wash one's face during courtship), that my bride-elect became frightened and cried off. Now, I have seen the Lady Bertha, and I am determined to marry her.'

'You? Ha, ha! Excuse me, but— Ha, ha!'

'Yes, I. But you will see that it is essential that as little time as possible should elapse between my introduction to her and our marriage.'

'Of course; and you want me to prepare her to receive you, and marry you there and then without delay.'

'Exactly; and if you consent, I will give you several gold mines, and as many diamonds as you can carry.'

'You will? My dear sir, say no more! "Revenge! Revenge! Revenge! Timotheus cried," ' (quoting a popular comic song of the day.) 'But how do you effect the necessary transformation?'

'Here is a ring which gives me the power of assuming human form once more during my existence. I have only to put it on my middle finger, and the transformation is complete.'

'I see—but—couldn't you oblige me with a few thalers on account?'

'Um,' said the gnome; 'it's irregular: but here are two.'

'Right,' said the Count, biting them; 'I'll do it. Come the day after to-morrow.'

'At this time?' said the gnome.

'At this time.'

'Good-night.'

'Good-night.'

And the gnome disappeared up the chimney.

The Count von Krappentrapp hurried off without loss of time to communicate to the lovely Bertha the splendid fate in store for her.

'Lady Bertha,' said he, 'I come to you with a magnificent proposal.'

'Now, Krappentrapp,' said Bertha, 'don't be a donkey. Once for all, I *will* NOT have you.'

'I am not alluding to myself; I am speaking on behalf of a friend.'

'O, any friend of yours, I'm sure,' began Bertha politely.

'Thanks, very much.'

'Would be open to the same objection as yourself. He would be repulsive.'

'But he is magnificent!'

'He would be vicious.'

'But he is virtuous!'

'He would be insignificant in rank and stature.'

'He is a prince of unexampled proportions!'

'He would be absurdedly poor.'

'He is fabulously wealthy!'

'Indeed?' said Bertha; 'your story interests me.' (She was intimately acquainted with German melodrama.) 'Proceed.'

'This prince,' said Krappentrapp, 'has heard of you, has seen you, and consequently has fallen in love with you.'

'O, g'long,' said Bertha giggling, and nudging him with her extraordinarily moulded elbow.

'Fact. He proposes to settle on you Africa, the Crystal Palace, several solar systems, the Rhine, and Rosherville. The place,' added he, musingly, 'to spend a happy, happy day.'

'Are you in earnest, or' (baring her right arm to the shoulder) 'is this some of your nonsense?'

'Upon my honour, I am in earnest. He will be here the day after to-morrow at this time to claim you, if you consent to have him. He will carry you away with him alone to his own province, and there will marry you.'

'Go away alone with him? I wouldn't think of such a thing!' said Bertha, who was a model of propriety.

'H'm!' said the Count, 'that is awkward certainly. Ha! a thought! You shall marry him first, and start afterwards, only as he has to leave in two days, the wedding must take place without a moment's delay.'

You see, if he had suggested this in the first instance, she would have indignantly rejected the notion, on principle. As it was she jumped at it, and, as a token of peace, let down her sleeve.

'I can provide my trousseau in two days. I will marry him the day he arrives, if he turns out to be all you have represented him. But if he does not—' And she again bared her arm, significantly, to the shoulder.

That night, the Baron von Klauffenbach and the Count von Krappentrapp kept it up right merrily on the two thalers which the Count had procured from the gnome. The Baron was overjoyed at the prospect of a princely son-in-law; and the shower of ink-bottles from the battlements was heavier than ever.

The second day after this the gnome appeared to Count Krappentrapp.

'How do you do?' said the Count.

'Thank you,' said the gnome; 'I'm pretty well. It's an awful thing being married.'

'Oh, no. Don't be dispirited.'

'Ah, it's all very well for you to say that, but— Is the lady ready?' said he, changing the subject abruptly.

'Ready, I should think so. She's sitting in the banqueting hall in full bridal array, panting for your arrival.'

'O! do I look nervous?'

'Well, candidly, you do,' said the Count.

'I'm afraid I do. Is everything prepared?'

'The preparations,' said the Count, 'are on the most magnificent scale. Half buns and cut oranges are scattered over the place in luxurious profusion, and there is enough gingerbierheimer and currantweinmilch on tap to float the Rob Roy canoe. Gretchen is engaged, as I speak, in cutting ham-sandwiches recklessly in the kitchen; and the Baron has taken down the "Apartments furnished," which has hung for ages in the stained glass windows of the banqueting hall.'

'I see,' said the gnome. 'to give a tone to the thing.'

'Just so. Altogether it will be the completest thing you ever saw.'

'Well,' said the gnome, 'then I think I'll dress.'

For he had not yet taken his human form.

So he slipped a big carbuncle ring on to the middle finger of his right hand. Immediately the room was filled with a puff of smoke from the chimney, and when it had cleared away, the Count saw, to his astonishment, a magnificent young man in the place where the gnome had stood.

'There is no deception,' said the gnome.

'Bravo! very good indeed! very neat!' said the Count, applauding.

'Clever thing, isn't it?' said the gnome.

'Capital; most ingenious. But now—what's your name?'

'It's an odd name. Prince Pooh.'

'Prince Pooh? Pooh! pooh? you're joking.'

'Now, take my advice, and never try to pun upon a fellow's name; you may be sure that, however ingenious the joke may be, it's certain to have been done before over and over again to his face. Your own particular joke is precisely the joke every fool makes when he first hears my name.'

'I beg your pardon—it *was* weak. Now, if you'll come with me to the Baron, you and he can settle preliminaries.'

So they went to the Baron, who was charmed with his son-in-law elect. Prince Pooh settled on Bertha the whole of Africa, the Crystal Palace, several solar systems, the Rhine, and Rosherville, and made the Baron a present of Siberia and Vesuvius; after that they all went down to the banqueting hall, where Bertha and the priest were awaiting their arrival.

'Allow me,' said the Baron. 'Bertha, my dear, Prince Pooh—who has behaved *most handsomely*' (this in a whisper). 'Prince Pooh—my daughter Bertha. Pardon a father if he is for a moment unmanned.'

And the Baron wept over Bertha, while Prince Pooh mingled his tears with those of Count Krappentrapp, and the priest with those of Gretchen, who had finished cutting the sandwiches. The ceremony was then gone into with much zeal on all sides, and on its conclusion the party sat down to the elegant collation already referred to. The Prince declared that the Baron was the best fellow he had ever met, and the Baron assured the Prince that words failed him when he endeavoured to express the joy he felt at an alliance with so unexceptionable a Serene Highness.

The Prince and his bride started in a carriage and twenty-seven for his country seat, which was only fifty miles from Tackleschlosstein, and that night the Baron and the Count kept it up harder than ever. They went down to the local silversmith to buy up all the presentation inkstands in his stock; and the shower of inkstands from the castle battlements on the heads of the villagers below that night is probably without precedent or imitation in the chronicles of revelry.

Bertha and Prince Pooh spent a happy honeymoon: Bertha had one, and only one cause of complaint against Prince Pooh, and that was an insignificant one—do all she could, she couldn't persuade him to wash his face more than once a week. Bertha was a clean girl for a German, and had acquired a habit of performing ablutions three or even four times a week; consequently her husband's annoying peculiarity irritated her more than it would have irritated most of the young damsels of Tackleschlosstein. So she would contrive, when he was asleep, to go over his features with a damp towel; and whenever he went out for a walk she hid his umbrella, in order that, if it chanced to rain, he might get a providential and sanitary wetting.

This sort of thing went on for about two months, and at the end of that period Bertha began to observe an extraordinary change not only in her husband's appearance, but also in her own. To her horror she found that both she and her husband were shrinking rapidly! On the day of their marriage each of them was six feet high, and now her husband was only five feet nine, while she had diminished to five feet six—owing to her more frequent use of water. Her dresses were too long and too wide for her. Tucks had to be run in everything to which tucks were applicable, and breadths and gores taken out of all garments which were susceptible of these modifications. She spent a small fortune in heels, and even then had to walk about on tiptoe in order to escape remark. Nor was Prince Pooh a whit more easy in his mind than was his wife. He wore the tallest hats with the biggest feathers, and the most preposterous heels to his boots that ever were seen. Each seemed afraid to allude to these extraordinary modifications to each other, and a gentle melancholy took the place of the hilarious jollity which had characterized their proceedings hitherto.

At length matters came to a crisis. The Prince went out hunting one day, and fell into the Rhine from the top of a high rock. He was an excellent swimmer, and he had to remain about two hours, swimming against a powerful tide, before assistance arrived. The consequence was that when he was taken out he had shrunk so considerably that his attendants hardly knew him. He was reduced, in fact, to four feet nine.

On his return to his castle he dressed himself in his tallest hat and highest heels, and, warming his chilly body at the fire, he nervously awaited the arrival of his wife from a shopping expedition in the neighbourhood.

'Charles,' said she, 'further disguise were worse than useless. It is impossible for me to conceal from myself the extremely unpleasant fact that we are both of us rapidly shrinking. Two months since you were a fine man, and I was one of the most magnificent women of this or any other time. Now *I* am only middle-sized, and you have suddenly become contemptibly small. What does this mean?'

'A husband is often made to look small in the eyes of his wife,' said Prince Charles Pooh, attempting to turn it off with a feeble joke.

'Yes, but a wife don't mean to stand being made to look small in the eyes of her husband.'

'It's only fancy, my dear. You are as fine a woman as ever.'

'Nonsense, Charles. Gores, Gussets, and Tucks are Solemn Things,' said Bertha, speaking in capitals; 'they are Stubborn Facts which there is No Denying, and I Insist on an Explanation.'

'I'm very sorry,' said Prince Pooh, 'but I can't account for it;' and suddenly remembering that his horse was still in the Rhine, he ran off as hard as he could to get it out.

Bertha was evidently vexed. She began to suspect that she had married the Fiend, and the consideration annoyed her much. So she determined to write to her father, and ask him what she had better do.

Now, Prince Pooh had behaved most shabbily to his friend Count Krappentrapp. Instead of giving him the gold-mines and diamonds which he had promised him he sent him nothing at all but a bill for twenty pounds at six months, a few old masters, a dozen or so of cheap hock, and a few hundred paving stones, which were wholly inadequate to the satisfaction of the Count and the Baron's new-born craving for silver inkstands. So Count von Krappentrapp determined to avenge himself on the Prince at the very earliest opportunity; and in Bertha's letter the opportunity presented itself.

He saddled the castle donkey, and started for Poohberg,

the Prince's seat. In two days he arrived there, and sent up his card to Bertha. Bertha admitted him; and he then told the Prince's real character, and the horrible fate that was in store for her if she continued to be his wife.

'But what am I to do?' said she.

'If you were single again, whom would you marry?' said he with much sly emphasis.

'O,' said the Princess, 'you, of course.'

'You would.'

'Undoubtedly. Here it is in writing.'

And she gave him a written promise to marry him if anything ever happened to the Prince her husband.

'But,' said the Count, 'can you reconcile yourself to the fact that my proportions are insignificant?'

'Compared with me, as I now am, you are gigantic,' said Bertha. 'I am cured of my pride in my own splendid stature.'

'Good,' said the Count. 'You have noticed the carbuncle that your husband (husband! ha! ha! but no matter) wears on his middle finger?'

'I have.'

'In that rests his charm. Remove it while he sleeps; he will vanish, and you will be a free woman.'

That night as the clock struck twelve, the Princess removed the ring from the right-hand middle finger of Prince Pooh. He gave a fearful shriek; the room was filled with smoke; and on its clearing off, the body of the gnome in its original form lay dead upon the bed, charred to ashes!

The castle of Poohberg, however, remained, and all that was in it. The ashes of the monster were buried in the back garden, and a horrible leafless shrub, encrusted with a black, shiny, horny bark, that suggested black beetles grew out of the grave with astounding rapidity. It grew, and grew, and grew, but never put forth a leaf; and as often as it was cut down it grew again. So when Bertha (who never recovered her original proportions) married Count Krappentrapp, it became necessary to shut up the back garden altogether, and to put ground-glass panes into the windows which commanded it. And they took the dear old Baron to live with them, and the

Count and he spent a jolly time of it. The Count laid in a stock of inkstands which would last out the old man's life, and many a merry hour they spent on the hoary battlements of Poohberg. Bertha and her husband lived to a good old age, and died full of years and of honours.

Jones' Victoria Cross*

I PASSED the greater part of the year 185— with my family at a small town in Germany, where we became acquainted with a Mrs. Jones. Her family, consisting of one boy and three girls, were of about the same age as our own children, and we soon got to be very intimate. She, poor lady, had much to trouble her; some unhappy domestic quarrel had caused a separation between her husband and herself. Mr. Jones did not, I believe, bear the best of characters; he was at that time living on his estate in the North of Ireland, and allowed his poor wife a miserable pittance of about £200 a year, with which she had to maintain herself and family in respectability, and give them a decent education. Mortimer the eldest, was a noble fellow, then of about sixteen or seventeen years of age, and a universal favourite. My boy was of about the same age, and they were bosom friends. There was a bachelor uncle, the brother-in-law of Mrs. Jones, of whom she always spoke in terms of gratitude. I fancy that he often assisted her, and that it was partly by his means that she was enabled to keep up the respectable position she held. One of her great anxieties was how to get her boy out into the world. Mortimer himself wished to enter the army; but with no means of purchasing a commission for him, and with no interest to get one in any other way, there was but little hope of his attaining the object of his ambition. In the spring of the following year we left Germany and returned to England; Mortimer was still without employment; he had privately confided to me that in the event of his not being able to obtain something to do in the course of that year, he should go to sea, as he was determined not to be a burden to his mother,

* For the *general* accuracy of this story the writer will vouch. The names of persons and places, of course, are all altered, as also are those circumstances which might by any possibility enable any one to identify the actors in it.

now that he was old enough to earn his own living. For some time we lost sight of Mrs. Jones and her family.

It was in the winter of this year, when reading the paper at my club, that my eye caught the name of Mortimer Jones. Yes, there was no doubt of it; the Gazette notified in the 150th regiment, 'Mortimer Jones, gent., to be ensign by purchase, vice Brown, resigned.' I was much pleased to see it, and before leaving the club I wrote to Mrs. Jones to congratulate her on her son's good fortune.

I had posted the letter and was leaving the house, when on the steps I met Mortimer himself. He had come to London about his outfit, and was staying with his uncle, who had been the means of obtaining him his commission; he was now on his way to pay me a visit. He was in high spirits at his good luck, as he called it; his only regret being that the regiment to which he had been appointed was stationed in Canada, and not in the Crimea. He joined the depôt shortly afterwards, and it was about ten years before I met him again.

One Sunday morning in the spring of 186—, as my wife and I were on our way to church at ——, we passed a tall, military-looking man with a long fair moustache, who looked fixedly at us, as I did at him, for I fancied I knew the face; after passing, he turned round, came up, and held out his hand.

'Mr. M—?' he said.

'Yes; but though I remember your face, I haven't the least recollection of your name.'

It was Mortimer Jones; a boy of seventeen or eighteen when I last met him, now a well set-up man some ten years older. He accompanied us to church, and afterwards I prevailed on him to come and partake of our early dinner; it was then he gave me this account of his wanderings since we last met. I had congratulated him on his having obtained the Victoria Cross—I had seen the notification some short time before in the papers; but I little imagined that I should have further to congratulate him on his having obtained a brevet-majority; I thought he was still a subaltern.

'Why,' I said, when I heard it, 'you must be the luckiest fellow in the whole service!'

'Well,' he replied, 'I *have* been lucky. When we last met I said good luck had befallen me; it has stuck to me ever since. A V.C. and a brevet-majority in little more than ten years' service is what anyone may call good luck.'

'But, of course, you had to purchase your company?'

'Yes, my father did that for me; but I got my lieutenancy without purchase; however, I'll tell you how it all happened.

'When I last saw you I was in town on that most enviable of all expeditions to a newly appointed ensign, getting my outfit. I joined the depôt at York and went out to Canada three months afterwards. I returned home with the regiment the following year. Our tour of home service was shorter than usually falls to the lot of regiments; in 185— we were suddenly ordered to India. At this time I was first on the list of ensigns, and here I might have remained, had not luck stepped in and befriended me. I had no means of purchasing, but a few days after landing at Bombay the senior lieutenant was accidentally drowned, and I was promoted to a lieutenancy without purchase in his place. The same Gazette which announced my promotion notified the appointment of the Honourable Herbert Fitz Lyon to be ensign in our regiment. It is to him, or rather to his mother, that I am principally indebted for the Victoria Cross and my brevet-majority. Fitz belongs to a very influential but not wealthy family; his mother, Lady Fitz Lyon, has somehow or other great interest in high quarters, and if Fitz had been senior instead of junior to me I should still be Lieutenant Jones and no V.C. Fitz Lyon was posted to my company, and the year following we were sent up the country. About that time my Captain was placed on the staff, we had now three captains on the staff and of course three of the subalterns had to do the captain's duty and their own too, which I have always thought a hard case. I was now in charge of Captain Graham's company, Fitz Lyon was my senior subaltern; he had just purchased his lieutenancy over the heads of six ensigns; my junior sub. had not then joined, his name was Williams. Some robber tribes had just then given great trouble to the poeple in the North, and troops were ordered up to disperse them and destroy their fortifications; for I assure you that word is not misapplied as to the way in which these rascals were entrenched. General H— commanded the division sent on this expedition, and he failed; a great loss of life on our part was the result, but the robbers remained victorious in their fastnesses, and as it was too late in the season for any further active operations, and sickness having set in among the Europeans, General H— ordered a retreat. For another year these robber tribes remained undisturbed. Meantime the news of the repulse had reached England, and the government were highly annoyed at the event. They determined to make another and better prepared attempt on the approach of the next cold weather, and instructions were sent out to the Commander in Chief to see to it.

'The time came round, and my regiment was one of the first ordered up to those districts. I was in command of No. 1 company; Fitz Lyon, and Ensign Williams, who had just joined, were the officers under me. A considerable force was collected, and we found ourselves, about the month of October, close to the forts occupied by these fellows. The general kept everything very quiet, and no one had the least notion when he intended to attack. On the night of October 28th, my company formed the advanced picket of the little army: we had no idea that anything was intended that night; but at break of day, one of the sentries passed the word that the division was getting under arms; a few minutes more and we could distinguish the different companies silently 'falling in.' Not a sound was heard; but after the lapse of a little time I distinctly heard the ring of some of the ramrods; they had loaded, and soon afterwards the tramp of many hundred men caught my ear—they were advancing! My first thought was, if anyone is to be the first I don't see why I shouldn't be the man. Fitz Lyon came up at this moment, and said "Those rascals yonder are wide-awake: I have just been round the hill, and see lights all over that part; depend upon it they are ready for us."

'The adjutant of the 200th came up just then from the main body, and brought the intelligence that the forts were really to be stormed, and my company was ordered to fall in immediately and join the main body as they came up. I ordered No. 1 to fall in at once, sentries and all; and before the division had come up to us we were ready to advance. I said to Fitz, "I don't see why we shouldn't go on ahead of the column."

' "All right," he replied; "give the word."

' "Fours right, quick march;" and we were on our way with the main body some hundreds of yards in rear of us.

'We got within forty or fifty yards of the nearest and strongest fort, and I began to think we had been unobserved; but at that moment the silence was broken by an awful discharge of guns, matchlocks, and all sorts of fire-arms, that laid many of my poor fellows on the ground. Williams, the ensign, was killed by this discharge. Forward! I shouted; and in a few moments we were close to the barricades. Here we found we could do nothing; there was a wall of some eighteen or twenty feet high to mount, and we had no ladders. For some minutes we remained in a sort of dry ditch, peppered at from above by hundreds of the villains; here we lost fourteen men killed, and twenty-five wounded, out of my company of seventy men. Just then the advanced party of the main division came up with ladders, &c. I seized one, and Fitz another; and about half-a-dozen were placed against the wall at the same moment. Followed by a crowd of our gallant fellows, we led the way, and reached the top, where, I believe, Fitz, myself, and a sergeant of the 200th, were the first to arrive. The robbers were nowhere to be found! from the moment of our reaching the top of the wall we were masters of the situation. Disheartened, I conclude, at the determined attempt we were evidently making, they thought prudence the best part of valour; and we could just descry them flying in a considerable body across the plain in rear of the forts towards some distant hills. My company was the only one that sustained much loss; there were not more than twenty casualties altogether amongst the rest. Poor young Williams and the men killed were buried that evening. The engineers set to work, and soon levelled all the fortifications with the ground.

'We returned after that little exploit to Ramilsuccor. Fitz Lyon obtained leave of absence soon after this, and left for England. I was now fourth on the list of lieutenants, the three above me were not for purchase, and as I was in a like case I had no more chance of getting my company than of being made a G.C.B. Fitz came two below me on the list. To my infinite astonishment I heard some weeks afterwards that he had been promoted to an unattached company. My friends wrote from England, How is it that your junior has been promoted over your head? *I* knew that Fitz's friends had unbounded interest, and I quite understood the thing, but I determined to *bide my time*.

'I now applied for leave of absence, and got it for 18 months. I landed in England not many weeks ago, and at the Waterloo Station I bought a penny newspaper, sent my things on to the hotel, and walked across the park to my uncle's house. On my way I sat down on an inviting seat half way over the park and scanned over the news of the day. One of the first things that caught my astonished eye was an announcement at the head of the "Gazette" to the effect that "Lieutenants Mortimer Jones and the Honourable Herbert Fitz Lyon of the 150th Regiment were to receive the decoration of the Victoria Cross, for distinguished conduct at the storm and capture of," etc., etc.

'I can safely say that I was never so astounded at anything in my life before. Scarcely believing what I saw, I presented myself at my uncle's door; the kind old man was at home, and welcomed me most warmly. He sincerely congratulated me on the honour that had been conferred on me; he had just read it in his own paper. After dinner he said "Well, Mortimer, I wish I had it in my power to do it for you, but you *ought* to have your company; surely you have as much right to a company as your junior, Mr. Fitz Lyon. Can you not make an application about it?"

' "My dear uncle" I replied, "Fitz Lyon's family have no end of interest, it is through *that* he got his company: with no interest and no money how can I ever expect to get mine, except through a death vacancy? I know there is a company just about to become vacant, my old Captain (Graham) is going to retire, but that will be purchased by Robinson, who is junior to me."

' "By Jove," said my Uncle, "this must not be: it *shall* not be. I'll write to your father to-night; he has never done much for you, but he *must* do something now; after gaining the Victoria Cross, he cannot refuse to purchase your company for you."

'My uncle's application was successful; my father came to town a few days afterwards and lodged the money at

Cox's. Very shortly afterwards, I was promoted to a company by purchase, "Vice Graham, resigned."

'I was now a captain and a V.C. but the thought that Fitz Lyon had been promoted over me rankled in my mind, and I determined to "circumvent" him if possible. I presented myself a short time back at a reception given by one of those who held the army reins. I was kindly received by Lord A—.

' "What can I do for you, Captain Jones?" said his lordship.

' "My lord,' I replied, "I beg respectfully to ask your lordship to recommend me for a brevet-majority."

' "Indeed:" said his lordship, referring to the Army List, "ten years' service only, and just got your company; on what grounds do you ask for this?"

' "My lord," I answered, "my junior subaltern was promoted over my head; he obtained the Victoria Cross on the same occasion as myself. I beg respectfully to say that I think I should have been promoted before him; or that I should demand a court martial." After much conversation, and many questions about the old robber-forts affair, his lordship said:—

' "Well, Captain Jones, we will think about the matter;" and so he dismissed me.

'Two weeks afterwards, I was gazetted a brevet-major—and here I am.

'It was Lady Fitz Lyon who did it all. She bothered them out of their lives, directly she heard of the part Fitz had taken in the affair, about giving him the Victoria Cross.

'At first she met with nothing but "Pooh! Pooh!"—then with "How can your son expect to receive the Victoria Cross when a senior officer was in command of the company, and distinguished himself equally?"

' "Oh," said her ladyship, "if that is all, *give it to both of them*;" and the end of it was that we both got it.

'Fitz got his company, and no doubt thought he had out-manoeuvered me, but I have beaten him hollow in the race. He can't expect to get his majority for some years; meantime, I am creeping up the list of captains, and shall probably be a lieutenant-colonel by the time he is brevet-major!'

DIAMONDS

I

I AM SORRY to have to begin a tale, which is really not intended to be objectionably squalid, in a public house. It is an unpromising opening, and one that is calculated to alienate the good opinion of a large section of readers, but I am not sure but that, after all, it has some artistic merit. It may be taken to stand to the coming chapters, in the relation that the opening scene in a pantomime does to the impossible glories that are to follow: it serves as a foil to them, and their effect is heightened by contrast with the dismal horrors which have preceded them. Please be good enough to suppose, for the moment, that the 'Jolly Super' theatrical house of call is The Abode of the Demon Alcohol, and that the pretty but supercilious barmaid is a carnal embodiment of his familiar, the malignant Djin; raise the curtain to the air of 'The Roast Beef of Old England,' encourage the fiction that the conversation is spoken through the levelling medium of a pantomime mask, and all will be well. I promise you that there are bright fairies, pretty shepherdesses, princes with black hair, and big-headed monarchs, waiting at the wing for their cue to come on; and you must not quarrel with me if I avail myself of my privilege to delay their appearance until the progress of the plot demands it.

The 'Jolly Super' is a dingy public-house in the immediate neighbourhood of the Theatre Royal Parnassus, and derives its main support from the custom of the 'Parnassus' company, and that of their friends and admirers. Its name would suggest that the establishment appeals exclusively to the sympathies of the humbler members of the theatrical profession, but this is not, in point of fact, the case; indeed, a standing rule of the house, tacitly acquiesced in by all concerned, makes it a breach of etiquette for any member of a dramatic company to enter the private bar, unless his theatrical status entitle him to avail himself of the green-room of his theatre—a privilege accorded at the Parnassus to those members only whose salary amounted to a minimum of thirty shillings a week.

Besides the Parnassus company, the 'Jolly Super' is much affected by members of a neighbouring Literary Club, known to themselves and to the publishing world as the 'Aged Pilgrims.' The 'Aged Pilgrims' are (as their name implies) a collection of young and middle-aged dramatic authors, novelists, reviewers, magazine writers, actors, 'entertainers,' and literary barristers. As a rule, the 'Aged Pilgrims' are appreciated by the publishing world alone, and utterly unknown to the rest of society. They are, for the most part, clever fellows, but their cleverness is expended, mainly, upon anonymous magazine articles and daily newspaper work; so, if it should happen that any members of the 'Aged Pilgrims' whom I may have occasion to introduce to you in the course of this story are not already known to you by name, you must not entertain a poor opinion of them on that account. You read all the novels that Mr. Mudie sends you, you know the peculiarities of their several authors, and you therefore suppose that you are acquainted with the name of every literary man, of any talent, in England. But you never were more mistaken in the whole course of your existence. Who, do you suppose, writes the leading articles and reviews in the morning and weekly papers and in the monthly magazines? Men, my good friends, of whom, twenty chances to one, you have never heard, unless you are behind the scenes in these matters. Men with clear logical brains, and great literary ability; keen satirists, pleasant humorists, but men whose names, with, perhaps, half-a-dozen exceptions, are totally unknown to you. They are men who have devoted themselves to anonymous literature; and to the world at large they are as distinct from their writings as the Punch-and-Judy man is from the puppets he works. You get your *Times* every morning with your hot rolls; you read the leaders from beginning to end, but you would as soon think of setting yourself the task of finding out the names of the men who wrote them as of seeking an introduction to a peripatetic showman, because you have derived some whimsical amusement from his wooden dolls. So I warn you beforehand, that if you expect to find many notabilities among the 'Aged Pilgrims,' you will be disappointed. But take my word for it that they are mostly clever fellows, that they may all be termed good fellows, if you have no objection to place a liberal construction on the words; and that whenever an 'Aged Pilgrim' falls sick, and is thereby prevented from earning his weekly income, he has no occasion to appeal to his brother Pilgrims for assistance, for assistance is volunteered with a liberality which only those who know how hardly the dole of a literary hack is earned can appreciate. I am bound, in justice, to admit, that good fellows as they are, they have for the most part a reprehensible yearning for bar-parlours, long clays, and spittoons; but you must bear in mind that I prayed you to understand the term 'good fellow' in its most liberal sense.

Of these 'good fellows' one of the best was Ralph Warren—a tall, fair-haired young fellow, with a clever but not a strictly handsome face; indeed, if the truth must be spoken, his appearance spoke much too plainly of extremely irregular hours, and extremely regular brandies-and-sodas, to justify any very complimentary remarks on that score. I am sorry to add that his clothes were rather mildewy, and his boots a trifle lop-sided; his linen, however, was clean, and so were his face and hands. I hardly know how to reconcile the term 'gentlemanly' with this rather unpromising description, but there certainly was an air of easy frankness about Ralph Warren—a genial gentlemanly *bonhomie*, combined with a suggestion of quiet, conscious power, that induced you to forget his seediness and his sodas-and-brandy, and to dub him 'gentleman' before you had enjoyed five minutes of his conversation.

In point of fact, Warren was a gentleman by birth and education. His father, Lieutenant-Colonel the Hon. Guy Warren, was the second son of Lord Singleton, an extremely wealthy but eccentric nobleman, who quarreled on principle with every member of his family, except his heir-apparent or presumptive for the time being. Lord Singleton had turned Ralph's father into the world at the age of sixteen, with an ensign's commission in a marching regiment and a hundred a year, coming to an unavowed determination to avail himself of the earliest opportunity that should arise of quarrelling with this unfortunate young officer, and of forbidding him the house, as a natural consequence. The opportunity soon arose. Guy 'went wrong' in the matter of debts before he had been six months with his regiment; his father paid the score without a murmur; intimated to Guy that he would not be cheerfully received at Singleton any more; and, indeed, determined to hold no further converse with him at any time, unless it should unfortunately happen that his elder brother, Spencer, were to die childless, in which case Guy, as the heir for the time being, would come in for all the gratifying consideration which, until the occurrence of that unlikely contingency, would be the hereditary right of his fortunate elder brother. At the same time Lord Singleton did not disguise from himself the bare possibility of such a complication taking place, and so, with the view of keeping Guy well before his eyes, so that he might be able to lay his hands upon him whenever he might happen to want him, he privately advanced that young officer's interests in the Horse Guards, and, indeed, went so far on one occasion as to pay the purchase-money for his captain's commission.

The old lord, however, was much too knowing a hand to do this good deed in his own name, and so lay himself open to the supposition of being accessible to the claims of impecunious kinsmen; he did it through a confidential valet, who, in the assumed character of a benevolent money-lender, called on Guy and offered to accommodate him with the necessary amount at insignificant interest, for any period he might choose to name, on his (Guy's) personal assurance that the money should be repaid as soon as Guy should find it convenient to do so. Of course the seedy lieutenant closed with the benevolent money-lender on the spot—the loan was there and then affected, and Guy sang the worthy usurer's praises to such effect among his brother officers and their friends, that that excellent person was embarrassed with innumerable applications from these straightened gentry for the loan of fabulous sums on the same security that Guy had given for the loan of the purchase-money for his captain's commission. It is, perhaps, hardly needful to add, that Lord Singleton's valet found it necessary to decline all the proposed negotiations.

It will not surprise the worldly-minded reader to hear that

the treatment that Guy experienced at the hands of his ungenial parent contributed to sour that officer's mind against his own offspring generally and against his second son, Ralph in particular. Guy retired from the army on captain's half-pay, and although he rose on the half-pay list to a lieutenant-colonel's commission, this accession of dignity contributed in no way to increase his income. He married a young lady with five hundred a year of her own, and this, with his captain's half-pay, formed the bulk of his income. The lieutenant-colonel lived, all the year round, at a cheap watering-place, with his wife and eldest son, a hopeless cripple; and when he had procured for Ralph a clerkship in a bad Government office, he considered that he had done his duty by the boy, and left him to shift for himself in London.

Ralph's method of shifting for himself was, at first, a failure. He took cheap rooms with a brother clerk in Islington, attended at his office, and did his work in a slip-shod way during the day, dined flashily and unwholesomely at a cheap but showy eating-house afterwards, spent his evening usually at one of the theatres or at Cremorne, knocked about at cheap places of disreputable resort, went to bed at two in the morning, not tipsy, but yet having drunk freely and unwholesomely, and woke up the next day with a hot head, a feverish pulse, and a mouth parched with cheap hot cigars. He got into debt with the money-lenders who infest Government offices, and was generally admitted by all who knew him to be going directly and unmistakably to the bad.

But Ralph was not a cad by instinct. A reaction set in, and although his life was anything but a spotless one from that moment, it was an immense improvement upon what it had been. He was a smart, clever fellow, with a natural turn for epigram and satire, and he began to turn these dangerous qualities to good effect in the columns of better-class periodicals. He began humbly and anonymously in obscure journals, but he obtained a certain measure of success in these, and this success induced him to aspire to greater things. He became, in course of time, a regular contributor to a weekly paper, and an occasional one to most of the monthly magazines. By degrees his income from these sources increased to such an extent as to justify him in throwing up his appointment in his seedy Government office, and taking to literature as his sole means of support. He joined the 'Aged Pilgrims,' with whom his smart, showy, conversational powers and irrepressible good humour made him an immense favourite. He had belonged to their brotherhood for about two years at the date of his introduction to the reader. I again apologize for bringing him into notice amid the unpolite surroundings of a theatrical house of call, but as, unfortunately, the 'Jolly Super' was the place where Ralph Warren was generally to be found, as it was here that he, in company with other 'Aged Pilgrims,' usually dined, always wrote his articles, and generally spent his evenings, it will be seen that I have an excuse for so doing. After all, he was more to be pitied than blamed. If he had had only an opportunity of making himself at home with three or four decent families of regular habits and with pretty daughters in them, he would have been as much disgusted with this Bohemian life as you yourself are. But this opportunity had never been offered to him, and so he stuck to his Bohemianism as the only form of life which was open to him.

Ralph was sitting in the club-room of the 'Aged Pilgrims,' on the first-floor of the 'Jolly Super,' with half-a-dozen other members of that sociable brotherhood. They were not particularly jolly at that moment, for news had just arrived of the failure of a new speculative magazine in which they were all interested, and of the bankruptcy of the proprietor. Poor Warren was especially down in the mouth, as he had been sent down to Sheffield by the editor with instructions to remain a fortnight, and to 'do' a chatty descriptive account of all the manufactures of that cheerless city for the magazine in question. By way of rider to his instructions, he was told to make himself as jolly as circumstances would permit, and not on any account to spare any expense. He had acted fully upon these hints—he had taken pains with the articles, he had spared no expense whatever, and he was anxiously expecting a cheque for a hundred and twenty-five pounds (seventy-five pounds for the papers, and fifty for his hotel bill and travelling expenses), when the news of the collapse of the whole thing arrived. They were endeavouring to restore the balance of their equanimity with their customary panacea—brandy-and-soda; but whether it was that brandy-and-soda as a remedy did not apply to losses above five pounds, or whether the irrepressible good humour and aggravating jollity of Sam Travers (the low comedian of the Parnassus), who had that day signed an engagement for the next season at an increase of five pounds a week to his salary, operated as a damper with which it was impossible to contend, I don't know, but certainly the conversation flagged to an extent almost unknown among the 'Aged Pilgrims.'

'They say,' said one of them, 'that there won't be a penny in the pound. The whole thing is mortgaged to the paper-makers.'

'Hang the paper-makers!' prayed another, while the rest chorused in 'Amen!'

'Thirty pounds a month for "Gnats and Camels", till it ran through, I was to have had.'

'Well, you'll get it off your hands in some other paper.'

'Devil a bit; it was written to order—written up to some confounded blocks that the beggar bought wholesale off Flicker and Dowse before they went to smash.'

'How much do you put your claim at, Ralph.'

'A hundred and twenty-five, and cheap enough, too, for a fortnight in Sheffield.'

'It'll be all right, my boys,' said Travers. 'Never say die! Down one moment—up the next! Look at me—I began as call-boy and sub-deputy assistant property-man, at eight-and-sixpence a week, and I've just signed an engagement for five-and-thirty pound. It'll be your turn next. Lor' bless you, it isn't half such a bad world as people think! The devil isn't half as black as he's painted!'

'Nor speculating publishers half as white as they're white-washed,' said Ralph. 'Oh, come in; don't stand knocking there.'

The door opened, and a waiter put a letter into Ralph's hand. A lawyer's letter—blue paper and a red criss-crossed wafer. At any other time Ralph would have kept it to stick, unopened, upon his mantelpiece, where it would have remained for months, while he and his friends amused themselves with lively conjectures as to its contents. But matters were getting serious, and he opened it with a solemn face.

'13, Lincoln's Inn Fields, Feb. 4, 1860.

'Sir,—We regret to inform you that intelligence has just reached us of the death of the Right Hon. Baron Singleton and his eldest son, the Honourable Hugh Warren, who were unfortunately drowned by the sudden capsizing of a yacht off Selsey Bill. We are instructed by your father, the present Baron Singleton, to communicate to you his desire that you should join him at Singleton without any delay.

'We are instructed that you are at liberty to draw upon us to the amount of £100 (one hundred pounds) to defray your necessary expenses.—We have the honour to be, Sir, your very obedient servants,

'Wardle and Tapp.

'To the Hon. Ralph Warren,
'The Jolly Super,' Bedfourdbury.'

II

Little Woman

RALPH WARREN rose and left his companions without a word. He walked moodily downstairs, paid his score, and strolled into the street. It was some time before he could quite realize his position. The whole thing was so sudden—so wholesale—the unexpected change in his prospects was so overwhelming, that he had to repeat the contents of the letter several times to himself before he could realize them. He walked up and down Covent Garden for nearly an hour, and after he had read and re-read the astounding letter three or four dozen times, he began to realize the fact that instead of drudging wearily and obscurely at half-paid author-work, he was to be suddenly removed to an almost brilliant position, with the probable command of what appeared to him to be unlimited wealth, and an almost certain prospect of a peerage; for his elder brother, the cripple, to whom allusion has already been made, would certainly never marry, and indeed was scarcely likely to live many years.

He put his hand into his breast pocket to open and read

for the fiftieth time the communication which had so agitated him, and he drew forth by mistake a poor humble little letter addressed to him in a girlish hand. It reminded him that he had that evening promised to meet one Mary Vyner at Oxford Circus, at eight o'clock. It then wanted but twenty minutes to eight, so he went into the Strand and mounted an omnibus which would take him past the spot.

It's a dreadful thing to confess, but Mary Vyner was a milliner's assistant in Vigo Street, Regent Street. I am afraid I must add that Ralph Warren had never been properly introduced to her; and while I am about it, I may as well admit that he was in the habit of meeting her about twice a week, in the evening, too, at eight o'clock, and of taking her to a theatre (he was on the free list everywhere) or some other place of amusement, where they beguiled the time until eleven, when Mary Vyner had to report herself in Vigo Street. This is all very shocking indeed, and quite indefensible, and, indeed, the only thing that anybody could find to say in palliation of its atrocity was, that Mary Vyner was, on the whole, a very good little girl, that Ralph Warren, although a free liver, was not an utterly unconscientious scamp, and that although they had known each other for about two years, no harm had ever come, or was ever likely to come, of their meetings. I don't mean to say that Mary Vyner was altogether a perfect character; she was rather thoughtless, rather too fond of admiration perhaps, and certainly imprudent in allowing Ralph Warren to meet her, time after time, without ascertaining how he proposed that these meetings should end. But notwithstanding this, Mary Vyner was a quiet, modest, ladylike girl, whose greatest fault was an absolute devotion to, and an overwhelming belief in, the merits of the rather graceless young gentleman who was then on his way to meet her. She had learnt to love him with all the fervour that her blind little heart was capable of; and if he did not reciprocate her attachment to its full extent, he was still a great deal too fond of Mary Vyner to do her any deliberate wrong. So these heedless young people met, and met, and met again, and beyond the fact that it was very shocking and highly improper, no harm whatever had hitherto come of it.

Ralph Warren was in some perplexity. He hardly knew

how to break the important news to Mary Vyner, and still less did he know how to act with reference to her, now that his position was so materially altered.

'Mary,' said he, when they met, 'I've good and bad news. My grandfather is dead.'

Mary had never heard of his having a grandfather, for Warren had purposely kept the aristocratic features of his family history a secret from her. However, he didn't seem very much distressed, and Mary condoled with him in the usual form. She was so matter-of-fact as to wind up by asking Singleton whether his position would be at all improved by it.

'Very considerably. He was Lord Singleton, and my father was his second son.'

'Lord Singleton! Then there is only one between your father and the title?'

'There is not one. My father's elder brother died with my grandfather, and my father takes the peerage.'

'Your father Lord Singleton? Oh, Ralph, you never told me this!'

'Why should I? It would have frightened you away from me.'

'It would. Oh, Ralph, you won't leave me—say you won't leave me! Promise me that!' said poor little Mary, her eyes full of tears.

'I must leave you for a short time to go to Singleton—my father's place; but—I will return.'

They walked on in silence. It was pretty evident that they would 'assist' at no theatre that night. 'Ralph,' said she, after a pause, 'you may go away from me if you like, and I will never, never follow you or trouble you again. I have loved you, oh, so much, so much! and I think I shall never be happy again if you go; but do go, dear Ralph, if you think it best. I shall be dreadfully sad and dull at first—Oh!' (bursting into tears) 'how sad and dull I shall be!'

'Little Woman!' said Ralph, placing her hand in his (it was quite dark), 'don't cry so terribly. Come into the Park, and we will talk it over.'

I am afraid that when Ralph went to meet Mary Vyner that night, he had made up his mind that that meeting must be their last. But the Little Woman's sobs had moved him, and he felt that the tie between them was not to be so easily broken.

'Listen,' said he, impulsively, but yet with a quiet force that astonished him, 'I never openly told you that I loved you because I never thought—well I didn't expect to be ever able to marry anyone. But if you will have me, Little Woman, now that my prospects are brighter—if you will take me with all my faults, as I am—we will be married, privately, as soon as the affairs connected with my grandfather's and uncle's deaths are settled.' They stood still. Little Woman laid her fair young face against his strong chest, and he, bending his head, kissed the big brown eyes that looked up so trustfully into his own.

And this was the plighting of Ralph Warren to Mary Vyner.

III

Lady Julia and Her Rival

RALPH WARREN went down to join his father at Singleton the next day. The meeting of the two is curious enough. Lord Singleton had neither seen nor heard from Ralph since that erratic young man left his government appointment to seek his bread as a journalist. As Lord Singleton's father had 'discharged' him on the first occasion of his running counter to his will, so did he discharge *his* son. It was a part of the family code, supported by many precedents, that erring second sons should be discarded at the first opportunity, until some important family convulsion rendered it necessary that they should be forgiven. The death of the old lord and his eldest son, and the consequent succession of Colonel Warren to the peerage, was an event of sufficient importance to bring father and son together again. They were extremely gentlemanly, and, indeed, courteous to one another at first, but this dignified state of things at length relapsed into a mere cold toleration of one another's presence. The health of the poor crippled elder son was failing fast, and it soon became evident that the ex-journalist would in all probability succeed to the style, title, and estates of Lord Singleton.

So it became necessary that he should marry, and marry well, and the lady selected for him by his father was that haughty, imperious beauty, Lady Julia Domner, the only daughter of the Earl of Sangazure, K.G., Lord-Lieutenant of the County, and Honorary Colonel of the Turniptopshire Yeomanry.

If I have conveyed the impression (and I am afraid I have) that all this was arranged the day after Ralph's arrival at Singleton, I must stop to correct it. It was the work of fifteen months. I should like to have conveyed some notion of that interval of time by expatiating at considerable length upon the demeanour of Lord Singleton and his son on stepping suddenly from the gloom of almost penniless obscurity into the full blaze of nobility, wealth, and county distinction. I should like to have told how the new lord made himself utterly ridiculous at first, how, by slow degrees, he arrived at something like a proper appreciation of the form of conduct which was expected of him, and how eventually he subsided into a fairly respectable type of a wealthy but rather foolish county swell. I should like to show how Ralph also made all sorts of blunders at first, more particularly in the matter of field sports and other county amusements, with which he was of course wholly unfamiliar. However, he had more of the natural gentleman about him than his father, and at the dinner-table or in the drawing-room his behaviour was unexceptionable. I should also like to have shown how, at first, he corresponded regularly (though secretly) with Mary Vyner—how Little Woman's eyes gradually, though surely, opened to the fact that Ralph was slowly 'getting out of it;' how she bore his faithlessness at first with sham pride which did not sit at all comfortably on her homely little shoulders, and how the sham pride eventually broke down and left her as weeping, heart-broken, deserted, and hopeless a Little Woman as any in wide London. But there are other matters more immediately to the point, and I must not run too long.

Lady Julia Domner was, as I have said, a cold imperious beauty. Her father was an impoverished peer, who hoped, by an alliance with the wealthy Warrens, to secure a becoming position for his only daughter. Lord Singleton saw, clearly enough, that his country position would stand all the more strongly for the shoring up that it would derive from an alliance with Lord Sangazure's family. Ralph, completely cut off from his old associates, and anxious to gain a good footing in his new position, didn't much care whom he married, so that that end was obtained. So the marriage was determined upon, and all parties were satisfied.

In justice to Ralph, I must admit that his desertion of poor Mary Vyner was not unattended by some serious qualms of conscience. He thought often and often of the poor little girl, read over and over again the long touching letters that she wrote upon its becoming evident to her that he was casting her off. But a sense that a public acknowledgment of her as his wife was out of the question, and moreover that he had gone too far with Lady Julia to render it possible that he could break it off with her without bringing himself into public contempt, reconciled him, to some extent, to the course of conduct he was pursuing.

He was not happy in his courtship of Lady Julia. He had always preferred the pretty to the magnificent, and her little brother's plump governess was very much more to his mind. Lady Julia began by treating him rather coldly, but she was a clever and intensely appreciative woman, and the singular charm of Ralph's conversation eventually exercised an extraordinary fascination over her. She began by rather disliking him than otherwise—she ended by loving him with as much devotion as her cold, undemonstrative nature was capable of.

The first novelty of the thing over, Ralph found that the fetters of a formal engagement bored him fearfully. The eternal rides and drives—always with the same companions; the eternal congratulations—always in the same form of words; the eternal evenings at Lord Sangazure's, each a *replica* of its predecessor, came to be looked upon by him with a feeling little short of aversion. He contrived to maintain an outward semblance of affection; but it was a hollow sham, and he knew it. His uneasiness was aggravated from time to time by receiving, at long intervals, letters from Little Woman, written in passionate bursts of grief, imploring him to send her some sign, if it was but a glove that he had worn. But Ralph could never make up his mind to open them—he kissed them and tore them up as they were.

He was altogether in a very unsatisfactory state of mind. He endeavoured at one time to revive the old happy Bohemian days by inviting Dick Pender, who wrote sporting novels, and two or three other 'Aged Pilgrims,' down to Singleton, but the scheme failed. Dick Pender was worth nothing on horseback, and the others spent the whole day in the billiard-room, and the evenings passed in a sort of genteel martyrdom on the drawing-room ottomans, listening to vapid county politics and stable talk, of which they understood never one word. Dick Pender made many notes on sporting subjects, of which he eventually made profitable use, but the others gained neither profit nor pleasure by the visit, and it was never repeated.

To return to Mary Vyner. The Little Woman fell dangerously sick shortly after her discovery of Ralph's faithlessness, and it became necessary that she should have country air; so she spent six months with her only relation, an uncle, who farmed a considerable number of acres in South Wales. She never breathed to any one the real cause of her illness, and when at length she recovered, and returned to Vigo Street to her work, it was supposed by her companions that her attachment to Ralph Warren was a thing altogether of the past, and her quiet, subdued demeanour was ascribed by them to the effect of the serious illness from which she had barely recovered. But Little Woman's thoughts still ran on the clever scapegrace who had left her. She made all sorts of excuses to herself for his desertion, and hoped and prayed that a day would come when he would return to her. It was silly enough in Little Woman to think such a thing possible, but in her seclusion in South Wales she had not heard of his engagement, and for aught she knew, he might be out of England, and so her letters might not have reached him.

But the young ladies at the establishment in Vigo Street subscribed to take in *The Times*, and in the columns of that paper she read one day that the alliance between the Hon. Ralph Warren and Lady Julia Domner, which had for some time been in contemplation, was definitely fixed to take place at Sangazure Hall, her father's seat, on the 15th of the ensuing month, and that the festivities on that occasion were to be on a scale of surpassing splendour.

She was an impulsive little girl. She only waited to get leave of absence from the Lady Superior, and off she started to Singleton. With a beating heart she inquired for Ralph, and was told that he had just left unexpectedly for the Continent, and it was not known when he would return. She then asked the way to Sangazure Hall, and finding that it was six miles distant, she hired a trap at the inn, and drove there as fast as she could induce the flyman to take her.

At Sangazure she learnt that Lady Julia Domner was very unwell, and unable to see any one, but on sending a message to the effect that her business was of the deepest importance, Lady Julia consented to receive her. Little Woman's big heart bounded within her as she was ushered into her presence.

Lady Julia was a very beautiful woman, with a marble face and blue-black hair, and Little Woman felt her blood rush home as she looked upon her magnificent rival. But she did not cry—she was too excited for that; she stood in the centre of the room with one hand pressed to her heart, and breathing heavily, as one who had overtaxed her strength in running.

'Who are you? what do you want with me?' asked Lady Julia.

'I have come all the way from town to see you; forgive me—I am so unhappy!' gasped poor Little Woman.

'But what business have you with me? I am unwell, and may not be intruded upon without good cause.'

'Lady Julia, I went first to Singleton, but he was not there.'

Lady Julia started.

'Has your business any connection with Mr. Warren?'

Little Woman nodded affirmatively—she had no breath to speak with.

'Speak out—don't be afraid; let me know everything.'

The proud woman seemed strangely agitated, although her countenance still wore the same cold marble rigidity as when Mary first entered the room. It was in the heaving of that magnificent bust, and the nervous clutching of those long firm fingers, that Mary saw that her words had worked some extraordinary effect on her rival.

'I am Mary Vyner—he loved me. Oh! I'm sure he loved me; give him back to me! Oh, Lady Julia, have mercy upon me!'

'*He* loved YOU!'

'Oh! so well; but that was long ago, when he was poor. He left me on his grandfather's death, promising to come back and marry me; but he never came, and I have been so ill.'

Little Woman's tears came now.

'You should not have come here to seek your paramour—'

The tears stopped, frightened away by the indignant flash of Little Woman's eyes. Lady Julia saw that she had made a mistake. 'I beg your pardon,' she said; 'I spoke in hot blood. Mr. Warren is not here; it will perhaps be some consolation to you to learn that he and I are utter strangers from this day. He has just left Singleton, and will never return.'

'Left you?'

'Left me. It is enough for you to know that. If it will tend to restore your peace of mind to learn that Mr. Warren is nothing whatever to me—'

The tears in her proud eyes belied it, and she turned aside to hide them. But they came all the more for that, although she strove with all the force of her strong will to repress them. At last she bent her head upon the arm of the sofa on which she was sitting, and let them have their way.

Little Woman crept timidly to her side, and with fear and trembling took her noble rival's hand. Lady Julia did not withdraw it.

'Lady Julia, you are a lady of high rank, I am a poor milliner's girl; don't let me forget that in what I am going to say. I loved Ralph (I must call him so) devotedly; I love him still, or I should not be here. Before he quitted me, each day was an earthly life that died and left me in heaven. He was so good to me, so kind to me, so true to me; he was so clever and I so common-place. He left me to go to Singleton, and I have never seen him since. I have been true to him—who would not be?—I have waited and waited for him, believed in him through the long dreary days and the cold black nights

—through a long, long illness which nearly killed me—through my slow recovery—even through the knowledge that he was on the point of being married to you. I loved him in my humble way as devotedly as you could have done. I suffered when he left me as you suffer now. Dear Lady Julia, I came here in hot anger to upbraid you for having torn my love from me; I remain to tell you how well I know how to sympathize with your bereavement, and to beg of you to pardon me for having broken in upon you with my selfish sorrow at such a time.'

Lady Julia bent her beautiful head upon Little Woman's shoulder. All sense of animosity, all distinction of rank, was swamped by their common grief.

'We are sisters in our sorrow. God bless you, Mary Vyner, for your sympathy. You must leave me now; but take this ring, which may serve to remind you of the strange bond between us. Now go, but come and see me when I am stronger.'

And Little Woman, with her hot sorrow strangely chastened, hurried back to town.

And there she found, at last, a letter from Ralph. A hot, fevered letter, written under a passionate pulse—a letter that told her how he had longed for her throughout his engagement to another, how her form had been in his mind all day, and in his eyes all night, how he had chafed under the fetters he had woven for himself, how he had freed himself from them at one reckless bound, and how he would be at the old trysting place at the old time that night.

And Little Woman kept the appointment.

An Elixir of Love

I

PLOVERLEIGH WAS a picturesque little village in Dorsetshire, ten miles from anywhere. It lay in a pretty valley nestling amid clumps of elm trees, and a pleasant little trout stream ran right through it from end to end. The vicar of Ploverleigh was the Hon. and Rev. Mortimer De Becheville, third son of the forty-eighth Earl of Caramel. He was an excellent gentleman, and his living was worth £1,200 a-year. He was a graduate of Cambridge, and held a College Fellowship, besides which his father allowed him £500 a-year. So he was very comfortably 'off.'

Mr. De Becheville had a very easy time of it, for he spent eleven-twelfths of the year away from the parish, delegating his duties to the Rev. Stanley Gay, an admirable young curate to whom he paid a stipend of £120 a-year, pocketing by this means a clear annual profit of £1,080. It was said by unkind and ungenerous people, that, as Mr. De Becheville had (presumably) been selected for his sacred duties at a high salary on account of his special and exceptional qualifications for their discharge, it was hardly fair to delegate them to a wholly inexperienced young gentleman of two-and-twenty. It was argued that if a colonel, or a stipendiary magistrate, or a superintendent of a country lunatic asylum, or any other person holding a responsible office (outside the Church of England), for which he was handsomely paid, were to do his work by cheap deputy, such a responsible official would be looked upon as a swindler. But this line of reasoning is only applied to the cure of souls by uncharitable and narrow-minded people who never go to church, and consequently can't know anything about it. Besides, who cares what people who never go to church think? If it comes to that, Mr. De Becheville was *not* selected (as it happens) on account of his special and exceptional fitness for the cure of souls inasmuch as the living was a family one, and went to De Becheville because his two elder brothers preferred the Guards. So that argument falls to the ground.

The Rev. Stanley Gay was a Leveller. I don't mean to say that he was a mere I'm-as-good-as-you Radical spouter, who advocated a redistribution of property from mere sordid motives. Mr. Gay was an aesthetic Leveller. He held that as Love is the great bond of union between man and woman, no arbitrary obstacle should be allowed to interfere with its progress. He did not desire to abolish Rank, but he *did* desire that a mere difference in rank should not be an obstacle in the way of making two young people happy. He could prove to you by figures (for he was a famous mathematician) that, rank notwithstanding, all men are equal, and this is how he did it.

He began, as a matter of course, with x, because, as he said, x, whether it represents one or one hundred thousand, is always x, and do what you will, you cannot make w or y of it by any known process.

Having made this quite clear to you, he carried on his argument by means of algebra, until he got right through algebra to the 'cases' at the end of the book, and then he slid by gentle and imperceptible degrees into conic sections, where x, although you found it masquerading as the equation to the parabola, was still as much x as ever. Then if you were not too tired to follow him, you found yourself up to the eyes in plane and spherical trigonometry, where x again turned up in a variety of assumed characters, sometimes as 'cos α' sometimes as 'sin β,' but generally with a $\sqrt[2]{}$ over it, and none the less x on that account. This singular character then made its appearance in a quaint binomial disguise, and was eventually run to earth in the very heart of differential and integral calculus, looking less like x, but being, in point of fact, more like x than ever. The force of his argument went to show that, do what you would, you could not stamp x out, and therefore it was better and wiser and more straightforward to call him x at once than to invest him with complicated sham dignities which meant nothing, and only served to bother and perplex people who met him for the first time. It's a very easy problem—anybody can do it.

Mr. Gay was, as a matter of course, engaged to be married. He loved a pretty little girl of eighteen, with soft brown eyes, and bright silky brown hair. Her name was Jessie Lightly, and she was the only daughter of Sir Caractacus Lightly, a wealthy baronet who had a large place in the neighbourhood of Ploverleigh. Sir Caractacus was a very dignified old gentleman, whose wife had died two years after Jessie's birth. A well-bred, courtly old gentleman, too, with a keen sense of honour. He was very fond of Mr. Gay, though he had no sympathy with his levelling views.

One beautiful moonlit evening Mr. Gay and Jessie were sitting together on Sir Caractacus's lawn. Everything around them was pure and calm and still, so they grew sentimental.

'Stanley,' said Jessie, 'we are very, very happy, are we not?'

'Unspeakably happy,' said Gay. 'So happy that when I look around me, and see how many there are whose lives are embittered by disappointment—by envy, by hatred, and by malice' (when he grew oratorical he generally lapsed into the Litany) 'I turn to the tranquil and unruffled calm of my own pure and happy love for you with gratitude unspeakable.'

He really meant all this, though he expressed himself in rather flatulent periods.

'I wish with all my heart,' said Jessie, 'that every soul on earth were as happy as we two.'

'And why are they not?' asked Gay, who hopped on to his hobby whenever it was, so to speak, brought round to the front door. 'And why are they not, Jessie? I will tell you why they are not. Because—'

'Yes, darling,' said Jessie, who had often heard his argument before. 'I know why. It's dreadful.'

'It's as simple as possible,' said Gay. 'Take x to represent the abstract human being—'

'Certainly, dear,' said Jessie, who agreed with his argument heart and soul, but didn't want to hear it again. 'We took it last night.'

'Then,' said Gay, not heeding the interruption, 'let $x+1$, $x+2$, $x+3$, represent three grades of high rank.'

'Exactly, it's contemptible,' said Jessie. 'How softly the wind sighs among the trees.'

'What is a duke?' asked Gay—not for information, but oratorically, with a view to making a point.

'A mere $x+3$,' said Jessie. 'Could anything be more hollow. What a lovely evening!'

'The Duke of Buckingham and Chandos—it sounds well, I grant you,' continued Gay, 'but call him the $x+3$ of Buckingham and Chandos, and you reduce him at once to—'

'I know,' said Jessie, 'to his lowest common denominator,' and her little upper lip curled with contempt.

'Nothing of the kind,' said Gay, turning red. 'Either hear me out, or let me drop the subject. At all events don't make ridiculous suggestions.'

'I'm very sorry, dear,' said Jessie, humbly. 'Go on, I'm listening, and I won't interrupt any more.'

But Gay was annoyed and wouldn't go on. So they returned to the house together. It was their first tiff.

II

In St. Martin's Lane lived Baylis and Culpepper, magicians, astrologers, and professors of the Black Art. Baylis had sold himself to the Devil at a very early age, and had become remarkably proficient in all kinds of enchantment. Culpepper had been his apprentice, and having also acquired considerable skill as a necromancer, was taken into partnership by the genial old magician, who from the first had taken a liking to the frank and fair-haired boy. Ten years ago (the date of my story) the firm of Baylis and Culpepper stood at the very head of the London family magicians. They did what is known as a pushing trade, but although they advertised largely, and never neglected a chance, it was admitted even by their rivals, that the goods they supplied could be relied on as sound useful articles. They had a special reputation for a class of serviceable family nativity, and they did a very large and increasing business in love philtres, 'The Patent Oxy-Hydrogen Love-at-First-Sight Draught' in bottles at 1*s.* 1½*d.* and 2*s.* 3*d.* ('our leading article,' as Baylis called it) was strong enough in itself to keep the firm going, had all its other resources failed them. But the establishment in St. Martin's Lane was also a 'Noted House for Amulets,' and if you wanted a neat, well-finished divining-rod, I don't know any place to which I would sooner recommend you. Their Curses at a shilling per dozen were the cheapest things in the trade, and they sold thousands of them in the course of the year. Their Blessings—also very cheap indeed, and quite effective—were not much asked for. 'We always keep a few on hand as curiosities and for completeness, but we don't sell two in the twelvemonth,' said Mr. Baylis. 'A gentleman bought one last week to send to his mother-in-law, but it turned out that he was afflicted in the head, and the persons who had charge of him declined to pay for it, and it's been returned to us. But the sale of penny curses, especially on Saturday nights, is tremendous. We can't turn 'em out fast enough.'

As Baylis and Culpepper were making up their books one evening, just at closing time, a gentle young clergyman with large violet eyes, and a beautiful girl of eighteen, with soft brown hair, and a Madonna-like purity of expression, entered the warehouse. These were Stanley Gay and Jessie Lightly. And this is how it came to pass that they found themselves in London, and in the warehouse of the worthy magicians.

As the reader knows, Stanley Gay and Jessie had for many months given themselves up to the conviction that it was their duty to do all in their power to bring their fellow men and women together in holy matrimony, without regard to distinctions of age or rank. Stanley gave lectures on the subject at mechanics' institutes, and the mechanics were unanimous in their approval of his views. He preached his doctrine in workhouses, in beer-shops, and in lunatic asylums, and his listeners supported him with enthusiasm. He addressed navvies at the roadside on the humanizing advantages that would accrue to them if they married refined and wealthy ladies of rank, and not a navvy dissented. In short, he felt more and more convinced every day that he had at last discovered the secret of human happiness. Still he had a formidable battle to fight with class prejudice, and he and Jessie pondered gravely on the difficulties that were before them, and on the best means of overcoming them.

'It's no use disguising the fact, Jessie,' said Mr. Gay, 'that the Countesses won't like it.' And little Jessie gave a sigh, and owned that she expected some difficulty with the Countesses. 'We must look these things in the face, Jessie, it won't do to ignore them. We have convinced the humble mechanics and artisans, but the aristocracy hold aloof.'

'The working-man is the true Intelligence after all,' said Jessie.

'He is a noble creature when he is quite sober,' said Gay. 'God bless him.'

Stanley Gay and Jessie were in this frame of mind when they came across Baylis and Culpepper's advertisement in the *Connubial Chronicle*.

'My dear Jessie,' said Gay, 'I see a way out of our difficulty.'

And dear little Jessie's face beamed with hope.

'These Love Philtres that Baylis and Culpepper advertise—they are very cheap indeed, and if we may judge by the testimonials, they are very effective. Listen, darling.'

And Stanley Gay read as follows:—

'From the Earl of Market Harborough. "I am a hideous old man of eighty, and everyone avoided me. I took a family bottle of your philtre, immediately on my accession to the title and estates a fortnight ago, and I can't keep the young women off. Please send me a pipe of it to lay down."

'From Amelia Orange Blossom.—"I am a very pretty girl of fifteen. For upwards of fourteen years past I have been without a definitely declared admirer. I took a large bottle of your philtre yesterday, and within fourteen hours a young nobleman winked at me in church. Send me a couple of dozen." '

'What can the girl want with a couple of dozen young noblemen, darling?' asked Jessie.

'I don't know—perhaps she took it too strong. Now these men,' said Gay, laying down the paper, 'are benefactors indeed, if they can accomplish all they undertake. I would ennoble these men. They should have statues. I would enthrone them in high places. They would be $x+3$.'

'My generous darling,' said Jessie, gazing into his eyes in a fervid ecstasy.

'Not at all,' replied Gay. 'They deserve it. We confer peerages on generals who plunge half a nation into mourning—shall we deny them to men who bring a life's happiness home to every door? Always supposing,' added the cautious clergyman, 'that they can really do what they profess.'

The upshot of this conversation was that Gay determined to lay in a stock of philtres for general use among his parishioners. If the effect upon them was satisfactory he would extend the sphere of their operations. So when Sir Caractacus and his daughter went to town for the season, Stanley Gay spent a fortnight with them, and thus it came to pass that he and Jessie went together to Baylis and Culpepper's.

'Have you any fresh Love Philtres today?' said Gay.

'Plenty, sir,' said Mr. Culpepper. 'How many would you like?'

'Well—let me see,' say Gay. 'There are a hundred and forty souls in my parish,—say twelve dozen.'

'I think, dear,' said little Jessie, 'you are better to take a few more than you really want, in case of accidents.'

'In purchasing a large quantity, sir,' said Mr. Culpepper, 'we would strongly advise you taking it in the wood, and drawing it off as you happen to want it. We have it in four-and-a-half and nine-gallon casks, and we deduct ten per cent, for cash payments.'

'Then, Mr. Culpepper, be good enough to let me have a nine-gallon cask of Love Philtre as soon as possible. Send it to the Rev. Stanley Gay, Ploverleigh.'

He wrote a cheque for the amount, and so the transaction ended.

'Is there any other article?' said Mr. Culpepper.

'Nothing to-day. Good afternoon.'

'Have you seen our new wishing-caps? They are lined with silk and very chastely quilted, sir. We sold one to the Archbishop of Canterbury not an hour ago. Allow me to put you up a wishing-cap.'

'I tell you that I want nothing more,' said Gay, going.

'Our Flying Carpets are quite the talk of the town, sir,' said Culpepper, producing a very handsome piece of Persian tapestry. 'You spread it on the ground and sit on it, and then you think of a place and you find yourself there before you can count ten. Our Abudah chests, sir, each chest containing a patent Hag, who comes out and prophesies disasters whenever you touch this spring, are highly spoken of. We can sell the Abudah chest complete for fifteen guineas.'

'I think you tradespeople make a great mistake in worrying people to buy things they dont want,' said Gay.

'You'd be surprised if you knew the quantity of things we get rid of by this means, sir.'

'No doubt, but I think you keep a great many people out of your shop. If x represents the amount you gain by it, and y the amount you lose by it, then if $\frac{x}{2}=y$ you are clearly out of pocket by it at the end of the year. Think this over. Good evening.'

And Mr. Gay left the shop with Jessie.

'Stanley,' said she, 'what a blessing you are to mankind. You do good wherever you go.'

'My dear Jessie,' replied Gay, 'I have had a magnificent education, and if I can show these worthy but half-educated tradesmen that their ignorance of the profounder mathematics is misleading them, I am only dealing as I should deal with the blessings that have been entrusted to my care.'

As Messrs. Baylis & Culpepper have nothing more to do with this story, it may be stated at once that Stanley Gay's words had a marked effect upon them. They determined never to push an article again, and within two years of this resolve they retired on ample fortunes, Baylis to a beautiful detached house on Clapham Common, and Culpepper to a handsome château on the Mediterranean, about four miles from Nice.

III

We are once more at Ploverleigh, but this time at the Vicarage. The scene is Mr. Gay's handsome library, and in this library three persons are assembled—Mr. Gay, Jessie, and old Zorah Clarke. It should be explained that Zorah is Mr. Gay's cook and housekeeper, and it is understood between him and Sir Caractacus Lightly that Jessie may call on the curate whenever she likes, on condition that Zorah is present during the whole time of the visit. Zorah is stone deaf and has to be communicated with through the medium of pantomime, so that while she is really no impediment whatever to the free flow of conversation, the chastening influence of her presence would suffice of itself to silence ill-natured comments, if such articles had an existence among the primitive and innocent inhabitants of Ploverleigh.

The nine-gallon cask of Love Philtre had arrived in due course, and Mr. Gay had decided that it should be locked up in a cupboard in his library, as he thought it would scarcely be prudent to trust it to Zorah, whose curiosity might get the better of her discretion. Zorah (who believed that the cask contained sherry) was much scandalized at her master's action in keeping it in his library, and looked upon it as an evident and unmistakeable sign that he had deliberately made up his mind to take a steady course of drinking. However, Mr. Gay partly reassured the good old lady by informing her in pantomime (an art of expression in which long practice had made him singularly expert) that the liquid was not intoxicating in the ordinary sense of the word, but that it was a cunning and subtle essence, concocted from innocent herbs by learned gentlemen who had devoted a lifetime to the study of its properties. He added (still in pantomime) that he did not propose to drink a single drop of it himself, but that he intended to distribute it among his parishioners, whom it would benefit socially, mentally, and morally to a considerable extent. Master as he was of the art of expression by gesture, it took two days' hard work to make this clear to her, and even then she had acquired but a faint and feeble idea of its properties, for she always referred to it as sarsaparilla.

'Jessie,' said Gay, 'the question now arises,—How shall we most effectually dispense the great boon we have at our command? Shall we give a party to our friends, and put the Love Philtre on the table in decanters, and allow them to help themselves?'

'We must be very careful, dear,' said Jessie, 'not to allow any married people to taste it.'

'True,' said Gay, 'quite true. I never thought of that. It wouldn't do at all. I am much obliged to you for the suggestion. It would be terrible—quite terrible.'

And Stanley Gay turned quite pale and faint at the very thought of such a *contretemps*.

'Then,' said Jessie, 'there are the engaged couples. I don't think we ought to do anything to interfere with the prospects of those who have already plighted their troth.'

'Quite true,' said Gay, 'we have no right, as you say, to interfere with the arrangements of engaged couples. That narrows our sphere of action very considerably.'

'Then the widows and the widowers of less than one year's standing should be exempted from its influence.'

'Certainly, most certainly. That reflection did not occur to me, I confess. It is clear that the dispensing of the philtre will be a very delicate operation: it will have to be conducted with the utmost tact. Can you think of any more exceptions?'

'Let me see,' said Jessie. 'There's Tibbits, our gardener, who has fits; and there's Williamson, papa's second groom, who drinks, oughtn't to be allowed to marry; and Major Crump, who uses dreadful language before ladies; and Dame Parboy, who is bed-ridden; and the old ladies in the alms-houses—and little Tommy, the idiot—and, indeed, all children under—under what age shall we say?'

'All children who have not been confirmed,' said Gay. 'Yes, these exceptions never occurred to me.'

'I don't think we shall ever use the nine gallons, dear,' said Jessie. 'One tablespoonful is a dose.'

'I have just thought of another exception,' said Gay. 'Your papa.'

'Oh! papa *must* marry again! Poor dear old papa! Oh! You *must* let *him* marry.'

'My dear Jessie,' said Gay, 'Heaven has offered me the chance of entering into the married state unencumbered with a mother-in-law. And I am content to accept the blessing as I find it. Indeed, I prefer it so.'

'Papa *does* so want to marry—he is always talking of it,' replied the poor little woman, with a pretty pout. 'O indeed, *indeed*, my new mamma, whoever she may be, shall never interfere with us. Why, how thankless you are! My papa is about to confer upon you the most inestimable treasure in the world, a young, beautiful and devoted wife, and you withhold from him a priceless blessing that you are ready to confer on the very meanest of your parishioners.'

'Jessie,' said Gay, 'you have said enough. Sir Caractacus *shall* marry. I was wrong. If a certain burden to which I will not more particularly refer is to descend upon my shoulders, I will endeavour to bear it without repining.'

It was finally determined that there was only one way in which the philtre could be safely and properly distributed. Mr. Gay was to give out that he was much interested in the sale of a very peculiar and curious old Amontillado, and small sample bottles of the wine were to be circulated among such of his parishioners as were decently eligible as brides and bridegrooms. The scheme was put into operation as soon as it was decided upon. Mr. Gay sent to the nearest market-town for a gross of two-ounce phials, and Jessie and he spent a long afternoon bottling the elixir into these convenient receptacles. They then rolled them up in papers, and addressed them to the persons who were destined to be operated upon. And when all this was done Jessie returned to her papa, and Mr. Gay sat up all night explaining in pantomime to Zorah that a widowed aunt of his, in somewhat straitened circumstances, who resided in a small but picturesque villa in the suburbs of Montilla, and had been compelled to take a large quantity of the very finest sherry from a bankrupt wine-merchant, in satisfaction of a year's rent of her second floor, and that he had undertaken to push its sale in Ploverleigh in consideration of a commission of two-and-a-half per cent. on the sales effected—which commission was to be added to the fund for the restoration of the church steeple. He began his explanation at 9 p.m. and at 6 a.m. Zorah thought she began to understand him, and Stanley Gay, quite exhausted with his pantomime exertions, retired, dead beat, to his chamber.

IV

The next morning as Sir Caractacus Lightly sat at breakfast with Jessie, the footman informed him that Mr. Gay's housekeeper wished to speak to him on very particular business. The courtly old Baronet directed that she should be shown into the library, and at once proceeded to ask what she wanted.

'If you please Sir Caractacus, and beggin' your pardon,' said Zorah as he entered, 'I've come with a message from my master.'

'Pray be seated,' said Sir Caractacus. But the poor old lady could not hear him, so he explained his meaning to her in the best dumb show he could command. He pointed to a chair—walked to it—sat down in it—leant back, crossed his legs cosily, got up, and waved his hand to her in a manner that clearly conveyed to her that she was expected to do as he had done.

'My master's compliments and he's gone into the wine trade, and would you accept a sample?'

After all, Mr. Gay's exertions had failed to convey his exact meaning to the deaf old lady.

'You astonish me,' said Sir Caractacus; then, finding that she did not understand him, he rumpled his hair, opened his mouth, strained his eye-balls, and threw himself into an attitude of the most horror-struck amazement. Having made his state of mind quite clear to her, he smiled pleasantly, and nodded to her to proceed.

'If you'll kindly taste it, sir, I'll take back any orders with which you may favour me.'

Sir Caractacus rang for a wineglass and proceeded to taste the sample.

'I don't know what it is, but it's not Amontillado,' said he, smacking his lips; 'still it is a pleasant cordial. Taste it.'

The old lady seemed to gather his meaning at once. She nodded, bobbed a curtsey, and emptied the glass.

Baylis and Culpepper had not over-stated the singular effects of the 'Patent Oxy-Hydrogen Love-at-First-Sight Draught.' Sir Caractacus's hard and firmly-set features gradually relaxed as the old lady sipped the contents of her glass. Zorah set it down when she had quite emptied it, and as she did so her eyes met those of the good old Baronet. She blushed under the ardour of his gaze, and a tear trembled on her old eyelid.

'You're a remarkably fine woman,' said Sir Caractacus, 'and singularly well preserved for your age.'

'Alas, kind sir,' said Zorah, 'I am that hard of hearin' that cannons is whispers.'

Sir Caractacus stood up, stroked his face significantly, smacked his hands together, slapped them both upon his heart, and sank on one knee at her feet. He then got up and nodded smilingly at her to imply that he really meant it.

Zorah turned aside and trembled.

'I ain't no scollard, Sir Caractacus, and I don't rightly know how a poor old 'ooman like me did ought to own her likings for a lordly barrownight—but a true 'art is more precious than diamonds they do say, and a lovin' wife is a crown of gold to her husband. I ain't fashionable, but I'm a respectable old party, and can make you comfortable if nothing else.'

'Zorah, you are the very jewel of my hopes. My dear daughter will soon be taken from me. It lies with you to brighten my desolate old age. Will you be Lady Lightly?'

And he pointed to a picture of his late wife, and went through the pantomime of putting a ring on Zorah's finger. He then indicated the despair that would possess him if she refused to accept his offer. Having achieved these feats of silent eloquence, he smiled and nodded at her reassuringly, and waited for a reply with an interrogative expression of countenance.

'Yes, dearie,' murmured Zorah, as she sank into the Baronet's arms.

After a happy half-hour Zorah felt it was her duty to return to her master, so the lovers took a fond farewell of each other, and Sir Caractacus returned to the breakfast-room.

'Jessie,' said Sir Caractacus, 'I think you really love your poor old father?'

'Indeed, papa, I do.'

'Then you will, I trust, be pleased to hear that my declining years are not unlikely to be solaced by the companionship of a good, virtuous, and companionable woman.'

'My dear papa,' said Jessie, 'do you really mean that—that you are likely to be married?'

'Indeed, Jessie, I think it is more than probable! You

know you are going to leave me very soon, and my dear little nurse must be replaced, or what will become of me?'

Jessie's eyes filled with tears—but they were tears of joy.

'I cannot tell you papa—dear, dear, papa—how happy you have made me.'

'And you will, I am sure, accept your new mamma with every feeling of respect and affection.'

'Any wife of yours is a mamma of mine,' said Jessie.

'My darling! Yes, Jessie, before very long I hope to lead to the altar a bride who will love and honour me as I deserve. She is no light and giddy girl, Jessie. She is a woman of sober age and staid demeanour, yet easy and comfortable in her ways. I am going to marry Mr. Gay's cook, Zorah.'

'Zorah,' cried Jessie, 'dear, dear old Zorah! Oh, indeed, I am very, very glad and happy!'

'Bless you, my child,' said the Baronet. 'I knew my pet would not blame her poor old father for acting on the impulse of a heart that has never misled him. Yes, I think—nay, I am sure—that I have taken a wise and prudent step. Zorah is not what the world calls beautiful.'

'Zorah is very good, and very clean and honest, and quite, quite sober in her habits,' said Jessie warmly, 'and that is worth more—far more than beauty, dear papa. Beauty will fade and perish, but personal cleanliness is practically undying, for it can be renewed whenever it discovers symptoms of decay. Oh, I am sure you will be happy!' And Jessie hurried off to tell Stanley Gay how nobly the potion had done its work.

'Stanley, dear Stanley,' said she, 'I have such news—Papa and Zorah are engaged!'

'I am very glad to hear it. She will make him an excellent wife; it is a very auspicious beginning.'

'And have *you* any news to tell me?'

'None, except that all the bottles are distributed, and I am now waiting to see their effect. By the way, the Bishop has arrived unexpectedly, and is stopping at the Rectory, and I have sent him a bottle. I should like to find a nice little wife for the Bishop, for he has Crawleigh in his gift—the present incumbent is at the point of death, and the living is worth £1,800 a year. The duty is extremely light, and the county society unexceptional. I think I could be truly useful in such a sphere of action.'

V

The action of the 'Patent Oxy-Hydrogen Love-at-First-Sight Philtre' was rapid and powerful, and before evening there was scarcely a disengaged person (over thirteen years of age) in Ploverleigh. The Dowager Lady Fitz-Saracen, a fierce old lady of sixty, had betrothed herself to Alfred Creeper, of the 'Three Fiddlers,' a very worthy man, who had been engaged in the public trade all his life, and had never yet had a mark on his license. Colonel Pemberton, of The Grove, had fixed his affections on dear little Bessie Lane, the pupil teacher, and his son Willie (who had returned from Eton only the day before) had given out his engagement to kind old Mrs. Partlet, the widow of the late sexton. In point of fact there was only one disengaged person in the village—the good and grave old Bishop. He was in the position of the odd player who can't find a seat in the 'Family Coach.' But, on the whole, Stanley Gay was rather glad of this, as he venerated the good old prelate, and in his opinion there was no one in the village at that time who was really good enough to be a Bishop's wife, except, indeed, the dear little brown-haired, soft-eyed maiden to whom Stanley himself was betrothed.

So far everything had worked admirably, and the unions effected through the agency of the philtre, if they were occasionally ill-assorted as regards the stations in life of the contracting parties, were all that could be desired in every other respect. Good, virtuous straightforward, and temperate men were engaged to blameless women who were calculated to make admirable wives and mothers, and there was every prospect that Ploverleigh would become celebrated as the only Home of Perfect Happiness. There was but one sad soul in the village. The good old Bishop had drunk freely of the philtre, but there was no one left to love him. It was pitiable to see the poor love-lorn prelate as he wandered disconsolately through the smiling meadows of Ploverleigh, pouring out the accents of his love to an incorporeal abstraction.

'Something must be done for the Bishop,' said Stanley, as he watched him sitting on a stile in the distance. 'The poor old gentleman is wasting to a shadow.'

The next morning as Stanley was carefully reading through the manuscript sermon which had been sent to him by a firm in Paternoster Row for delivery on the ensuing Sabbath, little Jessie entered his library (with Zorah) and threw herself on a sofa, sobbing as if her heart would break.

'Why, Jessie—my own little love,' exclaimed Stanley. 'What in the world is the matter?'

And he put his arms fondly round her waist, and endeavoured to raise her face to his.

'Oh, no—no—Stanley—don't—you musn't—indeed, indeed, you musn't.'

'Why, my pet, what can you mean?'

'Oh, Stanley, Stanley—you will never, never forgive me.'

'Nonsense, child,' said he. 'My dear little Jessie in incapable of an act which is beyond the pale of forgiveness.' And he gently kissed her forehead.

'Stanley, you musn't do it—indeed you musn't.'

'No, you musnt do it, Muster Gay,' said Zorah.

'Why, confound you, what do you mean by interfering?' said Stanley in a rage.

'Ah, it's all very fine, I dare say, but I don't know what you're a-talking about.'

And Stanley, recollecting her infirmity, explained in pantomime the process of confounding a person, and intimated that it would be put into operation upon her if she presumed to cut in with impertinent remarks.

'Stanley—Mr. Gay—' said Jessie.

'*Mr.* Gay!' ejaculated Stanley.

'I musn't call you Stanley any more.'

'Great Heaven, why not?'

'I'll tell you all about it if you promise not to be violent.'

And Gay, prepared for some terrible news, hid his head in his hands, and sobbed audibly.

'I loved you—oh so, so much—you were my life—my heart,' said the poor little woman. 'By day and by night my thoughts were with you, and the love came from my heart as the water from a well!'

Stanley groaned.

'When I rose in the morning it was to work for your happiness, and when I lay down in my bed at night it was to dream of the love that was to weave itself through my life.'

He kept his head between his hands and moved not.

'My life was for your life—my soul for yours! I drew breath but for one end— to love, to honour, to reverence you.'

He lifted his head at last. His face was ashy pale.

'Come to the point,' he gasped.

'Last night,' said Jessie, 'I was tempted to taste a bottle of the Elixir. It was but a drop I took on the tip of my finger. I went to bed thinking but of you. I rose to-day, still with you in my mind. Immediately after breakfast, I left home to call upon you, and as I crossed Bullthorn's meadow I saw the Bishop of Chelsea seated on a stile. At once I became conscious that I had placed myself unwittingly under the influence of the fatal potion. Horrified at my involuntary faithlessness—loathing my miserable weakness—hating myself for the misery I was about to weave around the life of a saint I had so long adored—I could not but own to myself that the love of my heart was given over, for ever, to that solitary and love-lorn prelate. Mr. Gay (for by that name I must call you to the end), I have told you nearly all that you need care to know. It is enough to add that my love is, as a matter of course, reciprocated, and, but for the misery I have caused you, I am happy. But, full as my cup of joy may be, it will never be without a bitter after-taste, for I cannot forget that my folly—my wicked folly— has blighted the life of a man who, an hour ago, was dearer to me than the whole world!'

And Jessie fell sobbing on Zorah's bosom.

Stanley Gay, pale and haggard, rose from his chair, and staggered to a side table. He tried to pour out a glass of water, but as he was in the act of doing so the venerable Bishop entered the room.

'Mr. Gay, I cannot but feel that I owe you some apology for having gained the affections of a young lady to whom you were attached—Jessie, my love, compose yourself.'

And the Bishop gently removed Jessie's arms from

Zorah's neck, and placed them about his own.

'My Lord,' said Mr. Gay, 'I am lost in amazement. When I have more fully realized the unparalleled misfortune that has overtaken me I shall perhaps be able to speak and act with calmness. At the present moment I am unable to trust myself to do either. I am stunned—quite, quite stunned.'

'Do not suppose, my dear Mr. Gay,' said the Bishop, 'that I came here this morning to add to your reasonable misery by presenting myself before you in the capacity of a successful rival. No. I came to tell you that poor old Mr. Chudd, the vicar of Crawleigh has been mercifully removed. He is no more, and as the living is in my gift, I have come to tell you that, if it can compensate in any way for the terrible loss I have been the unintentional means of inflicting upon you, it is entirely at your disposal. It is worth £1,800 per annum—the duty is extremely light, and the local society is unexceptional.'

Stanley Gay pressed the kind old Bishop's hand.

'Eighteen hundred a year will not entirely compensate me for Jessie.'

'For Miss Lightly,' murmured the Bishop, gently.

'For Miss Lightly—but it will go some way towards doing so. I accept your lordship's offer with gratitude.'

'We shall always take an interest in you,' said the Bishop.

'Always—always,' said Jessie. 'And we shall be so glad to see you at the Palace—shall we not Frederick?'

'Well—ha—hum—yes—oh, yes, of course. Always,' said the Bishop. 'That is—oh, yes—always.'

The 14th of February was a great day for Ploverleigh, for on that date all the couples that had been brought together through the agency of the philtre were united in matrimony by the only bachelor in the place, the Rev. Stanley Gay. A week afterwards he took leave of his parishioners in an affecting sermon, and 'read himself in' at Crawleigh. He is still unmarried, and likely to remain so. He has quite got over his early disappointment, and he and the Bishop and Jessie have many a hearty laugh together over the circumstances under which the good old prelate wooed and won the bright-eyed little lady. Sir Caractacus died within a year of his marriage, and Zorah lives with her daughter-in-law at the Palace. The Bishop works hard at the art of pantomimic expression, but as yet with qualified success. He has lately taken to conversing with her through the medium of diagrams, many of which are very spirited in effect, though crude in design. It is not unlikely that they may be published before long. The series of twelve consecutive sketches, by which the Bishop informed his mother-in-law that, if she didn't mind her own business, and refrain from interfering between his wife and himself, he should be under the necessity of requiring her to pack up and be off, is likely to have a very large sale.

Tom Poulton's Joke

A SOCIABLE CLUB of seventy or eighty choice spirits, calling itself 'The Serious Family,' and having for its president or chairman Mr. Tom Poulton, Barrister-at-Law in theory, and Nothing-at-All in fact, held its weekly meetings for some years in three or four large rooms in a dull gaunt house in Soho Square. The primary object of this association was the promotion of good-fellowship by the conciliatory medium of wholesome spirits and good tobacco. It possessed a secondary, or rather incidental, feature in the shape of a Provident Loan Fund, and according to the bye-laws of this fund, all members of the Club who had proved their general solvency by twelve regular monthly payments of one sovereign, were entitled to one loan of twenty-four pounds, to be repaid within six months of the date of borrowing. This fund was projected by Mr. Tom Poulton, who proved by statistics that, taking the general population of Great Britain and Ireland, including women and children, and excluding all members of the House of Peers and all registered paupers, only one person in four lived beyond his annual income; or, in other words, only one person in four had occasion to borrow money to meet his yearly expenditure. Assuming that these statistics were applicable to so many members of the Serious Family as elected to become subscribers to the projected Provident Loan Fund, it followed that for every four annual subscriptions of twelve pounds only one annual loan of twenty-four pounds would be applied for, leaving a clear annual balance of twenty-four other pounds in the fund's favour. But Mr. Tom Poulton did not close his eyes to the possibility that statistics which held good when applied to thirty-five million people, including women and children, might stand in need of some modification before they became applicable to an exceptional gathering of seventy or eighty young and middle-aged persons, among whom were no women and no children. He very fairly admitted the exceptional character of the Club, in the course of his speech on the motion that the fund should be instituted, but he contended that if as many as one in three, instead of one in four, were to apply at the year's end for the loan of twenty-four pounds, the result would show a clear balance of fifty per cent. in favour of the projected fund. He went on to show that if an application from one in three resulted in a profit of fifty per cent., an application from one in one and a half would result in a profit of twenty-five per cent.; or, carrying the principle still further, an application from one in three-quarters would result in a profit of twelve and a half per cent.; from which an easy calculation would show that if every member of the Loan Fund who had subscribed twelve pounds were to insist on borrowing twenty-four, the clear annual profit in favour of the Club would be fifteen and five-eighths per cent., and Mr. Tom Poulton would undertake, in writing, to be responsible for the accuracy of his calculation. It was immediately proposed that this fund be forthwith instituted, and the proposition was carried by acclamation. Mr. Tom Poulton was immediately elected Chairman, Treasurer, Secretary, and Trustee of the fund, and the whole Club became subscribers to it.

Now this was one of Mr. Tom Poulton's practical jokes. Mr. Tom Poulton had, among other valuable gifts, a keen sense of humour, so keen, indeed, that it was in no degree blunted if the joke turned against himself. Most of Mr. Tom Poulton's practical jokes turned against himself, and the particular joke that Mr. Tom Poulton perpetrated in connection with the Serious Family Provident Loan Fund, proved especially disastrous to Mr. Tom Poulton, and, in the long run, especially beneficial to his intended victims, the subscribers to the fund.

As the year drew towards its close, and as all the twelve-pound subscribers to the fund intimated their intention of applying for loans of twenty-four pounds apiece (leaving a clear annual balance of fifteen and five-eighths per cent. in favour of the fund, according to Tom Poulton's own showing), Tom Poulton began to cast about for another joke that should have the effect of eclipsing, by the richness of its humour, the humour of the fund joke, and of oblitering, by the force of its agreeable *dénouement*, all recollection of the disappointment that would be occasioned by the *dénouement* of the fund joke.

One morning Mr. Tom Poulton called upon Mr. Richard Harris, the Secretary of the Serious Family. Mr. Harris was the chosen abettor of Mr. Poulton's little jokes. He also acted the part of Traiter-in-Ordinary to that gentleman, and brought all his ingenuity to bear upon the best means of causing Mr. Poulton's jokes to recoil upon himself. But Mr. Poulton's keen sense of humour reconciled him to all misfortunes that proceeded from it, and he and Mr. Harris were on the best of terms.

'Harris,' said Tom Poulton, 'I've arranged another sell for the Family, and I want your help.'

'It is yours,' said Harris. 'Details?'

'You are aware that all the Family will be down on me, in six weeks' time, for their twenty-four pound loans? Well, before they fall due I'm going to die.'

'Don't do that,' said Harris.

'Yes, my mind's made up. Listen. I've found an old man of my name—Tom Poulton; I advertised for him. He is wretchedly poor, and he lives all by himself in Clump Cottages, Haverstock Hill.'

'Well?'

'Well, he can't live three weeks, and I've taken lodgings in his house.'

'Still I don't see—'

'You're very dull. He can't live three weeks—that is to say, in three weeks he'll die and he'll be buried. The Family must hear of it through you, they will all come to the funeral, and I'll turn up among them.'

'But if you die, and don't repay them their money they have subscribed to the fund, I don't think they *will* come to the funeral.'

'Yes, I've arranged about that. I'll make my will, leaving everything I have to be equally divided among them. The will must be opened by you immediately after my demise. I'll appoint you executor and I'll leave you—I'll leave you a hundred pounds for your trouble.'

'Thank you—thank you heartily.'

'Spend it judiciously, Richard—when you get it.'

'On the 17th November, at 3 Clump Cottages, Haverstock Hill, Thomas Poulton, Esquire, of the Inner Temple, Barrister-at-Law.'

The Serious Family were very angry at Tom Poulton's death. He had pocketed nearly a thousand pounds of their money, and out of this sum they had counted on borrowing two thousand at Christmas. But by their chairman and treasurer's demise, not only was there no prospect of effecting the contemplated loan, but it became a very serious question whether they would ever see any of the paid-up capital again. It was voted abominable on Tom Poulton's part to die at such a crisis, and nobody expressed any intention of going to his funeral. However, Mr. Dick Harris completely justified Tom Poulton's dying by producing his will at the next meeting; the will left everything that Tom Poulton possessed to the society, to be divided equally among its members, and as Tom Poulton had three or four hundred a year from house property, everyone expressed an intention of going to his funeral.

The funeral was plain, not to say meagre, in its appointments; but no doubt Dick Harris, as executor, did not feel justified in putting the Serious Family to any unnecessary expense. It was voted thoughtful in Dick Harris, and never did any body of men feel more thoroughly convinced of the vanity of funeral pomp than did the members of the Serious Family as they stood round poor Tom Poulton's grave.

But between the demise and burial of theTom Poulton who actually *did* die, Mr. Dick Harris had made an important discovery.

The Tom Poulton who *did* die turned out to be an extraordinarily wealthy old miser. His mattress was stuffed with bank-notes, and so was his easy chair, and under the boards of his room was gold to the amount of eight or nine thousand pounds. Moreover, he appeared to have died intestate; at all events, the only will that was found was the will made in favour of the Serious Family by the Tom Poulton who did not die. In the absence of any other testamentary document applying to the property of the Tom Poulton who *did* die, Mr. Dick Harris had no alternative but to apply to it the testamentary document drawn up and signed by the Mr. Tom Poulton who did *not* die. I will not attempt to describe how the grief of the Serious Family for the loss of Tom Poulton was tempered by the rapture with which they learnt that his estate was worth altogether some thirty or forty thousand pounds.

The day of Tom Poulton's funeral was a bitterly cold one. A drizzling November mist shrouded one half of the funeral party from the other half, and all were drenched to the skin. There had much moralizing among the mourners on the good qualities of poor Tom Poulton, on the eccentric taste that induced him to hoard away so much good money, and on the irreparable—almost irreparable—loss that his death would cause to the Family. As they stood round poor Tom Poulton's grave, dicoursing in saddened whispers to this effect, they were naturally rather surprised to find poor Tom Poulton standing among them, his eyes red with weeping and his general appearance carefully contrived to convey the idea that his grief at his own death was unbounded. It was natural enough that he should be sorry for his own death; the only unaccountable feature in the matter was his being present as a live mourner at his own funeral. This consideration appealed powerfully to Mr. Peter Hodgson, the member of the Serious Family who first became conscious of Mr. Tom Poulton's presence among them.

At first Mr. Peter Hodgson was not at all surprised. Mr. Tom Poulton was so thoroughly identified with all gatherings of the Serious Family, particularly with all funerals of deceased members (for it was a point of honour with the Family to muster in full strength on such occasions), that Mr. Peter Hodgson accepted his presence almost as a matter of course. His attention, however, was directed to the anomaly by Tom Poulton's first remark. 'Whose funeral is this?' said Tom. Peter turned dead white. 'Why it's—it's yours, Tom,' said Peter.

'Mine?'

'Yes, Tom—yours.'

'This is scarcely a place or time for a joke, sir,' said Tom, sternly.

'Joke!' said Peter, 'it's no joke! Didn't you die last week?'

'I? Nonsense!'

'Well, anyway we're burying you, Tom Poulton!'

'Why do you call me Tom Poulton?

'Aren't you Tom Poulton?'

'Certainly not—I don't even know the name—I happened to be passing through the Cemetery, and seeing a large crowd of mourners, I joined them from motives of mere curiosity.'

'Then, sir,' said Peter Hodgson, 'I never saw such a wonderful likeness of the very man we are burying in the whole course of my life?'

Tom glided mysteriously away from Peter Hodgson and made his way into the throng of mourners.

'Tom!' said another; 'why we are burying you!'

'My name, sir, is not Tom, and I have never been buried in my life.'

'Tom Poulton!' 'Tom Poulton!' 'Tom Poulton's alive and present!' passed from mouth to mouth, as the astounded Serious Family gazed in horror on his familiar, but by no means vulgar, features.

'Gentlemen,' said Tom Poulton, 'I must again assure you that you are deceived by an accidental resemblance; I am not Tom Poulton, and I never heard of him.'

And with a slight bow he walked away.

The principal topic of conversation that night, at the meeting of the Serious Family, was the miraculous appearance of somebody very like Tom Poulton, at Tom Poulton's funeral. It was held that it couldn't possibly have been Tom Poulton, because Tom Poulton was dead and buried, and Tom Poulton's will had been opened, by which he left thirty or forty thousand pounds in ready money to the Serious Family. This was held by implication only, as it never entered anybody's head to suggest that the mysterious stranger could possibly have been Tom Poulton.

The Club had resolved itself into a committee to consider the best means of investing or otherwise disposing of the handsome legacy which Tom Poulton had left them.

It was decided, as a first step, that, as a mark of respect to poor Tom Poulton's fund scheme, every member should be permitted to borrow twenty-four pounds from Tom's estate.

The question then arose whether it would be better to apply the balance to allowing every member a reasonable quantity of spirits and tobacco for life, without any payment whatever, or to divide it equally among the surviving members—a course of procedure that would give every member, after allowing for probate and executorial expenses, nearly one hundred pounds each.

As this interesting question was being put to the meeting by Mr. Richard Harris, Mr. Tom Poulton walked in.

Everybody looked very uncomfortable. Mr. Peter Hodgson, however, quickly recovered himself.

'Sir,' said he, 'this is a private club room, and strangers are not admitted unless they are introduced by members.'

'Ha! ha!' said Tom, 'bravo Peter!'

'Sir,' said another, 'we don't know who you are, but we must request you to withdraw.'

'Allow me to introduce myself,' said Tom, with much mock gravity. 'I am Mr. Tom Poulton, whose funeral you attended this morning.' And he took a chair and filled a pipe.

'If you imagine, sir, that because you bear a certain distant resemblance to our poor friend Tom Poulton, you are justified in horrifying his friends with a highly indecent practical joke—' began Peter Hodgson.

'A distant resemblance!'

'A very distant and shadowy resemblance, sir. Nothing more, I assure you.'

'Don't be a fool, Peter,' said Tom; 'we've had enough of this, haven't we, Dick?'

'We have, sir,' said Dick; 'I must insist on your withdrawing immediately.'

'Come, come' said Tom, rather chapfallen; 'it was only my joke. I impersonated a poor old chap who happened to bear my name, in order to sell you all. Dick Hodgson and I arranged it together; didn't we Dick?'

'Sir,' said Dick, 'I haven't the pleasure of your acquaintance. You will be good enough to withdraw, or we shall be under the necessity of expelling you by force.'

And as the members of the Club rose in a body with the evident intention of carrying Dick Hodgson's threat into effect, Mr. Tom Poulton withdrew with a very blank expression of countenance.

In order to test the feeling of the Club on the subject, it was immediately proposed by Mr. Dick Harris and seconded by Mr. Peter Hodgson that Mr. Tom Poulton was dead and buried. The motion was carried by acclamation.

It was then proposed by Mr. Peter Hodgson and seconded by Mr. Dick Harris, that if, by any miracle, Mr. Tom Poulton came to life again, the whole of the legacy should be refunded to him, if possible, without driving him into Chancery for its recovery. This motion also was carried by acclamation.

Finally it was proposed by Mr. Dick Harris and seconded by Mr. Peter Hodgson, that the person who had just represented himself to be Tom Poulton restored to life was not in the least like Tom Poulton, and that he had no claim, and never by any possibility could have any claim, to the legacy in question. This motion also was carried by acclamation.

The question was considered settled by all but Tom Poulton himself.

Tom Poulton beseiged the Club doors day after day, but to no effect. The Hall Porter—they had started a Hall Porter and many other conveniences since Tom Poulton's death—had received strict injunctions not to admit any person calling himself Tom Poulton. He treated Tom kindly enough, believing him to be a harmless monomaniac, but no consideration could induce him to admit Tom within the Club threshold.

Tom next tried the parish surgeon who gave the certificate of the dead Tom Poulton's death. But all the surgeon could prove was that the Tom Poulton who died was not at all like the Tom Poulton who stood before him. On the whole, this materially strengthened the Club's case; particularly as the description given by the surgeon of the dead Tom Poulton's personal appearance corresponded exactly with every member's recollection of the unfortunate chairman of the Serious Family. It was finally voted that, on the surgeon's evidence, poor Tom Poulton was more dead than ever.

Do what he might, Tom Poulton could *not* prove himself to be alive. Nobody would hear of it for a moment. He appealed (at some pecuniary loss) to his tradesmen for identification. They identified him without hesitation as the Tom Poulton who owed them money, but they furnished no clue that would serve to identify him with the Tom Poulton who had been chairman of the Serious Family.

He never rested. He prepared petitions, but no one would present them. He commenced actions, but he broke down at the declaration for want of money. He called day after day at the Club, but the Hall Porter was adamant. He addressed letter after letter to every member of the Club, and enclosed stamped envelopes for reply, but they tore up the envelopes and applied the stamps to other uses.

At first, these appeals amused the Club immensely, but after six or eight months' persecution, the Family began to get tired of it. The *soi-distant* Tom Poulton was voted a bore, and at length it was solemnly proposed that negotiations should be opened with him with the view of arriving at some compromise. Mr. Tom Poulton was formally invited into the Club-room, but he was informed that for the purposes of that meeting his name was Major-General Arthur Fitzpatrick. Tom was reduced to that condition of self-abnegation that he really had no objection to this arrangement.

It was then and there arranged with Major-General Arthur Fitzpatrick that so long as Tom Poulton continued to be dead, an annual salary of one hundred pounds should be paid, quarterly, to the Major-General by the Committee of the Serious Family. The Major-General accepted this proposition with alacrity, and he was forthwith elected an honorary life member of the Serious Family, *vice* Tom Poulton deceased.

And Major-General Fitzpatrick accepted his election, and eventually became Chairman of the Club. And poor Tom Poulton lies dead and buried at a salary of a hundred a year payable quarterly in advance. On one occasion, indeed, when the Major-General's quarterly instalment was some three weeks in arrears, poor Tom Poulton showed strong symptoms of revivification, but his disturbed spirit was eventually appeased by an additional advance of five pounds on account of the Major-General's next quarter's salary.

Creatures of Impulse

MISTRESS DOROTHY Trabbs was the buxom landlady of the 'Three Pigeons,' a pretty country inn on the road from London to Norwich, and Mistress Dorothy was held by competent judges to be the pleasantest landlady on that road, for she was very pretty, and very round, and very plump—too plump, some people said, but that was envy. She had a pretty daughter, Jenny, and a clumsy, cowardly, ill-conditioned, gawky nephew, named Peter; and these two, with a chambermaid and a nondescript 'odd-man,' constituted her staff of assistants.

Jenny was a very pretty little girl, but so absurdly shy that her prettiness went for nothing. I suppose it was this very shyness of hers that emboldened Peter to fall in love with her; for he was such a timid donkey that an ordinarily self-possessed woman frightened him into fits. At all events he *did* fall in love with her, and he told her so. And when he told her so, Jenny forgot, for the moment, her shyness and boxed his ears soundly. He felt this blow so much that he never opened the subject again. In fact, Jenny had a proper contempt for cowards, and like all women, shy or otherwise, adored manly courage. And Sergeant Brice, of Her Majesty Queen Anne's Foot Guards, who had just returned from Malplaquet with a bullet in his right leg, but otherwise well and hearty, and who had received a billet on the 'Three Pigeons,' was as brave as a man need be, So Jenny fell in love with him, but nobody knew anything about it.

At the time when my story opens, Mistress Dorothy was in a terrible state of perplexity. A strange Old Lady, who declined to give any name or any reference as to her respectability, and who had no luggage whatever, had taken up her abode at the 'Three Pigeons,' and steadily refused to pay any rent at all. This state of things had continued for three months, and seemed likely to continue for three more months, or three years for that matter, for the Old Lady was a fairy of malignant description, and had it in her power to inflict all sorts of punishment on anybody who displeased her. At first Mistress Dorothy declined to supply her with food, but the Old Lady explained that she could live quite comfortably without any food at all, and indeed would much prefer not to have any refreshment of any kind set before her. So, as I said before, Mistress Dorothy was in a terrible state of perplexity, and a council of war was held in the bar-parlour, in which council Sergeant Brice, Jenny, and the abject Peter assisted, together with a wealthy, but very disreputable, old miser named Verditter, who was collecting rents in the neighbourhood, and who had made the 'Three Pigeons' his headquarters because it was the cheapest as well as the best inn in the village.

Peter, abject coward as he was, had one redeeming virtue—he was not superstitious. He declined to believe in fairies at all, and especially in the particular fairy under discussion. He had, on one occasion, seen the Old Lady cleaning her teeth with a tooth-brush, and he argued, with some show of reason, that this proved she was not a fairy, as fairies did everything with a wand. So, as the Old Lady was a very weak and tottering old lady, he thought that he might venture to tackle her without incurring any serious risk. Moreover, as all the others most firmly believed in her supernatural character, he would no doubt acquire a cheap reputation for courage if he offered to undertake to get her out of the house. So he walked boldy into her room with the firm intention of bullying her out of it.

'Now, Old Lady,' said Peter, 'we've put up with you long enough. Pack up your tooth-brush, and be off, for your room is wanted, and your company is not.'

'Take care, Peter,' said the Old Lady.

'Take care! What have I to take care of? Why, I could manage two old women like you any day in the week!' and he stalked about like a swashbuckler.

'Take care, Peter,' answered she, 'or I shall give you a sound thrashing.'

But Peter didn't care any longer, indeed he was so rude

as to put out his tongue at her, and by his general demeanour he expressed the most marked contempt for her physical strength.

'Now, Old Lady, enough of this,' said he; 'you talk of thrashing me. ME? Come on!' And Peter took off his coat, and squared-up to her with great bravery.

'Peter,' said she, 'you have thought fit to square-up to me. You will continue to square-up at everybody you meet, until further notice.'

The Old Lady hobbled away into her bed-room, and Peter, to his extreme dismay, found himself compelled to be continually squaring-up, in an undaunted manner, at a roomful of invisible enemies. He retired in great confusion to his loft, shouting down to this friends in the bar-parlour, that he had altogether failed in his mission.

It was now Jenny's turn to try her luck with the Old Lady. The poor little timid girl set about her work with great reluctance.

'Well, my dear,' said the Old Lady, 'what do you want?'

Jenny, finding the Old Lady in an amiable mood, thought that she could not do better than endeavour to coax her out of the place.

'Dear Old Lady,' said she, 'you are so kind, and so good, and so amiable, that I am sure it is only necessary to tell you that we want your room or your rent, and you will immediately humour our little wishes in this respect. Now do, there's a dear, kind, pretty Old Lady.'

And Jenny began to kiss and coax the Old Lady, as no Old Lady was ever kissed and coaxed before.

'My dear,' said the Old Lady, 'this show of affection for one you don't care twopence about, is very disgusting, and, as a punishment, you will be so good as to kiss and coax everybody you meet until further notice.'

And Jenny retired in great confusion to her room, calling downstairs to her friends in the bar-parlour, that she had altogether failed in her mission.

The brave Sergeant Brice's turn came next.

'Go away, soldier,' said she. 'I hate soldiers!'

'But—'

'Go away; you're a bold, bad man!'

And she struck so hard at the brave Sergeant with her crutched stick, that he was obliged to dodge and duck all over the room in order to ward off her blows.

'As a punishment for your impertinence in entering my room without permission,' said the Old Lady, 'you will be so obliging to dodge and duck, as you are dodging and ducking now, before everybody you meet.'

And the bold Sergeant retreated in great amazement to his room, dodging and ducking at an imaginary foe all the way, and shouting downstairs to his friends in the bar-parlour, that he had altogether failed in his mission.

Old Verditter, the miser, had, in the meantime, been getting on very well with plump Mistress Dorothy, and having looked round the comfortable bar-parlour, and noticed the silver spoons and the silver tea-pot, and the large silver salver on the sideboard, he had settled in his own mind that Dorothy would make him a very comfortable and remunerative wife. Indeed he had got so far as to make two or three very broad hints on the subject, when Mistress Dorothy cut him short by begging him to be so good as to try what he could do to get the tiresome Old Lady out of the house. Verditter had a firm faith in the power of gold to work out any social problem, and readily undertook to get rid of Mistress Dorothy's unremunerative lodger.

So taking the big bag of gold, which he had collected from his tenants during the day, he walked fearlessly into the Old Lady's room.

'Now, ma'am,' said he, 'Mistress Dorothy wishes you to go, and I presume that you do not comply with her request, because you have no money with which to pay your travelling expenses to another town. Allow me to present you with this guinea, which I have no doubt will enable you to reach your destination.'

'You are an impertinent old scamp to dare to offer me money,' said the Old Lady; 'and, as a punishment, you will be good enough to offer guineas out of that bag to everyone you meet, until further notice.'

And the wretched miser retreated in great amazement to the smoking-room (which he knew was empty), offering guineas right and left to imaginary applicants, and screaming downstairs to Mistress Dorothy in the bar-parlour, that he had altogether failed in his mission.

Peter was getting hungry in his cock-loft, so he ventured to descend, squaring at nobody, with a great show of valour. His only hope was that he should not meet the Sergeant, and his hope was gratified, for the only person he met was Jenny, who had ventured downstairs in order to consult her mother as to the best means of breaking the very compromising spell that the Old Lady had thrown over her. But the mother had gone out to consult the village schoolmaster, who was a celebrated witch-finder, and a great authority on all matters connected with the Powers of Darkness.

The shy and prudish Jenny, as soon as she saw the abhorred Peter, ran up to him, and, to her extreme consternation, endeavoured to throw her arms round his neck and kiss him. Peter, who was delighted at this proof of affection from a girl who had hitherto detested him, would have offered her every encouragement if he had not felt himself unfortunately compelled to hit out right and left at her in unyielding compliance with the request of the mischievous Old Lady upstairs. 'Peter,' said the retiring girl, 'I hate and detest you.' And so saying she once more threw her arms round his neck, and he, delighted at her change of manner towards him, and attributing her angry words to the disappointment she felt at his rebuffing her, hit out from his shoulder so violently that she had the greatest difficulty in escaping the blow.

'Peter, you brute,' said she, 'I don't want to kiss you, but somehow I can't help it.'

And again she tried to embrace him, and again he struck out at her.

'Peter,' said she, 'I tell you I am doing this because I can't help it. Please don't hit me, because I am only obeying an irresistible impulse.'

And as she made a third attempt to get at him, the Sergeant walked into the room, dodging and ducking, as he dodged and ducked when the Old Lady ran after him with her stick. Peter, hearing the Sergeant coming, ran out of the room as fast as his legs could carry him.

'What!' said the Sergerant, 'do I see my shy and timid Jenny endeavouring to embrace that gawky nincompoop, and do I hear her excusing herself by attributing her behaviour to an irresistible impulse?'

And he dodged and ducked about the room in a wholly irrational and unaccountable manner.

'Sergeant, do not hastily condemn me,' said Jenny, rushing at the Sergeant, and endeavouring to embrace him as she before endeavoured to embrace Peter.

'Jenny, I'm ashamed of you—shocked,—disgusted!' said he, dodging and ducking, as she tried to throw her arms round his neck. 'I loved you for your remarkable and unexampled modesty: but really—'

'Don't, don't be hard on me, Sergeant,' said she; 'indeed, I am as timid and modest as ever, but an irrepressible impulse compels me to kiss every man I meet.'

And she once more threw her arms around him and embraced him. The Sergeant (who had been very carefully brought up) was horrified, and rushed from the room into the street in utter disgust, dodging and ducking all the way, Jenny following him with a most demonstrative show of affection.

In the street the Sergeant met Peter. Peter was in a terrible state of mind, and encountering the Sergeant, would willingly have run away: but the spell the Old Lady had thrown over him compelled him to square up at the Sergeant in the most reckless manner imaginable.

The Sergeant, who was furious at having discovered Jenny's apparent love for Peter, desired nothing better than to give Peter a sound thrashing, but to his own intense annoyance, and to Peter's unspeakable surprise and relief, the fairy's spell compelled the Sergeant to duck and dodge as Peter struck at him as if he (the Sergeant) were in a state of the most abject fear.

'Sergeant,' said Peter, 'please don't be angry; but indeed I can't help it.'

And he hit the Sergeant straight between the eyes.

'I sincerely trust that this will not hurt you much!'

And he struck the Sergeant full upon his military nose.

'I earnestly hope that you will derive no inconvenience from this round-hander.'

And he planted a round-hander just on the Sergeant's left ear, as that officer ducked and dodged about, apparently in a great state of terror, but really boiling with indignation and thirsting for his adversary's blood.

'Well,' said Jenny, hugging the odd-man (who was the only other person within sights, and who did not resist as the Sergeant and Peter had resisted, but who, on the contrary, patiently allowed her to do what she pleased)—'Well,' said she, 'I did think the Sergeant was a brave man; and see how Peter is giving it to him—Peter, who is such a coward!'

And she ran into the house, determined to have nothing to do with either of them.

In the house she met Verditter the miser, whom she heartily detested, the more so because there was every prospect that he would some day be her step-father; but nevertheless she ran up to him, and explaining that he was not to misinterpret the compliment as she was acting under an irresistible impulse, threw her arms round his neck and began to kiss him as she had kissed the others. Verditter was delighted (for he was a dreadful old Turk), but it was not on that account that he presented her with a succession of guineas from his long bag; he did that in compliance with the whim of the strange Old Lady.

Jenny was very much annoyed indeed, not only at having behaved in such a forward manner to old Verditter, but also because she considered his presenting her with guineas an act of extremely bad taste. However, she did not wish to offend him by refusing his guineas, for he was a vicious old man who always resented an insult, so she pocketed them with a very bad grace, and spent them the next day with extreme reluctance on a handsome brooch and earrings, which she wore ever afterwards as a kind of punishment upon herself for having taken the old man's money at all.

As old Verditter has handing over his guineas, with a most piteous expression of countenance, to Jenny, who could scarcely conceal her annoyance at having to take them, who should come in but Mistress Dorothy. Mistress Dorothy had been trying her hand to get rid of the Old Lady, and having fairly lost her temper, endeavoured to push the Old Lady by main force out of the house. So the Old Lady compelled her to go on pushing everybody away from her until furher notice.

As soon as Mistress Dorothy entered, Jenny ran away in great confusion, so old Verditter turned his attention to the buxom landlady and began, to his intense dismay and to her intense delight and astonishment, to offer her guineas from his long bag. But to *her* intense dismay, and to *his* intense delight and astonishment, she felt herself compelled to push him and his guineas away, although she would have liked to have pocketed the whole bagful.

'Ma'am,' said he, handing her a guinea, 'do not misunderstand me. I give you this money under an irresistible impulse.'

'Sir,' said she, 'you are extremely good, but an irresistible impulse compels me to reject it.'

Here the Sergeant entered, dodging and ducking as before.

'Sir,' said old Verditter, 'do not be alarmed. I am not going to hurt you. I feel myself compelled to offer you a guinea.'

'Sir,' said the Sergeant, pocketing the money, 'I never yet was alarmed in my life. I dodge and duck like this because I am acting under an irresistible impulse.'

At this point Peter entered, squaring-up in the fiercest manner at everybody.

'Sir,' said Peter, pocketing the money, 'I am far from being offended, and I sincerely trust you will take this in good part.'

And he knocked old Verditter down to the great astonishment of everybody. Jenny, hearing Mistress Dorothy scream, ran in to see what was the matter. By this time the state of affairs was as follows:

The miserly old Verditter, with tears in his eyes and the worst of language on his lips, was handing guineas to everyone as fast as he could get them out of his bag.

The hospitable Mistress Dorothy was trying to turn him and everybody else out of her inn.

The cowardly Peter was squaring-up at everybody, and particularly at the Sergeant, in an utterly reckless manner.

The valiant Sergeant was ducking and dodging from Peter and everybody else who came near him, as if he had been the most timid soul on the face of the earth.

And Jenny—the shy, modest, prudish, bashful, blushing Jenny—was kissing everybody right and left, as if her life depended on it. In short, there never was a more extraordinary scene in a bar-parlour since bar-parlours first became an institution in Great Britain and Ireland.

In the midst of this scene the Old Lady entered, for she was curious to see how the spell that she had thrown over the inmates of the 'Three Pigeons' was working.

Directly she entered, the attention of everyone was directed to her.

The Miser gave her gold.

The Landlady tried to push her out.

The Sergeant ducked and dodged at her.

The bashful Jenny kissed her.

And the cowardly Peter squared-up to her in such a determined manner, if she had not been surrounded by the others, he would have done her a serious injury.

In short, the Old Lady, who was much more than a match for each of them taken singly, was overpowered by numbers. She never thought of this when she entered the room, which was stupid in the Old Lady.

So she at once withdrew the spell she had over them, and they all resumed their natural attributes. Then the Old Lady, who felt very foolish at the error she had committed, hobbled out of the inn for good and all.

The really curious part of this story is that, after everything had been explained, and all had been restored to their normal courses of action, none of the personages in it married each other. They were all so annoyed at having made such fools of themselves that they walked out of the inn in different directions, and were never seen or heard of again.

Except Peter, who, seeing nothing to be ashamed of in having shown such undaunted courage, remained and kept the 'Three Pigeons,' and prospered remarkably to the end of his days.

THE WICKED WORLD

An Allegory

I

HERE IS a blank sheet of paper—several blank sheets of paper. What shall I put upon them? I declare I don't know. Shall it be a fashionable story of modern life? I know nothing of fashionable life. A mediaeval romance? It would take too much cramming. A sea story? I know nothing about the sea, except that it makes me sick. A fairy tale then? Well, a fairy tale be it.

'But,' says the acute reader, 'if you decline to write a story about fashionable life because you know little of Fashion, how is it that you propose to write about fairies, of whom you must know still less?' Exactly. I know nothing at all about fairies—but then neither do you. If I attempt to depict fashionable life, and make his Lordship the Duke dance a double hornpipe in September, at a Buckingham Palace ball, with the Right Honourable Lady Annabel Hicks, daughter of Sir Wickham Hicks, Puisne Judge, and Member for Birmingham-super-Mare, you may be down upon me for a group of solecisms; for no doubt you move in the distinguished circles I attempt to describe, and therefore know more about them than I do. But in Fairyland we meet on other terms, and there I am your lordship's equal. *Habes*. Let us get on.

The scene, then, is in Fairyland. Not the Fairyland of the pantomimes, but the Fairyland of My Own Vivid Imagination. A pleasant, dreamy land, with no bright colours in it—a land where it is always bright moonlight—a land with plenty of impalpable trees, through which you can walk, if you like, as easily as my pen can cleave the smoke that is curling from my cigar as I write—a land where there is nothing whatever to do but to sit and chat with good pleasant-looking people, who like a joke, and can make one, too—a land where there is no such thing as hunger, or sleep, or fatigue, or illness, or old age—a land where no collars or boots are worn—a land where there is no love-making, but plenty of innocent love ready made.

There are no men in this Fairyland. I can't have a man in my Paradise—at least, not at first. I know so much about men, being myself a man, that I would rather not think of them in connection with a place where all is calm, and gentle, and tranquil, and happy. I know so little about women, that I propose to people this happy, dreamy, peaceful place with none but women. There must be no envy, hatred, malice, or uncharitableness of any kind in my Fairyland. There must be nothing sordid, nothing worldly, nothing commonplace. Universal charity must reign in my Fairyland, and that, you see, is why I people it with women.

Well, they are all women, and all the women are supremely lovely. They wear long robes, high in the throat, falling loosely and gracefully to the very feet, and each fairy has a necklace of the very purest diamonds. They have wings—large soft downy wings—six feet high, like the wings of angels. And by some spiritual contrivance, which I will not detain you by enlarging upon here, these wings won't crumple and crackle under the fairies when they sit down. So you see, you theatrical managers, my Fairyland is not yours. When I conceive a Fairyland with creaky phenomena and indelicate inhabitants who take a pride in their baggy, bony knees, I will come to you for suggestions on the subject. But I have not yet conceived such a Paradise. Faugh!

My tale opens upon a group of fairies—beautiful, simple girls, with beautiful simple names. There were Mary, and Annie, and Janet, and Mattie, and Bessie, and Kate, and fifty others whose names you can select for yourselves. They were chatting pleasantly together—not talking all at once, as boisterous men will do—but listening cheerfully and patiently to one another; for all had something to say that was worth hearing, and each was ready to listen to the other. Mary was the Queen of the Fairies. I make Mary the Queen, because I like the name 'Mary' better than any other name I know. People are made kings and queens on earth for no better reasons, and many of them turn out fairly well. The conversation turned on the wickedness of the world. Kate had once been a mortal, but she died, and on account of her surpassing purity was translated to Fairyland. She was the only mortal who had ever been so distinguished. Among the fairies she was an authority on the subject of the wickedness of the world (though in truth she knew very little indeed about it), and all questions that related to the world were referred to her for her decision, which was final. For I should have told you that although my fairies exercised an influence over the destinies of mortals, they did not mix with them. They kept themselves to themselves: they were not obliged to do so, but they hated wickedness, and the world was very wicked.

Well, the Fairy Kate was relating some of her experiences, and the other fairies were affected almost to tears at the revelations she made. Not that the Fairy Kate's revelations would have shocked you and me very desperately, but the other fairies had no idea of the wickedness of which the world is capable, and listened aghast to matters which we gross mortals look upon with little or no disfavour. Indeed, the Fairy Kate did not enter very deeply into the subject of her remarks, for she had only an amiable, half-instructed good girl's knowledge of them, and she spoke according to her twilight.

She said, for instance, that whole nations devoted themselves to each other's annihilation for reasons which would not operate to produce a coolness between two private individuals. But then she forgot that a nation consists, perhaps, of fifty million private individuals, and that an affront offered to such a nation is fifty million times as great as the same affront would be if directed against an individual member of it. She also said that when people gave alms they required that the fact should be advertised in the public prints through the length and breadth of the land. But she forgot that as example is better than precept (which is also very good in its way), it follows that, although it is good to exhort people to acts of charity, it is still better to let them see that you are actively charitable yourself; and if an example is good it cannot be too widely diffused. I mention the statements of the Fairy Kate to show that her knowledge of the world was, after all, very superficial, and not at all to be relied upon.

The effect of the Fairy Kate's remarks was that the other fairies were so dreadfully shocked at her picture of the wickedness of the world, that they came to consider whether some steps might not be taken to improve its condition, and bring its inhabitants generally to a proper sense of their duties to one another.

It was proposed that, with a view to ascertaining the present state of the world, a Woman should be summoned to Fairyland, and interrogated on the subject. For, after all, the Fairy Kate's information was of no recent date, and matters might have improved since she left the earth. So the Fairy Bessie suggested that a Mortal Woman should be summoned forthwith. The suggestion was received with high favour by all the fairies, and Fairy Janet suggested, as an amendment, that the word 'Man' should be substituted for 'Woman.' A man, she argued, is naturally in a position to see much more of the world than a woman, and his information would, therefore, be more valuable. (Amendment carried unanimously.)

So a cloud was sent down to earth with instructions to envelop and carry up into Fairyland the first mortal it happened to see. These instructions had to be repeated several times, for the cloud was rather foggy, but eventually it was made to understand them, and it started on its mission.

The time that elapsed between the departure of the cloud and the arrival of a real live man appeared interminable to the fairies, but, at length, after many hours' absence, it did return with a magnificent young Prince. The stupid cloud, instead of bringing up the first man it saw (a very ragged drunken old beggar, who would have answered the fairies' purpose as well as anybody else), looked out for a young and handsome man, in the absurd belief that the presence of such a one in Fairyland would give pleasure to his beautiful employers. The idea was ridiculous, but the cloud meant well, and the fairies did not scold it.

II

Prince Paragon was a very brave and handsome youth, the son of a powerful King, whose dominions were situated in what, many thousand years afterwards, proved to be the (*soi-distant*) United States of America. He had many weaknesses, and a few vices, but they were not such vices as the world has ever dealt very hardly with. He was a generous young man, and had a profound respect for womankind.

His cousin, Prince Snob, was a handsome, boastful, courageous, reckless, unscrupulous young scamp. He was in the habit of boasting of his successful love affairs, which were, in truth, very numerous. One day, in the presence of Prince Paragon, Prince Snob told a long story how for a wager he had undertaken to break the heart of a young, beautiful, and innocent girl, and how he had succeeded in doing so—for she died of her love for him. Prince Paragon, who made love quite as successfully as Prince Snob, but who never broke hearts intentionally, was very indignant with Prince Snob, and challenged him to fight. The challenge was accepted; and it was as Prince Paragon was on his way to the meeting that the cloud enveloped him, and took him up into the skies. It will be easily understood that Prince Paragon was furious at this occurrence, for he felt sure that his disappearance would be attributed by his enemy to rank cowardice. When he arrived in Fairyland he was extremely sulky.

'Oh, what an ugly pout!' said Queen Mary. 'I hope our society does not displease you?'

'I don't know who you are, ma'am,' said the Prince, 'or how I came here; but I have an important engagement which I am now quite unable to keep.'

'Business?' said Fairy Kate—sober, thoughtful Kate.

'Um—m—m!' said the Prince considering.

'Pleasure?' said Fairy Bessie—light-hearted little Bessie.

'Um—m—m!' said the Prince. 'Both.'

'Well,' said Queen Mary, 'we are fairies.' The Prince bowed. 'We want to know all about the wickedness of the world, and we have sent for you that you may give us some information on the subject.'

'Ah,' said the Prince. 'Exactly. Do you want to know everything?'

'Everything!' they all exclaimed.

'Do you *insist* on my telling you everything?'

'Most decidedly.'

'What shall I begin with? Love?'

'Sir!' exclaimed the Queen of the Fairies, 'you forget that you are addressing ladies.'

'Pardon me,' said the Prince, 'but if the bare mention of love shocks you, I think I would rather leave the selection of the matters on which you wish to be instructed in your hands.'

'What was the nature of the business on which you were proceeding when we interrupted you?' said Queen Mary.

'I was going to fight a duel. I was going to kill a man if I could, and he was going to kill me if *he* could.'

'A duel!' exclaimed the Queen. 'Horrible! And why were you going to fight this duel?'

'Well,' said the Prince, 'there was a lady in the case.'

'Stop!' said the Queen, much shocked. 'Go on to something else. Are you in debt? You don't mind my speaking openly?'

'Not at all—Oh, yes; I'm in debt.'

'You owe more than you can pay?'

'I'm afraid I do.'

'Well!' said the Queen. 'Upon my word! And how did *that* come to pass?'

'Why, there was a lady in *that* case, too'—

'Stop!' said the Queen.

'I was in love with her, and gave her some handsome presents.'

'Will you stop when I tell you?' said the Queen. 'Your conversation is shocking.'

'Shall I go?' said the Prince.

'No—let me see. Do you ever tell stories?'

'I'm afraid I do, sometimes. I did yesterday.'

'Tell us all about it,' said the fairies eagerly, for they were dreadfully shocked.

'Well,' said the Prince, 'there was a lady in *that* case.'

'There seems to be a lady in every case,' said the Queen.

'There generally is,' said the Prince. 'There is no complication of human events in which a woman is not implicated. Such, at least, is my experience.'

'How old are you?' said the Queen.

'Twenty-two. How old are *you*?'

'Never mind,' said the Queen. 'Where were you born?'

'I was born in Bulgaria. There was a lady in *that* case, too.'

'Of course, you absurd creature! Do you love your fellow-creatures as you are taught to do?'

'About half of them.'

'Which half?—Stop, I know. I'm ashamed of you.'

And the fairies were so horrified that they could not take their eyes off his wicked handsome face.

'I think you are hard on me, and hard on the world,' said the Prince. 'I am not an anchorite, but I am not a scamp. I would not knowingly do an unhandsome thing. I never fight except in defence of my honour, or of the honour of someone who is dear to me. I only run into debt because I am liberally disposed. I only tell stories to prevent innocent people from getting into undeserved trouble. I only love women in an honourable—'

'*Will* you hold your tongue?' said the Queen. 'Go on,' she added, rather unreasonably.

'Really,' said the Prince, 'the world isn't such a bad world after all. I wish one of you would come down to earth with me, and judge for herself.'

'Yes,' said the Queen, considering; 'that's not a bad idea. But who would go?'

'I would go with him, dear Queen,' said all the fairies in a breath. They feared not the Wicked World, for they were strong in their own excellence.

'No,' said the Queen. 'the perils of the journey are great. It is fitting that I, your Queen, should set an example of intrepidity and unselfishness when such an example is necessary. At all risks I will go to earth: I will go for one year, and at the expiration of the year I will return and tell you all about it.'

And Queen Mary and the Prince got into a cloud, and descended to the Wicked World.

III

The Queen of the Fairies and Prince Paragon arrived safely on earth, and proceeded by train to his father's Court. But before getting into the train she unhooked her wings and left them at the cloak-room of the station 'to be called for,' so as not to attract attention. The Prince introduced her to his father as a lady of high rank. The old King received her very graciously, but his mother the Queen and his sisters thought she looked a great deal too demure and quiet.

The Queen of the Fairies was regularly installed in Court quarters, and—solely with a view of ascertaining what the wickedness of the world really was—entered into all the Court festivities. Her extraordinary beauty, her modesty, her simple grace, and her unaffected disposition enchanted everybody except the old Queen and her daughters, who saw through all this, and called it slyness.

Prince Paragon fell in love with the beautiful Queen Mary, and so did Prince Snob. But Queen Mary had been so horrified at Prince Paragon's reckless confessions in Fairy-land that she could not bring herself to like him at all. Prince Snob, however, gave her to understand, in so many words, that he, Prince Snob, was a good man, who had only committed one fault in his whole life (when he was only six years old, he had made use of the bad world 'D—v—l' on strong provocation). As he was a very good-looking man, she allowed herself to think leniently of his early error, and on the strength of his sincere repentance she eventually bestowed her heart upon him. For the Fairy Mary, when she came down to the world, invested herself with human attributes and instincts, and so fell in love, as other good girls have done, and will do, until the whole system of things undergoes a radical change.

For the present I must dismiss Prince Paragon (who, at first, appeared likely to become the hero of my fairy tale), for I have to occupy myself with the Fairy Queen's love for Prince Snob.

The poor lady became quite infatuated with the hypocritical scamp. In course of time she saw through his hypocrisy, but her love for him had taken so fixed a possession of her that she could not shake it off. She also learnt that Prince Paragon was really a very good young fellow—with certain human weaknesses, no doubt—but still a very good young fellow, as young fellows go. But she had a simple old-fashioned notion that a woman should only love one man in the course of her life-time, and she had made her choice and intended to keep to it. Still, although she loved Prince Snob devotedly, she resolved not to marry him until he reformed; for she had another old-fashioned idea, which was—that one ought not to marry a man one can't respect. So she went on loving him in her innocent way without respecting him a bit, hoping by her devotion to him, and by her good example and precept, to make a respectable man of him.

Prince Snob's affection for the Fairy Queen was born partly of his admiration for her beauty, but mainly of his admiration for her magnificent diamonds. He was dreadfully in debt, and he was mean enough to ask her, time after time, for jewels, which he sold, and so these jewels disappeared one by one, until at last there was none left. Prince Snob was very indignant when he found that the Fairy Queen had no more diamonds, and plainly told her that unless she could borrow some jewels or some money (he wasn't particular which), and by so doing prove that she did possess some mortal weaknesses, a sense of what was due to a Fairy Queen would compel him to feel wholly unworthy to possess her.

Terrified at this dreadful threat (for she had had to part with all her fairy attributes on descending to earth), she called upon Prince Paragon, who still loved her devotedly, and begged him to advance her some money. He gave her at once all that she required, and she returned with her pockets and her two hands full of gold, to Prince Snob, and poured the money into that disgraceful fellow's hat. Prince Snob embraced her, telling her that he was quite reassured now that he found she was not absolutely perfect—that she really was open to the influence of some mortal weakness (as if he had not already had proof of that!)—and he assured her that he began to think himself once more really worthy of her.

Well, this money was soon squandered, and again the Prince urged her to borrow more, and again she resorted to Prince Paragon, who again supplied her. This occurred so often that at length Prince Paragon asked her what she did with her money, and I am sorry to say that her regard for Prince Snob led her to tell Prince Paragon a story. So she told him that she had lost the money at play. Prince Paragon spoke to her very kindly and very sorrowfully, and represented to her how unladylike it was to gamble for such high stakes. The good Prince still loved her, and was dreadfully distressed to see her going, not step by step, but staircase by staircase (if I may so express myself), to her ruin. At length, actuated by his sincere regard for her, he refused to advance her any more money, and the miserable Fairy Queen was in utter despair.

A scene ensued with Prince Snob which is almost too terrible for description. However, here it is.

'Ma'am,' said the Prince, when he heard that she could supply him with no more money, 'I am terribly disappointed in you.'

'Dear Snob,' said the Fairy Queen, 'don't be hard on me. I've done my best—indeed I have.'

'Ma'am,' said the Prince, 'you have done nothing of the kind.'

'Indeed, I have borrowed money for you, until I can't induce anyone to lend me any more.'

'Yes, you have borrowed money—*but you have not yet stolen money*. Steal!'

'Oh, Snob, you are joking.'

'Do I look as if I were joking?' And indeed he did not. 'Steal immediately, or I have done with you.'

The Fairy Queen was at last aroused to a sense of her position.

'Prince Snob, you require of me that which is not ordinarily required of ladies by their lovers, and I decline to obey you.'

'Very good, ma'am; then you will understand that our association is at an end. I thought that, Fairy Queen as you are, you had, nevertheless, some mortal failings—some pardonable blemishes, which would serve to bring you down to the level of a human being. You are much too good for me: you are a Fairy Queen; I am an erring mortal,—for I know I have my faults—'

'No, no!' said the Queen, in an agony.

'Yes, indeed I have,' rejoined the Prince. 'I am an erring mortal, and I am wholly unworthy of you. Good morning, ma'am.'

And he left her abruptly.

The Fairy Queen was utterly miserable. She went to good Prince Paragon, and told him all about Prince Snob's treatment of her. Prince Paragon was furious. He sought out Prince Snob, and immediately challenged him to mortal combat.

'All right!' said Prince Snob, who had plenty of pluck. 'But no clouds this time.'

Prince Paragon was stung by the taunt. 'Come on!' he said.

And Prince Snob came on. They fought valiantly, but Prince Snob was eventually overpowered. He fell, and as Prince Paragon was about to pass his sword through the calf of Prince Snob's left leg (for Prince Paragon did not want to kill his adversary outright), the Fairy Queen rushed in and implored Prince Paragon to spare his rival.

'I won't hurt him seriously, ma'am,' said the Prince. I am only going to pass my sword through a fleshy part.'

He said this sarcastically, for Prince Snob's calves were notoriously insignificant.

'Spare him even that,' said the Queen. 'My year has just expired, and I must return to Fairyland. Let me take him with me. If I cannot bring myself down to his level, I can at all events raise him to mine.'

'Oh!' said Prince Paragon. 'Then I wish you good morning.'

'Stay,' said the Queen. 'Won't you come, too?'

'But I should be in the way.'

'You goose? I'm not going to marry him. I want to make a fairy of him; and I'll do the same for you, too.'

And a cloud descended and took them all up into Fairyland as soon as the Queen had redeemed her wings from the custody of the woman at the railway cloakroom.

IV

(I THINK this will be a very short chapter.)

The Fairy Queen arrived in due time at Fairyland with Prince Paragon and Prince Snob. They had not had a comfortable journey in the cloud, for they were crowded (it was only a cloud for one), and Prince Snob kept trying to push Prince Paragon out of it.

'Well,' said the Fairy Queen to the other fairies, 'here I am, safe and sound. Why, how cross you all look!'

'If we had known that we were to have had the pleasure of the society of these two gentlemen we would have prepared a larger cloud,' said Fairy Bessie, rather spitefully.

'Fairy Bessie,' said the Fairy Queen, 'I don't like innuendoes. Speak openly, I command you.'

'You—I beg pardon—you do what?' said Bessie, as if she had not understood the Queen.

'I *command* you!' said the Fairy Queen, with great dignity.

'Only the Queen commands *me*,' said Bessie.

'I *am* the Queen, miss!'

'Oh, dear, no! You are deposed. You *would* go to earth, you know, alone with that gentleman, and we all thought it bold, so we deposed you. Fairy Mattie is our Queen now.'

'Is this so?' said Mary to Fairy Lizzie.

'Certainly,' said Lizzie. 'We don't think your conduct respectable.'

'Will you tell your Queen that I am here, and would like to speak to her?'

'I can't. The Queen and I are not on speaking terms.'

'Will you tell someone else to tell the Queen?' said the poor ex-monarch.

'I can't even do that. In fact, we are none of us on speaking terms with one another.'

The poor ex-Queen went about from fairy to fairy, but from all she received the same answer: 'We are not on speaking terms with each other.'

At length the Fairy Kate came up. (I think it was the Fairy Kate who I said had once been on earth? Let me look back. Yes, the Fairy Kate.) Well, the Fairy Kate came up, and she alone of all the fairies seemed glad to see the ex-Queen.

'What in the world is the reason of this extraordinary demoralization among my late subjects?' said poor Mary.

'I think I can explain,' said Kate. 'The presence of the mortal whom we summoned into Fairyland a year ago has contaminated us. We were good and happy till he came, but since that unfortunate event we have fallen into all kinds of uncharitable ways of thinking. We quarrelled dreadfully, talked at one another, and said the most unkind things about each other's hair. We can't get on at all. He brought a wordly atmosphere with him (I recognized it directly), and this has worked its evil effect upon us. We are as so many women!' And the Fairy Kate burst into tears.

All the other fairies exclaimed, 'Yes that's the secret of it!' and they burst into tears.

'But,' said Fairy Bessie, 'independently of this, we have really heard such things of you! We hear that you fell in love with a man, and that you ran into debt, and that you borrowed money, and that you told stories, and that you actually were the cause of a duel between two of your admirers. All this is very, very dreadful!'

How they knew all this I cannot for the life of me imagine, as they had held no communication whatever with the world during the ex-Queen's absence.

'It is all true,' said the Queen, 'and, as you say, it is very dreadful. But make some allowance for me. See what evil effect the presence among you of one mortal, and that one a very good one, has worked! The mere fact of your having breathed an atmosphere in common with him has robbed you of those social excellences for which you were all so remarkable; you have become vain, tetchy, jealous, and morose. If this is the legitimate and necessary effect of the presence of one good mortal among you for half an hour, think what I have had to undergo, who have been compelled to associate for a whole twelve month with men and women of all descriptions! Believe me, fairies, we are too vainglorious, too proud of our excellence, too unmindful of the fact that we were good because we had no temptation to do wrong. We despised the world because it was wicked, forgetting that the wickedness of the world is born of the temptations to which only the inhabitants of the world are exposed. Let us forgive one another, and endeavour to think more charitably of the errors of those who are subjected to temptations from which we are happily removed.'

The fairies were much affected by the ex-Queen's remarks, and Queen Mattie resigned on the spot. The Fairy Kate approached Prince Paragon and Prince Snob (who were standing rather awkwardly apart during the scene I have just described), and welcomed them. She shook hands with Prince Paragon, but when she looked at Prince Snob she gave a shriek, and fell fainting into his arms. Prince Snob was the villain who had broken her heart when she was a mortal on earth.

Prince Snob was so much moved that he retired into a corner and reformed upon the spot. He offered to marry the Fairy Kate, then and there, but that, of course, could not be. So the Fairy Kate was sent down to earth as a mortal, with instructions to allow Prince Snob to marry her, and to return to Fairyland immediately upon his first act of unkindness; and Queen Mary received the same permission with respect to Prince Paragon. Neither the Queen nor the Fairy Kate returned until they were widows, when they resumed their fairy attributes for good and all. Their weeds were so much admired that widows' caps became the fashion in Fairyland, and are universally worn to this day.

This chapter is not so very short, after all.

WIDE AWAKE

I AM A remarkably good-looking middle-aged bachelor. Twenty years ago I sunk all my property in an annuity, and on that annuity I live very comfortably.

Ten years ago it occurred to me that I would very likely marry, so I ensured my life for ten thousand pounds.

I am a man of a particularly affectionate disposition. This amiable tendency has led me into many difficulties in my time—not the least of which was an engagement to marry my cousin Georgina Sparrow.

I supposed I loved Georgina when I proposed to her. Looking calmly back at Georgina, it seems improbable I admit—but still I *did* propose to her, and as I had no underhand motive in doing so (for I am rich and extremely handsome, whereas she is poor and singularly plain), I suppose I must have loved her more or less.

However that may be, there is no doubt at all that before I had been engaged to her for a week, I found myself wondering what on earth I had ever seen in her to admire. She was bony, angular, acid, and forty.

My uncle, old Sparrow (Georgina's father), and my aunt Julia, his wife, and Georgina's two horsey brothers, James and John, took the greatest interest in our engagement. They seemed to think it likely that I should try to get out of it, and they determined that I should not have a chance of doing so. I should have stated that I lodged at their house. I should have liked to lodge elsewhere, where I could have had more liberty and less fluff, but my natural amiability was more than a match for my sense of convenience, and I remained.

On one occasion I *did* hint at the possibility of my removing to a less dear, and less dirty sphere of action, but the indignation of Mr. and Mrs. Sparrow, the violent attitudes of John and James, and the appalling hysterics of Georgina, induced me weakly to confess that it was only my fun.

My natural amiability is such that I *must* love someone—and as it was out of the question to go on loving

Georgina, it became necessary to love somebody else. I found an appropriate object of homage in Bridget Comfit, a very plump and rosy widow lady of small independent property, who lived in Great Coram Street.

To make a long story short, I will at once confess that, being engaged to Georgina Sparrow, I nevertheless secretly made love to Mrs. Comfit. I even went so far as to make arrangements to marry Mrs. Comfit at St. Pancras Church, Euston Square. I did not tell Bridget about Georgina because I knew that it would distress her, and I did not tell Georgina about Bridget, because I knew that it would distress *her*. It would also have distressed her furious father, her fluent mother, and her two very violent and impulsive brothers, John and James. I acted for the best.

The day before the day appointed for my marriage with Mrs. Comfit arrived. I did not feel quite happy that evening. I did not enjoy my dinner. Uncle Sparrow seemed to have a reproachful something in his eye which I could not account for. Aunt Sparrow was surprisingly silent. The two brothers, John and James, looked moody, and Georgina was uncomfortably affectionate. I felt rather conscience smitten.

I began to think that in marrying Bridget secretly, I was perhaps acting an underhand part towards Georgina. I had never looked at it in that light before; it had always seemed to me to be the most natural thing in the world that a man who had engaged himself to Georgina should take the earliest opportunity of getting out of the engagement.

But there is a right and a wrong way of doing everything, and I saw, when it was too late, that it would have been better to have broken her heart in a more manly and straightforward way. Still I acted for the best.

The next morning—the morning of my marriage day—I had breakfasted in bed. I couldn't face the family. I am a tender-hearted old fool, and I could not feel at my ease in the presence of the woman whose heart I was deliberately breaking. So I pleaded a bad bilious headache, and remained in bed until Uncle Sparrow had started for the City (he was something—not much—in the City), and his two headstrong sons had betaken themselves to Aldridge's.

I knew that this would happen at a quarter to ten, and

that at ten o'clock Mrs. Sparrow and Georgina would go down to the kitchen to have their daily row over the cook's accounts—so at ten I determined to make my escape.

I dressed—reached the ground-floor safely—kissed a last farewell to Georgina's very long goloshes in the umbrella-stand, and eventually stood free and undetected in the street. I had yet an hour to spare before Bridget would arrive at the church, and I spent this in walking round Euston Square—which can be done in two thousand one hundred paces—and at a quarter to eleven I entered the church. There was no one there but the beadle.

I went up to him and said, 'Oh, I beg your pardon, but I've come to be married.' At that moment I was clapped on the back by Georgina's two headstrong brothers. My cousins and their father had been paying a visit to a money-lender in Euston Square. They saw me walking round, their curiosity was excited, and they followed me to the church. And so came about one of the most tremendously dramatic situations in Modern History.

'So, sir,' said Uncle Sparrow, 'you've come to be married?'

'Fire and fury!' said John.

'Zounds and the devil!' said James.

I was equal to the emergency. My natural kindness of heart prevented my admitting the truth to my uncle and my cousins, for I never distress a fellow-creature intentionally (unless she is ugly, and I am engaged to her), so I resorted to one of the most ingenious methods of getting out of a dilemma that I ever heard of. I gave a sudden start, gasped, rolled my eyes wildly, and exlaimed:—

'Where am I?'

They explained to me in language quite unsuited to the sacred edifice in which they were standing, that I was in St. Pancras Church.

'How did I come here? I don't remember anything about it! The last thing I can remember is being in bed with a bilious headache, and trying to go to sleep! And here I am, dressed and wide-awake, in St. Pancras Church. What is the inference?'

They admitted in disgracefully strong language, that they

were at a loss to draw any satisfactory inference from this statement.

'My dear uncle, my good (but violent) cousins,' said I, 'this is very distressing to me, for I thought I had quite shaken it off. I haven't done such a thing as walk in my sleep for years.'

They replied, sardonically, that they felt sure of it.

'I once remained for nearly a week in a state of somnambulism. It is most providential that you happened to be here.'

They quite agreed with me.

'Another time,' said I, 'don't wake me suddenly. It is very dangerous to wake a somnambulist with a violent shock. Better let him have his sleep out.'

This I said to keep up the illusion.

They promised that, now that they were aware of my infirmity, they would not wake me too suddenly on the next occasion.

'The best thing I can do,' said I, 'is to go home and go to bed again.'

They heartily concurred with this suggestion. John took one of my arms, James took the other, and Uncle Sparrow walked behind us, keeping the ferule of his walking-stick in the small of my back.

There was nothing for it but to give up all hope of being married that day. I was sorry for Bridget; but I felt that an explanation made at the earliest opportunity would set that right. After all, it would only delay our happiness for a few days. I could not help chuckling over my presence of mind, and the ready wit I had shown in escaping from a difficulty which would have overwhelmed ninety-nine out of a hundred. It is true I was rather surprised to find how readily my explanation was accepted by my uncle and my cousins; but that only showed how skilfully I had played my part.

I remained in bed all that day, for I really did not feel equal to facing the family in my disappointed frame of mind. But one can't remain in bed for ever, and the next morning I put a bold face on it, and came down, as usual, to breakfast.

'Good morning, uncle,' said I, in my most cheerful tones. 'How are you, dear aunt? Ha, John! Ha, James!

Georgina, my love, good morning.'

They looked at one another significantly, but made no response to my greeting.

'Lovely morning,' said I.

'It's just as I thought,' said Uncle Sparrow to Aunt Julia. 'He's at it again.'

'Hush,' said Aunt Julia, 'don't speak so loud. You'll wake him.'

'Poor boy,' said Georgina, in a half-whisper. 'his eyes are wide open, though he's evidently fast asleep.'

'That is always the case with somnambulists,' said Uncle Sparrow. 'The sleeping brain receives its impressions through the eyes, nose, and ears.'

'His nose and ears are wide open also,' said John.

'So they were yesterday,' said James.

'A very curious instance of somnambulism came under my notice in Italy a few years ago,' said Uncle Sparrow. 'A very respectable young girl was found under suspicious circumstances in the chamber of an Italian noble, and the most unfavourable inferences were drawn as to her moral character in consequence. Her forthcoming marriage with a handsome young peasant was broken off, and all her old companions repudiated her. Eventually, she was seen crossing a most dangerous plank over a watermill, in her petticoat body, and it became clear to all that the girl was a confirmed somnambulist. She was at once re-instated in the good opinion of her friends, and her marriage with the young peasant was celebrated with unusual rejoicings. I knew the family very well.'

I looked from one to another in blank astonishment.

'Am I to suppose,' said I, 'that you are under the impression that I am asleep?'

'Except that his utterance is thick,' said Georgina, 'there is very little difference between his sleeping and waking voice.'

I began to get annoyed.

'Is this a joke?' I inquired, as I sat down to breakfast.

'Take his knife away, Georgina,' said Aunt Julia; 'cut up his bacon and let him eat it with a tea-spoon.'

You can't eat fried bacon with a tea-spoon so as to enjoy it. I therefore protested against this interference with my convenience.

'I insist,' said Uncle Sparrow, 'on his knife being removed. John and James, sit one on each side of him and watch his movements very carefully. But be very careful not to wake him as that would be most dangerous. These trances usually last a week. John, feed him with a spoon. James, hold his tea-cup and give him a sip occasionally.'

'Uncle,' said I, 'I beg—I *beg* that you will allow me to have my breakfast in peace. I had nothing to eat yesterday (having had a bilious headache), and I am literally starving.'

'Now give him a bit of muffin,' said Uncle Sparrow. 'Now a spoonful of egg.'

'Indeed, indeed, I am quite awake. I can feed myself. I want no assistance from anyone.'

'Now a mouthful of tea—take care—it's running down his waistcoat.'

There was nothing for it but to submit to be fed by the hulking brothers.

I made several appeals to their intelligence, to their sense of humour, and to their feelings as human beings, but in vain. The only notice they took of my remarks was to direct each other's attention to the fact that I expressed myself quite coherently.

The farce was carried on through the whole day, and the next, and the next after that. Nothing would convince them that I was awake. I did all I could to persuade them to treat me like a rational being, but in vain. The two detestable brothers devoted themselves to taking care of me with extraordinary assiduity. They never left me. They took me out for a walk every day, fed me carefully at meal times, undressed me and put me to bed at night, and dressed me again the next morning.

My unfortunate condition was explained to all visitors, who took a deep interest in watching my movements, and everyone was enjoined to speak with bated breath for fear of waking me. No attention was paid by anyone to my remarks; but everyone made observations of the most unpleasantly personal description about me. And, curiously enough, no one entered the house who did not notice something unusual in my appearance and demeanour which was only reconcilable with the theory that I was walking and talking in my sleep.

Uncle Sparrow opened all my letters (including a very emphatic one from the disappointed Mrs. Comfit), and kindly volunteered to take care of them until I was in a condition to take care of them myself.

I am a man of easy temper, but there are limits to my powers of endurance. It was quite evident to me that they were simply 'paying me out' for the deception I had practised on them at the church. It was, perhaps, right that I should suffer some little mortification, but I felt that matters had now been carried far enough. I spoke out with furious indignation, and told them that unless they at once gave me an assurance in writing, and signed by the whole family that I was wide awake, I would appeal for protection to the laws of my country. I did not feel quite sure under which Act of Parliament my grievance would come, but I knew that a remedy was provided for every wrong, and that to insist upon it that a man is asleep when he is really wide awake, is a wrong of a most distinct and aggravating description. But my threats had no effect upon my relations, nor was I more successful with one eminent psychologist who came three times a day for a hour and a half each time to study my case for a work on dreams upon which he was then engaged.

As I sat fuming with impatience in an arm-chair in Uncle Sparrow's study surrounded by the whole family, a letter (addressed to me) was placed in Uncle Sparrow's hand. In spite of my emphatic protest, he took the liberty of opening and reading it.

It was from the office in which I had insured my life for the benefit of my widow (whoever that might be) for £10,000. It informed me that the annual premium on my policy was still unpaid, that the fourteen days of grace had expired, and that unless the secretary received a cheque for the amount (£320) in the course of the afternoon, the policy would, *ipso facto*, become null and void.

'You had better attend to this at once,' said he, handing the letter to me. '*At once*,' he added, with marked emphasis. 'I am surprised that you have neglected so important, so vital a matter.'

I saw my advantage at a glance.

'I will attend to it, Uncle, to-morrow, if I am in a condition to do so. These trances, however, usually last a week.'

'But to-morrow won't do. The secretary says expressly that the money must be paid this afternoon.'

'My dear,' said Georgina, 'pray do not risk a delay. The matter is of the highest moment. Please be good enough to write a cheque at once.'

'I will write a cheque for the amount,' said I, 'as soon as I am awake. But these trances usually last a week.'

'Come, come,' said Uncle Sparrow, 'the joke has been carried far enough. We were only chaffing you. You never were wider awake in your life. Come—write the cheque at once.'

'Uncle Sparrow,' said I, 'Aunt Julia, Georgina, John and James—you have done your best to persuade me that I have been in a somnambulistic trance for three days. At first I doubted it, but it became impossible to reject the evidence of so many disinterested witnesses, and I am quite convinced that you were right and I was wrong. I am, no doubt, fast asleep. I admit it cheerfully, and I am very much obliged to you for the great care and attention you have bestowed on me in this unfortunate and abnormal condition. It is not likely to last above three or four days longer, and as soon as I am thoroughly awake and capable of attending to business, I will certainly send a cheque for my premium. But not till then.'

'I tell you, sir,' replied Uncle Sparrow, 'that the whole thing was a joke. I freely admit it. But it is time that this fooling came to an end. Write the cheque, like a good fellow, or Georgina will be left penniless.'

'My own, my love,' said Georgina, 'don't be ridiculous. You are much older than I'—that wasn't true—'and in the natural course of events I shall survive you. If the cheque is not written at once, I shall be a penniless widow!'

'I will write it,' said I, 'when I awake.'

'Papa—Mamma—John—James,' exclaimed Georgina, in a frenzy, 'explain to him that he is labouring under a delusion! Oh, somebody, pray do something, or I shall be ruined.'

I was firm; I insisted upon it that a cheque written in a

state of somnambulism would be invalid, and that it would be a useless waste of a stamp if I were to write one in my then condition. The whole family went on their knees to me, but in vain. I stuck to my colours.

The hours crept on—it was three o'clock, and the office closed at four. Eventually, finding that nothing could shake my resolution, Uncle Sparrow rushed out to his bankers with the family plate, Aunt Julia's jewels, and a bundle of American stock, borrowed the three hundred and twenty pounds on the security, and paid my premium five minutes before the office closed.

The next day I came down to breakfast, wide awake. I felt that I was awake, and besides that, the whole family admitted it quite cheerfully. Uncle Sparrow begged me to favour him at once with a cheque for the amount of my premium. At first I did not understand what he meant, but a few words of explanation made his meaning clear. I expressed my natural surprise that he should take upon himself to pay the premium on a policy which I had no intention of keeping up, and I declined altogether to hold myself responsible for his act. An angry scene ensued, which resulted in a final rupture of my engagement with Georgina.

To-morrow I marry Mrs. Comfit.

Comedy and Tragedy

In 1745, Mdlle; Céline was 'leading lady' at the Théâtre Français. She was a very beautiful woman, twenty-five years old, and of irreproachable character. Mdlle. Céline was only her stage name, inasmuch as she was the wife of Philippe de Quillac, late a lieutenant in the Royal Bodyguard, and now an actor of small parts in the theatre of which his wife was a distinguished ornament. De Quillac was a young man of good family, and of some small fortune. He honestly fell in love with Céline while he was still a lieutenant in the army, and honestly married her, and as a conseqence of this social down-step (for actors and actresses were held as little better than outcasts in those days), he had to resign his commission. Having nothing better to do, he took to the stage, for which, it must be admitted, he had no special talent. Nevertheless, his own industry, backed by his wife's influence, obtained for him an engagement at the Français—a consummation which he had earnestly desired to bring about, in order that he might be constantly at his wife's side. In truth, she stood greatly in need of a protector, for the Duc de Richelieu had condescended to make two distinct attempts to carry her away, as she left the stage door.

Her personal beauty, which was considerable, would probably have been insufficient of itself to incite that distinguished blackguard to take such determined steps; but her reputation as a spotless woman was a standing insult to him, and he made up his mind to avenge it. He laid siege to her in the orthodox fashion of those clumsy times. He sent her flowers, with notes in them. He composed immetrical quatrains in her honour. He obtained access to her at rehearsals, and delivered monstrous compliments, puffed out with complicated allegory. He was so obliging as to invite her to supper on many occasions, and on one occasion he carried his condescension so far as to offer to sup with her. These delicate overtures were a source of incessant irritation, both to Céline and to her husband. De Quillac sent many challenges to the Duc de Richelieu, but they were treated with contempt. De Quillac was an actor, and it was impossible for a nobleman of Richelieu's rank to cross swords with him. Eventually Richelieu's attentions became more definite, and they finally culminated in two attempts to carry her off, as she was leaving the theatre after performance. These experiments were made, not by Richelieu himself, but by his servants, who, having no great interest at stake, allowed themselves to be readily defeated by De Quillac and other actors of the theatre.

These renewed insults, and the impossibility of bringing their instigator to account, rendered De Quillac's life intolerable, and at length he and his wife determined to lay such a snare for their distinguished enemy as would bring him fairly into De Quillac's power. To achieve this end, Céline gave out that as she found it impossible to get on with her husband, they had resolved to separate. She further explained that a life of respectability was a rather Quixotic end to aim at, and that she had resolved, thenceforward, to see a little more of the world, and to taste a little more freely of its pleasures; and to this sensible determination she was encouraged by the approval of many distinguished persons of both sexes, whose careers were so strictly in accordance with their proffered advice, that their good faith in giving it was placed beyond suspicion. The news quickly reached Richelieu's ears, and he, also, was pleased to compliment her, in an atrocious ode, on her extreme good sense. This was the more disinterested on his part, as his appetite for the chase was in direct ratio to the difficulty of the country, as he was candid enough to explain to her in the last verse but one. That she might not, however, be unduly cast down by this information, he assured her, in the last verse, that he intended, despite the facilities that this new order of things seemed to promise, to renew his solicitations at an early opportunity. Céline intimated her determination to signalize her new method of life by a pleasant supper party, to which Richelieu, and many other eminent debauchees of the Court of Louis XV., were invited.

The night of the supper arrived, and Céline received her guests in a *salon* on the ground floor of her hotel. She was, to all appearances, in admirable spirits, and received them with infinite good humour. Richelieu arrived last, and the frankness of her welcome, tempered as it was by a touch of profound respect for his exalted rank, seemed to him to be the very essence of good breeding. Supper was eventually announced, but at this stage Céline pleaded a headache, and on this plea contrived to remain behind. Richelieu, infinitely pained at the news, was so good as to offer to remain with her until she should feel well enough to rejoin her friends—an offer which Céline gratefully accepted.

Left alone with her, he, as a matter of course, condoled with her on her affliction, and suggested many remedies, which she pettishly rejected.

'Bah! Monsieur le Duc, are you so young a hand as not to understand that there are headaches for which a congenial *tête-à-tête* is the best remedy? These friends of yours—they worry me. They talk so much, and they do not talk well. I can listen to you, but not to them.'

'I am infinitely flattered, Madame, at the compliment you are so good as to pay me. I cannot doubt its good faith, for it is a conclusion that you have arrived at after some deliberation.'

'You allude to the silence with which I have hitherto received your attention. You must remember that I was not a free agent. The acts of a woman who is embarrassed by the incessant presence of a jealous husband must not be judged too stricly. But there, he is gone, and I am to all intents a widow.'

'You would have been a widow in very truth, long since, if I had found it possible to comply with his pressing invitations. But what could I do? Personally, I have the profoundest respect for his calling, but in my position I was helpless. Am I forgiven?'

And so saying, he took her hand affectionately in his.

'I did not desire his death, Monsieur, nor do I now. He has done for me all that was necessary; he has gone to Marseilles, and he has pledged his word that he will not return. Nay, Monsieur le Duc, be reasonable.'

The Duke had placed his arm round her waist.

'You must make some allowance. I am hungry—here is a feast. Have I not said grace enough?'

'Nay, Monsieur, I cannot allow this. Remove your arm, I pray; your friends will be returning. If they should see us thus—'

'My friends will not return yet awhile, and when they do they will give us fair notice of their approach. Céline, I love you. Céline, I have waited long and patiently. Céline, I—'

At this point he looked over her shoulder, and saw, standing behind her De Quillac, white and stern, with a drawn sword in his hand. The truth flashed upon Richelieu in a moment.

'This is a trap,' said he.

'It is a trap,' replied Céline.

'It is a trap,' repeated De Quillac. 'For many months you have grossly insulted my wife, and, through my wife, myself. I have sent you challenge after challenge, but my messages were ignored by you. Inflamed beyond endurance at the many outrages you have dared to inflict upon us, we have devised this plan to get you into our power.'

'And this is with your consent, Madame?'

'Entirely.'

'Those doors lead to the garden. You must fight me there, to-night.'

'And if I refuse?'

'I will kill you where you stand.'

'But you are an actor, and, by your profession, proscribed. I cannot fight an actor.'

'Monsieur, I have laboured long and wearily to attain the position which I have just achieved—that of a member of the Théâtre Français. It has been the aim of my ambition, and that long-coveted reward has, within the last few days, been conferred on me. Here is my engagement, signed and sealed. By this act'—and here he tore the paper into two pieces—'I annul my engagement, and I pledge you my honour that under no circumstances will I ever appear on the stage again. Now, M. le Duc, I am no longer an actor, and you cannot refuse to meet me.'

'Madame,' said Richelieu, turning to Céline, 'I have no desire to injure you or your husband. I have wronged you sufficiently, and I would willingly make amends. I implore you not to expose your husband to the danger he is courting.'

Céline's lip quivered for a moment; it was for a moment only.

'Monsieur le Duc, you must fight my husband.'

'Let me remind you,' said the Duke, 'that I am one of the most skilful swordsmen in France. Let me place distinctly before your eyes the fact that in going out with me your husband runs no risk, for he encounters a certainty. I implore you to use your influence to check him, if you have any regard for him, for if I cross swords with him, I assure you, on my honour, that I will kill him.'

Céline was deadly pale, but her resolution did not desert her.

'Monsieur le Duc, you must fight my husband.'

'Good. It shall be as you will. I make but one stipulation—that the fact that I have consented to meet an actor shall never be known to any but ourselves.'

'You have my promise,' said De Quillac.

'And mine,' said Céline.

'Then, sir,' said the Duke, 'if you will be so good as to lead the way, I will do myself the honour to follow you.'

De Quillac turned to his wife, and, taking her in his arms, kissed her fondly.

'I am ready, Monsieur,' said he.

And the Duke and the actor went through the double doors into the garden.

At this point the full significance of the Duke's warning seemed to dawn upon her. The loss that she was, almost to a certainty, about to sustain—the knowledge that this great risk was undertaken on her behalf, with her consent, and almost at her instigation, destroyed the stern stuff of which the woman was made. She rushed to the door that had just closed.

'Philippe!—come back! for the love of Heaven, come back!'

It was too late, for, through another door came her guests, warmed with wine. With a supreme effort she assumed a thoughtless gaiety of carriage, and entered, almost recklessly into the tone of *persiflage* which prevailed among those who had supped. She felt that it was impossible to be silent—she must say something, or do something incessantly, or her fortitude would assuredly break down.

'Come, what shall we do? Have you nothing to propose? Shall we sing—dance—what shall we do? But be quick! I cannot bear delay. Suggest something, for Heaven's sake—'

Several suggestions were made. Each in turn was eagerly acquiesced in by Céline. At length some one recollected that Céline had a singular faculty for improvisation. Give her a suitable subject, and she would extemporise a poem upon it, in excellent rhymed Alexandrines. It was suggested that she should favour the company with an example of her remarkable facility in this respect.

'With pleasure—anything you please—give me a subject—quick! quick!—I cannot wait.'

It was debated among the company whether the subject to be proposed should belong to the domain of Comedy or of Tragedy. Some were for one—some for the other. To Céline, it was a matter of indifference, so that the question was quickly settled. At length a gentleman present solved the difficulty by proposing that she should extemporize in Comedy first, and in tragedy afterwards. Céline was ready—all that she waited for was a subject.

A comedy-subject was proposed. An unsuccessful lover had surreptitiously obtained access to his mistress's chamber in a woman's disguise.

It was enough, Céline, in the character of the lady, commenced her improvisation. She detected the imposture, and proceeded, in withering terms, to ridicule the contemptible device to which her suitor had resorted.

At this point, one of the guests—a Monsieur L'Estrange—exclaimed:

'Hush! I pray your pardon for this interruption; but I am certain I heard a sound of swords clashing in the garden.'

'It is nothing, sir,' said Céline. 'My servants are amusing themselves. We are enjoying ourselves here—let them have their enjoyent also. It is nothing, I assure you.'

She proceeded with the improvisation. She pointed out to her disguised lover how well a woman's garb befitted such a woman's soul as his, and recommended him to adhere to a costume which he carried with such address. Her manner was buoyant and defiant—perhaps a little too much so; still everyone was delighted with the exhibition. At a critical point in the verse, L'Estrange, who had been listening at the garden-door, again interrupted her:

'Madame, I am bound to interrupt you again. The clashing of swords is distinctly audible. I am certain you cannot be aware of what is going on. You must permit me to examine the garden.

Céline rushed to the door, locked it, and withdrew the key.

'It is nothing, Monsieur, I assure you. You must not enter the garden. The fact is, that I am preparing a little surprise for you all, and if you go into the garden at this moment, you will destroy everything. Pray permit me to continue.'

So saying, she gave the key of the door to the physician to the theatre, who happened to be among the guests, enjoining him, at the same time, not to part with it on any consideration.

She attempted to resume her improvisation, but she found it difficult to take up the thread at the point at which it had been broken. It was, in truth, a struggle between Comedy and Tragedy, and Tragedy had the best of it, for a loud exclamation, as from a man in acute pain, broke upon her ear, and her resolution gave way at once.

'Gentlemen, I cannot go on. It is useless to attempt to disguise my agitation from you. You must see that I am terribly overwrought. Gentlemen, for the love of Heaven, interfere to save my husband. He is in that garden, engaged in a duel with the Duc de Richelieu! The shriek that we all heard was his—he is dying—perhaps dead! For God's sake interfere to save him, if it be not too late!'

And so saying, she endeavoured, but vainly, to break open the door which she had so recently locked.

At first the guests were alarmed, till they recollected that the exhibition of Comedy was to be succeeded by one of Tragedy, and they concluded that this was but the fulfilment of the second half of her promise.

'Admirable! What passion—what earnestness!' and a

round of applause rang round the room.

'Gentlemen, pray do not mock me. I am not acting; I am in earnest. My husband is dying, perhaps dead. For Heaven's love, help him while there is yet time!'

A murmur of admiration was the only reply that this appeal elicited. The spectators were as men spellbound.

'Doctor, you have the key; I gave it to you. I love him. He is in deadly peril. Give me the key, I say, give me the key, or I shall die!'

It was agreed by all present that Céline had surpassed herself—that is to say, by all but one.

'Gentlemen,' said the Doctor, 'this lady is not acting; she is in earnest. See her colour comes and goes.'

'Nonsense, Doctor! Madame is acting, and acting admirably. Strange that so old a hand as you should be deceived.'

'It would be strange indeed if I were deceived, but I am not. I take upon myself to believe that she is in mortal earnest, and in that belief I shall comply with her wish.'

Undeterred by the ridicule with which his resolve was received, he went to the door and unlocked it, Céline rushed eagerly towards it, when she saw, standing in the open doorway, her husband, pale, stern, and unwounded.

A few hurried whispers passed between them.

'You are safe?'

'I am.'

'And the Duke?'

'Wounded to the death.'

With a great effort she recovered her presence of mind, and taking her husband's hand, led him forward.

'This, ladies and gentlemen,' said she, 'is the little surprise of which I spoke. I am delighted to think that my attempt at improvised Tragedy has met with your cordial approval.'

A prolonged round of applause followed this announcement. It was admitted on all hands that, admirably as she had shone in Comedy, it was in Tragedy that she carried off the palm.

FOGGERTY'S FAIRY

I

'OH, DASH it all!' said Freddy Foggerty, 'he knows me, and I shall be tried for desertion!'

Freddy Foggerty was a confectioner on a small scale in the Borough Road. He did not begin by being a confectioner, for his career had been a chequered one, and his ups and downs had been many. He began life as a Gentleman's Baby, a situation which he filled for about three years with much credit, when he found himself promoted to the rank and standing of a Gentleman's Little Boy—a position which carried with it an improved scale of dietary, and an emolument of twopence per week, on a Judge's tenure, that is to say, *dum se bene gesserit.* He passed through the various grades of boyhood and adolescence without having distinguished himself, except as a remarkable and exceptionally ordinary kind of boy, with this one distinguishing feature—that he had developed no prominent characteristic of any kind whatever. At nineteen, he became a Government clerk in the Bitter Beer branch of the Malt and Hops Department of the Inland Revenue Office. In this capacity he distinguished himself by the invention of a new system of cooking accounts, but the Heads of his Department looked coldly and indeed suspiciously on his discovery, and, treating him with the jealous brutality that usually characterizes Government officials in dealing with humble inventors, required him to send in his papers without further delay. Too proud to discuss the question with his blinded superiors, he retired at once, and, finding himself penniless, enlisted in a regiment of Highlanders. He served with some distinction as a soldier for nearly three days, but the brutality of the regimental barber, who cut his hair so short as to be absolutely unbecoming (and this in spite of his earnest remonstrance), disgusted him with the service, which he quitted abruptly, to the surprise and consternation of his Colonel, and the bitter disappointment of the Field-Marshall

Commanding-in-Chief. Feeling that a life of comparative seclusion in some distant region would best harmonize with his then state of mind, he shipped himself as a stowaway on board the *Rattan* (A 1), 800 tons, Captain Gilgal P. Bonesetter, then loading in the London Docks, and to sail for New York forthwith. After a dignified seclusion of eleven days behind a pork cask, he was discovered by the boatswain, who introduced him to Captain Bonesetter, who received him with open arms and closed fists. The Captain's big dog Jupiter, had just been washed overboard, and Captain Bonesetter, with the unaffected hospitality of a true sailor, immediately placed the animal's kennel at Mr. Foggerty's disposal. The dog's spare collar was found to fit him admirably, and the dog's daily rations were quite as much as Mr. Foggerty's stomach could digest. It was the Captain's whim to treat him as if he had really been a dog, and Mr. Foggerty, entering fully into the spirit of the joke, barked, ran about on all fours, sat up on his haunches, and caught a biscuit off his nose, for all the world as if he had been trained to do so. The joke lasted nine weeks and five days, by which time the ship had sighted the American continent, and Mr. Foggerty, having been comfortably provided at the Captain's expense with an entirely new and perfectly well-fitting suit of tar and feathers, was placed ashore at Sandy Hook, with a roving commision to go just wherever he pleased, and do just whatever he liked.

Delighted with his newly-acquired liberty (for a long sea voyage, even under the most agreeable circumstances, is a cramping thing), Mr. Foggerty set off in the direction of New York, the singularity of his appearance in the Captain's suit evoking some amusement, and not a few comments, from the ladies and gentlemen of Port Monmouth. But Mr. Foggery set all conjecture at rest by explaining that he was the Duke of Northumberland doing it for a wager—adding that the feat he had undertaken was accomplished, and he would feel much obliged if somebody would kindly scrape him down and 'loan' him a suit or two of clothes, a gold watch, and an eyeglass, until he could communicate with his solicitor in London. He further stated that the wager was made with a certain Royal Personage of the *very highest possible* rank, and that he was prepared to settle the amount won (£37,000 and Balmoral) on trustees in trust to build a cathedral and found a bishopric for Port Monmouth. Upon hearing of this pious resolve the clergyman of the parish, the Rev. Hicks K. Plappy (who liked the idea of the bishopric), scraped him down and provided him with everything he could possibly require, including a marble bust of himself, and a cow with five legs, for many years the surprise and glory of the state of New Jersey. To these gifts he superadded his daugther Louisa, a beautiful young lady of twenty—marrying them himself that His Grace might not have a chance of changing his mind. The wedding was magnificent, and His Grace (who had stipulated, as the only condition upon which he could consent to marry Miss Plappy, that his *incognito* should be strictly preserved for ever) started with his blushing bride from New York, per *Cuba*, for England the same evening. On his arrival at Liverpool, his wife, who was anxious to assume her real station, urged upon her husband the propriety of immediately throwing off his *incognito*, a course which appeared particularly advisable as she had read of another Duke of Northumberland, then in England, and she was anxious to know which of the two was the right one. But Foggerty explained that the other Duke was an imposter who had taken advantage of his absence to assume his name and rank, and that he proposed to remain in obscurity for the present, just in order to see how far the sham Duke would carry his pretentions. His wife objected, naturally enough, to this course; but Foggerty was firm, and there was nothing more to be said. He proposed that while they were watching the movements of the sham Duke, they should amuse themselves by purchasing the goodwill of a confectioner's shop in the Borough Road, and play at being tradespeople. To this course Her Grace was obliged to consent. The game had lasted about twelve years, and was still going on, when our story commenced, for Foggerty (as he preferred to be called) had not yet done watching the movements of the sham Duke, who was now dealing with Northumberland House as if it really belonged to him. These are Freddy Foggerty's antecedents, which we have set out at some length because it is essential to a proper appreciation of his astonishing adventures that these details should be clearly understood.

Freddy Foggerty was seated on his counter in a very uncomfortable frame of mind. A sergeant of Highlanders had that morning entered his shop to purchase some acidulated drops. On seeing Mr. Foggerty it was observed that the sergeant stared at him in a very remarkable manner—so much so that Mr. Foggerty had said to him, 'It's lucky for you, sergeant, that it's me, and not my wife, you are staring at so rudely, for she is strong and stands no nonense.' Upon which the sergeant remarked that it was a fine day (which it was not, for it was snowing heavily), and went out of the shop, leaving the acidulated drops behind him in his nervous agitation. This little incident served to set Freddy in a roar, until he suddenly recollected that this very sergeant was very like the very sergeant who had enlisted him some thirteen years before, and it was this sudden recollection that caused him to use the exclamation with which this story opens—' 'Oh, dash it all, he knows me, and I shall be tried for desertion!'

He was terribly agitated, for he was really prosperous as a confectioner; moreover, he was extremely fond of his wife, and he had two children. The thought of his being torn away from his business and from them, with the shop going to rack and ruin while he served his time in the ranks, was too much for him, and he burst into tears.

'Cheer up, Mr. Foggerty,' said a pipy little voice.

He looked up, but could see no one. At last his eye rested on a small twelfth-cake in the window, and he was surprised to see the little plaster-of-Paris fairy which had crowned the top of it hop off her box of sugar-plums, and pick her way carefully through the tracery that decorated the surface of the cake. She travelled on slowly, tumbling over a harlequin, and getting her skirt entangled in the fringe of a gelatine 'cracker,' until she reached the edge of the cake. She looked over the edge of the little parapet that ran round it, and said:

'I'm afraid, Mr. Foggerty, it's too high to jump, and I shall tear my clothes if I try to scramble down. Will you kindly let me step on to your hand?'

Freddy, who had never seen anything of the kind before, was much interested in her movements, and helped her down at once with the utmost propriety, like a man of gallantry as he was.

'What is troubling you, Mr. Foggerty?'

'Why, miss, thirteen years ago I enlisted, and three days afterwards I deserted, and I have just been discovered, and now I shall be taken up, tried, and imprisoned, and then, perhaps, have to serve out my time as a soldier.'

'Indeed,' said the young lady, 'that will be a pity, for from what I have seen of Mrs. Foggerty I don't think she will do the shop justice. She's a respectable young woman, but with no taste for business.'

'Louisa is quite the lady, though,' said Freddy.

'Oh, a perfect lady, but I see things from my position in the shop that you don't see. Take my word for it, Mrs. Foggerty is no business woman. Only the other day a little girl came in for three-pen'north of chocolate cream. Well, Mrs. Foggerty not only gave her the chocolate for nothing, but added a Bath bun and a penny ice, and told her to come in again whenever she liked, and bring all her young friends. Now that's all very nice, but it's not business,' said the fairy, with decision.

'Mrs. Foggerty is all heart,' said Freddy; 'besides, she is a born lady, and can't bear the idea of selling anything.'

'I wish you would tell me your history,' said the fairy.

'Oh, with great pleasure,' said Freddy. And he told her his history, just as I have been telling it to you.

'It seems to me, Mr. Foggerty, that your career has been a very discreditable one,' said the fairy, when Mr. Foggerty had finished.

'I'm not proud of it, miss. I've done many things in my time that I've had reason to regret. There are many incidents in my career that I'd give anything to blot out.'

'Oh, indeed,' said the fairy. 'Now I think I can help you to do that. First of all, how many ornaments are there on that twelfth-cake?'

'Three large ones,' said Freddy; 'a Ship, a Harlequin, and a Policeman, besides crackers and other unimportant trifles.'

'Very good,' said the fairy; 'take these ornaments off the cake, and whenever you wish to obliterate any one deed of your life and all its consequences, eat one of those ornaments.'

'And the deed will be obliterated from my history?'

'Entirely,' said the fairy; 'you will be as though it had never been committed.'

'I am very much obliged to you,' said Freddy.

'Not at all,' said the fairy, 'I'm very glad to have had it in my power to assist you.'

And so saying she made her way back to the bon-bon box on the top of the cake, and became plaster-of-Paris once more.

Freddy scarcely knew what to make of his adventure. He was not so foolish as to believe in fairies, but still, without committing himself to a belief, *there she was*. As to his being able to obliterate an event of his life by eating one of the ornaments on the cake, why that was preposterous. He could understand that he might obliterate his life altogether by so doing, for they were coloured, for the most part, with arsenite of copper and chromate of lead, but *any one event*—it was out of the question.

As these ideas floated through his head he looked down the street, and saw a corporal's guard in the distance. It was marching straight towards his shop. A crisis was about to take place. It was too awful. To be torn away from his beloved wife and adored children—no, no! Drowning men catch at straws, and Freddy crunched the Ship, ejaculating at the same time a sincere wish that his return to England from NEW YORK, AND ALL ITS CONSEQUENCES MIGHT BE OBLITERATED FROM HIS HISTORY FOR EVER!

II

The fairy was as good as her word. A remarkable change took place in Mr. Freddy Foggerty's condition. The confectioner's shop, the twelfth-cake, the house, the street, the corporal's guard, all vanished in a moment, and Freddy found himself living in a comfortable cot in a ship's stern-cabin.

Freddy was wondering where he was, and how he got there, when the cabin-door opened, and a black man put his head in.

'Seven bells, Massa Foggerty.'

'Oh!' said Freddy; 'how's her head?'

'S.S.W. and by S.—light breeze freshenin', Massa Foggerty.'

'Oh! then I'll tumble up.'

Freddy felt it incumbent upon him to appear to know exactly where he was, and to be surprised at nothing. He determined to make no inquiries, but to leave it to time and accident to enlighten him as to the circumstances in which he found himself, and proceeded to dress himself in a pair of blue serge trousers (in the pockets of which were the Policeman and the Harlequin), a pea-jacket with gilt buttons, and a cap with a gold band. He completed his toilet and went on deck. He then saw that the ship was a fine bark, with raking masts, and perhaps a tonnage of 800. She carried two long carronades.

'Mornin', cap'en,' said a tall wiry Yankee mate. 'With a breeze like this I reckon we shall take tarnation snakes out of yon Britisher.'

'No doubt of it,' said Freddy. 'Where is the Britisher?'

'About three miles off the starboard quarter,' said the mate, pointing in the named direction with a telescope.

'I see him—that is *her*,' said Freddy.

'If this breeze lasts she'll never overhaul the *Flying Clam*.'

'And if she should,' said Freddy, 'who cares?'

He looked anxiously at the mate, to see if *he* cared.

'Wal, *I* du for one. The crew du for another. *And* the cargo du for a third.'

'The cargo? I don't see how it can concern the cargo?'

'Wal,' said the mate; Ho! ho! ho! that *is* a good'un. Don't see how it can consarn the cargo! No, no—you'll never beat that if you tries a year, cap'en! Bully for you, old man! Ho! ho! ho!'

'Ho! ho! ho!' laughed Freddy, mechanically; 'Bully for me, as you say.'

'You du make me larf, you bet!' said the mate.
'Can't consarn the cargo! No, not at all. Ho! ho! ho!'

'I think,' said Freddy, 'I should like to have another look at the cargo.' For he began to wonder what it consisted of.

'Whelps!' shouted the mate to the boatswain, who was serving out grog to five-and-twenty skulking-looking ruffians, 'the cap'en wants another look at the cargo. Take the cap'en into the hold.'

'Ay, ay,' cried the boatswain. He handed the pannikin to his mate, and went down the main hatch. Freddy followed him. On the main deck he lighted a lantern, and then descended a second 'companion,' and so reached the lower deck. He then raised a bolted and barred trap-door, and prepared to descend a third ladder. At this point Freddy perceived that the atmosphere in the neighbourhood of the cargo had a distinct and recognizable flavour of its own.

He descended the third ladder. The boatswain held up the lantern, and Freddy formed his first impression of the cargo, and his first impression was that it was cocoa-nuts. But a closer inspection showed that each cocoa-nut had two white glaring eyeballs, and he then formed his second (and right) impression, which was 'niggers.' As his eyes became accustomed to the darkness he saw that the hold contained from forty to fifty black people, of both sexes, huddled together in a dreadfully uncomfortable manner.

They were chained two and two, the chain of communication running through a staple in the deck. It flashed upon Freddy that he must be the captain of a slaver, at that moment hotly pursued by one of Her Britannic Majesty's ships of war.

It now becomes necessary to explain the circumstances under which Mr. Foggerty came to fill such a position. They are shortly as follows:

If Mr. Foggerty had not returned from New York to England, his career would have taken an entirely different course. He would have lived for some months on the speculative bounty of the Rev. Hicks K. Plappy, who would have secured himself from ultimate loss by taking bills at twelve months for his son-in-law's keep. Eventually, however, the reverend pastor's suspicions would have been aroused, and Freddy's pretentions to the dukedom would have undergone a through investigation before a magistrate. He would then have been tried, and convicted of obtaining money and goods under false pretences, and sentenced to twelve months' imprisonment, with hard labour, in the 'Tombs.' In this retreat he would have formed a bowing acquaintance with a seafaring man of evil countenance, and their sentences expiring on the same day, Freddy and the seafaring man would have set forth 'on the tramp,' to take whatever good or ill luck might turn up for them. At length the sailor would have found work on board a blockade-runner, and Freddy, who would have known very well that there was no chance of his being engaged as one of the crew, would have shipped himself once more in his old and favourite character as a 'stowaway.' A certain smartness and activity which characterized all of Freddy's movements would have recommended him to the skipper, and he would eventually have formed one of the ship's crew. In this capacity he would have distinguished himself so remarkably that he would in a couple of years, have been promoted to the rank of boatswain's mate. On the cessation of the American War his ship would have traded to the east coast of Africa in ivory and gold dust, and Freddy, who by this time would have saved about two thousand dollars, would have purchased a sixteenth share in her. From this point his promotion would have been rapid, and in six years he would have saved money enough to purchase her out and out, and trade with her on his own account. He would have discovered that the slave trade was still more profitable than that in gold and ivory, and (keeping it secret from Louisa, who would be living luxuriously somewhere in Florida, under the impression that her husband was a blameless merchant) he would have devoted himself to its prosecution with an energy which might with equal profit, and less risk, have been expended upon a more legitimate speculation.

However, Freddy knew nothing of what *would have happened*, if his return to England and all its consequences had been blotted out of his career, and felt himself somewhat at a loss to account for his position.

'Great heavens,' said Freddy, on realizing the exact character of the cargo, 'these must be slaves!'

'The cap'en will be the death o' me one day!' roared the boatswain in the middle of an uncontrollable fit of laughter.

'How horrible! how awful!' said Freddy. 'Torn from the bosom of their families—cramped and crippled in a filthy hold, and in an atmosphere in which a candle will hardly burn—it's horrible, it's appalling!'

'The cap'en's joke agin all others, I allers say!' screamed the boatswain, who in the excess of his merriment had to hold on by the ladder to save himself from falling. 'He acts it all to the life, that's sartin!'

Freddy recollected himself and forced a grim smile.

'Shut the devils up again,' said he.

'This yere's the slow match,' said the boatswain, pointing to the end of a piece of yarn which lay on the lower deck. 'It's in beautiful order, and burns two minutes.'

'Oh, to be sure,' said Freddy, 'that is the slow match. Quite right. Of course the other end communicates with—'

'With an open barrel of powder in the magazine, 'cordin' to your own orders, cap'en.'

'Quite correct. And now let me see whether you fully understand my instructions. When are you to set light to it?'

'As soon as the Britisher's first shot strikes our hull. Then up we goes, and there's an end of the *Flying Clam*, crew, cargo, cap'en and all.'

'Admirable!' said Freddy, white with terror, 'only—I've been thinking that—perhaps on the whole there is something rather contemptible, not to say downright cowardly, in this summary and comparatively painless way of evading the punishment our captors may have in store for us.'

'Wot!' yelled the boatswain.

'Why, reflect,' said Freddy. 'If we blow ourselves up they may say that we do so because we are afraid of them! The thought is unendurable! No, no—let us evince a truer and a nobler courage than that of the mere suicide. Let us rather express our indifference to penal servitude by submitting with sullen contempt to whatever punishment these bloodhounds may think proper to inflict upon us.'

And Freddy's nostrils dilated with a noble scorn that would have fitted a Protestant martyr in the reign of Queen Mary.

'Wal!' roared the boatswain, as he clutched at Freddy's collar. 'Of all the yelping cocktails—but stop a bit—stop a bit!'

He put his pipe to his mouth and blew shrilly upon

it—'Tweet! tweet! tweet! twilly, twilly, twilly,—twee-e-e—twip, twip, twip—twee-e-e-e! All hands on upper deck!' He ran fore and aft along the main deck, piping and shouting down each hatchway.

The crew tumbled up in all haste—men of all nations—many black and brown—all scowling and tigerish. They stood on both sides of the upper deck according to their watches.

'Mr. Slip!' shouted the boatswain, foaming at the mouth. 'Mr. Slip, and men all. Lookee yere. This yere cap'en of ourn—this yere lanky cocktail—this white-livered devil's chicken—he's showing the white feather—he's a cur—a slinkin' coward—a shiverin' cocktail! He won't fight, and he won't sink—he's going to give in—if you'll let him, mates, if you'll let him!'

The boatswain's fury had almost exhausted him, and he lolloped on to a carronade from sheer weakness.

'Shame! shame!' yelled the men, who seemed to contemplate a general rush at Freddy.

'Wot's this?' said Slip, taking Freddy by the collar and presenting a six-shooter at his head. 'Now, lookee yere, cap'en. Wot's your prog*ramme?* What do you pur*pose* to du?' Freddy recollected himself, for he felt that a crisis was at hand, and that his only chance lay in carrying it off with a high hand.

'To fight till the last drop of my blood shall trickle on these snowy decks, and then, mingling with the blue ocean beneath our feet, proclaim to all who may chance to see it that Rule Columbia, Columbia rules the waves, Yankee traders never, never, *never* will be done out of their slaves!'

A yell of joy rang through the air as the confused metaphors of their beloved captain sank into the souls of the crew. He perceived his advantage, and lost no time in following it up.

'Now, my men,' said he, 'what shall we do with these lying mutineers, who for ends of their own have endeavoured to stir you up against your captain?'

'Overboard!' was the universal verdict, and a hundred hands clutched at the mate and the boatswain. In another moment they were hurled, gurgling, into the deep.

In the meanwhile, the wind had freshened considerably, and the British frigate (to whom no one paid any attention during the excitement of this scene) came up, hand over hand.

'Here you,' said Freddy to a middle-aged person, who had been foremost in throwing over the first mate—and whom he concluded on that account to be the second mate—'take charge of the slow match on the lower deck, and when I give the word "go," set light to it.'

'Ay, ay, sir!' said the second mate. And he slowly and reluctantly disappeared (with a very pale face) down the main-hatch. 'Bang!' from the Britisher. The shot, a thirty-two, flew high over their heads, carrying away one of the main topsail lifts.

'Carpenter!' shouted Freddy.

'Ay, ay, sir!'

'Stave in the boats.'

'But—'

'Not a word, or I'll blow your head off.'

The carpenter took an axe and sullenly obeyed orders.

'Boatswain's mate!'

'Sir!'

'Can she carry any more sail?'

'Not an inch, sir.'

The chase lasted half-an-hour, in the course of which the Britisher rapidly overhauled the slaver, for the breeze had increased to half a gale. At length a round shot carried away the mizzen about two feet below the necklace, and with a fearful crash the mast and its cumbrous gear fell over the ship's quarter. Two men were carried overboard with it.

'Go!' shouted Foggerty down the hatch. He took out his watch; the crew held their breath, and each man nervously clutched at something.

'Go it is!' replied the muffled voice of the pale mate, as he obeyed the order from the lower deck. In another moment he rushed up the companion.

'The match is fired!' screamed he, 'and in two minutes we shall be blown to feathers!' And so saying he flung himself overboard—an example which was followed by the greater part of the crew.

Freddy looked at his watch for a minute and a half.

'I NOW WISH,' said he, very deliberately and distinctly as he masticated the Policeman, 'I NOW WISH THAT MY TARRING AND FEATHERING AND ALL ITS CONSEQUENCES MAY BE BLOTTED OUT OF MY HISTORY FOR EVER!'

III

With the muffled sound of a distant explosion ringing in his head, Freddy found himself sitting in a comfortable room fitted up partly as an office, and partly as a luxurious study. He was seated at a handsome mahogany writing-table, furnished with every little luxury that can reduce the toil and enhance the pleasures of pen-work. Above a handsome statuary marble mantelpiece hung a portrait of himself in the act of addressing society at large on the subject of a scroll of parchment with a pendent seal, and regardless of the threatening appearance of a raging thunderstorm, from which a pillar and a crimson curtain afforded an inadequate protection. Beneath his feet was an Axminster carpet of astonishing pile, and two or three easy-chairs, with a comfortable welcoming 'come along, old man' sort of expression, stood about the room.

'It is quite clear,' said Freddy, 'that I'm a banker's clerk of some kind. I wonder what Bank I belong to. Rather a prosperous concern apparently—or, what is still more likely, a flashy and unsubstantial one.'

He took some paper from a stand in front of him, and found it headed 'Royal Indelible Bank, 142, Threadneedle Street, E.C.' He then noticed that all the books on his desk were stamped 'Royal Indelible Bank' and the official seal, which stood ready to his hand, bore a similar inscription.

He walked to the door and opened it. He found that it communicated with a very large room, in which forty or fifty clerks were at work.

'By Jove!' thought he, as he contrasted their apartment with his own luxurious private room, 'banker's clerk be hanged! I'm a banker, or something very like it, and on a large scale too!'

At this moment the clock struck five, and all the clerks rose simultaneously, and began to wash their hands at little stands provided for the purpose. When they had completed their toilettes they went out in twos and threes, passing his door as they did so, and saying, 'Good evening, sir,' very respectfully, as they went by.

'I suppose,' thought Freddy, 'I ought to go too. I wonder where I live.' So he took down his hat from a peg and followed the last clerk out. He saw the porter (a stout responsible-looking person in a quiet business-like livery), at the end of a passage, holding the door open for him.

'Now,' thought Freddy, 'how the deuce am I to find out where I live? I can't ask the porter, he'll think I've been drinking.' He felt in his pockets for some cards, but he could not find any. 'I'll go back,' thought he, 'and look in the Directory. I'm sure to be a householder.'

But just as he was turning back the porter said to him, 'Your carriage is here, sir,' and as he spoke a quiet brougham, drawn by a pair of handsome greys, pulled up at the door. This relieved him of all anxiety. He stepped in, saying 'Home!' to the groom, just as if he knew where Home was.

He leant back on the soft cushions as the brougham drove off.

'Come,' thought he, 'this is better—this is something like. A good berth—secretary or manager perhaps—in a substantial Bank—at least we'll hope it's substantial—and a brougham and pair to drive me home to some snug little villa in the Regent's Park; or perhaps a good house in Bedford Square, and Louisa and the children waiting for me at home. I wonder how Louisa's looking. Dear Louisa! I'm glad she wasn't on board the slaver!'

The brougham drove down Oxford Street.

'Ha!' thought he, 'it isn't Bedford Square. Well, I am glad it isn't Bedford Square. I prefer the Regent's Park. By-the-bye, I wonder what my income is?'

He felt in his pocket, and found a pocket-book containing business appointments and important memoranda—all in his own writing, and many of them incomprehensible to him owing to their being written in a kind of cypher or shorthand with which he was not familiar.

'I hope,' thought he, 'I shall find the key to these, or I shall get into a mess.'

He read through several legible memoranda, and eventually lit on the following:—

'Sept. 29th, Qr's. Sal. £375.

'Fifteen hundred a year, eh? Well, that's pretty good—but this pair of horses can't be done on that. I hope I'm not exceeding my income; perhaps Louisa's come into money.'

He settled in his own mind that old Plappy was gathered to his fathers, leaving everything to his child.

The carriage drove past the Marble Arch, and along the road towards Bayswater. Tommy watched the progress of the carriage with much anxiety.

'I won't live in Bayswater,' said he. 'If it's Bayswater I'll move to-morrow. I do wonder where I live. I suppose if I asked the groom he'd think it odd.' However, it wasn't Bayswater, for as this thought passed through his mind the carriage drove into Lancaster Gate, and stopped at No. 352.

'Whew!' said he. 'Lancaster Gate, eh? Freddy, Freddy, this can't be done of £1500 a year, or anything like it. Something wrong, Freddy, I'm afraid.' And he shook his head at himself, and held up his finger in a very reproving manner.

The door was opened by a grave man in a very handsome livery, and Tommy entered the house with much misgiving.

'Anybody in?'

'Only my lady, sir,' said the man.

'Only your lady?'

'Yes, Sir Frederick. Her ladyship is upstairs.'

'Oho!' thought Freddy. '*Sir* Frederick, and her ladyship, eh? So I've been, knighted I suppose. Perhaps I'm a baronet. I hope I'm a baronet for Theodore's sake.'

'Any letters?'

'Only one, Sir Frederick.' It was directed to

'SIR FREDERICK FOGGERTY,
'&c., &c., &c.,
'352, Lancaster Gate, W.'

'Only a knight, eh? Well, it might be worse—I suppose

I've been a sheriff. Now to surprise Louisa!'

He ran upstairs without stopping to examine the pictures in the hall, or the handsome bust of himself on the first landing. He entered the drawing-room, a spacious apartment tastefully furnished in French grey satin and ebony, but it was empty. As he turned from the room he met a nursemaid coming downstairs with two children, a girl of three and a boy of two, whom he had not had the pleasure of seeing before.

'Papa tum 'ome!' cried the little boy. And the two children, released by their nurse, ran and possessed themselves of his two legs.

'Papa tiss Tiny!' said the little girl, making vigorous efforts to swarm up his right leg.

'My dear child,' said Freddy, who had a pleasant way with children, 'I'm not your papa.'

The nurse smiled a weak smile, as who should say, 'Master's joke is always so amusingly chosen.'

'Yes, yes—you papa!' chorused the two children, with an emphasis which carried conviction with it.

'Whose children are these, nurse?' said Freddy.

'I'm sure I can't say, sir,' replied the woman with an agreeable simper, as humouring her master's whim.

'Don't be a dashed fool, girl,' said Freddy, losing his temper. 'Whose are they—tell me directly?'

'Dear me, Sir Frederick, yours of course!' said the woman in great terror. 'Yours and my lady's, Sir Frederick. What a question, Sir Frederick, and on this day of all others!'

'Oh, Go!'

The nurse lost no time in hurrying herself and the children out of the presence of a master in whom she detected signs of incipient insanity.

'Mine, eh?' thought Freddy. 'I've no recollection of—I've made up my mind not to be surprised at anything, but really this discovery makes a greater demand upon my powers of self-control than I bargained for.'

However, he regained his equanimity, and went upstairs. He opened the door quietly. A lady was seated at the glass, and a maid was doing her hair.

'Boo!' exclaimed Sir Frederick, playfully.

The maid started, and the lady turned round—it was *not* Louisa!

'I—beg your pardon—I thought— that is, I was told—'

'Come in, darling,' said the lady, and a very stout, jolly-looking lady she was. 'Come in. I'm so glad you've come home early.' And so saying she ran to him and gave him a sounding kiss in the very heart of his right cheek.

It was quite clear that it was not Louisa, and it was equally clear that it was someone in whose room he had a perfect right to be. Who was she? He had a delicacy in asking the question—indeed he felt that his position was altogether a most delicate and difficult one.

'There's nothing wrong in the city, dear?' said she, noticing his embarrassment, and misinterpreting it.

'Nothing whatever—dear.'

'That's right. It wouldn't have a secret from its little wifey, would it, on this day, too, of all others?'

The truth flashed upon him. If he had never been tarred and feathered he would never have made the acquaintance of the Rev. Hicks K. Plappy, and so would never have married his daughter Louisa, but would probably have married someone else, to wit, the buxom jolly red-faced lady who was at that moment plumping kisses into the very heart of his right cheek. The delicacy of his position was not all diminished by the discovery.

'Poor Louisa!' exclaimed Freddy, with unaffected grief, for he was very fond of her. 'Poor darling Louisa!'

'Frederick!' exclaimed the stout lady.

'And the dear, dear children! I shall never see them again!'

'Frederick! on this day, too, of all others!' screamed the stout lady. 'Explain yourself this moment, I insist!'

Freddy pulled himself together in a moment.

'It's a sad story,' said he. 'I had a dear, dear sister—whose existence I have hitherto kept a secret from you, for, many years ago, she disgraced her family by marrying a villain—a pickle-merchant, who had extensive works in Lambeth. His business has gradually declined, owing to the rapid rise in the price of copper, and he and Louisa and her innocent babes have emigrated to New Zealand.'

It *was* a sad story, and he knew it, but there was no other way out of it.

'Dear Frederick,' said the lady, 'you always had a feeling heart. I knew there was something wrong, directly I saw you.'

Freddy felt dreadfully hypocritical, but what was he to do? If he had explained to Lady Foggerty that an hour ago he was a Yankee slave captain, with a dear wife Louisa and two beloved children in Florida, and that a few hours before that he was a confectioner in the Borough Road, and that Louisa assisted him in his business, Lady Foggerty would have declined to accept his explanation, militating, as it would have done, with her own experience of him during the last four years. On the whole, I think it was one of those exceptional occasions on which a story is allowable, and having to tell a story, I don't know that he would have pitched upon a better one.

He retired to his dressing-room to prepare for dinner. He found the room luxuriously furnished, with two large easy chairs of the most inviting description, and a comfortable sofa, on which his dress clothes were laid out. He threw himself into one of the chairs, and as he sank in it, he thought to himself as follows:—

'As a speculation, this change has not turned out so badly. I have exchanged a lawless life of continual peril for one of assured prosperity and perfect lawfulness. There are only two drawbacks to it. I am afraid I must be living considerably beyond my income, and I have exchanged a pretty and ladylike wife for a stout and vulgar one. I wonder how I came to marry so gross a person; for I was always a bit of an epicure in such matters. There must have been some reason for it,' said he, musingly. 'I wonder what it was?'—then with a sudden start, 'I have it! I must have married her for her money? That's it—she was a wealthy widow, no doubt, and I married her for her money.'

Having settled this point, much to his own satisfaction (for it quite accounted for his extravagant style of living), he proceeded, with the assistance of a quiet valet, to dress for dinner.

'Which studs will you wear to-night, Sir Frederick?' said the man.

'Oh, well, let me see, which did I wear last night?'

'The plain pearls, Sir Frederick.'

'Then I'll wear the plain pearls to-night.'

'Beg pardon, Sir Frederick, but if you remember one of the pearls came off, and you told me to take it to the jeweller's.'

'True, how stupid of me! Well, I'll wear the others.'

'Which others, Sir Frederick?'

'Which others?' said Freddy angrily. 'Why, *the* others to be sure! Which others *should* I mean, you donkey?'

The valet shrugged his shoulders, and Freddy finished his toilet. As he was putting the final touch to his tie, the lady's maid rapped at the door.

'Please, sir, my lady says will you hurry please, as some of 'em have arrived.'

'Who has arrived?'

'Mr. and Mrs. Bortle, and Lord Portico, Sir Frederick.'

'Oh, I'm coming. Dinner party, eh?' said he to himself as he went downstairs. 'Rather awkward.'

He entered the drawing-room and shook hands very heartily with Lord Portico, telling him it seemed an age since they met (which it must have done, as this was the first time they had seen each other), and asking very cordially after Lady Portico, who had been dead about six months. Lord Portico's indignant stare proved to him that he had made some mistake, so he was more careful in his demeanour towards Mr. and Mrs. Bortle, bowing coldly but respectfully to them, which was not right either, as Bortle was his wife's father and had procured him his appointment, and Mr. and Mrs. Bortle had just returned from India after an absence of six years, and the meeting ought to have been a very effusive one. Several other guests arrived, including Mr. and Mrs. Crabthorne (Mrs. Crabthorne was Lady Foggerty's sister) and Sir John Carboy, the eminent accoucheur, who had presided at the birth of Freddy's two little children. In short, it was quite a family party, as Freddy took occasion to observe in an under-breath to Lady Foggerty, who replied, 'Well, I should think so, and on this day, too, of all others!'

'I wonder what day of all others this is! I don't like to ask,' thought he.

'By-the-bye, dear,' said Lady Foggerty, 'I forgot to give you this.' And she slipped into his hand a piece of paper containing the list of guests told off into couples. He was rather taken aback, because he only knew the Bortles and Lord Portico by sight, but by dint of listening to the conversation, he contrived to hit on the right people, and when dinner was announced down they went.

He managed to get through his dinner pretty comfortably. He had Lady Carboy on his right, and Mrs. Bortle on his left, and as he contrived to confine the conversation to general topics, he did not 'put his foot into it' more than twenty or five-and-twenty times during the course of the meal. He was much puzzled, however, by Lady Carboy's and Mrs. Bortle's continual reference to 'this day of all others,' and he determined to find out what day of all others it really was. He could scarcely ask them without seeming absurd, so he called the butler to him and whispered—'Here, what's your name? In the name of mischief, tell me, *what* day *is* this?' to which the butler, thus solemnly adjured, replied 'Tuesday, Sir Frederick,' which afforded him no clue whatever to the mystery.

After dinner, Sir John Carboy rose and said—

'Ladies and gentlemen, it is not usual to drink healths at modern dinner parties, but there are occasions when the strict forms of etiquette may be relaxed, and I think you will agree with me that this day of all others is one of them. I need not detain you by dilating on the auspicious character of the event we are here to celebrate—the circumstances are known to you all. I will content myself with proposing that we drink the health of my dear old friend, Sir Frederick Foggerty, and my still older, and (may I add?) my still dearer friend, his admirable wife.'

This short and (to Freddy) unsatisfactory speech was received with much applause, and Freddy observed, with some apprehension, that two fat tears stood in Lady Foggerty's little eyes. At last a bright thought occurred to him—'It must be the anniversary of our wedding!' Primed with this fortunate suggestion, he rose and spoke—

'Ha—hum—sir!' (*he had forgotten Sir John's name*). 'My dear, my very, very dear old friend, in rising to reply to the toast with which you have been good enough to couple my name, and that of my dear, my dear (*he had never heard his wife's name*), my dear wife, I feel no little embarrassment. On this day, never mind how many years ago (*with a deep sigh*), Heaven blessed our union—I say—Heaven blessed our union'—

'Hear, hear, my dear boy, my very dear boy,' from old Bortle, who was boo-hooing in his handkerchief.

'It's all right,' thought Freddy, 'it *is* the wedding day.' Then he continued—'Yes, on this day, never mind how many years ago—more than I care to look back upon—'

'Four years, only four, my dear boy,' sobbed old Bortle from behind his handkerchief.

'On this day four years ago, my wife and I were married.'

'Frederick!' exclaimed Lady Foggerty, springing to her feet, 'pray recollect yourself.'

'I said, my dear, that on this day four years ago, on this day of all others, you and I were happily married—'

Lady Foggerty screamed and fainted. Mr. Bortle, her father, rose, purple with rage, and thus delivered himself:

'Fred! Fred Foggerty! you're drunk—drunk at your own table! He *must* be drunk—to insult his wife in this manner—on this day of all others! Look, sir! Look at your work, scoundrel! She's fainted! Confound you, sir, she's fainted!'

'Be composed, Mr. Bortle,' said Lord Portico.

'Be composed! No, sir, I shall *not* be composed. I am not here to be dictated to by anybody, whatever his rank, Lord Portico—be he baron, viscount, earl, marquis, duke, or king. We are invited here on the pretence of celebrating the fourth anniversary of the birth of my daughter's son and heir, and this insolent joker, whose fortune I and my daughter have made, rises and publicly states at his own table—*at his own table, mind*—that on this day four years ago, and on this day of all others, and not until this day, he and she were happily married—were happily married—happily married!'

At this point the purple old gentleman fell back gasping in his chair, and was carried out of the room on the very verge of apoplexy, followed by all the ladies in tears.

'I am sorry, my friends,' said Foggerty, when the door was closed, 'that my poor little joke should have been so unfortunately misconstrued by Mr.—by my very dear father-in-law. Pray let us forget that it happened, and be as jolly as though I had replied in terms that had melted you to tears.'

Sir Frederick was readily excused, and after a short interval of rather forced conversation, the gentlemen rose to join the ladies. At this moment the butler put a telegram into Sir Frederick's hand. It was as follows:—

'GONE COON, *to* SIR FREDERICK FOGGERTY,
'Cripplegate, 352, Lancaster Gate.

'Crumph jagger puntiboom rubbleburby cowk.'

Sir Frederick stood in the hall, puzzling himself with this document, when the street bell rang and a servant opened the door to two tall stout persons, who inquired for Sir Frederick Foggerty.

'I am he,' said Freddy.

'Sorry to trouble you at this time of night, sir,' said one of the men, 'but business is business, as you very well knows.'

'My maxim through life,' said Sir Frederick.

'I suppose you can guess our errand?'

'I conclude it has something to do with this,' said Sir Frederick at a guess, handing them the mystic telegram.

'Exactly. So the Gone Coon is in it?'

'The Gone Coon is in it. Indeed, he has been in it some time.'

'Much obliged for the information. It seems from this telegram that we were just in time.'

'Just in time.'

'I suppose in another ten minutes you'd have been off?'

'Five. Five minutes. But I'm glad you managed to catch me at home.'

'So are we, Sir Frederick,' said the man with a chuckle. 'I suppose you'll come quietly?'

'As a mouse. Shall I go with you, or follow you in an hour's time?'

'Well, I think it would be more satisfactory if you were

to go with us,' said the man, grinning to his companion. 'Well, you *are* a game one, I will say that. 'Taint every man in your position as could cut jokes on the brink of penal servitude.'

'WHAT?'

'I'm afraid it'll be that, Sir Frederick. There's the bonds and the two bills on Pogson and Blythe—you know.'

'Forgery!' said Sir Frederick, throwing himself back into an arm-chair. 'It's monstrous! Come here, all of you,' shouted he up the stairs,—'come at once, will you?'

'I say, Sir Frederick, none of this, you know,' said the men, drawing their truncheons; 'you said you'd come quietly, and if anything of a rescue is attempted—'

'Nonsense, I'm coming quite quietly.' By this time the guests had lined the staircase, listening in great astonishment to the excited proceedings in the hall.

'Look here,' said Freddy to his friends. 'It's several degrees too bad. Five hours ago I commanded a slaver, and at four this afternoon I was a confectioner in the Borough with a wife and a fine boy. I have during the last few hours been apparently a prosperous banker, with another wife whose acquaintance I had much pleasure in making, and a couple of children for whom I can't account in any way whatever. No matter, I have a fine house in Lancaster Gate, and a circle of agreeable friends—more or less titled, some them—and all of them agreeable in many respects. Now, it seems I'm to forfeit all these advantages, because in some bygone time while I was not me but somebody else, Sir Frederick Foggerty and an unknown person called the 'Gone Coon' (probably an *alias*) forged certain bills and securities. Not I, mind you, but me, before I was I!'

The guests received this lucid statement of facts in mute surprise. 'Gettin' up the scaffolding for a plea of lunacy!' whispered one of the detectives to the other.

'Frederick!' screamed Lady Foggerty from the top of the stairs (she had gone upstairs to bathe her eyes, and only rushed down in time to hear the latter part of Sir Frederick's speech). 'Frederick—my darling, my beloved husband—don't take him gentlemen—he loves me so dearly—it's not true—he never did a dishonest act in his life—don't, don't take him—and on this day of all others!' and so saying, the poor soul fell fainting at his feet.

'Lead on,' said Sir Frederick.

And so they handcuffed him, and drove him off to Marlborough Street Police Station.

He had no substantial defence, but threw himself upon the mercy of the Court, in a speech which has been preserved in the annals of the Old Bailey, as the type of what such a speech should be.

He said, 'My Lord, and gentlemen of the jury, I canot deny that I, before I was me, may have been guilty of the charge imputed to me by the learned counsel for the prosecution, to whose very able and very lucid recital of the varied incidents of my career I have listened with much curiosity. That I have rendered myself amenable to the law I admit. But reflect. I have been for some hours past the toy and sport of a Twelfth Cake fairy, who has tempted me to change my original condition—that of a confectioner in the Borough—for, firstly, that of a slave captain; and secondly, that of a fraudulent banker. Was I a banker or only a manager to a bank? A manager—thank you. Don't you see the difficutly of my position? That fairy, gentlemen, has been the curse of my life. Let it be a warning to you all in that box, and above all to you my Lord on the bench, to beware of supernatural assistance. Trust to your own exertions, gentlemen, and you'll all do very well. I am very much obliged to you all for the attentive consideration you have devoted to my case, and as I know you are about to return a verdict of guilty (*here the jury bowed*), which will probably be followed by a sentence of penal servitude for life from my lord up there (*here the learned Judge bowed*), why, the best thing I can do is to make another change in my condition with all possible haste.'

So saying, he drew the Harlequin from his pocket, and put it into his mouth, uttering at the same time these remarkable words, 'I WISH THAT THE FAIRY ON THE TWELFTH CAKE, AND ALL THE CONSEQUENCES THAT SPRUNG FROM MY ACQUAINTANCE WITH HER, MAY BE BLOTTED OUT OF MY CAREER FOR EVER.'

And, behold, Mr. Frederick Foggerty found himself

once more in his little confectionery shop in the Borough Road in the act of selling the Twelfth Cake, with the Policeman, the Ship, and the Harlequin and the Fairy on the top of it, to a very bilious old lady with whom it was sure to disagree.

And Louisa was in the back shop with Theodore, and whenever Mr. Foggerty related the history of his adventure with the Twelfth Cake, she indignantly stopped him, telling him that he was a donkey, and had been dreaming.

Which I think was very likely the case.

The Burglar's Story

When I became eighteen years of age, my father, a distinguished begging-letter imposter, said to me, 'Reginald, I think it is time that you began to think about choosing a profession.'

These were ominous words. Since I left Eton, nearly a year before, I had spent my time very pleasantly, and very idly, and I was sorry to see my long holiday drawing to a close. My father had hoped to have sent me to Cambridge (Cambridge was a tradition in our family), but business had been very depressed of late, and a sentence of six months' hard labour had considerably straitened my poor father's resources.

It was necessary—highly necessary—that I should choose a calling. With a sigh of resignation, I admitted as much.

'If you like,' said my father, 'I will take you in hand, and teach you my profession, and, in a few years perhaps, I may take you into partnership; but, to be candid with you, I doubt whether it is a satisfactory calling for an athletic young fellow like you.'

'I don't seem to care about it, particularly,' said I.

'I'm glad to hear it,' said my father; 'it's a poor calling for a young man of spirit. Besides you have to grow grey in the service before people will listen to you. It's all very well as a refuge in old age; but a young fellow is likely to make but a poor hand at it. Now, I should like to consult your own tastes on so important a matter as the choice of a profession. What do you say? The Army?'

No, I didn't care for the army.

'Forgery? The Bar? Cornish Wrecking?'

'Father,' said I, 'I should like to be a forger, but I write such an infernal hand.'

'A regular Eton hand,' said he. 'Not plastic enough for

forgery; but you could have a writing master.'

'It's as much as I can do to forge my own name. I don't believe I should ever be able to forge anybody else's.'

'Anybody's else, you should say, not 'anybody else's.' It's dreadful barbarism. Eton English.'

'No,' said I, 'I should never make a fortune at it. As to wrecking—why you know how sea-sick I am.'

'You might get over that. Besides, you would deal with wrecks ashore, not wrecks at sea.'

'Most of it done in small boats, I'm told. A deal of small boat work. No, I won't be a wrecker. I think I should like to be a burglar.'

'Yes,' said my father, considering the subject. 'Yes, it's a fine manly profession; but it's dangerous, it's highly dangerous.'

'Just dangerous enough to be exciting, no more.'

'Well,' said my father, 'if you've a distinct taste for burglary I'll see what can be done.'

My dear father was always prompt with pen and ink. That evening he wrote to his old friend Ferdinand Stoneleigh, a burglar of the very highest professional standing, and in a week I was duly and formally articled to him, with a view to ultimate partnership.

I had to work hard under Mr. Stoneleigh.

'Burglary is a jealous mistress,' said he. 'She will tolerate no rivals. She exacts the undivided devotion of her worshippers.'

And so I found it. Every morning at ten o'clock I had to present myself at Stoneleigh's chambers in New Square, Lincoln's Inn, and until twelve I assisted his clerk with the correspondence. At twelve I had to go out prospecting with Stoneleigh, and from two to four I had to devote to finding out all particulars necessary to a scientific burglar in any given house. At first I did this merely for practice, and with no view to an actual attempt. He would tell me off to a house of which he knew all the particulars, and order me to ascertain all about the house and its inmates—their coming and going, the number of their servants, whether any of them were men, and, if so, whether they slept on the basement or not, and other details necessary to be known before a burglary could be safely attempted. Then he would compare my information with his own facts, and compliment or blame me, as I might deserve. He was a strict master, but always kind, just, and courteous, as became a highly polished gentleman of the old school. He was one of the last men who habitually wore hessians.

After a year's probation, I accompanied him on several expeditions, and had the happiness to believe that I was of some little use to him. I shot him eventually in the stomach, mistaking him for the master of a house into which we were breaking (I had mislaid my dark lantern), and he died on the grand piano. His dying wish was that his compliments might be conveyed to me. I now set up on my own account, and engaged his poor old clerk, who nearly broke his heart at his late master's funeral. Stoneleigh left no family. His money—about £12,000, invested for the most part in American railways—he left to the Society for Providing More Bishops; and his ledgers, daybooks, memoranda, and papers generally he bequeathed to me.

As the chambers required furnishing, I lost no time in commencing my professional duties. I looked through his books for a suitable house to begin upon, and found the following attractive entry:—

Thurloe Square.—No. 102.

House.—Medium.

Occupant.—John Davis, bachelor.

Occupation.—Designer of Dados.

Age.—86.

Physical Peculiarities.—Very feeble; eccentric; drinks; Evangelical; snores.

Servants.—Two housemaids, one cook.

Sex.—All female.

Particulars of Servants.—Pretty housemaid called Rachel; Jewess; open to attentions. Goes out for beer at 9 p.m.; snores. Ugly housemaid, called Bella; Presbyterian. Open to attentions; snores. Elderly cook; Primitive Methodist. Open to attentions; snores.

Fastenings.—Chubb's lock on street door, chain, and bolts. Bars to all basement windows. Practicable approach from third room, ground floor, which is shuttered and barred, but bar has no catch, and can be raised with table knife.

Valuable Contents of House.—Presentation plate from grateful aesthetes. Gold repeater. Mulready envelope. Two diamond rings. Complete edition of 'Bradshaw,' from 1834 to present time, 588 volumes, bound in limp calf.

General.—Mr. Davis sleeps second floor front; servants on third floor. Davis goes to bed at ten. No one on basement. Swarms with beetles; otherwise excellent house for purpose.

This seemed to me to be a capital house to try single handed. At twelve o'clock that very night I pocketed two crowbars, a bunch of skeleton keys, a centre-bit, a dark lantern, a box of silent matches, some putty, a life preserver, and a knife; and I set off at once for Thurloe Square. I remember that it snowed heavily. There was at least a foot of snow on the ground, and there was more to come. Poor Stoneleigh's particulars were exact in every detail. I got into the third room on the ground floor without any difficulty, and made my way into the dining-room. There was the presentation plate, sure enough—about 800 ounces, as I reckoned. I collected this, and tied it up so that I could carry it without attracting attention.

Just as I had finished, I heard a slight cough behind me. I turned and saw a dear old silver-haired gentleman in a dressing-gown standing in the doorway. The venerable gentleman covered me with a revolver.

My first impulse was to rush at and brain him with my life-preserver.

'Don't move', said he, 'or you're a dead man.'

A rather silly remark occurred to me to the effect that if I *did* move it would rather prove that I was a live man, but I dismissed it at once as unsuited to the business character of the interview.

'You're a burglar!' said he.

'I have that honour,' said I, making for my pistol-pocket.

'Don't move,' said he; 'I have often wished to have the pleasure of encountering a burglar, in order to be able to test a favourite theory of mine as to how persons of that class should be dealt with. But you mustn't move.'

I replied that I should be happy to assist him, if I could do so consistently with a due regard to my own safety.

'Promise me,' said I, 'that you will allow me to leave the house unmolested when your experiment is at an end?'

'If you will obey me promptly, you shall be at perfect liberty to leave the house.'

'You will neither give me into custody, nor take any steps to pursue me.'

'On my honour as a Designer of Dados,' said he.

'Good,' said I; 'go on.'

'Stand up,' said he, 'and stretch out your arms at right angles to your body.'

'Suppose I don't?' said I.

'I send a bullet through your left ear,' said he.

'But permit me to observe—' said I.

Bang! A ball cut off the lobe of my left ear.

The ear smarted, and I should have liked to attend to it, but under the circumstances I thought it better to comply with the whimsical old gentleman's wishes.

'Very good,' said he. 'Now do as I tell you, promptly and without a moment's hesitation, or I cut off the lobe of your right ear. Throw me that life-preserver.

'But—'

'Ah, would you?' said he, cocking the revolver.

The 'click' decided me. Besides, the old gentleman's eccentricity amused me, and I was curious to see how far it would carry him. So I tossed my life-preserver to him. He caught it neatly.

'Now take off your coat and throw it to me.'

I took off my coat, and threw it diagonally across the room.

'Now the waistcoat.'

I threw the waistcoat to him.

'Boots,' said he.

'They are shoes,' said I in some trepidation lest he should take offence when no offence was really intended.

'Shoes then,' said he.

I threw my shoes to him.

'Trousers,' said he.

'Come, come; I say,' exclaimed I.

Bang! The lobe of the other ear came off. With all his eccentricity the old gentleman was a man of his word. He had the trousers, and with them my revolver, which happened to be in the right-hand pocket.

'Now the rest of your drapery.'

I threw him the rest of my drapery. He tied up my clothes in the table-cloth; and, telling me that he wouldn't detain me any longer, made for the door with the bundle under his arm.

'Stop,' said I. 'What is to become of me?'

'Really, I hardly know,' said he.

'You promised me my liberty,' said I.

'Certainly,' said he. 'Don't let me trespass any further on your time. You will find the street door open; or, if from force of habit you prefer the window, you will have no difficulty in clearing the area railings.'

'But, I can't go like this! Won't you give me something to put on?'

'No,' said he, 'nothing at all. Good night.'

The quaint old man left the room with my bundle. I went after him, but I found that he had locked an inner door that led up stairs. The position was really a difficult one to deal with. I couldn't possibly go into the street as I was, and if I remained I should certainly be given into custody in the morning. For some time I looked in vain for something to cover myself with. The hats and great coats were no doubt in the inner hall, at all events they were not accessible under the circumstances. There was a carpet on the floor, but it was fitted to the recesses of the room, and, moreover, a heavy sideboard stood upon it.

However, there were twelve chairs in the room, and it was with no little pleasure I found on the back of each an antimacassar. Twelve antimacassars would go a long way towards covering me, and that was something.

I did my best with the antimacassars, but on reflection I came to the conclusion that they would not help me very much. They certainly covered me, but a gentleman walking through South Kensington at 3 a.m. dressed in nothing whatever but antimacassars, with the snow two feet deep on the ground, would be sure to attract attention. I might pretend that I was doing it for a wager, but who would believe me?

I grew very cold.

I looked out of the window, and presently saw the bull's-eye of a policeman who was wearily plodding through the snow. I felt that my only course was to surrender to him.

'Policeman,' said I, from the window, 'one word.'

'Anything wrong, sir?' said he.

'I have been committing a burglary in this house, and shall feel deeply obliged to you if you will kindly take me into custody.'

'Nonsense, sir,' said he; 'you'd better go to bed.'

'There is nothing I should like better, but I live in Lincoln's Inn, and I have nothing on but antimacassars; I am almost frozen. Pray take me into custody.'

'The street door's open,' said he.

'Yes,' said I. 'Come in.'

He came in. I explained the circumstances to him, and with great difficulty I convinced him that I was in earnest. The good fellow put his own great coat over me, and lent me his own handcuffs. In ten minutes I was thawing myself in Walton Street police station. In ten days I was convicted at the Old Bailey. In ten years I returned from penal servitude.

I found that poor Mr. Davis had gone to his long home in Brompton Cemetery.

For many years I never passed his house without a shudder at the terrible hours I spent in it as his guest. I have often tried to forget the incident I have been relating, and for a long time I tried in vain. Perserverance, however, met with its reward. I continued to try. Gradually one detail after another slipped from memory, and one lovely evening last May I found, to my intense delight, that I had absolutely forgotten all about it.

THE FINGER OF FATE

I AM GOING to give you an instance of the desperately strong measures Fate will take in order to bring about an event she has set her mind on.

I am a middle-aged bachelor, of staid and careful habits. I am pretty comfortably 'off,' having an independent income of £400 a-year, and a Civil Service pension of £700 a-year. I was for many years Secretary of the Warrant Officers' Shirt-frill and Shaving-Soap Department, a branch office under the Admiralty, Somerset House.

I have led a quiet and retired life—shunning society in its gayest sense, and associating intimately with three or four other heads of subordinate departments, and with no one else. I am naturally nervous, and, I am afraid, irritable. I hate bright colours, unnecessary conversation, useless noises—such as vocal and instrumental music, and the neighing of horses—and I can't bear to see people in quick motion. If I had my way, no one should speak to me except on matters of pure business, and only then when the communication could not be conveniently reduced into the form of a memorandum. Above all other things, I detest forward people—and above all other forward people, I detest strangers, who address me on immaterial topics in public conveyances.

I had occasion, a few weeks after my retirement from official life, to travel to Liverpool by the limited mail on my way to Jamaica. A railway journey to Liverpool is detestable, but posting is worse, and walking out of the question.

It was a cold night in April. There were very few passengers by the limited mail. There were only four first-class carriages to Liverpool: of these, three were occupied by ladies—one in each carriage; the fourth was a smoking carriage and empty. I don't smoke, but the train was on the point of starting, and the guard assured me that it was unlikely that we should take up any first-class passengers on our way. It was a new carriage, and had never been used. At all events I should be safe from female intrusion; so I jumped in. The train started, and I had my carriage all to myself. The train did not stop till we reached Rugby. At Rugby a lady opened the carriage door. She was a stout plain middle-aged woman—five-and-forty, I should say. She was extravagantly dressed in showy colours. Her complexion was very dark—she was, in fact, a Mulatto—and she wore a respectable moustache.

This wouldn't do; I could settle *her* at all events.

'I beg your pardon, ma'am, but this is a smoking carriage.'

'Exactly,' replied the lady, with a strong foreign accent, 'but I smokes.'

This was a contingency that I had never contemplated.

'You give me light, sar?' said the foreign lady.

Here was a chance of escape.

'I have no lights, madam.'

'Ah, dash!' she said. 'But, no consequence—Guard!'

The guard came up.

'You give me light?'

And he gave her a light, and then he disappeared.

I was nearly choking with the fumes of her detestable Havannah. At last I could stand it no longer.

'I beg you pardon, but I object to smoking.'

'Ah,' replied the lady, 'you object to smoke—you travel in smoking carriage. Donkey—jackass donkey!'

She said these last three words with the air of one who had done a short addition sum, and was stating the total.

I had never travelled abroad, but I knew that foreigners are remarkable for their politeness.

'I entered this carriage to avoid the society of ladies.'

'Me, too,' said the foreign lady. 'Dash! I hate lady. I like gentleman.' Then she added as an afterthought, 'You are haughty old customer, but I like *you*—you rummy old passenger!'

I was exceedingly annoyed at this. I plume myself upon my good taste in dress—that is to say, I study to dress myself in such a manner as to call for no remark of any kind, which I hold to be the perfection of good taste. My personal appearance is simply gentlemanly, without anything remarkable about it. It has been my constant study to be gentlemanly but usual; and to be called a 'rummy old passenger' was under the circumstances an irritating thing. However, I maintained a dignified silence.

It was a very cold night, and having regard to the strong dash of negro blood in my fellow-passenger's veins, thought it would irritate her if I let down the window.

Accordingly, I did so.

'Thank you, old passenger,' she said 'I like fresh airs. I let this one down too!' And she lowered the other window.

I couldn't stand the draught so I put up my window—and she put up hers. Something like this occurs in 'Box and Cox.'

I was sulkily furious by this time. In half-an-hour we should reach Stafford, and I determined to change my carriage at that station. In the meantime I tried to sleep, but the foreign lady kept up such an incessant clatter that sleep was out of the question.

'Where you going, old passenger? You not tell? Secret, eh? Ah, sly old dog! You old cashier, perhaps, bolting with bank moneys, eh? Confidential clerk with employer's cash-box in portmanteau, eh? Old boy going up north to marry old girl on the sly, eh? Bagman and ashamed of it, perhaps, eh, you old passenger? Bah! Bagman good as anybody else! Never be ashamed—look at me! Me not blush at myself. What you say I am?—eh? You not guess. Duchess? No! Countess? No! Lady of large property—wife of Liverpool merchant? Devil a bit! Missionary woman? No! Tight-rope dancer? No! Stewardess on West Indiaman spending pay? Yes—Hullo! What's that?'

I did not know what it was, but there was a sudden snap and our carriage suddenly slackened speed, and eventually stopped. I put my head out of the window. The coupling had broken, and our carriage and the guard's van had been separated from the rest of the train. The driver knew nothing about it; and there we were, half-way between Rugby and Stafford at 12 p.m. on a very cold April night!

'Good Heavens!' said I, in the very greatest alarm, 'the coupling has broken and we are left behind by the train! We shall be smashed by the next down train!'

'Not a bit, you old strange one!' replied she, without even looking out of the window. 'Guard at end of train. If we broke off, he broke off too.'

The guard had, in point of fact, rushed forward, moving his lantern in the faint hope of being able to attract the attention of the driver, but in vain. So he returned, very excited, but very sulky.

'What in the world are we to do?' asked I.

'Get out of this, you and your old woman, while I run back to Tamworth to telegraph. Come, out you go—'

'But where are we to go? It is raining hard, and we shall be soaked through and through.'

'There's a light yonder across the common. You'd better trot over there, you and your old woman, and knock 'em up. I don't know the country just here.' And off he went like lightning.

'His advice very good, my old man,' said my companion. 'I take your arm, and we trot. Come, rum chap.'

There was no help for it. I succumbed, and we had a squashy walk over a pathless and furzy common, half a mile in diameter. My companion had a knack of tumbling down in a sitting attitude at the faintest provocation; and if I lifted her up once I lifted her up twenty times. Twenty times sixteen stone is exactly two tons—which represents the weight I lifted off Copley Common that night. (I have since had reason to believe that her actual weight was fifteen stone three, but I say sixteen stone because I take into consideration the moisture with which her clothes were saturated.)

At length, after twenty minutes' difficult walking, we reached the light that had attracted our attention. It proceeded from the window of a very small cottage. We knocked, and eventually the door was opened to us. In the meantime, my companion, who had informed me that her name was Dolly Fortescue, sang negro songs in a deep contralto.

'Wot is it?' said the cottager.

'There has been an accident on the line, and we want shelter.'

'Wot'll you give?'

'A guinea,' said Miss Fortescue. 'This rum old card give a guinea.'

'Well, you can lie in the stable. My cottage is chock-full.'

He took a lantern and showed me the way to the 'stable,' which was a hut with one stall and a loose box in which was a very untidy donkey. I at once declined to share this stable with Miss Fortescue, preferring to risk a night in the rain. I stated my intention.

'Old boy is quite right. He's a rummy old passenger, but he's quite right. Come along, queer little old man—we walk somewheres else.'

'Now, lookee her,' said the man. 'Wot's your game, you two? Wot are yer up to? Is this here a lark? Where's my guinea! Come!—be a gentleman afore ye goes! None of this with ME you know! Give us 'old of my guinea! Come!'

'Old man,' said Dolly to me, 'pull out employer's cash-box and give guinea like bird.'

'Wot's this here about cash-boxes?' said the man. 'Come, out with that guinea! We hears a good deal about it, but we don't see none of it. Come, let's see some of it. Be a man!'

'I shall give you nothing,' said I. 'You are an insolent scoundrel!'

'Wot!' said the man. 'Wot's this here about cash-boxes? Come along o' me!' and he laid his hand upon my collar.

'You scoundrel!' said I, 'if I were a stronger man than you are I'd—'

'Wot, assault the perlice? My eye, here's a go! Come along o' me! I'm the constable. *I'll* give you a lodging. So it's cash-boxes, is it? Come along o' me—both on yer!'

And he led us to a square building at the back of his house, and, unlocking the door, pushed us in.

'Now,' he said, 'I'm a-going to search you.'

And he did; but he found nothing except a few sovereigns—for my money was in my dispatch box which had been placed in the luggage van.

'Now,' said he, 'how about searching your good woman? *I* ain't a-goin' to do it—and I ain't got a missus. Lookee here, suppose *you* do?'

'Sir, this lady is a total stranger to me.'

'Ah! separate responsibilities, eh? The hold story. Now, lookee here, ma'am, I ain't a-goin' to search you, because I've been properly brought up: but I'm a-goin' to shake you to see if you rattle.'

Miss Fortescue made no verbal reply, but pulled out a gigantic clasp knife.

'All rights,' said she. 'Come on policeman!'

He hesitated.

'Look, policeman, I tell you what I do. I walk out of this. Good nights!' and she did.

The policeman turned pale and civil.

'Ain't you goin' along with her, sir?' said he.

'I am not. I pass the night here.'

He retired, swearing fluently, and locked the door on me.

I could not sleep—but, at all events, I was free at last from my persecutrix. I was so pleased that I sang a merry song, and carved my name on the wall with a rusty nail, as other prisoners have done before me. The next day I was taken before a magistrate, who dismissed the case at once, and I resumed my journey.

When I reached Liverpool I found that my ship was on the point of sailing. My luggage had been placed on board, and my half-cabin was ready for me.

We had dreadful weather at sea; we were driven many hundred miles out of our course, and for three weeks after leaving Liverpool I was terribly ill, and did not leave my cabin. I believe I should not have left my cabin at all if I had not been thrown bodily out of it by a tremendous concussion one stormy night.

I rushed on deck, and found everything in the wildest confusion. A fearful storm was raging, and the ship had shifted her cargo. There was absolutely no hope for her, and it was impossible to launch a boat, even if it could have lived in such a sea.

I don't want to harrow anybody, so I will content myself with explaining that, amid the shrieks of three hundred people, the vessel foundered.

I always take the precaution, when at sea, of wearing a little india-rubber apparatus round my neck, which I inflate, and in that condition it prevents my head from going under. I inflated it hastily, and I found that it answered admirably. I was tossed about violently for some hours, and when the gale at length subsided, I looked around me. No land was visible; and as I rose and fell in the sulky lopping sea, I felt that my hour was at hand. I looked eagerly towards the horizon on all sides, in the vain hope of seeing a distant sail, but I saw none. There was, however, one thing in view—a dark round thing floating on the waves a mile or so from me. I struck out for it, and I was horrified to find that it was alive! Still I approached it, reflecting that death from a sea-monster was preferable to death from starvation, and to my amazement I found that it was making straight in my direction. On approaching it, I was appalled to find that it resembled nothing so much as a human head in a floating plate; and on coming within three or four yards, I discovered that it was the head of Miss Fortescue, supported above water by a contrivance similar in character to that which I myself wore. I should add that her great fat bouncy body and (I had no doubt) her legs were still connected with it.

'Not Miss Fortescue?' said I.

'Rummy old passenger, by Gar!' said she. 'What are you doing here, sar?'

'I am not here by choice. I was wrecked in the *Aurora Borealis*.'

'Me, too!' said she.

'You!' said I, 'Were you on board the *Aurora*?'

'—*Borealis*,' added she. 'Yes, me stewardess. How are you?'

'I am very cold, and this confounded thing has given me a crick in the neck.'

'Situation damp,' said she. 'Try this, you queer one!'

It was a flask of brandy. She held it to my lips until I had taken a comfortable draught.

'Two shillings,' said she, holding the bottle to the light to see how much I had taken.

'Here it is,' said I.

'Stewardess a shilling—make three.'

I determined to resist this extortion, for on that line of packets the steward's fee is included in the fare. I told her so.

'You mean old chap,' said Miss Fortescue. 'I give you nothing more.'

I tried to look dignified and indifferent, but it was of no use. You can't look dignified when you are perpetually bobbing up and down on a lopping sea supported entirely by an india-rubber bag round the neck. Besides, I was very hungry, and she had a large waterproof basket on her arm, so I gave her the shilling, which she bit and pocketed.

'Now then,' said she, 'what's to do next?'

'What have you got there?' said I.

'German sausage—cucumber—carrot—bottle barley-water—two tomatoes—a bloater—two eggs—one pound macaroni—head of endive—stick Spanish liquorice—three pounds snuff.'

'What are your terms for the carrot?'

'Carrot very dear out here, you peculiar old one. Carrot a guinea.'

'Hand it over.'

I gave her a guinea, and ate the carrot.

'Now,' said she, 'I go straight on in that direction for shore. Come along, old one!'

'Never!' said I; 'I will take the opposite point of the compass, and run my chance. Good bye.'

And I struck out vigorously in the opposite direction.

After a day and a half's vigorous swimming, I reached the point of a low sandy shore, which seemed to stretch for miles in a direction due south, as I judged from the position of the sun. I was well satisfied to feel dry ground under my legs again, and I landed with much gratitude.

I was extremely hungry, and I walked for miles along the shore picking up mussels and periwinkles, and eating them raw. I saw no trace of a human being of any kind, and as the sun went down I began to wish myself in the sea again. Night came on and I was hungry and alone. However, I still wandered on in a listless purposeless way until I fell over something that fell across my path. To my intense joy I found, on investigation, that it was a sleeping, breathing human being. I could not tell whether it was a man or a woman, as there was no moon, and the clothes he or she wore would have suited either sex equally well. I endeavoured to awaken the figure, but in vain, so I determined to sit by his or her side until morning. Accordingly I dropped myself into a sitting posture, when, to my extreme amazement, an explosion of fire took place immediately under me! The fearful idea flashed across me that the island was a mass of slumbering fire, only waiting for accidental contact with an exciting cause to blow itself and everything for miles around into the air! On closer examination, however, I found that I had sat down upon a box of vesuvains, and one of them had exploded.

It suddenly occcurred to me to use these vesuvians as a means of identifying my companion. I ignited one, but it was not a flaming vesuvian; it smouldered, and fizzed, and smelt, but afforded no assistance. I lit another and held it close to the person's nose, but it only illuminated a small circle as big as half-a-crown. I lit a third, and this time the red-hot end tumbled on the sleeper's cheek. The sleeper started up. It was Dolly Fortesque!

I was not a bit surprised. I had brought myself to look upon Dolly as my Fate. Dolly was not a bit surprised. She looked at me—grinned—and spoke.

'That hot, you odd one!'

When morning broke we looked about us. The island we found was about twenty-five miles long, and seven broad, principally rock—no vegetation—no fresh water. The island was crescent-shaped, the two horns being twenty miles asunder. I had landed on one horn, she on the other, and we had met in the middle. The only native inhabitants were periwinkles and mussels. So we set to work to make ourselves comfortable.

The object of this narrative is not to give a detailed account of the highly ingenious manner in which we continued to live comfortably, and even luxuriously, on our island, but rather to exhibit the caprices of a determined destiny.

I detested Dolly with all my heart, and avoided her whenever it was practicable; but she paid me every attention, and, notwithstanding her unpleasant appearance, she was really valuable to me. She christened the island 'Fortescue,' and crowned me its monarch. My first act as king was to try her for drawing her knife on the policeman in Bembridge lock-up, and by that means breaking out of custody. She was found guilty by an impartial jury of ME, and sentenced to transportation for life to the other side of the island. She went meekly and uncomplainingly, but, as she took all our cooking implements with her, I was obliged to follow.

This inconvenient life went on for thirteen years. At the expiration of that period my kingdom was visited by a missionary ship, which had driven out of her course. I signalled, and my signals were answered. A boat full of Baptist missionaries put off to us, bearing many bales of tracts for our conversion. They were very much disappointed and disgusted when they heard we were Christians, and when we added we were Protestants, they moodily returned to their boat and mechanically put to sea.

I screamed aloud in my terror at their contemplated departure without us.

Their chief explained that their mission was to convert, and that we needed no conversion.

'You are Christian,' said he—'Protestant, and no doubt, Baptist. What can we do?'

'No,' said I, as a ray of hope broke through the clouds that were gathering around us, 'not Baptist—Church of England!'

'Ha!' said their leader; 'will you let me make a Baptist of you, if we take you with us?'

'I am open to conviction,' said I.

'And your wife?' said he.

'This is NOT my wife!' said I, in a passion.

'Shocking, indeed!' said he. 'Will you marry her if I take you off?'

'Yes,' said Dolly, 'he will marry me; you melancholy old Presbyterian!'

So he took us into the boat, and we left the island. We were married as soon as we reached England.

In a week my wife had had enough of me. The arrears of my pension amounted to something considerable, and she ran off with them. I ran after her, but I could never find her. I suppose, now that I want her, I never shall.

Little Mim

THE ONLY point on which Joe Paulby and I could ever bring ourselves to agree was that his cousin Mim was the only young lady in the world who was worth falling in love with. Joe Paulby was eight, I was seven, and his cousin Mim was six. Joe was a strong, rough, troublesome boy, and I was small and weak and delicate; and if it had not been that we were both deeply in love with the same young lady I believe I should have hated him. That solitary bond of sympathy served to bind us more or less firmly to each other, and I seldom quarrelled with him except when his regard for her showed signs of cooling down.

She was a pretty, fragile little lady, with quaint ways of her own, and a gentle frightened manner of dealing with her boisterous playmate which seldom failed to bring him to a sense of order. She loved us both very dearly, but I think Joe was her favourite. Although a rude, unpleasant boy to others, to her he was quiet and gentle enough; but perhaps this palpable submission appealed more directly to the little lady than my undemonstrative and colourless affection. But she was very fond of me for all that.

Neither Mim nor I had any parents, and we lived with Joe's papa in a great gaunt, draughty house in Bloomsbury Square. Captain Paulby was our guardian—a tall, bony, unsympathetic widower—who governed his house as though it had been a regiment of soldiers. A scale of dietary was hung up in the nursery, and from it one learnt how many quarter-ounces of cocoa, how many half pounds of bread, and how many tablespoonfuls of arrowroot we consumed in the week. An order-book was brought into the nursery every morning, in which the detail of the day's duties was carefully set out, and to the instructions it contained implicit and unmurmuring obedience was exacted. It regulated the hours of rising and going to bed, the school hours and the hours of relaxation, when and where we were to walk, and what we were to wear.

We were placed in charge of a nurse—Nurse Starke—a

tall, muscular, hardened woman of forty. She had a stern unrelenting face, close lips, hard grey eyes, and a certain smooth roundness of figure, which on looking back, suggests the idea of her having been turned in a lathe. I never see the masculine old woman who lets lodgings in a pantomime without thinking of Nurse Starke. I am bound to say, however, that she was scrupulously, indeed aggravatingly, clean and neat, and in that respect of course, the analogy falls to the ground.

Nurse Starke was not actively unkind to us. Indeed, I believe she had cheated herself into a belief that she was rather weak-minded and indulgent than otherwise; but in this she was in error. I believe she was fond of us in a hard unyielding way, but she was sudden and impulsive in her movements, and never handled us without hurting us. There was a housemaid—Jane Cotter—who occasionally helped to put us to bed, and sometimes Nurse Starke undressed us while Jane put our hair into curl papers, and sometimes Nurse Starke did the curling while Jane undressed us. And the manner in which these duties were to be divided became a matter of no light speculation to us as evening approached, for it was Nurse Starke's custom to pull the locks of hair out to their full length, and then roll them round a piece of paper, twisting the ends together when the curl had been rolled well home, whereas Jane Cotter first made the curl up flat with her fingers, and then encased it gently in a triangular paper, which she pinched with the tongs. Jane Cotter's flat curls were pleasant to sleep upon, but Nurse Starke's corkscrews placed a comfortable night's rest out of the question. It is impossible to sleep in peace with a double row of balls, each as big as a large chestnut, round your head. You can't move without giving four or five of them a wrench.

I think we must have been sufficiently happy as a rule, or Sunday would not have stood out in such gaunt and desolate contrast to the other days of the week. There reigned in our nursery an unaccountable fiction that Sunday was a holiday; and in deference to this tradition we endeavoured to cheat ourselves into a belief that we were glad when that day arrived. Sunday began at a very early hour in Bloomsbury. It began to ring itself in at half-past seven when we got up, and continued to ring itself through the day at short intervals until it finally rang itself out, and us into bed, at half-past eight in the evening. There were drawbacks, however, to our enjoyment of the day. I think we were required to tackle more Collect than is good for a child of six or seven, and perhaps we did not quite understand the bearing of that Shorter Catechism which a bench of thoughtful Bishops has prepared for the express use of very young children. Even Nurse Starke, a high authority on all points of Church controversy, never succeeded in placing its meaning quite beyond all question. But Nurse Starke had a special Sunday frame of mind which discouraged close questioning, and on that day of the week, she was exceptionally short and sharp in her replies. She baffled our interrogatories by pointing out to us that there was nothing so unbecoming as a tendency to ask questions; which seemed to us a little unreasonable, when we considered the inquisitive character of *her* share in the Catechism.

I believe I liked going to Church, though I am sure Joe Paulby did not. That rugged boy never looked so hot or so rumpled as he did during Divine Service. As I look back upon Joe in church, I am always reminded of the appearance of restless decorum presented by a Christy Minstrel 'Bones' during the singing of a plaintive ballad. Joe occupied himself during the service in laying the foundations of a series of pains and penalties which usually lasted well into Thursday, for Nurse Starke had a quick eye for misdemeanours, and every crime had its apportioned punishment. Poor little Mim was too delicate to go to church, and used to sit at home in theological conference with Jane Cotter, whose picturesque and highly dramatic ideas of future rewards and punishments had a special interest for the poor little lady.

For Mim had been told that even children die sometimes, and both Nurse Starke and Jane had a long catalogue of stories in which good little people were cut off in their earliest years, and bad little people lived on to an evil old age. Mim was often weak and ailing, and at such times the recollection of these stories came upon her. Nurse Starke's grim, hard manner relaxed when she was speaking to the little sick child, and her kindness to Mim, gaunt and grudging as it was, seemed to increase with the trouble the child gave her—a never-ceasing source of wonderment to Joe and myself, who were only in favour when we ceased to occupy Nurse Starke's attention. Nurse Starke had a brother, a boy of twelve or thereabouts (though we believed him to be eight-and-twenty at least), who was a page at a doctor's in Charlotte Street; and Nurse Starke, as a great treat, used to allow this young gentleman to spend the afternoon with us, and entertain us with his varied social powers. Gaspar—for that was his unfortunate name—was a talented boy with a taste for acrobatics, conjuring, killing flies, and putting lob-worms down Mim's back; but notwithstanding these powerful recommendations we looked coldly upon him, and, on the whole, discouraged his visits. He had a way of challenging Joe and me to fight him with one of his hands tied behind his back, by way of a handicap, which was not what you look for in a visitor, and moreover compromised our reputation for valour in Mim's eyes. On the whole he was not popular with us, and eventually he was proscribed by Nurse Starke herself on a charge of filling the nursery candle with gunpowder, which exploded and burnt poor little Mim's eyebrows and eye-lashes. Gaspar eventually got into trouble about some original draughts of his own composition, which he supplied to his master's patients as healing waters made up in accordance with that gentleman's prescriptions, and spent several years in a reformatory.

I have a dismal impression of the wretched afternoons that Mim and Joe and I used to spend together in our great bare play-room. We were locked in by Nurse Starke at about five every afternoon, and not released until seven, when we had supper, and as the shadows deepened and the fire got lower and lower, we crowded together in a corner for warmth, and told each other strange stories of princes and noblemen who were tortured by cruel and vindictive page-boys; with an occasional touch from Joe Paulby upon caverns, demons, vampires, and other ghostly matters until poor little Mim screamed aloud with terror.

She was a pretty, fragile, sweet-tempered, clinging little soul, far too delicate for the coarse inconsiderate treatment to which she was subjected in common with ourselves. So at last she became seriously ill, and we noticed that the poor little child grew paler and thinner in her cot, day after day, day after day. She was very cheerful, although so weak, and when the tall, grave, kind doctor came—once a day at first, and then toward the last (for she died) two or three times a day—she would say in reply to his question, 'And how is our Little Mim?' that she was much better, and hoped in a day or two to be quite well again. After a time she was removed to another room which was always darkened, and to which we were seldom admitted, and only one at a time. An odd change seemed to come over us all. Nurse Starke was quite kind now, and used to read to her (but now about good children who lived and were very happy), and tell stories, and make beef-tea for her, and turn the cold side of the pillow to her poor little fevered head. And the oddest part of the thing was that Nurse Starke was kind to us too, and used to come of her own accord to tell us how Mim was (she was always a litte better), and what messages she had sent to us, and how she seemed to take a new pleasure in the toys she had once discarded. And then she would take us, one at a time, to the sick room, and we were allowed at first to speak to her, but afterwards only sit on the edge of the bed, (it was such a big bed now!), and hold her little dry hand. Joe Paulby would come back crying (it was a strange thing to see *him* cry, and it touched me as it touches me now to see a strong man in tears), and he would spend his half-pence—they were rare enough, poor fellow—in picture-books for our poor little dying wife. But a time came when even the picture-books were forbidden, and then the whole house was enjoined to silence, and the grave doctor—graver now than ever—came and went on tip-toe. And if we stole to the little girl's bedroom as we often did, we were pretty sure to find great hard Nurse Starke in tears, or with traces of tears upon her face; and once when Joe and I crept down to the room, and looked in at the half-opened door, we saw the shadow of Nurse Starke on her knees, thrown by the flickering firelight on the wall. Then we knew that the end was near.

One day Captain Paulby came home earlier than usual, looking very grave, and with him came the kind doctor, and with them another doctor, an older man, but also very kind. They went up into little Mim's room, and they stayed so long that Joe and I stole down from our old dark play-room to hear, if we could, the reason of his father's unexpected return. And Joe and I cried as if our hearts would break, for our dear little wife was dying.

Captain Paulby came out of the room, and seeing us in the passage, told us quite kindly to go back to the play-room. Joe Paulby went, but I begged Captain Paulby to let me see my dear little playmate once more, and alarmed by my excited manner and my choking sobs, he admitted me.

I had not seen her for two days, and she was greatly changed. She looked so little in that big bed that the two doctors and Captain Paulby and Nurse Starke seemed absolutely gigantic as they all bent, silently and without motion, over the little child. I think we must have remained so for nearly two hours, the silence undisturbed except by an occasional whisper from one of the doctors, and a sob from Nurse Starke. When I first went into the dark room Mim was asleep, but eventually she recognized me, and begged to be allowed to kiss me as she was nearly quite well. They laid me on the bed by her side, and her little thin arms were placed round my neck, and there we lay motionless, both of us in deep silence. At length I became conscious of a movement among the doctors, and then a loud ringing wail from Nurse Starke told me that my little wife was quite, quite well again.

ANGELA

An Inverted Love Story

I AM A poor paralysed fellow who, for many years past, has been confined to a bed or a sofa. For the last six years I have occupied a small room, giving on to one of the side canals of Venice, and having no one about me but a deaf old woman, who makes my bed and attends to my food; and there I eke out a poor income of about thirty pounds a year by making water-colour drawings of flowers and fruit (they are the cheapest models in Venice), and these I send to a friend in London, who sells them to a dealer for small sums. But, on the whole, I am happy and content.

It is necessary that I should describe the position of my room rather minutely. Its only window is about five feet above the water of the canal, and above it the house projects some six feet, and overhangs the water, the projecting portion being supported by stout piles driven into the bed of the canal. This arrangement has the disadvantage (among others) of so limiting my upward view that I am unable to see more than about ten feet of the height of the house immediately opposite to me, although, by reaching as far out of the window as my infirmity will permit, I can see for a considerable distance up and down the canal, which does not exceed fifteen feet in width. But, although I can see but little of the material house opposite, I can see its reflection upside down in the canal, and I take a good deal of inverted interest in such of its inhabitants as show themselves from time to time (always upside down) on its balconies and at its windows.

When I first occupied my room, about six years ago, my attention was directed to the reflection of a little girl of thirteen or so (as nearly as I could judge), who passed every day on a balcony just above the upward range of my limited field of view. She had a glass of flowers and a crucifix on a little table by her side; and as she sat there, in fine weather, from early morning until dark, working assiduously all the time, I concluded that she earned her living by needle-work. She was certainly an industrious little girl, and, as far as I could judge by her upside-down reflection, neat in her dress and pretty. She had an old mother, an invalid, who, on warm days, would sit on the balcony with her, and it interested me to see the little maid wrap the old lady in shawls, and bring pillows for her chair, and a stool for her feet, and every now and again lay down her work and kiss and fondle the old lady for half a minute, and then take up her work again.

Time went by, and as the little maid grew up, her reflection grew down, and at last she was quite a little woman of, I suppose, sixteen or seventeen. I can only work for a couple of hours or so in the brightest part of the day, so I had plenty of time on my hands in which to watch her movements, and sufficient imagination to weave a little romance about her, and to endow her with a beauty which, to a great extent, I had to take for granted. I saw—or fancied that I could see—that she began to take an interest in *my* reflection (which, of course, she could see as I could see hers); and one day, when it appeared to me that she was looking right at it—that is to say when her reflection appeared to be looking right at me—I tried the desperate experiment of nodding to her, and to my intense delight her reflection nodded in reply. And so our two reflections became known to one another.

It did not take me very long to fall in love with her, but a long time passed before I could make up my mind to do more than nod to her every morning, when the old woman moved me from my bed to the sofa at the window, and again in the evening, when the little maid left the balcony for that day. One day, however, when I saw her reflection looking at mine, I nodded to her, and threw a flower into the canal. She nodded several times in return, and I saw her direct her mother's attention to the incident. Then every morning I threw a flower into the water for 'good morning,' and another in the evening for 'good night,' and I soon discovered that I had not altogether thrown them in vain, for one day she threw a flower to join mine, and she laughed and clapped her hands when she saw the two flowers join forces and float away together. And then every morning and every evening she threw her flower when I threw mine, and when the two flowers met she clapped her hands, and so did I; but when they were separated, as they sometimes were, owing to one of them having met an obstruction which did not catch the other, she threw up her hands in a pretty affectation of despair, which I tried to imitate but in an English and unsuccessful fashion. And when they were rudely run down by a passing gondola (which happened not unfrequently) she pretended to cry, and I did the same. Then, in pretty pantomime, she would point downwards to the sky to tell me that it was Destiny that had caused the shipwreck of our flowers, and I, in pantomime, not nearly so pretty, would try to convey to her that Destiny would be kinder next time, and that perhaps to-morrow our flowers would be more fortunate—and so the innocent courtship went on. One day she showed me her crucifix and kissed it, and thereupon I took a little silver crucifix that always stood by me, and kissed that, and so she knew that we were one in religion.

One day the little maid did not appear on her balcony, and for several days I saw nothing of her; and although I threw my flowers as usual, no flower came to keep it company. However, after a time, she reappeared, dressed in black, and crying often, and then I knew that the poor child's mother was dead, and, as far as I knew, she was alone in the world. The flowers came no more for many days, nor did she show any sign of recognition, but kept her eyes on her work, except when she placed her handkerchief to them. And opposite to her was the old lady's chair, and I could see that, from time to time, she would lay down her work and gaze at it, and then a flood of tears would come to her relief. But at last one day she roused herself to nod to me, and then her flower came, day by day, and my flower went forth to join it, and with varying fortunes the two flowers sailed away as of yore.

But the darkest day of all to me was when a good-looking young gondolier, standing right end uppermost in his gondola (for I could see *him* in the flesh), worked his craft alongside the house, and stood talking to her as she sat on the balcony. They seemed to speak as old friends—indeed, as well as I could make out, he held her by the hand during the whole of their interview which lasted quite half an hour. Eventually he pushed off, and left my heart heavy within me. But I soon took heart of grace, for as soon as he was out of sight, the little maid threw two flowers growing on the same stem—an allegory of which I could make nothing, until it broke upon me that she meant to convey to me that he and she were brother and sister, and that I had no cause to be sad. And thereupon I nodded to her cheerily, and she nodded to me, and laughed aloud, and I laughed in return, and all went on again as before.

Then came a dark and dreary time, for it became necessary that I should undergo treatment that confined me absolutely to my bed for many days, and I worried and fretted to think that the little maid and I should see each other no longer, and worse still, that she would think that I had gone away without even hinting to her that I was going. And I lay awake at night wondering how I could let her know the truth, and fifty plans flitted through my brain, all appearing to be feasible enough at night, but absolutely wild and impracticable in the morning. One day—and it was a bright day indeed for me—the old woman who tended me told me that a gondolier had inquired whether the English signor had gone away or had died; and so I learnt that the little maid had been anxious about me, and that she had sent her brother to inquire, and the brother had no doubt taken to her the reason of my protracted absence from the window.

From that day, and ever after during my three weeks of bed-keeping, a flower was found every morning on the ledge of my window, which was within easy reach of anyone in a boat; and when at last a day came when I could be moved, I took my accustomed place on my sofa at the window, and the little maid saw me, and stood on her head (so to speak) and clapped her hands upside down with a delight that was as eloquent as my right-end-up delight could be. And so the first time the gondolier passed my window I beckoned to him, and he pushed alongside, and told me, with many bright smiles, that he was glad indeed to see me well again. Then I thanked him and his sister for their many kind thoughts about me during my retreat, and I then learnt from him that her name was Angela, and that she was the best and purest maiden in all Venice, and that anyone might think himself happy indeed who could call her sister, but that he was happier even than her brother, for he was to be married to her, and indeed they were to married the next day.

Thereupon my heart seemed to swell to bursting, and the blood rushed through my veins so that I could hear it and nothing else for a while. I managed at last to stammer forth some words of awkward congratulation, and he left me, singing merrily, after asking permission to bring his bride to see me on the morrow as they returned from church.

'For,' said he, 'my Angela has known you very long—ever since she was a child, and she has often spoken to me of the poor Englishman who was a good Catholic, and who lay all day long for years and years on a sofa at a window, and she had said over and over again how dearly she wished she could speak to him and comfort him; and one day, when you threw a flower into the canal, she asked me whether she might throw another, and I told her yes, for he would understand that it meant sympathy for one sorely afflicted.'

And so I learned that it was pity, and not love, except indeed such love as is akin to pity, that prompted her to interest herself in my welfare, and there was an end of it all.

For the two flowers that I thought were on one stem were two flowers tied together (but I could not tell that), and they were meant to indicate that she and the gondolier were affianced lovers, and my expressed pleasure at this symbol delighted her, for she took it to mean that I rejoiced in her happiness.

And the next day the gondolier came with a train of other gondoliers, all decked in their holiday garb, and on his gondola sat Angela, happy, and blushing at her happiness. Then he and she entered the house in which I dwelt, and came into my room (and it was strange indeed, after so many years of inversion, to see her with her head above her feet!), and then she wished me happiness and a speedy restoration to good health (which could never be); and I in broken words and with tears in my eyes, gave her the little siver crucifix that had stood by my bed or my table for so many years. And Angela took it reverently, and crossed herself, and kissed it, and so departed with her delighted husband.

And as I heard the song of the gondoliers as they went

their way—the song dying away in the distance as the shadows of the sundown closed around me—I felt that they were singing the requiem of the only love that had ever entered my heart.

THE FAIRY'S DILEMMA

I WAS BORN, a good many hundred years ago (never mind how many—a lady never likes her age to be known), in a rather gaudy and extremely complex arrangement of large gilt lilies, metallic leaves of curious scroll-like structure, revolving wheels of a glittering silvery material and large marine bivalves, constructed entirely of mother-of-pearl. My birth was accompanied by a shower of what looked at first like silver rain, but as it only shook, and wetted nobody, it must have been something else. One of the large bivalves opened, and I issued from it, not in the form of spat, like a mere oyster, but full grown and dressed in a very low and extremely short white Tarletane frock, with about fifteen skirts to it, each fifteen inches long. I wore a wreath of metallic flowers (which caught my hair in a very tiresome manner), and I carried a light wand with a tin star at the top of it. My arms were bare (except that I wore several diamond bracelets of extraordinary value), my legs were covered with a pink silk webbing—which had a strong tendency to 'go in ladders'—and on my feet I wore white satin shoes much too short in the toes. And so I was born. I have often thought that a medical practitioner would have considered it an interesting case to attend. It might have been worked up into a very readable paper for the *Lancet*.

It happened that I was the heir-presumptive to a Fairy Crown, and consequently very considerable pains were taken with my education. I was placed under the tutelage of a stout but experienced old Fairy, who had long retired from the active exercise of the profession, and who confined her energies to teaching polite accomplishments to half a dozen promising young fairies of good family. These accomplishments included the art of dancing (of which all fairies are extremely fond, though very few attain to anything like excellence in that graceful exercise)—the nice conduct of a silver wand, so manipulated as to bring about surprising and unexpected dusty mechanical changes at will—the art of hanging from the firmament on the end of a stout wire, of reposing motionless and in apparent comfort on the sharp edge of a large tin leaf, and the very difficult manoeuvre of shooting up through the solid earth and down again without losing my balance. Nothing is so calculated to cover a fairy with confusion as tumbling forward on her nose when shooting up through the floor, except, perhaps, being taken with a fit of sneezing when hanging from the petals of a metallic lily. I also received some rudimentary instruction in the process of interfering (quite unwarrantably, as it seemed to me) with the course of a true and honourable attachment by transforming the young people who had formed it into a couple of dumb mountebanks, who were compelled to dance for all futurity in more or less insufficient costumes through the muddy streets of London—and why always London, and never Constantinople or Paris, goodness only knows. This is done with the humane design of rendering them an inestimable service, but it always seemed to me to be a misplaced attention. Another unaccountable part of my duty was to pretend to punish a couple of persons of vicious tendencies by changing them into a pair of prosperous profligates, whose privilege it became to perpetrate every kind of dishonesty, every description of brutality, every form of unbridled depravity, with conspicuous success and absolute immunity from the penal consequences usually attendant on a course of deliberate violation of laws human and laws divine. Finally, I had to acquire the difficult and (as I think) unnecessary art of carrying on all my conversation in rhymed couplets. I have no ear whatever for metre or for rhyme, but, happily, that defect is not so important as it might, at first sight, appear to be, for in fairyland considerable latitude is allowed in this respect. A syllable or two more or less than the academic allowance to a line is not regarded as a serious lapse, and a liberal latitude is permitted in the matter of rhyme. For instance, you may rhyme 'well-wisher' with 'extinguisher,' or even 'sideboard' with 'School Board,' without any fear of incurring reproof. Still, with all this latitude, it is most tiresome to be compelled to carry on the business and pleasure of one's life in decasyllabic couplets. It is especially hampering when one is quarrelling.

I don't know that I need trouble you at any greater length with the details of my education, because this is not so much a history of my life as a history of a most unfortunate error which I committed in the course of my duty as a fairy guardian to two young people who had formed an attachment to each other, and whose arrangements were interfered with by a malignant demon called Alcohol. I should perhaps have stated that the great object of a fairy's existence is to thwart the schemes of a demon. Her interest in the fortunes of her *protégés* is purely incidental. She really cares nothing about them, personally, but if a demon should happen to concern himself with their love affairs it becomes her duty to defeat that demon's schemes, whatever they may be, and on the last occasion upon which I was called upon to discharge this duty I made a pretty mess of it, as you will presently see. But it is some comfort to reflect that in this particular case I am about to narrate the demon made as great a donkey of himself as I did. I am sorry to have taken up so much space with these preliminary details, but so much misapprehension exists as to the nature and occupation of fairies that I find it difficult to resist the temptation of explaining what commonplace people we really are and how much ridiculous and unmeaning drudgery we have to go through. It is, moreover, a great treat to be allowed to express myself in prose, and when I begin I feel as if I could go on for ever. But I won't.

One day, while I was practising 'battements,' holding on to the edge of a waterfall to preserve my balance, news was brought to me that the Demon Alcohol had, for some reasons best known to himself, arranged to give his counsel and support to a wicked Baronet, Sir Trevor Mauleverer, whose errant fancy had rested, for the moment, upon a beautiful young governess named Jane Collins, employed by a wealthy Nonconformist sugar broker on Clapham Common. Jane was engaged to a struggling medical practitioner, Arthur Perkins, who (owing perhaps to his incessant struggling) had failed to establish anything like a remunerative practice. As a matter of course, it became my instant duty to foil the demon in his designs by doing everything in my power to enable the worthy young surgeon to marry Jane as soon as possible, and take her, once and for all, beyond the sphere of Sir Trevor's temptations. Accordingly I lost no time in introducing myself into the laboratory of the Demon Alcohol.

The Demon Alcohol resided in a vast pantomimic cellar, hung about with heavy growths of a fungoid nature and furnished with wine and spirit vats of Brobdingnagian proportions. Being on the whole a kind-hearted fiend, he kept a great many domestic pets about him, such as huge toads, slimy lizards, big dusky bats, and gigantic hairy spiders of forbidding aspect. Large black beetles, with human arms and legs, crawled over the floor, and unpleasant speckled snakes wriggled in every direction. His domestic establishment consisted of a dozen green imps who went about their household duties with torches of blazing spirits in ther hands—a dangerous practice, as it appeared to me, having regard to their immediate surroundings. These imps were dumb, but not deaf; they expressed obedience and submission by bowing their heads with their arms stretched out and their legs very far apart. It was not a prepossessing household, but they seemed to understand their work and to do it satisfactorily. Still I think they might have killed the black beetles. The Demon himself I rather liked, for, except that he erred in the direction of a tendency to convivial excess, he was rather an amusing companion. However, he was undoubtedly a fiend of lax principles, and I was rather glad, on the whole, that my duty required that I should protect myself from the effects of his dangerous fascinations. He was an entertaining scamp.

I interrupted the Demon as he was confiding to his domestic household the plans he had formed for fostering the unworthy attachment of Sir Trevor for poor Jane Collins. The wall opened at my command (it was only lath and plaster), and I appeared in all my glory with a revolving silver star behind me.

The Demon seemed much surprised at my unannounced intrusion. He exclaimed: 'Why, who is this?'

I replied: 'The Fairy Rosebud.'

THE DEMON: '*Is* it?'

Greatly indebted to you for this visit.
What do you want?'

(*This was not polite, but it was his whim to cultivate an abrupt Abernethian manner which was not without its charm.*)

I replied: 'I've come your plans to thwart—
Your plans to carry off Miss Collins.'

THE DEMON (*spinning out the word to an absurd length*): Wha-a-awt? (*He made such a funny face that I could have kissed the dear.*)

'How are you going to do it, ducky?'

MYSELF (*looking much more offended than I really was*): 'Sir!!!
No liberties, I beg.'

(*The Demon was at an obvious loss for a rhyme to 'Sir' that would do. I heard him muttering to himself 'her—fur—stir—purr—cur—occur.' This last seemed to answer his purpose.*)

THE DEMON: 'Does it occur
To you that this is interference?'

MYSELF: 'Yes;
It's meant for that.'

(*I took good care so to break my lines that the responsibility of supplying the rhyme would always fall upon him. This is a dodge much cultivated in Fairyland.*)

THE DEMON: 'You cause me much distress!'

(*Here he pretended to weep so amusingly that I could scarcely keep my countenance.*)

Well, I needn't detail all our conversation. The upshot of it was that he was to do his best to help the Wicked Baronet to carry off the Virtuous Governess, and I was to do all I could to enable the Blameless Medical Practitioner to marry her, and so foil both the Wicked Baronet and the Amusing Demon. Our interview ended in a duet and (you will be surprised to hear) a step-dance. It is another anomaly of my calling that we have to be ready with extemporised parodies of all the commonest music-hall songs of the day, and that every duet must end with an absurd step-dance, even when the duettists are on the very worst of terms. However, the Demon was very clever at step-dancing, and his performances in this direction were always entertaining. Altogether, and in spite of his being distinctly plain, he was a very fascinating person.

My next act of duty was to call upon Dr. Perkins at his residence in Little Magog Villas, Little Magog Hill, East Brixton. I introduced myself (unannounced as usual) into his consulting room while he was engaged with his principal patient, Mr. Pharpar Whortle, a stout gentleman of serious aspect who suffered from gout, and who was pulling on his sock after having had his foot professionally examined. Dr. Perkins appeared to be surprised and not a little confused at my abrupt and unexpected appearance. Mr. Whortle, whose countenance flashed crimson with virtuous indignation, put on his boot and took up his hat and umbrella, and expressed, in an unnecessarily prolonged speech, his extreme disapproval of my conduct in presuming to appear before him—an elder of his chapel—in what he described as an unpardonably indelicate costume. He not only denounced my appearance as an outrage on his moral sense, but was good enough to explain (for my information) in what particular respect my costume fell short of what it should be. Having pointed out to me again and again the shocking impropriety of fifteen-inch skirts (he dwelt on this at a length wholly out of proportion to the subject of his discourse), he sternly reproved Dr. Perkins for permitting a young woman so imperfectly clothed to enter his consulting room (particularly when engaged with a sockless chapel elder), and having repeated all the aguments he had employed in his previous address to me, that there might be no mistake about his being in earnest, he took an indignant but reluctant leave of us, expressing his determination never to consult Dr. Perkins again. However, he returned in a minute to give me a card of admission to a Tea Party for the Reformation of Young Women who Required It.

Dr. Perkins was extremely angry with me.

'Who in the world are you, and what the deuce do you mean by coming into my consulting room without knocking?'

I replied:—

'I am the Fairy Rosebud, from above,
I watch young lovers and protect their love;
When they're in serious danger I descend,
And from all ill their courtship I defend.'

'Now look here,' said Dr. Perkins, 'I've no time for any nonsense; you've done me an irreparable injury, and the sooner you remove yourself the better.'

'But I'm the Fairy Rosebud,' I exclaimed.

'I don't care who you are. Be off at once. I've nothing for you, and if you don't go I'll send for the police.'

'It's very hard,' said I. 'I came here to do you a service, and you treat me as if I were I don't know what.' (I dropped into prose when I found that he did not consider it necessary to carry on the conversation in metrical form.) 'But I can make allowance for you—you're angry and upset, and I don't wonder. So I shall help and protect you all the same, whether you like it or not; and whenever you find that the course of your true love doesn't run smooth you've only to invoke the Fairy Rosebud, and she will pull you through.'

While I was speaking, Dr. Perkins rang a bell. A general servant with soapy arms entered.

'Go for a policeman,' said he.

Thereupon I vanished. I thought it the wiser course to take.

Of course it was extremely rude of Dr. Perkins to treat his guardian Fairy so abruptly, and, if I had consulted my own inclinations I should have washed my hands of him and his tuppenny-ha'penny love affairs, once and for all. But I had a duty to discharge. I had to defeat the machinations of the Demon Alcohol at any cost, so I affected to take a more kindly and considerate view of the Doctor's conduct towards me than I should otherwise have done.

As my visit to Dr. Perkins was not attended with all the success that I could have desired, I determined to introduce myself to Miss Collins at her employers' residence at Clapham in order to assure her of my goodwill and protection. Thinking that I had perhaps placed myself in a false position by not appearing before Dr. Perkins under sufficiently impressive circumstances, I determined to show Miss Collins that in dealing with me she was dealing with a Fairy Queen of a very high order. So I ordered forty-eight subordinate fairies to meet me in her employers' back garden and open the proceedings with a magnificent ballet, in which I arranged to take the part of *première danseuse*. There was plenty of room on the croquet lawn after the sticks and hoops had been removed, and I am bound to say that my fairies acquitted themselves admirably. But in the middle of my *pas seul* I was not a little confounded to discover that our proceedings had been watched by no less a person than Mr. Pharpar Whortle, in whose house (as I was surprised to discover) Jane was employed as governess.

'Stop!' shouted Mr. Whortle, when we had quite finished. 'So here you are again! How dare you intrude with these disreputable young baggages into my private premises?'

'I am the Fairy Rosebud,' I began.

'I don't care who you are. I've already expressed my opinion of you. Be off at once. I won't allow it.'

We all began to move off, rather disconsolately.

'Stop a bit,' said he. 'I should like Mrs. Whortle to see the lengths to which persons of your class presume to go.'

He called for his serious butler, and, ordering him to stand with his back towards us and close his eyes, directed him to ask Mrs. Whortle to come into the garden. He also instructed the serious butler to send all the male servants to the front of the house. Mrs. Whortle, a grave lady of mature years, soon made her appearance.

'Pharpar!' said Mrs. Whortle, 'what is the meaning of this disgraceful assemblage?'

'My love,' said he, 'I agree with you—it is perfectly outrageous. I was engaged in watering that geranium when this mob of young women suddenly came into the garden and began to dance in a most unseemly manner. I have sent for you that you may see with your own eyes the lengths to which feminine audacity will go.' Then addressing himself to me, 'Be good enough to repeat your disgraceful dance from the very beginning—right through.'

My forty-eight subordinates immediately ranged themselves for the *adagio* movement with which the ballet opened. We had scarcely reached the sixteenth bar when Mrs. Whortle interposed.

'Stop!' said she. 'Go down on your knees, every one of you. Even now your skirts hardly touch the ground!'

'Hadn't you better let them dance it through, my dear?' said Mr. Whortle timidly.

'On no account,' replied she. 'Not another step, if *I* know it!'

'But I think you ought to see it all,' urged Mr. Whortle, 'otherwise you won't know how shocking it is.'

'I will not allow it on any consideration,' said she. 'I've seen too much already. Now pack off, all of you. What would Sir Trevor Mauleverer say if he were to call at this moment?'

The bare mention of the Wicked Baronet's name aroused me to renewed exertion. I determined to make one more effort.

'I am the Fairy Rosebud, hear me, pray!
Jane Collins is my lonely *protégée.*'

'What!' said Mrs. Whortle. 'The hussey shall go this very hour!'

'Nay do not look so angry and so grim,
For Dr. Perkins loves her—she loves him.'

'Does she?' exclaimed Mrs. Whortle. 'A pretty pair of turtle doves! I'll pack her off this very minute. Nice goings-on, upon my word!'

Feeling convinced that we were not wanted—at all events by Mrs. Whortle—I dismissed my fairies and floated invisibly along the Brixton Road, disconsolately wondering what course I had better take. About an hour after this I saw Miss Collins, who had just been turned out of Mr. Whortle's house. To my surprise and delight, whom should I see coming from an opposite direction but Dr. Perkins!

They met. They didn't rush into each other's arms as I expected they would. He merely raised his hat, and she bowed. I at once made myself visible to them.

'Who is this person?' said Miss Collins.

'I am the Fairy Rosebud—I am here
To help both you and Dr. Perkins, dear.
Such love as yours we fairies much admire,
And I'll afford the aid that you require.
Take him—take her—'

'But stop,' said Dr. Perkins, 'There's some mistake here.'

'Mistake,' said I. 'Oh, no! We fairies never make mistakes.'

'If you are really a Fairy,' said Miss Collins, 'you must know, I should imagine, that my acquaintance with Dr. Perkins is of the slightest possible description.'

'Miss Collins and I have only seen each other twice—in fact I scarcely recognised her when we met,' said Dr. Perkins.

'Then you don't love each other?' said I.

'Oh, dear no!' said both of them in a breath.

'I'm afraid I have been hasty,' said I.

'Hasty and most imprudent,' said Dr. Perkins. 'You have lost me my only valuable patient by your impertinent interference.'

'And you've caused me to be turned out of my situation at a moment's notice and without a character,' said Miss Collins, beginning to cry. 'I couldn't imagine what Mrs. Whortle meant when she talked of hussies, but now I know.'

'I'm very sorry,' said I. 'I've been misled. I don't think I can do any good by remaining here. Pray, excuse me; I meant well.' And I vanished without more ado.

This was most mortifying. I at once repaired to the Subterranean Abode of the Demon Alcohol. He was at home, but in a tearing rage; kicking the nasty black beetles and boxing the hairy spiders' ears.

Although he was my official enemy, I was quite sorry to see him so upset. I was upset myself and could sympathise with him. So I addressed him politely and with a certain touch of tenderness which I never could quite suppress when talking to him.

> 'Excuse me, pray. I fear I am intruding.
> On what ill-starred occurrence are you brooding?'

He replied:—

> 'Of fish I've just prepared a pretty kettle,
> Enough the very dickens to ensettle.'

(*Then, looking cautiously round*):—

> 'There's no one listening to us, I suppose?
> Will you excuse me if I speak in prose?'

'By all means,' said I.

'Thanks so much,' said the Demon. 'The fact is, I'm much too upset to talk fluently in rhyme.'

'So am I, gracious knows,' rejoined I. 'But what in the world is the matter?'

'Oh, the whole story—I've made a donkey of myself again. Sir Trevor Mauleverer—you know whom I mean?'

'Of course,' I replied, 'the Bad Baronet.'

'There—that's just it,' said the Demon. 'He ain't a Bad Baronet—he's a Good Baronet.'

'A *Good* Baronet!' I exclaimed. 'There's no such thing as a Good Baronet.'

'There you mistake, my dear,' said he. 'I rashly assumed, as you did, that, being a Baronet, he must be a bad one. Such a name, too—Sir Trevor Mauleverer! There's villany in every letter of it! But (it's just like my luck) when I appeared to him and offered to help him to carry off Miss Collins, he indignantly rebuked me and gave me this tract! (producing a leaflet headed "Where the Devil are you Going?") He turns out to be a Nonconformist Baronet of the very strictest principles, and actuated, in everything that he does, by the nicest possible sense of honour! I never felt so small in my life!'

'But—his intentions towards Jane?'

'Punctiliously honourable. Hears that she has been discharged without a character for encouraging the visits of disreputable young women—'

'That's me and my fairies,' said I, turning purple. 'Never mind—go on.'

'And expresses his intention to marry her forthwith. The ceremony is to take place at Little Bethlehem Congregational Sub-Diaconal Chapel, in Fox Court, Borough Road, this very week! My only consolation is that this will completely capsize the matrimonial apple-cart of your estimable young friend, Dr. Perkins.'

'Not at all,' replied I. 'I've also been on a wrong tack.

Dr. Perkins and Jane Collins care nothing for each other. They are the merest acquaintances, and (if I may judge from their emphatic disclaimers of anything like an understanding between them) they rather dislike each other. It's a nice muddle, altogether!'

'Humph!' said the Demon. 'The only question is, what's to be done?'

'It must never get about that we've made such noodles of ourselves,' said I.

'Oh, it wouldn't do at all. I could never look my imps in the face after such an *exposé*,' replied the Demon.

'I think the best course,' said I, after a moment's reflection, 'will be to transport them all, at once, to the Revolving Realms of Radiant and Refulgent Rehabilitation, and effect the customary transformation before the scandal leaks out.

I should explain that the Revolving Realms of Radiant and Refulgent Rehabilitation (telegraphic address, 'Realms') is my laboratory, or Fairy Operating Theatre, in which alone the usual transformation can be effected. It's a sweet spot.

The Demon Alcohol jumped at the idea, and thanked me very heartily, and rather affectionately, for my ingenuity in getting him out of a very awkward predicament. A wave of my wand did all that was necessary—the beetles, toads, and spiders crawled off—the sides of the Demon Wine Vaults slid away—the gigantic vats sunk through the floor, and what was left of the Vaults rose into the air—and behold we found ourselves, at once, in the very heart of the Revolving Realms, with Sir Trevor Mauleverer, Mr. Pharpar Whortle, Dr. Perkins, and Miss Collins—all looking not a little bewildered, as though wondering where they were and what was going to happen to them.

I placed myself on my official throne, in the middle of a group of silver ferns, and addressed Dr. Perkins:—

'Dear Doctor Perkins, a new life begin
As twinkling, twirling, sparkling Harlequin.'

Dr. Perkins's professional frock-coat and tweed trousers vanished, to his intense confusion, and he appeared dressed in the costume of his new character.

He seemed quite thunderstruck. Quite against his will he assumed the usual attitudes, rolling his head about and posturing with his legs uncomfortably far apart. As soon as he could speak he attempted a formal expostulation, but I wouldn't listen to him. I addressed Miss Collins:—

'Miss Collins, to reward you I design,
Be you his faithful, loving Columbine!'

'But I don't love him,' she began.

'Do as I tell you directly,' said I. And her demure merino frock and cloth jacket disappeared as she suddenly made the requisite change of apparel.

'Dance.' said I.

'I really couldn't—and they're so short!'

But she had to, and she did, as though actuated (as she really was) by a power that completely overmastered her.

It was Mr. Whortle's turn next:—

'And as for you, you priggish old buffoon,
Be changed at once to senile Pantaloon.'

Quite bewildered, he submitted without protest—toddled forward in his new character, and, leaning on his crutch-stick, coughed heavily three times, and then, exclaiming 'Oh, what a pretty butterfly!' tried to catch Miss Collins, who neatly evaded his grasp in three twirls.

Only Sir Trevor remained to be disposed of.

'Sir Trevor, sport yourself in London Town,
As merry, mischievous, dishonest Clown!'

'But I energetically protest,' said he.

'You must do it—you can't help yourself,' said I.

And he couldn't. He became a Clown in a moment—turned three cart-wheels and four somersaults—made a grotesque grimace, felt deep down in the capacious pockets of his Jacobean costume as he exclaimed:—'Oh lor! I've lost my Sunday farden!' Then, turning to me and drawing himself up to his full height, 'Remember, Madam, I hold you personally responsible for this outrage. I shall at once place the matter in the hands of my solicitor.' Feeling no inclination to discuss the point with him, I transported them at once into Oxford Street, and left them to their devices.

Jane Collins and Dr. Perkins, greatly annoyed at having to go about together under such compromising circumstances, nevertheless found themselves compelled to dance hornpipes, polkas, and cachuchas all day long in the London mud—Dr. Perkins nervously anxious lest any of his patients should recognise him. As to Jane's confusion, I would rather not dwell upon that circumstance. It was painful in the extreme to have to transform her into Columbine; and I wouldn't have done it for the world if I could have seen any other way out of my difficulty. However, I must say, I rather enjoyed Dr. Perkins's annoyance, for he had been rude to me when I wished to do him (as I thought) a good turn. He was a prig, who hated dancing, and it is always a pleasure to turn such a person into Harlequin.

Sir Trevor and Mr. Whortle had a very uncomfortable time of it. Greatly distressed at having to appear in the London streets in the outrageous costume of Clown, and devoured by jealousy at the intimate relations which appeared to exist between his beloved Jane and Dr. Perkins, Sir Trevor Mauleverer's life became a burden to him. Compelled by supernatural power to commit acts of the most consummate villainy in crowded public thoroughfares, he never lost an opportunity of expressing his horror and disgust at the crimes which his unhappy Fate required him to perpetrate. It was really pathetic to see the worthy Baronet's remorse after blowing a policeman out of a cannon or knocking the crutches from under the arms of some pitiable martyr to an acute attack of gout in both feet. Mr. Whortle—a model of correct behaviour in his original capacity, was in his way equally disconcerted. On one occasion Sir Trevor and Mr. Whortle found themselves outside Buszard's in Oxford Street. Mr. Buszard came out of his shop with a card inscribed, 'Wanted, a Handy Young Man,' pointed to the placard, placed it against the shop front and retired. Sir Trevor pointed out the placard to Mr. Whortle, and, enjoining silence, slapped three times on Mr. Buszard's doorpost and then lay down at full length across the doorway. Mr. Buszard, always attentive to the call of duty, came hurriedly out of his shop (under the impression, perhaps, that some customer wanted a Bath bun), and, not seeing Sir Trevor, fell heavily over the prostrate Baronet, which was just what the prostrate Baronet intended. Mr. Buszard arose, and, naturally indignant at the childish but most dangerous trap laid for him by the excellent Baronet, began an expostulation accompanied by much emphatic action. The Baronet (who prided himself upon his ability to comport himself, under whatever circumstances, with the very nicest discrimination) made an exaggerated bow to Mr. Buszard, placing his hand on his heart, and exclaiming at the same time, 'Oh, I beg yer parsnips!' which, however incomplete as an explanation of the Baronet's unaccountable conduct, seemed to have the effect of so far appeasing Mr. Buszard as to induce him to entertain Sir Trevor's offer to fill the situation for which the 'Handy Young Man' was required. Mr. Buszard (whose time was, no doubt, extremely valuable) neglected to make the usual inquiries as to the respectability of candidates for employment in his extensive business, and accepted Sir Trevor Mauleverer solely on the strength of his unsupported recommendations, investing him then and there with the white cotton apron of office, and hurrying off without affording the slightest clue to the nature of the duties he had to discharge. The Baronet's conception of the duties of a Handy Young Man in the employment of Mr. Buszard was eccentric to the last degree, but if his conduct had the effect of proving to Mr. Buszard the folly of engaging servants without strict inquiry into their characters and antecedents, it was, perhaps, not altogether without its value. Sir Trevor and Mr. Whortle simply gorged themselves with Mr. Buszard's pastry, they licked the sugar off Mr. Buszard's wedding cakes, threw dozens of Mr. Buszard's cold plum puddings at the passers-by, and finished up by jumping through Mr. Buszard's expensive plate-glass window and rolling out through the lower part of Mr. Buszard's shop front on to Mr. Buszard's pavement. In fact, Sir Trevor displayed so much unfitness for the duties of Handy Young Man that Mr. Buszard found himself most reluctantly compelled to dispense with Sir Trevor's services. At the same time he pressed a sausage-roll into Sir Trevor's hand, and told him he might always look in and help himself whenever he was passing. The fact is that Sir Trevor was gifted with a singular fascination which attracted people to himself, notwithstanding his enforced social lapses.

Left to themselves, Sir Trevor and Mr. Whortle discussed the unpleasant condition into which their atrocious conduct had plunged them.

'It is most painful to me to find myself compelled to a line of conduct which is utterly opposed to my own instincts and habits as a gentleman. This kind-hearted tradesman who has repaid my unwarrantable outrages upon his stock and premises with—with this excellent confection—has not deserved the disgraceful treatment to which I have subjected him. I feel the degradation deeply.' And Sir Trevor ate the sausage-roll with an air of profound preoccupation.

'How long is this fearful state of things to last?' said Mr. Whortle. 'And what is to become of my sugar-broking business? I cannot possibly present myself at the office in this tom-fool costume. Think what the clerks would say!'

'Our only consolation,' replied the Baronet, 'is that we are acting under the influence of an irresistible force which compels us to commit profligacies at the very thought of which I stand aghast. I see a nursemaid advancing with a double-perambulator, and escorted by a trooper of the 2nd Life Guards. It becomes my very painful duty to trip up that soldier and rob the poor girl of her hat, feather, boa and cloak, while you sit upon the perambulator and squash her smiling innocents! Come along.' And with a deep sigh Sir Trevor and Mr. Whortle proceeded to put their nefarious scheme into operation. I will not pursue the adventures of Dr. Perkins, Miss Collins, Sir Trevor and Mr. Whortle at any greater length. The theme is excessively painful to me because I feel that I condemned them to their present disreputable course of life for no better reason than to enable myself and the Demon Alcohol to escape from a very uncomfortable predicament of our own creation. The four unhappy people are still engaged in their compromising duties—indeed, I saw them only yesterday afternoon making butter-slides for bishops outside the Athenaeum Club. You may come upon them at any moment.

A common calamity is as a bond of sympathy. I felt so deeply for the Demon Alcohol's disgrace that I consented to overlook certain physical disadvantages that were only too patent to his dearest friends, and notwithstanding his unwholesome, green-foil complexion, we there joined in holy matrimony. It was arranged for the settlements that, in the event of our being blessed with a family, the girls should be Good Fairies and the boys Demons.

We are quite happy so far. Like many another, he is a very good husband when sober.

The Lady in the Plaid Shawl

A Scrap of Autobiography

[NOTE.—*The following anecdote is literally true in every detail, even to the singular coincidence at the end.]*

IN THE autumn of 1870, a fortnight before the German army reached Paris, I was appointed war correspondent to the *Observer*, and required to start for Paris at six hours' notice. I should state that, at that time, the rule as to passports was strictly enforced.

I reached Dover at midnight, and found a heavy gale blowing. As I was going on board I heard an altercation between a young and rather attractive lady, who wore a red plaid shawl, and one of the steamer's officers at the gangway.

'They'll never let you land at Calais without a passport,' said the officer.

'But I *must* go,' replied the lady. 'My husband is at St. Valérie, at the point of death, and I must go to him at any cost.'

'Very sorry, ma'am,' said the officer. 'We can take you across, of course; but they certainly won't let you land unless you have a passport.'

'Nevertheless, I must go and take my chance, as it is a matter of life and death.'

I happened to be furnished with a passport made out in the names of my wife and myself, and, as I was travelling alone, it occurred to me that it might be useful in this emergency. So I said to the lady: 'I happen to have a passport which will carry two. If you like to go on shore in the assumed character of my wife, I shall be very pleased that you should do so.'

The lady expressed her thanks, and I saw no more of her until we met at the gangway when we were alongside Calais pier. My passport covered the lady, and she was permitted to land without question.

We found that we had about an hour to wait before the train started, and I offered her some supper at the *buffet*, which she gladly accepted, as the rough crossing had seriously inconvenienced her, and she stood in need of substantial restoration. After we had supped we had still about twenty minutes to wait, and we passed them in a carriage of the train.

So far my story is, I believe, almost identical with the opening pages of a novel called 'My Official Wife,' which was published some fifteen years ago, but which I have never seen. Possibly my story may have reached the author's ears, and he may have found it adapted to his purpose. This, of course, is mere conjecture, based on the vivid similarity of the two incidents. At this point, however, the novelist's story and my own diverge.

As we were waiting in the train the lady explained to me that she would be my fellow passenger only as far as Boulogne, as she would have to change at that station into another train that would take her to St. Valérie, where her husband, whom she described as a post-captain in the Navy, was lying seriously ill. She asked me to be so good as to get her a ticket for Boulogne or St. Valérie, I forget which. I bought the ticket and it cost five francs. When I returned to the carriage, she explained that she had come away in such a hurry that she had only brought a few shillings of change with her, and that this had been expended on the journey. I begged her not to distress herself about so small a matter, and she went on to explain that all the money she had with her was two ten pound notes, and she was afraid she would find it difficult to get them exchanged at St. Valérie. It so happened that, in the belief that I should be detained in Paris for some weeks, I had brought with me a hundred and twenty gold sovereigns, and I offered to give her twenty of these in exchange for the two notes. She gratefully accepted my offer—the train started, and on arriving at Boulogne she left me after we had exchanged addresses.

On the journey to Paris I had a narrow escape of being

arrested as a spy. I had with me a leather handbag upon which my name, 'W. SCHWENCK GILBERT,' was printed in unnecessarily conspicuous gold letters. At Amiens a couple of Frenchmen of the *commis-voyageur* type entered the carriage and, after a time, they began to mutter mysteriously to one another, and eventually one of them said to me:

'*Mais Monsieur est Prussien?*'

I denied the soft impeachment, and assured them that I was English to the backbone.

'*Pourtant*,' said my interrogator, pointing to the unhappy name 'SCHWENCK' on my gold-lettered bag, '*voilà un nom allemand.*'

I admitted that the name was German, and explained that it was given to me by my godfathers and godmothers at my baptism, and that I had not been consulted when they took that liberty, or I should certainly have declined to present myself at the font. As they still muttered, I concluded that my explanation had not been considered satisfactory and as I had no ambition to be handed over to a posse of infuriated soldiery on arriving at Paris, and possibly shot then and there, I thought it better to explain the business upon which I was travelling. So I produced a visiting card upon which I had written the name of the newspaper I represented, for use in getting through *cordons* and into public buildings.

'*Voilà, monsieur*,' said I. '*Cela vous expliquera mon affaire.*'

They looked at the card rather doubtfully, and, after a little more muttering, one of them said to me (in the tone of a General of Division addresssing troops):

'*Mais, monsieur*, '*Observer*'—*cela veut dire espion.*'

I admitted, not without some trepidation, that the word might possibly be considered to bear that construction, but I suggested to them that even they, imbued as they were with all the prejudices that, at that time, animated their countrymen, might understand that, if I were really a Prussian spy in pursuit of my vocation, I should hardly be so imprudent as to advertise the fact on my visiting card.

'*Monsieur*,' said my friend, '*un Prussien est capable de tout!*'

However, I succeeded eventually in making my position

clear to them, and we became very good friends. They explained to me that every Frenchman in Paris would shed his last drop of blood in its defence, and that the women would give their back hair to make bowstrings—which seemed to argue an imperfect acquaintance, on their part, with up-to-date methods of defence. I asked if he proposed to remain in Paris and assist in its defence. He replied, '*Non, monsieur, je pars ce soir pour Marseilles.*'

When I reached Paris I put up at the Grand Hotel, and after I had been there a few days I proposed to pay my bill. With this object I went to the bureau, and presented one of the two ten pound notes I had received from the post-captain's wife in exchange for my twenty sovereigns, and I was rather taken aback when the clerk, after examining the note, expressed his belief that it was a forgery. I was on the point of offering the other, when it occurrred to me that if the clerk should be of opinion that that also was a forgery, I might find myself in an unpleasant predicament. So I paid in gold, and there was an end of that incident. I left the hotel in order to visit the ramparts and outworks, and on my way to the Arc de l'Etoile I met a journalistic friend who had also come to Paris to remain through the seige. He was in very low spirits because, wanting money, he had drawn a cheque for twenty pounds and presented it at a bank where he was well known; but the bank declined to cash it, on the ground that telegraphic or other communication between Paris and London might be cut off at any moment, and, for the present, at all events, no cheques except those drawn by their own customers could be cashed. Thereupon I told him that I was the possessor of two ten pound notes, one of which had been refused by the cashier of the Grand Hotel as doubtful, and that, as to the other, I knew nothing, but if he liked to take them in exchange for his twenty pound cheque he was welcome to them, but it must be distinctly understood that I did not quarantee their honesty. My friend jumped at the suggestion; he took my notes and I took his cheque (which was duly cashed in London), and there the incident ended. He got rid of the notes without difficulty, and they may have been perfectly genuine for anything I know to the contrary.

After I had passed about ten days in Paris, waiting for

the Prussians, I was recalled by telegram, as the proprietors of the *Observer* had reason to believe that no letters from Paris would be likely to reach them after the investment. Accordingly, I packed up my traps and left Paris by the last train that *did* leave Paris. In point of fact, the French engineers obligingly waited until we had crossed the bridge at Creil, and then they blew it up. I heard the explosion. On arriving at Boulogne I called at Merridew's Library for newspapers and letters, and told Mrs. Merridew that I had just arrived from Paris. 'That is impossible,' said the lady, rather rudely, 'for the bridge of Creil was blown up this morning.' 'Exactly,' said I, 'I heard it.'

While I was waiting for the Folkestone steamer to start, I met an old friend, Admiral Hathorn, on the *port*. I told him of my adventure with the lady in the plaid shawl and the two ten pound notes.

'I can tell you a good deal about that lady and her husband,' said the Admiral. 'They are two notorious swindlers. He was a second officer of a merchantman, and he has assumed the rank of a post-captain in the Navy, for purposes of deception.' He told me other things about them, but as they do not bear upon my story I need not repeat them.

A few weeks after this I received a letter from the so-styled post-captain, written upon paper which was headed (in manuscript) 'Army and Navy Club,' stating that he was anxious to meet me, in order to thank me for my attention to his wife, and generally to cement a friendship which had begun so auspiciously. He stated that he was then in London, but was on the point of starting for St. Valérie (to which place my reply was to be addressed), but that on his return, later in the year, he would do himself the pleasure of calling on me. I at once called on the secretary of the Army and Navy Club, and showed him the letter. He confirmed Admiral Hathorn's statement that the man was a notorious swindler, who had frequently dated letters from the Club for nefarious purposes, and that the Committee were extremely anxious to find him. He took charge of the letter, but I never heard the result of any investigations that he may have made.

Some months later I was on my way to a performance at the Princess's Theatre, accompanied by my wife and a lady who is the wife of an accomplished and highly esteemed actor-manager. As we were driving to the theatre I happened to tell to this lady the history of my adventure with the lady in the plaid shawl, very much as I have told it on this paper. My friend, who is not unacquainted with a certain talent for imaginative romance, with which I have sometimes been credited, threw some doubt upon its details, under the impression that I was concocting a 'cock-and-bull' story for her amusement, and as she spoke we reached the box we were to occupy. 'Not only is my story absolutely true in every detail,' said I, 'but there,' pointing to a box immediately opposite to me, 'is, by a most amazing coincidence, the very lady in question!'

Sure enough there she was—the lady, no longer in a plaid shawl—accompanied by a tall, burly-looking man, wearing bushy ginger-coloured whiskers! The coincidence was quite uncanny. At the end of the first act a box-keeper knocked at the door.

'Gentleman wishes to speak to you, sir.'

I went into the box lobby, which was full of people who had left their places during the *entr'acte*, and I found the tall, burly, ginger-whiskered gentleman waitng for me.

'I believe, sir,' said he, in a loud quarter-deck voice, 'that you addressed my wife on board a Channel steamer six months ago.'

The sauntering people, anticipating a row, stopped and gathered round us as I admitted that I had been guilty of that imprudence.

'I am deeply indebted to you, sir, for your great kindness to her on that occasion.'

The sauntering people, finding that there was to be no row, dispersed.

'I believe you were good enough,' said he, 'to pay for her railway ticket.'

I replied that it was a small matter of four shillings, and not worth mentioning.

'I must insist upon getting out of your debt as far as a mere money payment is concerned,' said he, and he gave me a couple of florins.

'And now, sir,' said he, 'it will afford me the greatest

pleasure if you will allow me to call on you. My wife is especially anxious to have an opportunity of thanking you for your great kindness and courtesy to her at a very trying crisis.'

'Nothing,' said I, 'would give me greater pleasure, but I have ascertained, unfortunately, that you are a professional swindler.'

'What do you mean, sir? Who has presumed to describe me in such terms?'

'Well,' I replied, 'my informant was Admiral Hathorn, who told me that your rank was that of a rank imposter—a former mate in the merchant service, who assumed the rank of a post-captain in the Navy; and my second was the secretary of the Army and Navy Club, to whom I showed the letter that you were good enough to send me three months ago.'

'I see,' said he, thoughtfully.

'You appreciate the difficulty of my position?' said I.

'Perfectly,' said he.

'Not another word, I beg,' said he.

'-it would have given me the greatest pleasure—

'You are most kind.'

'But—a swindler!'

'Out of the question,' he replied.

'You acquit me of intentional discourtesy?'

'Absolutely. I quite understand. Good evening.'

And so we parted, and so ended my adventure with the Lady in the Plaid Shawl.

TRIAL BY JURY

An Operetta

SCENE,—A Court of Law at Westminster.
Opening Chorus of Counsel, Attorneys, and Populace.

HARK! The hour of ten is sounding,
Hearts with anxious hopes are bounding,
Halls of Justice crowds surrounding,
    Breathing hope and fear—
For to-day in this arena
Summoned by a stern subpoena
EDWIN, sued by ANGELINA,
    Shortly will appear!

Chorus of Attorneys.

    Attorneys are we
    And we pocket our fee,
Singing so merrily, 'Trial la law!'
    With our merry ca. sa.,
    And our jolly fi. fa.
Worshipping verily Trial la law!
    Trial la law!
    Trial la law!
Worshipping verily Trial la Law!

Chorus of Barristers.

Barristers we,
With demurrer and plea,
Singing so merrily, 'Trial la law!'
Be-wigged and be-gowned
We rejoice at the sound
Of the several syllables 'Trial by law!'
Trial la Law!
Trial la Law!
Singing so merrily Trial la law!

Recitative.

Usher.—Silence in court, and all attention lend!
Behold the Judge! In due submission bend.

(*The Judge enters and bows to the Bar. The Bar returns the compliment.*)

Recitative.

Counsel for Plaintiff.—May it please you, my lud!
Gentlemen of the Jury!

Aria.

With a sense of deep emotion
I approach this painful case,
For I never had a notion
That a man could be so base
Or deceive a girl confiding,
Vows, *et cetera,* deriding!
All.— He deceived a girl confiding,
Vows, *et cetera,* deriding!

Counsel.— See my interesting client,
Victim of a heartless wile,
See the traitor all defiant
Wear a supercilious smile:
Sweetly smiled my client on him,
Coyly woo'd and gently won him!

All.— Sweetly smiled their plaintiff on him,
Coyly woo'd and gently won him!

Counsel.— Swiftly fled each denied hour
Spent with this unmanly male,
Camberwell became a bower,
Peckham an Arcadian vale;
Breathing concentrated otto!
An existence *à la Watteau!*

All.— Bless us, concentrated otto!
An existence *à la Watteau!*

Counsel.— Picture, then, my client naming
And insisting on the day,
Picture him excuses framing,
Going from her far away.
Doubly criminal to do so
For the maid had bought her trousseau!
All.— Doubly criminal to do so
For the maid had bought her trousseau!

Recitative.

Counsel—Angelina!

(Angelina steps into the witness box.)

Solo.

Judge.— In the course of my career
As a judex, sitting here,
Never, never, I declare,
Have I see a maid so fair!

All.—Ah! Sly dog!

Judge.— See her sinking on her knees
In the Court of Common Pleas—
Place your briefs upon the shelf
I will marry her myself!

(*He throws himself into her arms.*)

All.—Ah! Sly dog!

Recitative.

Judge.— Come all of you—the breakfast I'll prepare—
Five hundred and eleven, Eaton Square!

Final Chorus

Trial la law! Trial la law!
Singing so merrily, Trial la law!

CURTAIN.

www.ingramcontent.com/pod-product-compliance
Lightning Source LLC
LaVergne TN
LVHW091041080826
845145LV00002B/579

* 9 7 8 1 9 3 3 9 9 3 3 0 0 *